Evah & the Unscrupulous THWARGG

Evah & the Unscrupulous THWARGG

Longoria Wolfe

an MRG STORY

First published in 2020

Text © Longoria Wolfe, 2020

Cover design © M. R. Garcia, 2020

Editing, typesetting and ebook production
by Laura Kincaid

ISBN: 978-1-7345365-3-9

Contents

TERMINUS

How shall a poison eat itself in all its brilliant forms?
By face or eye or word of war?
How well devised, where creeping adders lie
through sin or saint o'er shapes of woe?

DARK EYE

DARK EYE

Chapter 1
Monsters & Flora

Evah lived in fear. She lived with worry. It was not the fear you feel when you think something will be served for dinner that you don't like, or the worry that your shoes may come untied when you played thack ball at school, or even the fear of Pearly Shyen, who pushed Evah around and called her a nobody from nowhere because her skin was a different color and her hair would never grow straight and long below her shoulders. No, Evah worried over things she imagined. But it was worse. She worried over things she imagined that then became real.

Once there was an eight-eyed monster with five arms and tongues flipping about from every palm, and sometimes a deep dark hole appeared beneath the flinging bars where she swung and dangled at school. The hole went on forever, and fire flashed out of it like a hungry beast smacking its lips in anticipation of a sumptuous meal. But these were only things Evah thought up as she played to make her games more adventurous, or when she was in her room at night and didn't really want to go to sleep. She realized what other children could only imagine, for her could become very real.

Now, others were beginning to see the workings of her imagination too. It was the dark fiery hole beneath the flinging bars that caused the children to stop playing with her. One day, while

Corvy Bane was swinging on the bars with Evah, he saw that deep dark hole, and it made him cry. He ran away and, afraid to tell anyone about the extraordinary sight he saw, Corvy lied to the teacher and the other children, saying Evah had pinched him hard and smelled like a rhino's butt. He was not very nice, and afterward, neither were the other children. On top of that, the news that a boy thought Evah smelled like a rhino's butt just gave Pearly one more reason to be mean, even though it couldn't have been farther from the truth. You see, her happiest time was tending to the flowers in the garden with Father Segura.

Her favorite flower was the glillin. It smelled sweet and fresh, and as it was her strange and unknown gift to make things real out of nowhere, she manifested the scent of the glillin flower where ever she went. That was the real reason Corvy had wanted to play with her, and why Pearly Shyen hated her so much. She was jealous. Both because she wished she smelled so good and because she had a secret crush on Corvy.

Evah was different, and it made her feel alone. She didn't understand the wonders she could make happen, or why Corvy Bane could see that deep dark hole to nowhere. No one had ever witnessed the things from her mind before—not that she knew of anyway—and she convinced herself that she could never let it happen again, because it could only lead to sorrow and more cruelty. So she lived a lonely life. As you may know, the fear of not being liked does only one thing really well: It keeps you from making new friends. It can also make you run away from friends you've known for a long time. It is in this way that loneliness only makes more loneliness, and then more, and more, until you feel like you don't even have a reason to live.

Now, you may think all of these things would be more than enough to cause great fear and worry, but even they were not the most profound source of Evah's troubles. She hid herself away from the other children and the time she spent with Father Segura in the garden became empty of the joy it once brought. She stared deeply. She sometimes seemed confused. Once, walking up the steps to her classroom, she lifted her foot high, as if not to harm some pretty bug, then tripped, and made her knee bleed on the concrete. You can bet Pearly Shyen had some laughs that day. Then, Evah seemed to hear someone calling her. Playing on the flinging bars, she stopped suddenly, hopped off into the grass and stared at the vacant space of the field before her. I was becoming concerned.

I should introduce myself. Now is probably the right time. My name is Felin, and I'm a rat. A church rat as a matter of fact. A big fat black church rat in one of the last two broken-down old churches of its kind in the entire Spirean system, and it's a strange fate that's brought me here. How many rats do you know who tell stories and watch over children?

My life has its challenges too. To say the least, people don't like church rats. It's not like having a little mouse around, peeping sweetly, being soft and white and barely making a ruckus. I clomp around loudly pretty much everywhere I go. My teeth dangle weirdly from my mouth. My fur is thick and coarse. It's hard not to notice me in a quiet church, padding and pounding with a smack-smack-smack of my feet. My tail is absurdly big, and it flops and bonks on every hard surface, from the stone floor tiles to the highest beams of the arches above the pews. That's where I live—fifteen feet in the air and twenty feet from the view of the chorus balcony.

I have a puzzling secret of my own. One that even I can't understand. I'm more than just a rat, and I know Evah. I've known her longer than only one life could allow, though she would never recognize me now. We were about to meet again. The last time I talked to Evah, she was five. Her skin was like chocolate, and she was an adventurous spirit.

Now, a rat's got to eat, and with the schoolyard just outside the east wall, you can hear me thumping and skittering up and down and in and out of the walls, to satiate my unyielding instinct to snack. It should be known that I am blind to boot. Everything to me is dark as night, so I'm clumsy as a buffoon, banging into walls and beams and trash cans alike. But I do see a little—enough to figure out shapes anyway. I peer at the mysterious shadows of the children from the garbage cans, but mostly I watch Evah. I have a keen nose, and that's how I found out for sure that Evah had a bizarre gift.

One day, when Evah was tossing away part of her sandwich— Her sandwiches were very good. Packed with cheese! My mouth waters just thinking about it!

But I stray from the point. One warm day, while I was rummaging for something good to eat, the trash cans were reeking like raw sewage—all baked-up disgustingness. Personally, I don't enjoy this aspect of trash-can dining. Evah saw me, and you know, she didn't scream. She looked at me and twisted her lips, examining me with a somewhat annoyed expulsion of breath. A breath like water popping from the spout of a whale.

"Are you real?" she said, examining me like some vague figure hidden in a painting.

What should I say? I stood up on my rear feet, sniffing at her, as uncertain she was real as she was of me, I suppose.

Evah slipped a bottle into the recycling compressor. It vibrated vigorously, spraying its disinfectant chemical inside, then made three nearly deafening slamming noises as it compacted its contents. The sound made my wits fly into overdrive. I stumbled downward, jittered in a frantic circle, and banged into the trash can so hard it lurched forward with a grind.

The compressor finished with an automated voice reporting, "The Constellation of Spirea thanks you! Good work!"

"Huh. Never seen that before. Sorry. Maybe you are real." She knelt down and dropped the remains of her sandwich where I could easily tug at it with my teeth. "Here. Are you hungry?"

I grabbed at the sandwich like a dart through the wind.

"This place stinks," she commiserated. "Ever smell a glillin flower?"

Before I knew it, I was laden with the delicious smell of something like candy in spring rain. I felt the way I did when the church chorus sang in perfect harmony. My chest was warm, and my head was light, as if all my burdens were gone. I stopped my chewing for a moment and turned my nose in her direction. All the reek of the garbage cans was transfigured into bliss.

As lovely as this moment was, rats know not to outstay their welcome, so I picked up the remains of the sandwich and started for the church door that was always left ajar.

"Have a nice day," Evah whispered, watching my escape.

Before disappearing from sight, I stopped, and without even thinking, I spoke. "You too!" I knew not to do that: Talk to a human. Even one that you've loved for two lifetimes. There are just some things that don't seem natural. It could cause more trouble than any good you may hope for.

I hunched there, stunned for a moment, and then I was gone. As long as I had waited to be reunited with her, there was still a part of me that hoped she hadn't heard me. After all, even a rat that loves you can be more trouble than they're worth.

Chapter Two
The Constellation of Spirea

On the far side of the Eagle Galaxy, you will find the Constellation of Spirea. That is what we call our home, though it is not a system of stars at all. They're planets. Our planets are like states—seven free-floating orbs in the same gravitational field near the Eagle sun. They are ruled by the Magisteria of Constance who are unified under a prime minister. Constance, a small world rich with trees and water, serves as the capital of the Constellation system, with its cobblestone streets and historic buildings. Here in the Constellation of Spirea, starslides connect each world in a commuter system. They hang in the skies like tubes of blue light on every world. There are eight worlds altogether, but only six are inhabited. Those six worlds are Constance, Thwargg, Hypathia, Scabeeze, Sabia, and Sharvanna.

In all the galaxies of all the universes, there is something you may know as dark matter, but to us, it is not dark at all. It is filled with mirror worlds to the one you know and some even a little more different like ours.

Our home is an obscure place. It is like an undetectable solar system inside a solar system, a destination hidden inside the invisible landscape of the unseen mystery of the cosmos. But we do have a connection to Earth. At the end of Earth's history some survivors were escaping to a habitable planet by way of a

wormhole, but when they came out the other side they didn't reach their intended destination—they wound up here instead, some 2,500 years in the past, Earth time. We tried to contact Earth at first, but they were absolutely primitive. Now they're more evolved.

So many things are the same here, but some are very different. The survivors from Earth settled with the Sharvannas. They brought the embryos of animals from Earth and populated much of the system with them, but things have a way of growing and breeding in peculiar ways, and many of the species changed.

The earthlings changed too. Though they could not rebuild any world exactly as their home, they brought something more essential to the constellation than any animal or food or even religion—they brought humanity. Before long they united many of the worlds and the Great Experiment was born. Still, things are different here. Some things go up here that some think only go down, and there are some who can breathe in and out of water.

The magisteria strive for peace between all living things, all the alien races, by ensuring everyone has a place where they belong by the time they reach adulthood. Before growing up, things are still sloppy, and at one time or another, every boy or girl thinks they may never belong anywhere, like Evah so desperately believed. Life isn't perfect though. Some get called to duty never imagined, and sometimes, even in the Constellation of Spirea, people are left alone or unexpectedly find themselves in a life that doesn't make sense, the way it should, for everyone to be happy.

In the Constellation of Spirea, there are many things, like rats and rhinos—rhinos with their rhino butts. But there are other creatures too that you may only find here, such as giant barb fish. They make kepplequer when their offspring are born. Kepplequer, if never exposed to ultraviolet rays, is a powerful form of energy that fuels nearly everything here. It powers the cities and polar thrums that make sure people don't get lost on starslides; it even

powers the scotschoots that carry citizens from place to place around the cities and stimulates the graviton repulsors that make them fly. There are some barb fish here on Constance, but the water planet of Deiphera is where they originate from. That is a world they inhabit with other marine life and none of our alien races are permitted to reside there. Well, almost none.

Mankind is here, but there are other beings too. Some like man, others not so much. The citizens of Constance consist of beings from the five other inhabited worlds. It is an endeavor of collaboration in pursuit of longer, happier living in the planetary system known as the Great Experiment. Certain beings do certain things really well, and it is on that fundamental concept that the Magisteria of Constance found their first ordinance of social consistency.

Hypathians are dreamers. It is thought that one can make a satisfying life for a Hypath by determining the strength of their abilities, and then appointing them to one or other positions where they may be most beneficial to all life.

Thwargg are logical. They calculate plans well. Over many hundreds of years, they have become social directors who monitor the minds of all citizens using sleep technology. They can adjust a person's course of causality to actuate their highest potential, and make them the most productive citizens they can be.

Now, not all dreamers are like Hypathians. We all dream, after all. And not all Thwargg wish to actuate the dreams of others, preferring to realize their own dreams instead. This is one unfortunate problem with the ordinance of social consistency. Though there are suitable places in every industry for each type of planetary being, sometimes conflicts of personal freedoms occur. But the magisteria see it this way: A fish may one day decide it doesn't want to live in water but the desert. Now, even if it could breathe well in the desert, it's not made for walking, so how far would that get them? It isn't even made for slithering, so life could get deathly boring, right? It would be a terrible struggle to do anything, and it would require a lot of resources

from a compassionate society to make that life work. Thus, the ordinance of social consistency dictates that if you're a fish, do wonderful things in the lifestyle of a fish. Or dull stuff for that matter. It's up to you.

If you're a Hypath, dream. If you're a Thwargg, facilitate; actuate. If you're a Scabeeze, scheme. Or, as the magisteria seem to think of it, if you're a Scabeeze, organize business and commerce so that citizens have a certain amount of satisfaction. But that's something we'll talk about later on in this story because, well, let's just say it will be a *big* problem.

I guess I should tell you that the magisteria are most often Sharvannas. Being finely tuned to compassion, sometimes spiritual enlightenment, but always interested in balance and equality of life, their traits make them fair leaders. Every world, though, chooses their own magisteria representatives. In this way, the magisteria can more fairly represent everyone in the system.

Now, you may be wondering what Evah has to do with any of this.

Evah is a Hypath, and not just any Hypath. Evah is an extuiter. Indeed, she may be one of the most exceptional classes of extuiters.

Some Hypathians are singers or writers. One good line from a song can change the way people think about themselves and others for many years, but an extuiter can change what people see, hear, or smell without them giving much thought to how it came to be. Some can even change what people think of each other, what they think they know about each other, and in that way, how they want to treat each other. That makes up the majority of an extuiter's casework when employed by the state.

Say you're a kid like our Evah, with a Pearly Shyen who bullies you and seems like she'd do anything she could to hurt you without any reason at all. Well, if Pearly were brought to the attention of an extuiter, they might put into her mind that whenever she sees you, she would see something of someone she loves deeply in you. They might make your voice sound like her mom or dad's voice, or they could make you smell like a chocolate chip cookie, if that would change the way she treats you.

It could go farther too. When she's away from you, she may see something of you in her mom or dad, or hear your voice coming from them. It's complicated, but an extuiter can make that bully see your face in the clouds when they play their favorite game outside. Now, I am simplifying their work. It can be quite complicated. It can even be dangerous, but having such gifts they can perform miraculous deeds. It has been suggested that an extuiter may be like an angel. Maybe. There are still many mysteries, even here in the Constellation of Spirea, and where extuiters came from and where they are going is one of them.

What we do know about extuiters, though, is that they can die. And there are extuiters who do good and extuiters who, well, do just about anything wrong that they can think of. We know too that it can be frightening learning to be an extuiter because they can sometimes get lost between reality and the powerful workings of their minds.

Evah has much to learn about extuiting, and we have much to learn about the nature of her being.

Chapter 3
Unsought Sight

E vah entered the church seventeen times to visit me. She came with a sandwich every day. If someone wandered in, she learned to hide, searching through many places to find one where she would be undetected. First, near the door, then behind the altar, but that gave her uneasy feelings. On the fourth day, she settled finally under a stained-glass window of clouds, near the second to last row of the sanctuary. It was on the west wall, clear across from the schoolyard. At first, she was quiet, but on the fourth day, after she had finally found her safe spot, I heard her speak. She tried to be self-assured and remain unnoticed.

"Hey, rat!"

The room was quiet, and I wasn't about to blow my cover. Rats don't get many visitors, even in the Constellation of Spirea. Unless they're coming at you with a broom. I could smell her sandwich from twenty feet away. *All the cheese*! The truth was, though, that my interest in her had nothing to do with cheese. I wanted to know what she was seeing that gave her so many troubles. The ones that made her stumble on the stairs. I knew she wasn't blind. She climbed freely on the flinging bars and bravely leaped from one to another. What I could see of her anyway.

I stayed still. The first time we met, she seemed to not know if I was even real. I wanted to talk to her, but if I did, she might think she was really losing her mind. I'd mucked things up pretty good, speaking before, and I didn't know what to do.

She ate her sandwich and left, but not without leaving a handsome helping beneath the cloudy window.

Yeah… I ate it.

She did this four more times. I thought it was quite nice.

On the ninth day, she found a large garnet on the floor where she left my helping. Well, it was large for me. How big a stone could a rat carry? Well, it was that big! It took some real muscle for a rat. I found it in the trash. It smelled like Corvy Bane, but I didn't think Evah would notice. I had seen him throw it away after trying to give it to Pearly Shyen on her birthday. She was mean and told him to go give it to old rhino butt.

Evah admired the stone, holding it up to the light of the cloudy stained-glass window. She tapped it on the floor then gave it a squeeze, eating her sandwich. I watched her from above. Well, I watched the shape of her and wished I could see her face. I wished I could see her hair and her eyes, see her fingers, and the clothes she wore. See if she was smiling. She was quiet for a long time, and then the bell rang in the distance.

"Thank you!" she said, scuttling to her feet as she gathered herself up to leave.

Her words startled me, I was watching her so attentively. I nearly fell from my beam when I scuttled backward to keep her from discovering my hiding place.

She stared into the air. "Maybe next time!" her voice rose up. Then, more confidently: "Bye!" And she was gone.

On the tenth day, sitting under the glassy clouds, she spoke as if no one would ever bother with her wherever she was.

"You don't have to worry about me. Have all my sandwich. No one likes me, and I don't like much of anything myself. Corvy saw the hole to nowhere, and he ran away crying like a little baby. I don't know how he could see it. I'm having a terrible day. I'm such a stupid head I'm talking to rats. I can barely put one foot in front of the other. Father Segura was talking with a strange man about stewards or something. I think he was someone important. I think they're going to take me away. If you could just make everything stop, I would like that very much. Is he a doctor? He was so serious. He never smiled once. I think I'm in trouble—"

"You're a Hypath."

Evah froze. She stared at me, sitting on my duff four feet from her, beneath the cloudy image of a perfectly lovely day.

"Don't be afraid."

"You can ta— Are you— Oh my God."

"You're all right, Evah. I'm real. It's all right. Breathe."

Evah gripped her stomach in a hunched bundle. "I wanted a talking rat and that's what I got. The truth is I don't even care if you're real."

"Well, I am. You must know you're a Hypath?" I said, attempting to help her reason.

"Hypaths are supposed to be neat. I sure don't feel neat."

"There are no others here like you, but there are others. And—"

"And what?"

"You aren't alone. Sometimes Hypathians are more powerful than they realize, and they don't understand everything that is happening to them."

"But who is this steward? And what are they going to do to me?"

"They think you're an extuiter. That's someone exceptional, Evah."

"How do you know any of this?" she quipped shrewdly.

"Well... I... I haven't always been a church rat," I said, a little shaky from her tone. "I've seen some things. I've been places," I offered timidly. "That man may have been an advisor to the Thwargg."

Her ears pricked up at that.

"What would they want with me? They don't watch kids' dreams! I'm only eleven."

"Did Corvy Bane tell anyone what he saw with you on the flinging bars?"

"I don't know. I don't think so. He was too scared. I scared Corvy Bane!"

"Well, he's only eleven too. I think Corvy Bane thinks a lot of things about you. And not bad things. Listen, Evah." I moved in closer to her. "Is it possible you made contact with Corvy Bane?"

"No. What do you mean?" she asked with concern.

"Well, when an extuiter's power is weak, sometimes the only way another person can see what they're thinking is if they are touched. It could have been anything. Something insignificant."

"Yes. There was a… His hand grabbed the same bar I was hanging from. His hand touched mine."

"That's it. You were having a good time playing, and that can have a magic all on its own, but to an extuiter that could be just enough to transfer something they see. It doesn't usually happen so young. But that's it. It's simple. All you have to do is be careful about that. You can learn to control your gift. And hide it too."

"If it's exceptional, why should I hide it?"

"I just mean if you wanted to," I said, a little unsure. "I mean, you said you were afraid of having to go away. They'll send someone to observe you. Maybe ask some questions."

"You know a lot about these things."

"I used to know an extuiter. An extuiter who did some important work."

"What? You mean like she was famous?" Evah said, perking up.

"No. Extuiters don't get famous. Usually. But they can be involved in important work."

"Hmmm," she emitted. "Sounds boring."

"Trust me it isn't boring. You must tell me something, Evah. What are you seeing on the steps?"

"Ohh… that. I see animals. Tiny animals. Little stuffed animals. But they're alive. They're walking around. I see them everywhere." Her tone deepened with seriousness. "At first, I thought they were so cute. But I wasn't making them up, and they seemed so happy! Then the worst part of it started to happen."

"Yeah?"

"Well, they made me laugh and then… then I heard a baby laughing too. And then I saw a baby. Crawling around like it was perfectly normal to crawl around schoolyards. And then it was in the field near the flinging bars. I heard it laughing all the time. Saw it sitting in the grass. And then there was a voice. A man's voice. It called my name, but there was no one there. Then I started to hate the baby's laughing because it made me sad. And the animals too. I hated the little animals with their smiling faces. But they won't go away."

"Do you see them now?"

"No."

"What kind of animals?"

"They're like stuffed animals. There's a chigraff all yellow and spotty with a long neck and big smiling teeth like it's happy to see me. And then there's a monkey all brown and furry. It says, 'Eeh, eeh!' like it's trying to surprise me. Like I'm supposed to like it. And I did at first, but now they won't go away, and they make me sad. Them, and that baby, and that voice."

"Does the voice say anything else? Did it tell you its name?" I snapped back seriously, unable to censor my concern.

"No." She stopped to observe me attentively. "Why? Should I be afraid?"

"No." I tried to convince both her and myself. "All these things could be something you read or something from a cartoon."

"No cartoon I can think of."

"You say you don't see them now?"

"No, I don't," she said, allowing herself to relax a little.

"Good," I said, after thinking a moment. "I like spending time with you, Evah. If it makes you feel better, if you don't see those things, or hear those things when we're together, then I want you to come and visit me every day."

"All right," she said, as if her fears may have a remedy.

"Do you have the stone I gave you?"

"Yes." She held out her hand towards me, uncurling her fingers.

I shrank away from her fast, sniffing the air rapidly, and looking up and down. My confusion was unmistakable.

"Hey... you can't see, can you?"

"No," I confessed in a whisper. "Not too good."

"It's your stone. I have your stone. I have it with me all the time."

"Do you see anything when you hold it? I mean anything—"

"No."

"Hmm," I expelled, puzzled. "Then you hold on to that, and when you're nervous, give it a squeeze and think about glillin flowers or something else that makes you happy."

The school bell rang. Evah started to leave, then stopped and turned to me.

"I've been seeing them less since you gave me my gift." She was silent for a moment. There was something heavy on her mind. "I don't want to go away and be in a strange place."

"Well, I want you to stay too, Evah."

"I'll see you tomorrow."

Evah left. She seemed relieved to have a friend. Maybe even relieved not to be seeing those things that troubled her as often. But she knew there could be some considerable changes in her life soon.

There was something else bothering me—I knew something she didn't. I had a suspicion about why she was seeing those little animals, and the infant, and why she heard the voice calling her too. I couldn't help but think there was another extuiter at Holy Heart School. Maybe a very unpleasant one.

Chapter 4
Skenkin's Paradox

We cannot change the arrow of time. I cannot change the error of my choices. The arrow of time can be interfered with, and in the history of the Spirean system, we have done so—by accident. Space and time curve. They can be bent into a circle, establishing a loop where one can travel back and forth. But when this occurs it's expected that the subject becomes two of the same person. So even in the transcendence of time, I may not be able to change the error of my choices.

There may be another life for me, but it is not where I am or where I can claim it. In my other life, I would affix the record of my thoughts into a digital source or on the pages of some journal, but in this life I cannot. I am a murderess, a conspirator to murder, and to make such recordings of my thoughts is to create evidence. So, without such fixed points of reference, I am adrift in time. Like the feather of a bird adrift upon the endless sea of the water planet Deiphera, where I am now.

My name is Skenkin. Standing before the window of the South Rock Station observation room, through the transparent image of my reflection, I see the riotous waves crashing on the rocks before me and the endless backsplash lapping over the surface.

My eyes. My eyes are wearing away beneath the lapping of worry and regret for the things I've done, and for my losses.

The pale blue of my skin is darkening with age and spidering into webs of broken purple vessels. Even the firm impression of my face is slipping into the endless abyss of history. So I have written an equation for the achievement of a traversable acausal retrograde domain in space-time on the window, just across my heart. I can wipe it away there. It's as essential as I am to this life as of late. I may always be non-essential. Theoretically speaking, of course.

I'm the third child to the Claren Thwargg. My hair is black, my legs are not so long, my hands are fair, and my eyes glow like orange solar winds in the northern sky of Deiphera. I wish I could say I chose this planet for my home in hiding because the beauty of the skies reminds me of my eyes, but people don't associate the Thwargg with beauty. The person who placed me here doesn't think I'm beautiful. They know this world is haunted for me. I lost someone here, or perhaps I sent someone to their death here. How I secretly wish they would return.

It was not my place to rule the upper stations in the Thwargg wards, like my father, but I have had a privileged life. My parents took liberties in cooperation with a Scabeeze club looking to have a seat among the Magisteria of Constance. I have had two loves. Both were extuiters. It is not like the Thwargg to do such things as marry their children to the gifted dreamers, but in their plans to take power with the Scabeeze conspirator, it was convenient for my parents to use me thus. I'm more than simple but have a place in the Constellation of Spirea I should not have sidestepped to be where my parents put me.

We Thwargg have a gift to direct life, and when it comes to extuiters, one would think it only natural we should belong together. The magisteria think otherwise. Extuiters can do magical things, but they're often not ambitious, and so their gifts are not applied to achieving ambitious ends.

My first extuiter died. He realized that my parents had discovered his powers and then set a course for us to be together. When he realized his love life was fabricated, he stopped using his gifts for anything; he thought everything he was set out to do was really only to serve the desires of selfish people; to serve my father's whims and his ambitions. Now, I know he was right. That was years ago.

My father had him murdered when he became useless. One day they set a course for him that led him to starslide platform T36, where he had been convinced I'd met another boy. They sent me there to travel to Thwargg, where I was to meet my brother. When my extuiter saw me step into the slide, he followed me, and it was arranged that the polar thrum machine governing that slide should stop, and so he was lost forever, the structure of his fermion particles ripped apart in the gravitational fields. I thought they were right to do that at the time. I believed it was my destiny to be with a great extuiter, not one who had given up on living, but as I started to feel remorse for my deception, it became clear to me I knew no other way to live.

I knew no other way to build a life, and there was no one else who understood me. I didn't know where else to go other than my family and wait for them to set my life on a course to a new extuiter. If I could only have a child, I thought. Then I would have something that was my own. The child of a powerful extuiter would likely have such abilities, and then we could have a life together with or without their father.

And so I did. But now I know I was only making a slave. My child was hidden from me. And though, in truth, I knew I could have found her somehow, in my heart, I wanted her to be free. Clinging to the hope that these plans my family had for me were the right ones, I stayed with them for years after my second extuiter was lost, waiting for my child to be found. I knew they wanted her too. But I recognized that if I ever were to be with my little girl in a way that was right, I would have to leave them. And so I did.

Now I wait on Deiphera in a mining observation facility on the white banks of South Rock Promontory. I have made contact with a Constance magistere. He's the one who placed me here.

I'm sure he knows where my child is. As sure as he knows the things I've done. I believe he's waiting for me to tell him all the horrible secrets I know, but I don't want to convict myself. Time is running short because the Constellation of Spirea may not be big enough to keep me safe from my father and the Scabeeze master he works for. With his suspicions, the Magistere has done little to help us be reunited, and I understand why. I am a danger. I am a selfish danger… to my child.

The great waves of the Deiphera seas rise and fall like mountains beneath the sky of dancing lights, and four moons maraud through space, reflecting light from the nearby Eagle sun. Counting the days is all I can do, waiting for someone to give; someone to break. I don't know how much longer I can bear the isolation.

Chapter 5
Plancks

S tarslides stream about the Constance night sky like electric blue rivulets over a black velveteen canvas. They dangle all about the horizon in every direction up and around the fishbowl of the skies to the other planets in the Constellation.

I have memories—memories I cannot deny. I was a Hypathian boy. I remember, as that boy, thinking if I were a giant I could grab hold of one of those starslides and swing through the heavens from one to another. I could run my hands through the solar winds of Deiphera like a giant and splash its waters at the Eagle sun. I could swing to the nebula of the Pillars of Creation and fly into its hazy mysteries, tumbling around through the million new heavenly bodies that burst to life in that second. And like a being, big in the property of time and space, an eon would be like a day.

But starslides are for traveling through, not for swinging on, and lately, a day feels like an eon. Time has moved so slowly while I've waited for Evah. Though my fantasies as that boy still well up a thousand transcending hopes, I am not a giant. I am not even a Hypathian boy anymore. I am a rat of mixed experience, perhaps as confused about my own being as Evah is about hers. I can only hold fast to the laws of time and space that rule my current incarnation, so I refrain from the fantasy life of being so much in the tides of creation and devote myself with all the strength I have to be proactive for the child I love.

There is another kind of transport, unlike the starslide, that can be accessed by a device called a planck thurometer triangulator. These devices create a teleportation gate between two points in reality. If used correctly, you could utilize one to step from, oh say, a beam near the top of the Holy Heart Church to the trash cans on the school playground in only a second of time. That would be a welcome convenience for a blind rat, but getting one of those devices way up to where I live, or anywhere, would be, to say the least, problematic for a creature with my stature. But there is a gateway up here triangulated from another point in reality. The Office of the Honorable Magistere Sanje, Constance Governance Division, Liberty Square. I don't like to use this gate, because a planck thurometer triangulator does not guarantee a perfectly convenient entry location on its far side and that's where I am.

The evening of Evah's tenth visit, I knew something had to be done to help her. She did not want to be taken by the Thwargg any more than I wanted her to go. There were some unscrupulous Thwargg, and one thing was for sure: She could not fall into their unequivocally calculating hands.

I scuttled along the most northern beam, way up at the top of the Holy Heart Church—the place where there was nowhere left to roam. I stopped to peer over the edge. Beneath me was a sheer drop of twenty feet to the stone and wood below, but at the right angle, the planck gate could be seen. It was three feet wide and emitted radiant bands of blue light around a circle of what looked like waves of water continually cycling outward from the center. Well, black water to me. Knowing it was there made the depth of the fall beneath it no less daunting.

"Oh, here we go," I said, flapping my lips around a disconcerted exhale.

I could not close my eyes for fear I would miss it. I let my body drop off the beam into the air, but a final doubt instinctively caused my tiny hand to shoot out and grab the rough wood. Swinging for a moment, I expelled, "Well, if there were a day made for doing something, today's the day!" And with a final glance, I let go.

"OOOOOOOOOOH…"

Ffffhhhhhuuuum bhuump!

"…BROTHER!"

I landed on all fours with a solid *bhomp* on a stack of papers, cranking back my neck so as not to touch down with my face at matching ferocity. When I thought I was secure, my feet and hands started flailing, grasping wildly for something solid. The papers shot rapidly into the air behind me, then the entire stack tumbled to the ground, taking me with them.

"It took me an hour to organize those," said Magistere Sanje in a matter-of-fact tone, still in his seat and leaning over his desk, where he was busy studying something. I could hear the sounds of some scientific procedure, perhaps a surgery, playing through the zaria, a unit that picked up signals from the far-off world of Earth.

"We really have to talk about moving that gate," escaped my open toothy mouth, as I tried to acclimate to my new environment.

"It's been some time since I've seen you," Sanje offered mildly.

"Please don't make me try and climb that desk." Staring up at Sanje, I could smell his disinterest in engaging my request.

"You know I don't like you on my desk," he said, then released a slather of gentle exasperation. "You're filthy. No offense."

"None taken. You try being a rat." I leaned back to observe him the best I could, but I could make out little of him.

"They're coming for her, Sanje."

"What on Constance do you mean?"

"She's an extuiter. Segura has consulted with the Thwargg ambassador. They're going to find her."

"A consultation is a far step from the worst happening."

"No, but it's a beginning."

Sanje watched me. "She is young, but there are processes that can't be avoided. If she's exhibiting something out of the ordinary," he said, as if suggesting a remedy.

"I've already thought of that. I'm trying to persuade Evah to hide her powers."

"You've had communication with her?"

"She's hiding in the church every day. She saw me and… I don't get to talk to, well, anybody, and all I do is think about her, and words just came out."

"Well, I can't imagine how she took that."

"The children are bullying her." I reached for reason. "I didn't know what else to do. She extuited to some boy. I think she's extuiting quite a lot actually. Not images but… smells. It's really quite impressive actually. But there's another problem. Something more serious. Something she may not be able to have any control over."

"What?"

"She's seeing things that she isn't thinking up."

"But that's impossible, isn't it? Do you think it's Haytoo?" He leaned in toward me, his mood turning serious.

"No," I said in deep contemplation. "I don't know."

"Well. Let's hope there's another answer."

I was lost in thought.

He continued, "You understand it would draw unwanted suspicion if I intervened before they've even filed one report on the matter. The Claren family will have a natural claim over her. That will have to be contended with. I know you don't want her out in the open, but I must have an official reason to sequester on the grounds of being an extuiter for the Constellation of Spirea."

"You're a magistere! You can do whatever you want."

"You know that's not so. There are processes—"

"You want to use her."

"Everybody has a place. There are reasons that extuiters come along when they do. It's like anything or anybody else. If we try to do things outside the boundaries of the ordinances, we provoke endless angles of dissent."

"I can't believe this." I was losing my veneer of consideration.

"I don't want to use anybody. Please understand, my friend. We haven't had an extuiter for years."

"And for good reason too. It's as much a curse to be an extuiter as a blessing!" I told him sharply. "You people don't deserve to have an extuiter."

"No, it's not that," he replied with calmness. "It's just that there's so much we don't know."

"Well, perhaps what we don't know is that they should be allowed to live the same as anybody else."

"But they aren't the same as anybody else. And their effect on others can be…" He thought for a moment to choose his words wisely. "Dangerous. When they don't get the help they need to understand what they can do."

I had no reply to give because I knew he was right. Evah needed to be guided.

"You know, Felin, that I'm patient. And that I give great latitude for the best to transpire in extraordinary matters. You are the most extraordinary phenomenon I have seen since an extuiter. I don't have conversations with other rats. I've tried," he admitted, as if he had experienced a significant disappointment in himself. "And since the day you appeared in my office, with your stories and your ideas, I had to come to terms with the fact that there was no sensible place that you belonged in the order of things here. No other place than the one you seemed perfectly made for—to watch over Evah as you were told by Varin. I have given you what help I could. I have given you information. I had Evah hidden from her mother and the Claren family. And most of all, from Galneea. And I understand your concern. I don't want anyone to be used wrongfully."

"She's stronger than Varin."

"She must be gifted if she's already extuiting to others, but that surely doesn't mean she's stronger. It could be that she is much more fragile. That's why there are processes. To help her become strong with *wisdom*."

Understanding there was nothing else he felt he could do that would be right for Evah, I conceded. "I will try to help her."

"And I will closely monitor the Thwargg communications," he said with comfort. Then he continued. "You know, there *is* one option.

"What?"

"Skenkin has left the Clarens. She wants to find Evah, and if I know the conditions of a guilty mind, she will soon be willing to cooperate in an official investigation."

"No!" I gasped. "She's as bad as them! She'll do anything to get her, then she'll take her to them."

"She was a child too when all of that began. She asked me for help, and I have put her up on Deiphera."

"I'm sorry, but that can't be an option. Please promise me, Sanje—promise you won't give her to Skenkin," I pleaded softly.

"I promise I will watch her. And see if the Thwargg make any attempt to contact her or she them. I will find out her true intent, and I will tell you the truth."

"She doesn't know how to be anything else than what she has been. Varin said to keep her away at all costs. You have to believe that. She's dangerous. She'll trick you if she can."

"She's been alone there for many moons, and nothing so far. I'll watch her. And I won't do anything you don't want me to do. All right?"

"All right," I agreed, freeing myself from the gripping concerns enough to move on. "Well, go ahead and throw me up into the"—I swallowed disconcertingly, flopping back to all fours, gesturing to the circle of waves floating in the air at the end of his desk—"into the gate. Let's get this over with."

He drew back from his desk, opening the large lower drawer and took out a pair of rubber mittens. "I am sorry about the inconvenience of that planck gate. It seems the best we can do to make sure you don't end up in the middle of a beam instead of close to it. Are you hungry?"

"No, I had a big sandwich today."

"Lucky rat," he said, still peering into his drawer. "Oh, there is something else here that belongs to you."

"To me?"

He pulled an object from the drawer, placed it on the table, and opened it. "Something that might help you see."

"Really?"

Sanje lifted something from the box. It looked like a jumble of twisted straps, something helmet-shaped, and what appeared to be goggles, which glinted in the light enough for me to know they were metallic.

My chin dropped with confusion. "Am I supposed to eat out of that or wear it?"

"We don't make many of these for rats. It was a special order, to say the least."

"Well, why stop there? Next time have 'em make a big metal suit for me?"

"Really?" he said, not getting the humor.

"No. Of course not. How am I supposed to get around in that thing?"

"Well, don't knock it till you try it." And with that, he placed it on my head and tried to tighten a buckle fashioned on the straps.

"Uh, here, let me do that." Feeling around to understand the contraption, I finally pulled the buckle snuggly under my chin until it was latched sufficiently and opened my eyes. My head bobbed up and down as I learned to manage the weight. "Oh, geez!"

"What?"

"A little heavy."

"We had to use a helmet to track the neural patterns."

I stared into space. "Wait a minute. What's this?"

"What do you mean?"

"Well, all I see is light."

"Well, it's a particle field enhancer. You're seeing more than a human eye could ever see. Or a rat for that matter."

"It used to be that all I could see was shadows. Now all I can see are lights."

"Oh, I've seen what that technology can do. There should be clear differential clarity between static and moving matter."

"Uh, yeah," I said with a little shaky astonishment.

"And plenty of tonal variety for an effective experience of spatial awareness and depth perception."

"Oh, yeah…" Though he didn't know it, I had memories of Sanje from before I was blind, like I had seen a planck gate. I had seen his silken yellow magistere garments, the long violet robe that draped from his shoulder down along the chair. I had seen the smooth top of his head, his reassuringly kind face, and his dark skin, which had an inner light to it. Now, what I saw before me was a freakishly smiley head with giant vividly lit eyes. Everything was radically rushing flows of sparkling light whipping over contours of shape I only could intuitively recognize, all in a spectrum of color from deep murky golds to a nearly brilliant hot white. Drawing back a little, I could make out the difference in the space around him—the shape of his chair, the desk, and the walls in the distance, even some apparatuses on his desktop, but nothing like the vision I was once used to. I slumped with despair.

"I really… I needed to see. Like you see. Like Evah sees. I don't think I can help her like this. I don't know if I can help her at all."

"I'm sorry, Felin. It's the best we could do with what we had to work with."

"Well," I said, still a little dejected, "it's better. Thank you. Maybe I can learn to do something with it."

"Shall we get you through that gate?"

"Yeah… All right." Putting his mittens on, Sanje lifted me up and carried me to the planck gate.

"Oh, by the way…"

"Yeah?"

"What scents does Evah make for people to smell?"

"Glillin flowers," I informed him.

"Oh, that's nice." Then with one giant heave and a, "Goodbye," he flung me fast into the air.

Fffffhhhhhuuuum bhuump!

I was soaring upward above the church floor, out of the gate, towards the old heavy beam. My new goggles did afford me slightly better vision that helped me to grab hold tightly and hoist myself up. Sitting on my rear, I looked around a moment in hopes that my new goggles would see something more of ordinary sight, but no such luck.

Removing the visual gear, I set it down in front of me with a clack, sniffed the air, and, holding the new gizmo securely, wondered what could be in store for all of us next.

Chapter 6
Eye

O rder. This is a process in nature that does not move in one direction. I am the process. I am elemental. I am the universe, from the beginning to the end. I am in all things—far more than anyone could think. I am the disquieted ghost of a child's hope. I am the color yellow on a magistere's garments. I am a thread that does not move only in a straight line through space. I am infinite threads. I am the white in the coarse, thick fur of a grimy black rat that wants to be an angel. I am the pixels of reality ad infinitum, the fragile hands of a Thwargg girl, the snorting snout of a Scabeeze, the leaping, self-hating ambition of a Thwargg father. I am a teeming sea with wretched blue waves that tower over withered compassion. I span from galaxy to galaxy and wish to swell above the eastern coast of America. I am the least important value, the unneeded adventure that was the last and should have been avoided. I am the reconciliation of salvation, the martyred casualty in the causation of saved humanoid structure. And though I do not have a shape, for I am like a mist of all that is unseen, you may see me like the shadow of a little girl named Evah, for she is the one I've chosen.

I bet you thought this was a quaint story. One where right and wrong made a difference. Here's the worst part of it: I don't care if it does. What I do know is that I am not a story of past, present, and future. I am an event.

To an extuiter in Spirea, existence as we know it is made up of fragmented fields of consciousness—what we think we know is real; what we believe we see. They are like blankets and veils with funny seams we casually want to believe are immovable, safe, and logical. Reality is an agreed-upon secondary fantasy of what was, at a single point in time, once true. Everybody plays a part in agreeing what is true in the present moment, and conflicts arise because truths of single points collide in a difference of opinion of what should be. The loosely stitched edges of these agreed-on merges of reality are called thrines.

Beneath the Deiphera sea, way down beneath a league of pressure, I awoke as the extuiter tugged upon the greedy Scabeezes' thrine. Smoke, and gambling chips, and their rodent pets crammed the hidden mining decks with stink. How I loved my extuiter. He fooled the eyes hung over their Scabeeze snouts so they could not see him slipping in and out of their pavilion entryways. These were the doors to the source of their plots.

Beyond the cabin windows were whipping currents, coral, and sponges. I was the dark energy in every inch of thick air. All around the extuiter, I made warmth and comfort to perfect his will and timing. I pressed the salty pounds of water outside. I softened the fall of his step. As Scabeezes creaked their seats and chunked their chips into a pile saying, "I raise that bet!" I thought on how I may save my extuiter from a broken fate.

Chapter 7
The Varin Logic

"**B**at, ball?"
   "Hit."
   "Girl, kiss?"
"Boy."
"Tree, fall?"
"Crunch."
"That's right," said Thwargg Eine Claren, Division 7, Constance Ward. "Now, three. Ring, smile, finger?"
"Proposal," said the handsome young extuiter.
"No," Claren sneered, disappointed. "Focus on the sensation."
"Slide. Cool."
"Better."

These were the preparedness processes for extuiter class. The objective was to connect logical progressions of stimuli to inform a fully detailed illusion. An extuiter used logic training for two important reasons. First, to make an illusion more seamless and complete, ensuring the intended receiver or receivers would not question it, and second, to help the extuiter logically dispel any hallucinations that were self-generated, using the simple laws of cause and effect and reasonable linear expectation.

For instance, you see an empty canvas, you walk away from it into another room, but when you return a few moments later, the canvas is filled with a brilliant portrait of someone who despises you. This cannot happen logically. There is no time for someone to have painted a portrait, to mix the colors and to clean up, leaving only an extraordinary finished product.

"Two more," Claren announced.

"All right," the extuiter conceded.

"Man, woman, dance?"

"Music."

"Yes. Evening, breeze, hair?"

"Refreshing. Cool."

"Good enough. Now. Here is our friend, the rat." Claren lifted a small plastic box onto the table between them. "Our friend, the rat, needs nourishment. He hasn't eaten today. Put some food in the cage."

Noticing the young extuiter was looking at him with a slightly puzzled grin, Claren interrupted the process. "Something on your mind?"

"Well, it's just… this is logic processing class."

"Yes?"

"But that isn't a 'cage.'"

"Right," he mumbled with disgust. "What? You don't want to do this?"

"No. It isn't that. I'm just trying to be—"

"Then let's continue." Claren picked up his clipboard and started scribbling notes a little furiously.

The extuiter stared at the rat. He stared at the dish in the corner of the habitat where some food may be found. After a moment, he sighed with disappointment and shook his head gently as if not knowing what to do.

The Thwargg reached up and opened the plastic door on top of the habitat. "Go ahead," he directed, as if things could be much better.

The extuiter reached inside with care and gently touched the rat. It looked to the corner, immediately sniffing with ravenous fervor, then sprang like mad in the direction of the dish. Its head bonked against the dish's surface, its little hands grasping through the air at something it could not seem to get a hold of.

"You can extuit the feel of something solid, you know. And the sensation of taste. Even the feeling of being full. What is the purpose of these exercises if you choose not to make connections from—"

"But then he wouldn't eat. He'd think he'd already eaten. I don't want him to starve," the extuiter declared.

Pushing a dish of black pellets towards the extuiter, the Thwargg exclaimed directly, "You have more important things to be concerned with than whether a rat isn't in the mood to eat properly. And it's more than past the time you begin extuiting your illusions without tactile contact." He gathered his textbook data screen, clipboard, and pen neatly.

The extuiter took a pinch of pellets from the dish on the table and delivered them into the rat's dish. "I know, Sire Claren. I'm sorry. I'm working on it."

"Take the rat with you. Practice. I don't want to see any further oversimplifications. Details! Details!"

*

It was the twelfth day that Evah had visited when I began to tell her of extuiter training and uses of extuiter gifts that exhibited growth tempered with wisdom.

"But I thought the extuiter was a girl."

"I don't remember saying that. I'm sorry to disappoint," I said.

"Well, what was his name?"

"His name was Varin. And he was from right here in the Constance capital. In fact, he even attended Holy Heart."

"Really?"

"He came from a poor, undereducated family of Hypathians and no one ever thought he would make much of himself."

"Were you the rat?"

"Oh, yeah… yeah, I was the rat. But—"

"What did he look like?"

"Well, Evah… he looked like you. But with shorter hair. And he was taller. Varin did have more advanced skills than the Thwargg thought. He just didn't like to get into the minds of living things, especially people. He felt it was a person's private space, and there should really be good cause to extuit into someone's mind. It was around that time that he got involved with Skenkin."

"Who's Skenkin?" Evah questioned.

"Skenkin was a Thwargg girl." I sat down near Evah and let out a deep sigh. "Skenkin was not what many people would think of as beautiful, but Varin thought her the prettiest girl he'd ever seen. I don't want to scare you, but there were reasons for that that Varin would only realize much later."

"Like wh— What do you mean?"

"Well, it became clear to Varin that logic wasn't all they were putting into his mind with all their lessons. In particular, Sire Claren of Division 7. Everything they said to Varin had two meanings. On the surface, they were lessons in logic designed to help him build illusions and keep his mind from troubling thoughts, but there was a deeper meaning—one of suggestion."

"Like what?" Evah wondered.

"Like, many of the words were perfectly used to direct Varin to see Skenkin and fall in love. She would seem perfectly on the mark for many of the thoughts Varin had swimming around his young head about girls."

"That's sort of like making an illusion. Like an extuiter."

"That is what a Thwargg director does. And that is why Thwargg do what they do. Watch dreams and direct people to the best outcome that fulfills their desires while serving society. It's complicated, Evah." I did not want to overburden Evah with these concerns, but at the same time, I knew it was going to be important that some understanding was established. She needed to understand how important her gift was to people with ideas on how they'd like to use it.

"And did it work?"

"It did. He loved Skenkin immediately. And though he may have thought from time to time how strange it was that everything was so perfect, it only confirmed for him that he was special and meant for happiness and a life of great accomplishment. But, Evah, even though it may have been a circumstance manufactured by an unscrupulous Thwargg, it doesn't mean that Varin's love wasn't real. Or that the things he did for that love weren't real. Because he was in love. And Varin believed love was the greatest reason to extuit to others."

"Tell me something he did," she requested, so I did.

*

He had seen Skenkin outside the Thwargg offices. She always did her college homework on the steps of the Constance Thwargg ward, in the afternoons, at the same time Varin left to go home. They had talked now and then, with a passing, "Hi." He had a big crush on her. He loved her black hair and the way the sunlight danced on it. Her eyes glowed orange like the solar winds the Thwargg had him practice making in his lessons to master a sense of light in his illusions. On that day with the rat, as he descended the stairs, she spoke to him.

"Nice rat!" she said with a smile.

"Thanks!" Varin said. "They just gave him to me," he told her, hoping her interest would be peaked.

"What's his name?" she asked, as if it might reveal something about him.

After watching the rat with an *aren't we handsome* smile on his face, he replied, "I don't know."

"Nice habitat," she said admiringly and tapped the plastic with the long nail on her pretty index finger, as if to say hi.

"That's the word I was looking for," he continued.

"What do you mean?" she asked with an energy that confirmed how handsome he was.

"Well, my teacher kept calling it a 'cage.'"

"Oh, well, it's not all that bad. What does he know? A cage seems so cold and mean."

Varin watched her, happy to be so close. Skenkin looked down to her data screen and other study materials, gathered them up, and slipped them into her bag.

"All done?"

"Yeah. The sun is nice here, but it's going to start getting cool pretty soon." She slid a ring on her middle finger that had been laying on a step beside her onto her middle finger. Then she stood up and put her bag over her shoulder, looking at him with her dancing orange eyes.

"Headed home?"

"I am." She meandered a little on the stairs, with her eyes on him.

"I'm going that way," he said, pointing.

"I know." She continued smiling.

"Oh. Right."

"I see you every day. Me too. To the dormitory. I usually take a scotschoot."

"Well, why take a transport when you can walk with someone as handsome as me," he quipped playfully.

"Hm. All right," she replied.

They walked along as evening eased its purple color into the sky. The stars were beginning to shine. The planets brightened into focus, and the starslides with their electric blue curving tubes started to glow into the appearance of some heavenly trapeze.

He took her home, and they talked of things it would be nice to do in the future. Varin was mesmerized by her and wanted to show her his gifts. It was a strict rule that extuiters were not to reveal themselves, but he wanted to give her a memory to think on when they were apart.

And so he did after they had visited awhile and she stood to leave. Stepping to a table near the front door and picking up her bag, she noticed something falling to the floor over her shoulder with a little flash of white light. She stepped back to find a flickering glow all around her head of luxurious black hair. Stars floated over the surface and in and around her shiny locks.

"Wow," she said, lifting a lock of hair lined with the oscillating stars. She turned to admire her image in the mirror on the wall before her. With her orange eyes glowing and her dark hair surrounded with stars, she looked like some deity of the heavens. With the tip of one finger on her lovely hand, she lifted one star into the air for a closer look.

"It's warm," she said, her tone hypnotized. She studied it a moment, then looked at him.

"Make a wish," he encouraged.

And drawing in a deep breath, she blew on the star. It shot through the air, leaving a stream of glittery light in its trail, whipped around like a firefly, then shot straight into the rat's habitat, through a tiny ventilation hole and ricocheting directly into the rat's bowl, where it made a splash, filling it with water. The rat made a quick dash to the bowl and started lapping with joyful indulgence.

*

"What did it taste like?" Evah asked with a smile.

"It tasted like the best water a rat ever had!"

*

Skenkin turned to look at Varin with astonishment.

"Huh," Skenkin exclaimed. Varin smiled but asserted his modesty and gave no boast.

"I have to go." Skenkin gathered her things and flew out the door in a rush. But that was the beginning of their life together.

*

In the distance, the school bell rang. Evah jumped to her feet, and before making a run for the schoolyard, she looked at me.

"Thank you for telling me that story." Then after observing me a moment, she added, "Bye!" and then she was gone.

That is what I told her on the twelfth day because something deep inside me was hammering away. She needed some perspective on her gifts. There was more going on inside Evah than she had let on at first. Something more mysterious.

The day before, she'd done most of the talking. She told me about the glillin flowers—how they sprang into the air from the garden soil, like long exquisite birds standing on one foot, the new blossoms like heads with long, open mouths. As they grew, they turned into a tall, thick stock of vibrant colors—purple, pink, and blue. She and Father Segura would cut them and bring bouquets inside. That's when she fell in love with their smell.

Then she told me about the readings in church. They gave her the idea about that deep dark hole to nowhere under the flinging bars. They were readings about fire and incineration for things that were not so good.

"I couldn't decide if I was good or bad. You know, with everything...? And sometimes I wanted to be both," she'd told me like it was a secret.

Then, she'd explained that her class had taken a tour of the Constance Natural History Museum. All the halls were filled with strange creatures—deep-sea creatures. It was then she started imagining the eight-eyed monster with five arms in her closet at night.

"Were you scared?" I asked.

"I was. And I was so tired, but I couldn't sleep. Then one night, I was staring at the closet, and that horrible thing was there. Father Segura walked into the room like nothing at all strange was happening. He walked right over to that monster and poured salt on it. It melted away, and I fell right to sleep. I guess I must have imagined him too."

I wondered as she talked if my new goggles would have helped me see her better. I left them behind, thinking they may raise too many questions.

All of these stories seemed to not be too difficult for her. The toy animals and that crawling baby gave her the most trouble. That and the mysterious man's voice that called her in the afternoon. But, that wasn't the only time she heard it. She had seen the marching toy animals less and less since her time with me, but the voice persisted. One night as she watched TV in the orphanage and the other children colored together, she heard the voice calling to her. Looking in its direction, she saw the deep night sky and all its stars through the window.

"It seemed like the sky and stars were supposed to mean something," she told me.

Then, another time, flipping through the pages of a thick book, she'd come across a picture of a tempestuous blue sea.

"Yes," she heard the voice whisper, as if to tell her something about it.

Then, in class one day, something even stranger occurred. The voice called to her from outside a nearby window again.

"That," the voice informed her, and as she looked to see what it may be talking about, she caught a view of the wind blowing through a giant tree. One great leaf tumbled to the ground, then, all at once, right in front of her eyes, plain as day, came the sight of an enormous red leaf waving back and forth. When it finally moved, there was a man's face so close they were nose to nose.

"I could see him. But I couldn't see him. He was holding the leaf's stem between his fingers. He had on gloves. His face was dark, and his eyes were bright and brown. He was wearing something like a scrunched-up black cap, but it wasn't a hat. It was more like a mask he had pulled back, and he had something on his neck."

"Have you ever heard the voice when we're together?" I asked.

"No. When I was looking for a place to hide here in the church, I looked at that big stained-glass window with the blue sky and the clouds it said, 'There,' like it was telling me where to go."

That was strange indeed. It was that same window I watched every day when I lay down and slipped into my afternoon nap. I'd watch that window until my eyes were subdued by the glowing blur and I abandoned my efforts to make some extuition. I knew there was something to this, but I did not understand it—did not know what to think of such coincidences. And it was then I was suddenly in a strange way. I was thinking of the Thwargg ambassador appearing, Evah's experiences with the voice, and her coming to discover me after all these years of waiting. I was even thinking of Skenkin, waiting alone on Deiphera. These details had a bigger picture I could not discern a logic from. Why was everything starting to happen in such a short space of time? It felt like there was a hidden hand bringing all these things to pass.

It was then that I'd been struck dumb, every receptor in my nervous system flush. The past and present boomed together in my head, a chilling desperation was all over me. I felt pressed to tell her all that I knew, but I couldn't speak. I was crushed with fever and fell into a darkness.

When my eyes opened again, Evah was still there, staring into space, deep in thought. It seemed like nothing at all had happened. And I would have believed it but beneath my head was a tiny puddle of drool. *Was I drooling?* I wondered. That was something I was not accustomed to doing.

Everything remained a strange trance for the remainder of that eleventh day, even after she had returned to class. That's why I told her of Varin and the logic training on our twelfth visit. I didn't know for sure if she had anything to do with my blackout, but just in case, I needed to try and focus her. And prepare her. Because she needed to know something of unparalleled importance: She needed to know about the Haytoo virus.

Chapter 8
Flit

A melody of plucked strings in tumbling cycles that I knew from long ago rose softly in volume on the kalodia. It was sweet and calm. The same song that used to play on my child's animal mobile years ago. The mornings on Deiphera were always the same.

My eyes drew open to see the Zaizon moon through the window. One might think they could reach out and touch it, it seemed so close on the horizon at the start of every day. It seemed to stand just on top of the long rippling seas, wrapped in a warm indigo light, and hearing the kalodia play that plucking tune like fragile springs hopping, I awoke.

The light of my eyes illuminated my pillow, and outside the wide cloudy sky with its heavy, salty atmosphere was like a mirror to the feelings inside me. I rose up. The covers pulled around me like heavy cascading sand.

Morning came day after day. Morning. Waiting. Morning. The feeling of falling sand was all around my body as I told the forces that kept the planet in its place among the stars, I must rise today. And then that same kalodia song that used to play while my child contemplated the orbit of animals on the mobile above her crib so long ago snuck in to haunt me. Circles. Circles like the days of my life. Circles like the tumbling patterns of music. Circles like the path of Zaizon around my new home. Only to return to similar moments again and again.

Eat. Watch the waves crash on the South Rock Promontory, all craggy and wet. Read in the lounge. Sit in the captain's chair. Lie on the floor. Feel the warmth. Feel the cold—a cold that made me believe one day I could wake to find the sea waves frozen. Cook in the kitchen. Listen for life. Greet the infrequent sun.

The past and present seemed to be merging in one current event. So the mobile spun. Monkey and chigraff. Warm day, cold day. Fox and rhino. I'm in the chair, I'm on the floor, and so on, and so on.

Then, on the morning that old tune played on the kalodia to call me from my sleep, something different happened. Cozy inside the control room, as I watched the waves splash on the promontory rock and contemplated jumping into the sea for some variety, I spotted something out of place. I was not sure at all if I even saw them. Fog rose over the farthest point of the lookout, the waves receded, and as the haze stirred in the salty air from dense to a thin veil, there appeared what looked like flowers growing straight up from the barren white rock. First, long green stems sprouted up in an unnatural quantity of time, then a blossom—large and white. Then from another a pink blossom burst.

Donning my fur-lined coat, I braved my way out onto the unwelcoming rock surface to see the blossoms more clearly. The salty air saturated my skin, and it was cold, but the closer I stepped towards the flowers, the warmer it seemed to become. And though there was no brilliant sun in the air, subtle rays of sunlight radiated around the succulent new buds.

Another blossom peeled free of its long tender sepals. I wanted to reach out and touch them, but I was afraid a wave may sweep me away. The wind whipped over the rock surface, and my hair blew long, high, and sideways. It was so brisk, my hair seemed a permanent fixture of the sky.

I heard the crash of a wave and slowly raised my hand, the hard wind pressing against my will to reach my goal. My scarf blew off fast. Robbed by nature, it snaked into the heavy cloud, which was only scarcely held back beyond the flowers as if some mysterious force possessed it. Its intent seemed somehow indecisive, or it was in jeopardy of losing its control over the wild elements.

My ankle twisted on the uneven rock and I drew back in fear. The blossoms continued to pop open as if time were advancing faster. They almost seemed impatient with my cautious retreat, but the wind jammed hard against my face, and it seemed the same force that wanted me to approach was simultaneously forcing me away. I closed my eyes, trying to press into the wind. When I opened them, the flowers turned to lifeless water, giving up their shape to rain down onto the rock in a fast release.

The foggy cloud drew back as if commanded by some god to form a wall twenty feet from the edge of the rock. Before it, a possessed sum of shadowy blue water trembled and swelled up like a tidal wave that filled me with terror. As it did so, a slimy purple creature rose from the rock where the flowers had stood. Five arms sprang out of it in every direction, and on the palms of every hand, sickening tongues jutted wildly from salivating fangy mouths. Eight bulging eyes squeaked up on eight squirming tentacles. They twisted around, frantically searching the space until they finally settled their focus on me. The wall of ocean water towered fifteen feet high. My hand shot to my mouth, sure this was my time to die. If that wave collapsed on me, it would dragged me out to sea.

"No!" was drawn from my lips like a long bit of intestine might be drawn from deep inside my guts.

All the elements hung still. Then, in a heartbeat, everything came crashing straight down to its former place. In the sickening eight eyes, before they gave up their form, was a look of self-loathing, as if the creature loathed to be something so unwanted. Its eyes were filled with sorrow, with abandonment.

The resulting expulsion of water soaked my body and I fell to the ground, ready to hold tight to any crag I could dig into. Those eyes. My mouth was stunned open in shock.

I made my way back inside to the operations room and stared long at the staging area of that terrifying drama. I did not know how much of it was real. Or if it was something of a dream, as my days ran one into the other and some days everything was like a dream.

I returned to the blankets that drew about me like heavy sand and slept in hopes I might awake into the clarity of something more real.

Chapter 9
Eye Two: The Pearly Hornets

I don't know all things. I do not know myself. But, through others, I can know many details of goings-on. If you empty your pocket on any given busy day, you may find surprising things. Things that are needed and things that need to be thrown away. That is what it is like to empty a mind. There are things that have meaning and must be kept, and some things that remain of what needs to be done.

This is what Felin's head was like to empty, though it was deeper than one would think a rat's mind might be. I could see his Sharvanna magistere friend. I could remember their words as if they were my own. There were other things too, but many I could do nothing about. Not yet anyway.

There was a mother named Skenkin on a watery planet. But there was history too. A dirty scheming Scabeeze and rotten-willed Thwargg. I knew their faces well, as they had been in my scope of being for many years. They swam through the presence of the dark energy of which I was a part. But to get to the crux of a humanoid's experience in the field of time, you must obey the laws of time as they inhabit it. I was going to have to get closer.

In the morning, on the underside of a wave of light, I awoke with Evah. She rose from her bed in the Holy Heart Orphanage that morning, bathed, dressed, and made her way to the kitchen

where she ate her breakfast, holding tight to the pretty stone from her rat friend. She then proceeded to the asphalt playground and got in line, where she waited with the other children from class for their teacher to take them inside. The children laughed and chatted as they waited, and Pearly Shyen whispered with her friends about getting a new coat for winter. As always, she was right next to Evah, way too close for comfort. One boy was sharing the story of a riveting adventure his family had had at the Constance zoo. To some of the children, who did not get to do many things with their parents, if anything at all, for there were orphans present, this was annoying. The boy did not seem to notice, or he didn't care.

"The elephant was ginormous," the boy said.

"Really?" another inquired.

"Yeah. Big as my house. Taller. They let me feed it. I put out my hand, and my mom was so afraid she musta crapped her pants, 'cause she held on to me like I was gonna get sucked up by the monster thing. Its tusks were so big it had to hold them over my head and reach down to get the nuts with its trunk. Freakin' tusks were big too. Like they could have gone right through me and flung me through the air over to the lions!"

"Dang!" the boy listening said with amazement.

"I bet you never saw an elephant with tusks so big they could pick up your big fat mother!" said Corvy Bane to the little storyteller.

"Ah, you're just jealous 'cause you're lucky if your mom takes you to see crap on the street," he shot back.

"Ah, why don't you just shut up. Your breath smells like your mother fed you crap for breakfast."

"Dang, man," said the other boy with a smile, still hoping to hear the end of the story.

This humored meanness that seemed to come so easily to the other children was a perfect reason to tickle Evah's mind with discomfort. She sank her hand into her pocket to find the stone she squeezed when she was worried. I informed the stone to

have an imperfection not seen before, and she pulled it from her pocket, turning it around in her hand and rubbing the surface with her thumb. She then held it up to the light.

Nothing, she thought. *That's weird.* She stared at the deep red surface. She could see one side was perfectly flat and the other beveled into many angles.

"Uhh!" Pearly Shyen gasped. "Where d'ya get that stone?" She snatched it from Evah's hand. "Oh my God, Corvy, you are so desperate! You really went and gave that crummy old bow to rhino butt! I can't believe you really did it! Rhino butt doesn't know what to do with a bow, her hair's so nasty. She probably thought it was a bone! She chewed the stone right out of it! Probably spit the rest out in the trash can when she realized she couldn't eat it!"

The other girls laughed, and Pearly was drawing the attention of all the other children, including Corvy Bane. Evah noticed his staring eyes.

"I didn't give it to her! I don't know what you're talking about," he added with disdain.

"Rhino butt and Corvy sittin' in a tree!" she quipped to her girlfriends. "I'm surprised you didn't eat that stone! Go ahead!" She lifted the stone to Evah's mouth. "Go ahead! Swallow it!"

Evah moved her mouth away.

"Go ahead—swallow it!" She pushed Evah with one hand, goading her harshly. "Swallow it, stupid!"

When Evah gave no response, Pearly turned and threw the stone at the school building wall a few feet away. It made a smacking noise and bounced back onto the ground.

"Geez, Pearly, leave her alone," Corvy said.

Evah was still for a moment. She was in shock and did not know what to do. She didn't want the kids to think she needed the stone because she had a crush on Corvy, but she didn't want to leave it there either. She wished her friend Felin was there, and that she could run away.

There was a moment of stillness. Evah felt the morning chill, then she awkwardly walked over to the stone to pick it

up. Her muscles and bones were wonky like they couldn't work well together. She ran her thumb over the surface to feel for any damage.

"Yeah, fetch, rhino butt," Pearly added for a further jab.

Evah drew in a big breath that seemed to have no end, thinking she might cry, when suddenly the garnet melted in her hand. It separated into vibrating droplets, rolling around her palm, and up and down her fingers. They agitated violently and changed into angry black hornets, buzzing and flitting their wings. Growing enormous, they swarmed about Evah's hand and sprang in the direction of Pearly's head. The other children backed away, scrambling for a safe distance. Amazed, they could not stop watching.

Pearly swatted furiously at the angry hornets, letting out a whimper of fear that quickly became a scream of terror. The first sting cracked through Pearly's right hand. She howled in pain, shaking her hand like a wild creature losing its mind.

She slapped at her face as another sting welted her left cheek. The swarm was all about Pearly's long soft hair, spinning about the axis of her head like zipping satellites, crashing into the surface of her head, one after the other. They buzzed through her hair, disappearing and reemerging as through a dusty cloud, then one crawled onto her shoulder and stung her hard. Reaching up to sweep it away, three more hornets attacked, stinging her hand three more times with brutal conviction. She fell to her knees on the unforgiving asphalt and burst into a hail of tears. I made sure of that.

Evah ran to Pearly, putting her hands on her as if to comfort her and brush away the hornets. They disappeared faster than they'd burst to life. A few of them collapsed into one single hornet and shot back into Evah's pocket, out of existence. The buzzing was gone, and all was calm, though Pearly was a sobbing wreck. Only some of the children remained, staring at her as she moaned, but the others had run off. Father Segura appeared to help the two girls.

"What's happened, Evah?" he asked.

"There must have been a bee," she replied.

Father Segura lifted Pearly's chin with a cautious finger, and she brushed away a tear. All the stings were gone except one swelling welt on her right hand. The hand that she made so busy pushing Evah.

"Let's get you to the nurse, Pearly." Father Segura stared at Evah a moment, searching her expressions. "Thank you, Evah, now get back in line. Everybody get back in line! It's all right now. Your teacher's on her way. Come on. Back in line everybody," he said, reclaiming some order. Then Pearly was gone.

Chapter 10
Heartbeat

S hadow swirled open like a dusty fume, revealing the coursing waters of the Constance city canals. The water streamed along, turning this way and that through the branches of the aqueduct system. On its surface, the moon, the stars, and warm yellow lamps of the commons area shimmered and hopped upon its surface, as it banked from the sea deep into the water district. It flowed beneath one of the many stone bridges into a broad arterial passage, the force of the water revealing its strength in a torrent of sound like deafening white noise—like a million whispers at once.

From somewhere unseen, the long tones of a church organ could be heard. The dark waters flashed with the hot white light of explosions from beneath its surface, the bursts beginning in the large channel and reaching far into the distance on either side. *Pop, pop, pop* they blew, the hot white light escaping up into the air like an ancient photographic flash.

Some dock workers could be seen preparing themselves on the bank. They stood before the landing bay of the Constance Kepplequer Depository Factory, as noted on the sign atop the port opening. In the sky above, a wide shipping starslide could be seen and in it an incoming pulse of energy from Deiphera.

Crack shhhluuup!

A Prowler 239 shipping vessel slammed into sight, hovering above the docking bay, and shifted down from turbo thrust. It made a screaming howl like a giant predatory cat and levitated slowly into the light towards the depository bay doors. Its hydraulics revved to a hum and the prowler's wings folded in tightly around its hull. The dock workers scrambled—one latching hooks from the craft into the ground, another inputting data on the screen of a communication station.

Drawing away from there, and moving through the darkness between the surrounding stone buildings of the city, there was an apartment window, not too far away. Inside, was a softly lit nursery room. A furry black rat slipped clumsily, trying to keep his balance, on the rail of a crib near the window. He dangled from the rail, his little feet flailing as if he might fall, but he recovered a solid stance. In the crib, a baby girl lay looking up to a mobile of soft animals slowly turning around in a circle. The sound of streaming fluid could be heard and then a baby's heartbeat, pumping fast. The baby's eyes blinked as she studied the circular movements of the mobile's animal menagerie. Her single rapid heartbeat became two slower beats pumping in synchronicity like a pounding rhythmic conversation, one responding to the other.

A male figure was standing quietly over the baby, his hands resting on the rails. He was wearing a black bodysuit that covered him from head to toe. The chigraff from the mobile appeared on the footboard of the crib. It did a silly march and smiled as its head bopped back and forth to the music-box sounds of the spinning mobile.

"Oooiii, eeh, eeh, eeh, eeh, eeh, eeh!" exclaimed the monkey from its place on the mobile then stopped and restarted its jovial expressions again and again like a game of peek-a-boo. Noisy then so quiet you'd think it didn't move at all. Then again. Then quiet. Then again. And the baby laughed at its mischief. The monkey swung happily, sticking its tongue out at the girl with a grin, and her laughter grew.

White shimmers flashed around the child. Outside the window mysterious stars shined. Another identical man sat in a chair on the other side of the room. He seemed to be watching himself in the jovial interplay at the crib. This version of him sat still and upright, his hands on his lap, cloaked in a long black coat.

A white light began to glow from inside of him. It flared and emitted dancing golden bands. The lights grew brighter and then all the substance of his being disappeared, leaving only the outline of his figure, like a door. Through the door of his body, a blue sky could be seen. White clouds streamed past. Around him, the sturdy room still stood in its shadowy dim glow.

The two heartbeats responding to one another could be heard again. The clouds raced inside the outline of his body, and the plucking of the mobile made its pretty tune. The blue sky within him turned black. Peering into the black door of his being, far in the distance, a singular point of light could be seen, but just as the point of light seemed to be turning into something else, I sleepily opened my eyes.

It was afternoon. I was lying on a beam high above the church floor. A great droning chord blew from the organ across the sanctuary. Maddy Poole, the music director, stood up from her organ, collected her music, and quietly walked away, exiting through a door behind the altar.

I realized I had failed again. I dedicated my late mornings to deep meditation, and I thought with enough focus, I could make my own extuition. Extuit something to clog the pipes of Maddy Poole's organ. But no. All my meditation was good for was taking a nice nap. Maybe it was my rat brain. I guess I just didn't have the right equipment for it.

After a few moments of silence, the east door opened and Evah stepped inside. It was the thirteenth day she visited me.

Chapter 11
Epidemic of the Mind

Haytoo was a guitarist. He was popular in the nightclubs and cafes of the Constance Commons. His melodies were so informed with an understanding of the living experience, listeners found it more profoundly moving than any other music of his time. His ability to extuit became most potent a little later in life. Though he trained for a short time as an extuiter, Thwargg, Division 7 declared him inadequate. But Haytoo had decided he did not want to work for the Constance government and fooled his educators. Everyone but Eine Claren, who allowed him to go free under the condition that Haytoo would periodically do some secret work for him and his associates.

The more Haytoo had learned about the Constance Ordinances, the more he despised them. He detested the idea that persons with certain gifts should only be able to do certain work and that certain persons were not allowed to love whomever they pleased. It was suggested he fell in love with a Scabeeze girl, which was not permitted. An extuiter might make someone in business powerful beyond limits, and he committed terrible crimes, but no one really knew why. Some thought he was angry with the destruction of his people's ways. But, he was popular in music and heard on kalodias across the Constellation of Spirea. What was believed for sure was that his music had the power of extuition in it.

At one of the nightclubs where he played, there was a back-room Scabeeze club where business went on between those who were law-abiding and those who were a little more shady. Many Constance businesses were owned by Scabeeze, so this was quite common. The Scabeeze got a little wild there and went around with their gravity modulators set to zero. They could be seen floating around tables and flying through the air as they indulged in their debaucheries.

One night after a musical set that overwhelmed the crowd, Haytoo was invited to an audience with the owner, an influential Scabeeze named Phodak. Phodak was one of an elite Scabeeze club—one of the richest of all. Haytoo entered the back room and approached Phodak as he levitated with a circle of friends he was entertaining.

"Scladeesh," he told the others, who departed with impressive manners for the greediest of Scabeeze. While Phodak was distracted with the departure of his friends, Haytoo turned to a waiter and took an empty glass from their tray. Giving it a tap he made an expensive purple liquor appear inside it then traced the rim with one quick turn of his index finger.

"I've brought you a drink, great Phodak," he said and pulled up a stool to sit beside the floating master. He sat the drink on the table beneath Phodak's looming figure.

"I don't drink gifts from strangers," the master replied, looking down at him.

"It's the custom when brought before such a great master to bring a gift, is it not?"

"You know the Scabeeze ways?"

"I've known a Scabeeze or two." Haytoo gestured to the waiter. "Two glasses!"

He pulled a small sealed bottle of liquor from his long coat, set it on the table and grabbed the drink he had prepared for Phodak and swallowed it down in one big gulp and smacked the glass back down on the table. "What can I do for you, Master Phodak?

"It is a matter of what I can do for you. I want to put your music on every kalodia in the Constellation system."

"It sounds like a way to make a buck," Haytoo responded lightly but with some interest.

"I will be your new producer," Phodak put forth.

"My songs are already on kalodia playlists."

The waiter brought two glasses. Haytoo gestured to the bottle. The waiter picked up the bottle, unscrewing the top with a crack as the seal broke, and poured the liquid into the glasses.

"To your health," Haytoo said, lifting the glass, then shot back the second drink.

Phodak grabbed his glass and, bringing it up in a salute, he said, "I will triple your profits. I'm an influential man. There are some distributing companies who are more inclined to work with me." Then he too shot back his drink.

"It's nothing like what can be made in kepplequer." He poured Phodak another drink.

"What do you know about kepplequer? You're a musician? Kepplequer is for me to worry about."

"I know that you are the biggest distributor off-world. As big as Constance regulations will allow. Everybody needs power. And where there is something that everybody needs, there's money. That's where I want to be."

"I will make you much more money with the music than you could ever use."

"No."

"Do you know who I am?" he asked, offended.

"I think I made that pretty clear."

"Why would you offend me in such a way?"

"Because I'm confident," he responded with a smile.

"Well, maybe too confident, little Hypath."

"Fine. I'll make another partner."

"No one's going to put you in the kepplequer business!" Phodak recoiled, pushing away from his table to levitate higher above the irritant, his spindly arms gesturing with contempt.

"Somebody already has," Haytoo responded with control. "I have to be going."

"Who? Who is it? Someone trying to take business from me? Who is it? Tell me."

With that, Haytoo slipped off his stool and began to retreat to the exit.

"I have the biggest interest in the system. And that's all the system. Wait. It's that mealy worm Blossa! What does he want with you, ya talentless wire plucker? Kepplequer is mine."

Phodak's rising temper was drawing attention. His friends sputtered their propulsors, drawing into a circle around him. A guard put his hand out and grabbed Haytoo, but the man's hand lit up in flames and trying to put out the fire only made it spread faster. He started screaming, and the crackle of burning flesh could be heard.

"This man needs help! Someone help this man," Haytoo demanded and kept walking to the exit. As he reached the door, an argument erupted at Phodak's table. Phodak drew a short heavy blade from his belt and laid into another of the Scabeeze. The blade made a loud wet thwack, sticking deep into his newly established enemy.

"That's mine, you filthy thief!" Phodak said.

Another started yelling at Phodak in Scabeeze and ripped something from Phodak's garment at the arm, then he too drew his short sword and laid into Phodak. Before any sense could be made of what was happening, they were all hacking at each other in one fast, bloody opera of yelps. And Haytoo escaped.

*

"He put something in his drink?" Evah guessed.

"Even the drink wasn't real."

"The bottle?"

"None of it. None of that was real. Everybody saw it. Even interacted with it," I said, pressing the point.

"Did they really hurt each other?" Evah asked, deep worry in her expression.

"Yes, Evah. All of those Scabeeze are gone now."

"They died?"

"Yes. And although it only looked like a bad argument at the time, it was really something else altogether."

"What? What was it?" Evah inquired.

"It was the first time we know for sure that the Haytoo virus was used."

"But how did they get sick? The drinks weren't real."

"He extuited it. Some Hypathians are doctors or scientists. It takes a lot of imagination to innovate, but Haytoo's father was a microbiologist. They study tiny things—tiny lifeforms that interact with other lifeforms. Lifeforms that can be destructive to others. Haytoo spent his childhood looking through his father's electron microscope studying things like that; studying how they interact with the cells of animals and all the races here in the constellation system. So he imagined one apparently. One that made people think that others around them were guilty of unspeakable things, sometimes their worst fear and sometimes the truths that most disgusted them about themselves—the secrets they felt guilty about. They saw that in others, and something more too. It reacted differently in different planetary races. Apparently, they thought they were getting messages or something that informed them about others around them."

"But they were lies?"

"Usually. Usually, they were lies. Sometimes there was some little element of truth. Even then, it was only a corrupt instinct. Conjecture. Guessing. When the virus was at its worst, when it spread to many people, it caused them to be cruel to those they were suspicious of. It reflected their nature somehow. The most violent would kill or beat others, but the more mild and loving became cruel and alienating. So much so that people started hurting themselves to make up for wrongs they may or may not have been a part of at all. Some even killed themselves. The pressure of suspicions and paranoia can cause tragic responses in gentle people. All I can say is that it was a sickness, and even the purest were vulnerable."

"But why did he do it?"

"Haytoo had made a deal with Phodak's partner in the kepplequer business. He was paid extremely well to kill the Scabeeze master, even given shares in the business. Phodak's partner Galneea, who owned another large kepplequer refining company, basically took possession of both companies in a way that the Constance regulations could not condemn."

"Big money," Evah said.

"Yeah, big money. And big power too. There wasn't much a little rat like me could do about it."

"Did you get sick?"

"Yes, well, I guess so. But that's a complicated story. You must understand, Evah, why I'm telling you this. What you can do with your gift is a decision you must make every day. You can hurt, or you can help. I think you're a good person, Evah. I want to help you do what's right. That's why you must tell me everything that's going on. You can't hold out on me, like not telling me that the voice said so many things."

"But there are things I don't understand."

"Like what?"

"I… I don't have control," she said with a little despair.

"What happened? Did something happen?"

"Yeah. But there was something there. I felt different all day."

"Tell me."

"I felt big. Like I could see down the block and into the city. Into the ocean. Up to the clouds. Like I was a part of all those things."

"That isn't so bad."

"No. But in line before our first class, Pearly hurt me. She embarrassed me. And she tried to hurt my stone."

"I'm sorry."

"She threw it against a wall and when I picked it up, that thing—what made me feel so different… all I know is suddenly I was looking at the stone, and it changed into something horrible. Big bees. And they stung Pearly. And I was… It felt like I was swimming—like I was drifting in warm water. Like I was sleeping with my eyes open and warm currents were pressing all around me. When I saw what was happening, I went to her, and it stopped. I wished away all the stings, but they didn't all go away."

"Is she all right?"

"She looked fine when she left."

"Did anyone see?"

"Everyone saw it. Father Segura too."

"He was there?"

Evah nodded.

"Okay," I said, distracted with the realization of how serious the incident was, but I didn't want to scare Evah any more than she already was.

"Could Father Segura know for sure you caused it?" I put forth, hoping for some relief.

"No. He only came because Pearly was making such a scene. Well, all the kids were. But I don't think anyone knew it was me. Father Segura looked at me like maybe it could be me, but then he just took her away, and that was it."

"Well, that's good. Maybe nothing will come of it at all. Listen, Evah, everything has a solution. And sometimes the solution may seem scary or waiting for the solution to reveal itself may feel scary, but in the end, things have a way of turning out the way they should."

"What do you mean?"

"I mean, I don't want you to fear anything. Don't even fear going to see the Thwargg if that's what has to happen. I've talked to someone, and he's going to look out for you. He's one of the most important men on Constance."

Evah's eyes started to tear a little. "I *am* afraid, Felin. I don't want to hurt anyone."

I smiled at her. "You're good, Evah. You have to believe that. You tried to help Pearly, didn't you?"

"Yes."

"You see. Whatever happened, you wanted to help, right?"

"Yeah."

"Good."

"Do you think I have the Haytoo virus," she braved.

"No."

"How can you be sure?"

"Well, nothing is for sure. But what's most important is that even if you had it, you could still choose what you want to do. If you want to hurt people, that is a choice you make. And when you feel you're doing something or you're about to do something you wouldn't like done to yourself, you can stop and do something else. Sometimes doing nothing is better than doing harm." I looked at her to assure her. "You have control. Do you believe me?"

"I sure didn't feel like I did today."

"You must believe it. And you must want it. To choose not to do something you will regret."

"All right. I believe."

But I could sense her fear.

"Say it as if you mean it."

"I believe I have control. I believe."

"Good. Now listen. What you can understand, you can find a way to manage. You can understand problems, and there may not always be all the answers you need to solve the problem, but there will be ways to help the situation. So things can be better than only suffering. You can strengthen your mind; you can strengthen your body. There are things you can have power over. You are an extuiter, and sometimes knowledge can conquer the most overwhelming odds. If Haytoo can extuit a virus, you can know how the virus works. The Haytoo virus was a DNA virus. That's what makes up what we are. A DNA virus gets into the body through membranes around the eyes, the nose, the mouth. It lands on these cells and melts into them or is sucked in. Then, the virus tells the other cells around it to make more cells that have the virus in it.

"Some viruses stay in one place, and others spread through the body. The Haytoo virus affected special areas in the brain: The anterior cingulate cortex, the fronto insular cortex and the insula. The first two, the anterior cingulate cortex and the fronto insular cortex, have special cells that help us sense what others are feeling. Like if I cut my foot, you would feel sorry for me because you could imagine what it feels like to hurt that way. The insula takes information from the other areas in the brain and helps us make moral decisions. To do things that are right or responsible—things that are important for ourselves and the people around us. Furthermore, there was an abuse to the functionality of the amygdala that caused a retardation in the response to guilt and aggression. The hormonal and metabolic effect on all these regions led to a profound impulse of displaced aggression and self-hatred. That is what the Haytoo virus did."

"Oh, brother," Evah moaned. "I don't know those things. I'm e—"

"You're eleven. I know. But look at me. I'm a rat. I can know these things. And so can you."

"Well, stay in school, Evah, in case you run into a brilliant psycho," she said.

"Well, that would be good for a lot of reasons." With all the worry, I could not help but roll on my side and start to laugh, loud and hard. "Okay. It's a lot to know," I admitted.

"Yeah," she said and laughed a little herself. "I know there are 206 bones in most bodies in the Spirean Constellation," she added with a smile.

"Oh, that's very good. There's a lot to learn, but I can tell you this: Varin didn't know any of that when he finally came in contact with the Haytoo virus," I tried to reassure her.

*

The Scabeeze master Galneea took over all of Phodak's business interests. This made him exceedingly powerful on his planet, though some felt this was too much power for one Scabeeze.

One of the magisteria, a magistere named Sanje, together with a slim majority of the magisteria, passed a motion to have the highest court in the Spirean system dismantle all the companies that made up Galneea's kepplequer interests. A court date was set, and a judge selected to weigh the facts in a special evidentiary hearing that would decide whether the full-scale case should move forward. Everything depended on that judge's decision.

But the magisteria connected with the initiating motion started to suffer great misfortunes from the moment it was passed. One had ended his life; he left a note telling his associates that there was no other way he could think of to make right the losses people had suffered under his rule. Another had to go on leave from office because she had a terrible fight with her child, causing them to run away. Together with her husband, they had needled the boy with accusations until he lost hope and left, not to be seen or heard from until a report got back to her that he was involved with bad people and living on the streets. She felt responsible, and her leave was indefinite.

A third magistere attacked a man on his commute to the office, claiming he was spying on him and was going to blackmail him. He was placed in jail, for the beating he gave the stranger was severe.

A day or two before the hearing, Sanje was alone in his office, and Haytoo paid him a visit.

Sanje was busy with his affairs. He had been drinking clafenein from a cup on his desk. He emptied the cup and went back to his work, but after a moment he looked up to see it still had some clafenein left inside, so he picked up the cup and drank it up fast. A few moments later, upon standing to retrieve another beverage and reaching down to grab the cup, he saw that it was full yet again and stopped cold with astonishment.

At that moment, a group of court officials passed his office door. His listening became heightened. He could hear them talking, though he could make little sense of it until nine words sprang out strangely clear above the milieu of conversation.

"That judge is bought—"

"She'll destroy your little motion."

Sanje was not a vain man and did not think all things had to do with him, but this alarmed him, and he quickly looked after the passing crowd. He recognized no one, but the strangeness of the moment, the odd self-filling cup of clafenein, and the strange calling out of the words got the better of him. He thought he was having a spiritual experience, as he was a Sharvanna, and they were prone to experiences of extreme clarity.

Paranoia soaked his every thought, and within an hour, he was on the kalodia talking to every magistere remaining that had called for the hearing. They wrote a letter of complaint and had an investigation started to prove the judge presiding over the hearing was dirty. Within two days, the paranoia spread not only to the magisteria but to the investigator running the case. On top of that, an analysis of the judge's dreams from the Constance Thwargg ward reported the judge was having dreams about "power and riches." The judge was removed and subsequently found guilty of conspiracy, though it could not be proven for sure who the judge's contact was. The woman was ruined, fined, and suspended from her judgeship. Then, during the hearing to dismantle Galneea's company, the new seated judge made quick work of denying the motion altogether. Concurrently, another member of the magisteria group met a tragic fate in an argument with his wife. Sanje's suspicions that something foul was at work persisted, but this time he decided to do something else.

"I'm not myself, extuiter. I'm sure that everyone is involved in a conspiracy against the government. Even worse, against me, personally. I'm having to apply the utmost discipline to being clear-minded about these issues, and despite my rapidly deteriorating faith in anybody or anything, I am going to put my trust in you. Can you tell me if something has happened here? Something that someone like you might have done?"

Varin stood before Sanje, analyzing the magistere seriously. Sanje's clothes were wrinkled, and his eyes appeared dilated and tired, as if he was not sleeping. Varin had never been called to investigate such a situation. He had never done anything for the government, aside from social work, and had become sure he was only being paid to stay out of the way and not muck things up on some grand scale with his gifts.

"Well, this isn't something I usually do. I can manipulate reality, but I've never tried to see what someone else has done." He thought of what he might do in the office. First, he considered how he could not be seen. He could see the seams of perceptions from the perspective of the desk. He examined the thrines from the door to the desk and tugged at the edge of one with his mind to pull the illusion of the room around him so he could not be seen, disappearing before Sanje's eyes. "Yes. There is dark energy here." His voice came out of the empty space. "Like a residue around these thrines."

"Thrines?" Sanje repeated.

"The edges in time, space, and light that influence perception." Varin reappeared closer to the desk. "It's sort of like walking through a quilt—a really multidimensional quilt." He smiled and shook his head a little as if to say, *Isn't that neat?*

Sanje was not interested in "neat," so Varin went back to his work with an applied focus. Then, pointing gently to a place on the desk, he asked, "What was here? Do you keep something here?" The magistere watched him but did not want to tell Varin anything.

"Hmm. You drank something." He disappeared out of sight again. "I'll bet it was good too." His voice hung in space, seeming to move methodically along the desk to a filing cabinet. "You've got something here. Something I've never seen. Someone's tried to clean it, but they couldn't see it. Do you have somebody clean your office?" he said, still a voice without a body.

"Yes."

"It wasn't them. Looks like they couldn't see it and spread it around with a broom or something. It's got a weird energy signal to it." He popped back into sight, kneeling at the bottom of the file cabinet. "I think you should have it looked at."

"Clafenein," Sanje said finally spoke. "I was having a cup of clafenein here. And it kept refilling on its own." He said a little shakily.

"Oh, well, yeah. That should have been your first clue, there. That doesn't happen every day." Varin could not help but smile a little.

"Thank you," Sanje replied with a little irony. "How did you know about the liquid? Did it leave some trace of energy?" he asked, mystified.

"I couldn't see a liquid. There's a ring mark where you set your cup. I just put two and two together. My mom would tell me to use a coaster."

*

"What's dark energy?" Evah interrupted.

"Well, to put it simply, we only see with our eyes about fifteen percent of what's actually around us. Then there's dark matter—that's another fifteen percent which we don't see. And then there's dark energy. That makes up the other seventy percent or so. At least that's what some scientists say. On the whole, a lot is going on that we can't see. It's sort of a mystery, but when extuiters work on the seams of reality, a build-up of dark energy clings to that place like a residue. After closer examination by several teams of investigators, it was determined that what Varin found was radioactive dust. And there's only one logical place something like that is likely to be found."

"Where?"

"On the old world of Spirea."

"The trash planet?"

"Well, it used to be a lot more than a trash planet. A long time ago, that's where the Constellation of Spirea used to have its government."

"I always wondered why we called it the Constellation of Spirea when all we did was dump our junk there."

"Yeah. There are whole cities there. Civilizations, really. But there was a natural disaster on the surface. It didn't even happen in a big area, but it spread and killed everything. That's when they moved the capital to Constance and, not knowing what to do with the old world, they started using it as the system's dumpsite."

*

Luckily there were only a few active starslides to Spirea, and one in particular was used by Scabeeze industries. Sanje and his associates wanted to find proof Galneea was involved, so they set out to launch an investigation there. First, they sent someone from law enforcement, but he didn't return, so after a few more days, they decided to send Varin, since it was clear there was an extuiter involved. They sent five military personnel with him—a cold fire team. They packed up weapons and communication gear then launched to Spirea on a dump transport through the starslide.

On arrival, the transport was fed into the separation fields where junk was sorted from reusable materials. The military team's transport was one of thousands of open vessels that streamed through the plant and out to the surface world.

The giant automated arms of the separation facility proved dangerous enough for a start. One militia member nearly lost his life due to the meticulous machinery. They chose to enter the planet this way so they weren't detected starsliding right into the open on the visible platform. Varin watched as the landscape grew into what was hundreds of miles of waste. It was the garbage of seven planets, and hundreds of dump shipments streamed along on hover crafts to incineration fields.

The atmosphere here was thin, and the beta decay so intense that the environment was covered by a thin, effervescing rust-colored fog. Particles fumed upward all around them, and interspersed along the horizon were vivid red smoking fires that sometimes appeared as molten flows of lava. The team was outfitted with atmospheric suits that protected them from the deadly gases and oxygenated their bodies. The suits were white but quickly became layered in ashy pink silt. It was afternoon, but the poisonous atmosphere blotted out the sun, making a strange light between night and day. All seemed removed from any normal state of reality. Fire and emptiness loomed harshly in the planetary vista, and there was no sign of the mysterious extuiter.

Sanje had looked into the formal logs of previous extuiter candidates, but nothing could be found to identify the suspect.

"Dump schematics show an inhabitable structure in the fourteenth sector north of here." said one of the militia members, working on a handheld terminal. "There's a fast track module that can be accessed from the platform ahead."

The module couldn't be reached soon enough for comfort. The first incineration field was coming up fast, like a funeral pyre for giants out of hell. Varin fought back thoughts of being burned alive and tried to stay logical. He was a little concerned his gifts may spring unfortunate delusions that could be perilous for everyone.

They jumped onto a steel platform lined with holes to ventilate the undercurrents of heat. Diaphanous spires of smoke spit up around the team's boots. One of the command militants stepped up to a lever and yanked it back. Heavy machinery cranked to a start, and a blast of steam flowed up around the module dock. A long wailing ring sounded as the module whipped towards them from the far-off distance, and some sickening forms of life squirmed out from beneath the platform, slithering through the nearby cinders of refuse. They were like furless swollen rodents with multiple eyes and long horrible teeth. They slithered instead of crawled, devouring their meal and smacking their slimy mouths at each other.

"I guess the time for subtlety is done," Varin said, pressing the charging unit on his rifle, which spit out a high-pitched whine as it readied itself to fire.

Varin saw something large in the distance, leaping over flaming piles. They were the color of hot white ash, with bodies nine feet long and mammoth mouths, easily bigger than a bear's. Most were scattered along the horizon but some were closer. One perched upon a pile of junk and pulling back its great jowls, let out a piercing scream.

"Are you guys seeing these things?" Varin asked.

"Definitely," one militant replied. "Howlers."

Suddenly a harmony of rifle chargers whistled loud. The module was in sight and racing towards them, finally breaking hard into the dock. Nearing the edge of the platform to be sure the module was safe for boarding, they peered inside.

"We got a body," said the battalion leader.

It was the investigator Sanje had sent before. His body was without any atmosphere suit, only clothing, and his whole person was pink and swollen. One of the squirming furless rodents was feeding on his exposed guts. The investigator's face was twisted into a horrible contortion of wailing, teeth-gnashing sorrow.

One of the soldiers loosed off a shot from his rifle that blew the dining creature nearly in two. Another man dragged the investigator from the module and then swung the sickly creature out into the scatter of decay and fire by its tail. They filed inside and sat down, bracing themselves for the unknown journey ahead.

"You better hold on," said the team leader. Varin grabbed hold of the bracing handle, squeezing it tight.

"Launching," the technician remarked and kicked down hard on a stubborn foot pedal.

They all lurched back as the module propelled them towards the deeper sectors...

*

Suddenly the school bell rang and, lost in my story, Evah was startled.

"I've gotta do that sorta thing?" she asked, overwhelmed.

"No. No, of course not. You don't have to do anything you don't want to. These were special circumstances. You better go. Everything's all right."

Chapter 12
Primus

L ight buckled in the mouth of the Deiphera starslide as a
D-39 Shipping Scotschoot thrust into view over the igneous
surface of the South Rock Promontory. Fog was whipping in
and out of sight as I watched through the observatory window.
At first, it was nothing out of the ordinary from the usual bi-
weekly arrival. Sanje had arranged for food and other necessities
to be brought to the surface. The shipment delivery man was
a nice Spirean who always had some pleasant story to share
about Constance, but that day another man made the trip.
I moved to the entrance monitor for a better view, and my
heart filled with dread to see the scotschoot was operated by a
Thwargg man. My first instinct was to hide, but this was something other than just a strange delivery person standing on the
rock face preparing my packages. It was Blouty Duthane. He
was a boy from school that I had known years ago. One I could
never forget.

Dressed for the Deiphera cold, I walked out to meet him. As he
pushed his floating cart towards the observatory building, he gave
a knowing smile. Keeping his head down, he raised a muscular blue
finger to his lips. His eyes were like mutating emerald clouds.

"Shhhhhh," he whispered and continued through the sliding
doors.

I stared at him as the doors slid closed behind us. I was scared. But more than scared, the sight of him aroused a comforting nostalgia somewhere deep inside me. I did not want to reveal my joy. In some ways, I wanted to throw my arms around him and smell the scent I had loved so much in my youth. Once I dreamed of kissing his cheek day and night. I dreamed of having my cheek close to his and feeling his breath on my ear. He was my first love, and some feelings never seem to fade once you have loved someone.

He smiled widely, watching me before him as if we shared a million secrets, and we did. I made no movements but observed how he had grown. He was taller than most Thwargg. He wore an orange industrial smock and under it a class 1 Thwargg uniform that made him look dashing. It made him look the way I fantasized he would when I was a girl.

"I've wanted to see you for so long, and here you are," he said, awaiting some response, but I was in a daze. "Well? Is that all? Come! Give me a hug! It's been so long!" With that, he threw his arms around me and held me tight for a moment. Oh. The smell of him.

"How did you find me?" I said, diverting my eyes from his gaze. I walk towards the lounge but paused for a moment at the door to encourage him to follow.

"Are there observation monitors?" he asked without losing his beautiful smile.

"No. Not in the lounge. Only in here." Time seemed to slip away, and before I knew it, we were on the couch in the lounge. He had removed the orange smock and loosened the buttons on his coat as he sat comfortably beside me, all the while keeping his smile and his eyes on me. He projected such happiness to be with me. I was wearing a long soft skirt and sweater. I did not want to appear too comfortable. I kept a safe distance with my legs crossed. The Zaizon moon hung full and heavy in the window.

"You must get so bored here. I can't imagine being alone so long."

"I'm here for good reason. But no one is supposed to know that." I tried to contain myself in the moment.

"Oh, you have no reason to fear having me here." He continued to smile with expectation, then when he saw I was not budging, he relaxed his gaze as if to say, *Oh, come on.* He rose, took off his coat, and walked over to the kalodia. He was like a prize animal. Touching the screen with a few commands, he cued up a song.

"Do you remember this one?" It was something from our youth. The song achieved his goal of putting me in a fond mood.

"Of course. I could never forget that song."

"I can't stay long, Skee. I have to move out in a reasonable time, back to Constance."

"All right."

"I could stay with you forever."

"Things have changed, Blouty."

"Have they?"

"They have," I said, not feeling so convinced.

"You've done the things you had to do, Skee. We all have things we have to do, and you did that."

"No. It wasn't like that."

"I know you loved me. Your father knows you loved me. Do you know how broken-hearted I was when you left school to do what you had to do? I mourned you to an unbearable measure. I never stopped loving you. You were the big one, Skee. The one you never forget."

He crossed back over to me and sat on the couch, a little closer now, but respectful. "I finished school and worked on Thwargg for a few years. I never wanted anyone else. I guess I wanted to believe in something real. Something natural. It's time for me now. My time is now. I'm on Constance, in the ward there."

"That's wonderful, Blouty. I'm happy for you."

"I have a home on Thwargg still, Skee. A nice place. A place that's right for a family. It's only going to get better. We could do all that we dreamed of when we were kids." His demeanor and words were rapt with kindness, his bright eyes sincere. I tried to keep my thoughts diverted from fantasies.

"Your father came to me. He was filled with remorse, Skee. He said he was sorry for ever getting between us. He regretted that he had pushed you away. He's sorry. He wants you to be happy. He'll give you whatever distance you want, but he wants you to come home. He gave me his blessing to make a home for you. And I want to, Skee."

"I'm waiting for my child, Blouty," I said with a force I did not expect.

"And she's welcome too. We can give her a family—"

"You're talking like a dream. Life is more than dreams."

"What I'm saying is more than a dream. It's real," he interjected convincingly.

"If you know what my father has done to me, then know it isn't real. My father is a murderer."

"There's no proof of that, Skee. You may want to believe that because you had a rough time, but sometimes we make up stories so we don't hurt so much. Now, listen, I know. I made up stories about you and wanted them to be true. If I'm coming to you, ready to forget the past and move on, I know you can too. I'll protect you from your father. If we get married, he can have no power over you. Only what you give him. And you can decide. I won't tell you how much he should be in your life or Evah's. I swear to you."

I looked down with a desperation barely concealed. I wanted to believe Blouty. I wanted to have the things he was talking about. I didn't know if I would ever see Evah again. And the waiting was horrible. In my heart, though, I had a terrible fear this was only another man to whom my father would auction me off, so he could keep control over me, and over Evah, if she was found. At the same time, it was glaringly obvious I would never be rid of my father if he knew where I was now. I could never escape him and his plans.

"You have to go!"

He tried to take my hand. I pulled it away, but he grabbed it again.

"No, listen—" But he stopped. He stood and picked up his coat. His body language was relaxed, calm, showing no sign of animosity. "It's all right, Skee. There's nothing to be afraid of. Not from me. I don't want to hurt you."

Then he was silent for a moment, his eyes watching the floor. "You're my beginning and my end." He said the words we used to say to each other when we were kids. Words we said when we were young, and our love was like the power of the gods. "You're everything I want in my life, and everything I want on the other side of it."

Emotion rose in me fast and unexpectedly, but I fought to contain it.

"I will wait for you. I know that may sound stupid and like a lie, but it's not. I will wait."

I watched Blouty board the D-39. He cranked the brake and started the engine. It rose up in a hover. His green eyes reached out to me one more time from the shroud of his orange smock, and then he spoke once more.

"The ward thinks they've found Evah." He smiled lovingly, with that endearing stare, as the ship backed away from the rock, and with a *crack* he disappeared through the vacuum of the starslide.

Back inside, I walked to the kalodia and connected my call.

"Yes." Sanje started on the other end of the communication.

"Did you hear? Did you see everything?"

"Yes. Everything."

*

Across the space between our planets, in Sanje's office, the magistere was drying my furry body off after I'd had my first bath in years. We were careful not to let on that anyone else was listening. I gave a vigorous shake of my body to shed some excess water. This was a rare event in many ways. He never let me on his desk. So for a rat, I tried to be well mannered, sitting up to listen in on the conversation.

"I know this isn't easy for you, Skenkin," Sanje continued.

"He told me they found Evah," she said, hoping for information.

"I'll have to get back to you about that." Sanje was diplomatic.

"Tell me, Sanje. You know I'm being truthful with you."

"I'll tell you when I know something for certain," he said, remaining formal. "Goodbye, Ms. Claren."

And with that, he ended their connection.

"My honorable colleagues, are you still there?" Sanje continued.

Two voices responded simultaneously.

"Yes."

"Yes." Then the male voice of the two continued. "There's still no proof of any murder. There's no proof that anything the Claren Thwargg have said isn't true."

"I don't agree with any of this, Sanje," said the female magistere. "If you have been withholding that child from her family there will be immeasurable consequences for you."

"I will have to allow my two decades of experience to represent the value of my choices."

"Where is the girl?" the female continued.

"This is something that is safer kept secret for now. Soon enough, the girl will go before the Thwargg, and everyone will know where she is."

"I want to believe there was never an extuiter conspiracy, Sanje, but Magistere Cordura is right. And if no evidence can be found of a connection between Galneea and Claren, you run a steep risk of being proven a component of that conspiracy. Beware."

"Be sure to have someone on Galneea. There must be a connection somewhere. If we have to, we will talk to this Blouty. He clearly has some details."

I rolled on the towel, getting the last of the water from my fur.

"Galneea is an official now. He's a magistere, and he has more loopholes than ever to slip through," the female magistere pressed.

"Well, I just hope you will stay on my side until we see what happens. Good day, fellow magisteria. I will be in contact." And with that, he ended the communication.

"That went better than I thought it would," I told Sanje.

"Well, I'm glad you feel positive about it. You just remember you're a rat. They don't jail rats."

"I know you've risked a lot here," I confessed.

"If I had more to risk, I certainly wouldn't have."

"I know. I know, Sanje. But Blouty had to get his information from somewhere about how to find Skenkin, and he made it pretty clear it was Claren. We have to root out Claren's source. And I smell a big, rich, powerful Scabeeze. I'm just saying. And what does he mean 'there are things we all must do before we live our lives?' He makes it sound like it's common for people to seduce others for personal financial gain. Now I've gotta go; I'm late for lunch. Strap that inoculation shot on me so I can get outta here."

"Keep it clean. You don't want to give Evah some other virus trying to clear her of the Haytoo."

"You know, I'm not really that filthy," I exclaimed.

"Right. Okay."

"Why do you have so many of these shots on hand anyway?" I asked.

"If you talked to little animals you'd wonder, too, if you had a delusional condition. I shoot these regularly."

"Okay. Okay. I get it."

Sanje finished strapping a box onto me containing the inoculation shot. I picked up my goggles and brought them down over my eyes. I felt like a new rat. I hadn't anticipated how nice that bath would feel.

Sanje picked me up, readying to toss me into the Planck gate.

"How is it going with the girl?"

"Some things are better, and some things aren't so much. But the better part is good. Hopefully, the shot will clear up any other concerns."

Sanje walked to the vortex at the end of his desk.

"Good luck," he told me and tossed me high into the air.

Ffffhhhhhuuuum bhuump!

Grabbing hold of the church beam on the other side, I grappled to a firm stance and realized I had entered into an unexpected event. Evah was sitting in one of the wooden pews with Father Segura. They were talking quietly in the calm of the sanctuary, sitting side by side, looking on to the quiet service area. They were alone. I could see a devotional candle was flickering before the steps of the altar. The moment seemed solemn. I pushed up my goggles and focused to hear their words.

"There are many mysteries in God's kingdom, Evah. Especially gifted beings." Segura paused and took a deep breath. "I know what happened with the hornets. What I don't know is if you meant to hurt her."

"No. I swear." She was worried.

"I've known another who could do things like you. There are people who can help you to understand how your gift works, and I have invited them to talk with you. They won't hurt you."

"All right."

"You will always be my glillin girl."

"When will they come?"

"In a couple of days, I think."

"Should I say some prayers or something?"

"No. No acts of contrition necessary." He laughed a little under his breath. "I don't believe you've done anything wrong necessarily."

"Is it all right if I stay here… if I'm here during lunch?"

"That's why I leave the door open. Let's try not to draw a crowd though. I know you've felt alone, but you aren't. I hope, in here, you feel loved. I have to go."

Father Segura stood up and quietly walked out onto the schoolyard. I knew our time was running short. I laid my goggles aside and made my way down to the floor, doing my best to keep the inoculation case safe. When I reached the ground, I found Evah lying on the wooden pew as if she might be taking a nap.

She seemed to have her hands tucked up under her head as she stared into the ceiling above.

"I waited for you," she said, not looking at me.

"It seems we've been found out."

"Well, I have. Did you hear?"

"Yes," I said, and struggling to relieve myself of my cargo, I fell onto my side with a *clomp*!

"What's that?" she said, finally looking up at me.

"It's the answer to some of our worries."

She started towards me. "Ooh, a mystery. Let me help." She loosed the ties that fastened the case upon me. "Wow. Where did you get this?"

"From that friend I was telling you about."

She opened the box. "That doesn't look fun."

I expelled a sigh of concern. All of this was so much to take, but we had come this far together, so I continued with my plan. "That is the cure to the Haytoo virus."

"Isn't there a pill I can take or something?"

"No. Sorry. It goes in your arm below your shoulder. I wish you didn't have to—" In an instant, she took the cap from the needle and plunged it into her arm then quickly tucked the syringe back into the box and clapped it shut.

"There. It's done." Though she tried to look stoic, she could not fake it. "Dang it! That hurt." She held her arm. "Oweuuuuu." Then she was calm and silent for a moment. "I don't know how much time we have, and I want you to tell me as much as you know. Tell me the story. Start with what happened on Spirea."

"You'll be all right now."

"Will it make me sick?"

"No. But it will hurt for a while."

"Tell me about Spirea." She wanted me to take her away from the moment, so I did.

*

They were racing on the module to the far-out sectors. In the distance, a metropolis could be seen, empty of life and still. Everything was covered in a hue of red. Skittering along the course with a jolt here and there, they braced themselves as they entered a region free of fire. A circular concrete island came into view. At its center, there was a circular building with windows wrapping all the way around its circumference.

They whizzed past a howler that hopped up with its huge white body and blew a horrible scream in their direction, but it was blind with its passion, seeming only to reflexively hurl a command of domination at the sound of the speeding module. Varin could see an amethyst light shimmer around the circumference of the building from the endless curve of its window. Beyond the island, two mesa plateaus rose off the horizon like landscape guardians to the dead city that was far out of reach.

"Breaking!" shouted the module driver, and the ride skittered to a slow drag. It gave up its charge and slipped into a gentle glide before coming to a stop at the island dock.

Only twenty feet before them now, they could see two doors that appeared to be an elegant pressure hatch barely breaking the symmetry of the alien structure. Its surface was pearl-like. Varin and the squad filed out onto the cement. As Varin walked a few feet ahead, two men filed into a flanking position on the island perimeter with their weapons ready for howlers. One of the men dropped to his knees, cracking open a communication center, while another prepared scanning equipment. Their captain kept his eye on Varin with his weapon ready. The last man brought up the rear.

"We have a reading. One life form that seems to be inside," reported the man scanning the island, but there was some apprehension in his voice, as if the reading was strange.

A voice crackled from the communication gear. "We read you Collector One." the major's voice rose from the control room on Constance where Sanje was waiting with him.

"We've reached a ziggurat compound and identified one life-form reading on the interior. Permission to commence entry?"

"Commence entry when ready," the major commanded.

"Wait," Varin spoke up.

"What's on your mind, extuiter?" asked the captain.

"Whatever is in there, I don't think it's guns. The body in the module didn't have any visible injuries. Not from weapons anyway."

"So?"

"I think I should go in first. Whoever's in there may be far more dangerous for you than for me."

"Okay, but listen, my squad isn't exactly safe just hanging it out in the wind in this environment. Get that shock barrier up! We may be here a little while. Let's go! Let's go!" The three free men scrambled to set an electric barricade. The captain stalked over to the communications terminal. "Extuiter is requesting permission to enter alone." Varin scurried to join the conversation.

"Command, this is extuiter. Nothing would please me more than having these guys go in and light this subject up, but I think there's a real danger they might end up shooting each other instead. This person is powerful, Sanje!"

After a moment of silence, the major spoke. "Copy that, extuiter. Go ahead."

The captain put his hand out to hold Varin back. "Look. Getting the target's one thing, but we're here to protect you too, cause apparently, you're something important. So keep your comms on and, the minute it's clear for entry, you say so. You got that?"

"Yeah. All right." Varin turned to the doors and stepped up close. A light traced up and down the center of them and then, with no sound at all, the doors slowly disappeared into thin air, revealing a dark space inside. A rushing wind of decontamination vents kicked on full blast, and Varin looked to the captain. They were both amazed. Varin started in with his weapon ready. He could hear the captain speaking into the comms.

"Uh, Command, we have some strange phenomenon here." Varin tried to stay steady, having no idea what to expect. "Well, the doors just seemed to evaporate."

Varin was in the darkness. His eyes blurred white, and when his vision cleared, he was standing under a clear blue sky. All around him, in every direction, was the concrete island and the plains of an alien planet. The view stretched on for miles. But there was something different about the planetary illusion. It wasn't only that it was an alien world. No, the illusion seemed to be lifted from a photograph in a book. The air seemed temperate, and at the center of the island sat Haytoo. His hair was long, dark brown and twisted into thick locks. His skin was pale for a Hypathian. He was tall and wore a long coat that flowed to touch the white ground beneath him. Not far from him was a table and there was something on it. To his left was a stringed instrument propped on a stand. There was nothing else. From the air came a voice.

"Where is she? Bring her here! I see you," the voice whispered then the presence bobbed away.

"You're Haytoo Valaire."

Haytoo sat lazily in the chair. A finch flew past Varin's face. It startled him and, jolting back, he saw the white gloves of his atmosphere suit were empty. His weapon was gone.

Haytoo watched the extuiter to judge his opponent. Then he ran his right hand gently over his mouth, breathing in deeply through his nostrils. "It's safe, extuiter."

"Is it?" Varin watched him a moment then depressed the seals on his helmet, taking it off cautiously. He set the helmet on the ground and breathed the fresh air into his lungs. "Is this your work?" He raised his hand, gesturing to the sky. "Or is this a hologram environment?"

"Hm. You have a lot to learn."

Suddenly, Skenkin was standing in the distance beyond the table, and another man was kissing her. In a heartbeat, Varin was closer, only a few feet from Haytoo. He was amazed at his movement. Had he moved or had Haytoo? Skenkin and the man were gone. Varin looked at Haytoo seriously.

"Don't do that again." Varin's tone was dead cold.

A finch flew at Haytoo's face. He dodged it without much worry.

"Hm. You've got a girlfriend. And she's a monster."

"You know nothing."

"Oh, but he does."

From the mechanism on the table came a crackling sound. The bending of some high sound wave and a song started playing. A woman with a haunting voice lamented over it being too late for love and not knowing what went wrong.

"It's his favorite song," Haytoo said with a smile. She continued singing sweetly. The melody was playing from something like a rudimentary radio, but it seemed to fill the emptiness of the sky with rapture. "I just can't fake it," she sang.

"What is that?" Varin dared.

"That's a zaria. It picks up sounds from Earth. From where we're descended."

Varin searched Haytoo's words for meaning.

"Well, you really should know, being who you are. No one's more old school than you. Old-time allegiances. Old-time education. Old-time religion."

"You have your history mixed up. The earth babies settled on Sharvanna."

"No. There's more. Before that. Long before that. Hypathia and Earth have been connected since the beginning of time."

Varin thought on this for a moment, but he did not want to allow Haytoo to capture his imagination; the source from where Varin's power thrived.

"Who's favorite song is this?"

"Someone who's been to Earth. Someone who's been… everywhere… since your girlfriend put him in a blender and shot his atoms across the universe. Somebody I owe a favor. He says you can go to Earth."

That's it, Varin thought. The alien landscape looked like some old photograph or painted rendering of Earth.

"I got a bone to pick with you." The whisper came in fast, like something alighting upon Varin's cheek.

"I know you can hear him. Frankly, I don't think he knows what he wants. One minute he wants her dead, the next minute he wants to kill you, the next minute he wants her father. He's jealous, and he hates her. I first heard him at Constance Ward. I let on I could hear him, and that was… that was it. We are bigger than this. With his help, I could do more than I ever imagined. Now I'm beholden to him. That's why I'm here."

"Why?"

"To put you on the trash heap."

Varin didn't budge. He didn't know what to believe. What Haytoo didn't know was that Skenkin was pregnant. And they were going to be married. This voice didn't know, but he couldn't understand why. Then the zaria went silent.

"He was another extuiter. They made him love her, and then they prepared to use him. Those persnickety Thwargg. They sometimes get the idea to rule the Constellation system. Her first boyfriend figured it out and gave up on life, she broke his heart so good. Nothing was real. Not even love. And you know extuiters need to know which way is up and which way is down. They need to know what's real, so they aren't lost in their divine making. It is divine. I truly believe that. He cried a thousand tears when he realized the Thwargg tricked him into thinking she was moving on to someone else. He was disgusted by her, but he needed her, to know what was real. It turns out some Thwargg lies are as potent as a great extuiter's illusion. They got him stalking her jealously through a starslide and shut off the polar thrums, and he was spilled all over the universe."

"We're having a child," Varin informed the weird savant.

Haytoo began to giggle, barely getting out the words, "Oh, no, maybe we should leave you alive."

Suddenly the blue sky was grey, and thunder wracked the idyllic world. A petri dish appeared on the table. Haytoo dragged his long fingernail, grown for playing guitar, along the inner surface. "No?" he said, as if to the new dark clouds. And with that, he slashed open Varin's bottom lip. "Now you're really sick."

Varin stared in shock. His lips were agape, and blood poured from his mouth. He lifted his finger to wipe away the mess.

The sky turned red, and scummy effervescence rose around him. He was choking, hands clenching at his chest. Lines of golden dots swirled and waved around him. He was seeing the thrines of reality bending before his eyes now.

He fell to his knees, gasping, dragging himself to his helmet. As he wrestled to put it on, he could feel himself suffocating and clawed at the helmet seals. Then those squirming, furless pink rodents that had fed upon the gooey dump were feasting on him. They were well through his suit, feasting on his flesh. The scream of a howler seemed so close, Varin thought it was going to join the dining party.

Then the illusion disappeared. He was writhing on the filthy concrete, screaming. The squadron was closing in around him. They were confused to see him and no ziggurat compound at all. One of the men flew back against the ground, getting the wind knocked out of him. Behind the men, the fast-track module bobbed up and down, the brake cranked, and the module revved with a shrill whine, bolting off towards the starslide that had brought them in.

Two of the men leaped on top of Varin. He was raving mad with horror. Another of the men brought a sedative and jammed the shot into Varin's thigh.

"It's gonna be all right! You gotta hold still! You're all right!" the captain shouted.

Varin blacked out.

Chapter 13
Misericordia

Heavy sedatives could not control Varin's power and he slammed in and out of consciousness. Every time he found the strength to break open his eyes, he was in a new environment. It seemed to go on this way for days. Something changed each time he awoke; the lights were different or the restraints that held him down. He felt into and out of deliriousness so often, he lost all sense of time and could barely recognize his loved ones or colleagues. Then there was darkness for too long a time and nothing.

Then Sire Claren was there.

"Shoe, tree, coin. Please repeat what you can remember," said the rigid Thwargg, peering deep into Varin's pupils with some electronic magnification headgear.

But Varin could scarcely drool out a syllable.

"Too much. Still too much," the sire assessed.

Another time Varin awoke to a hustle of movement and rushed words. His mind was not his own. The spirit of the dead extuiter had possessed his body, and from his vocal cords escaped a hissing hatred. The spirit writhed through him, his head shaking, tight and tense.

"I'll show you how to be torn apart!" he said and spat at the scene before him in disgust.

"Let's hope the stone hasn't merged with his body! Carefully," said one of two physicians troubled over some shocking scene. The sound of power tools grinding and chunking away at something hard filled the air. Varin didn't think it was him they were working on. White lights flashed around him, and he was gone again.

In a nightmare, he was suffocating, locked away in a rat's habitat and Skenkin was watching him like a pet. She tapped on the glass with one of her pretty fingers.

Opening his eyes again, he found Skenkin was talking to him.

"I love you. You must control yourself, Varin, or they're going to put you in a coma."

"Who ya foolin'?" Varin slobbered out. "Catch 'em on the stairs. Like honey."

Then Varin was sitting with Sire Claren in a white room. They were talking backward.

"reh touhtiw si dlrow eht fo dne ehT," Claren said in a reasonable tone.

"aeenlaG morf tfig reh dnuof egduj ehT," Varin told him and saw himself dragging a child's crib down the steps of the Constance Thwargg ward.

Upon waking next, he confessed, "I made something for the judge." But, though it was a clue that helped to destroy the judge that first presided over the kepplequer preliminary hearing, it was not incriminating on its own. Claren's eye peered at him through a magnifier pulled down over the right eye of his headgear. His glowing blue eye was huge behind the glass.

"You're talking nonsense," Claren said with annoyance.

Finally, he woke up. He was in a large weapons-testing facility lit with white light. He was standing upright, strapped to a padded panel. The leather restraints were tight. Behind a high-density, protective glass twenty feet away sat Sanje. Skenkin was standing over his shoulder. They watched him from the safety of a control room. Sanje and Skenkin exchanged some words, then she disappeared from view. The extuiter felt something like a shock of spasms quake his body, but he was connected to no wires—it was the spirit. Sanje's voice started in through an intercom system. Varin thought of the zaria and the haunted love tune playing to the empty blue sky on Spirea.

"Can you remember what happened to you? Do you remember anything?"

"My mind is full," Varin muttered.

"I know. You have become—well, it seems… delusional, my friend."

Varin aimed his faculties towards listening with calm.

"You went to Spirea. Do you remember that?"

"Yes."

"You went with a team. Do you remember?"

"Yes. Oh my God!" Varin jolted, looking down at his body. "They didn't eat me." He fell into a peal of dark laughter, not quite sane.

"You are perfectly fine physically." Sanje was direct and reassuring. "That's more than I can say for many people in the city."

"I don't know what's real anymore," Varin said with hopelessness.

"We may not have much time, Varin. Who else was with you on Spirea?"

"Valaire. Haytoo Valaire."

"The musician?"

"But there was something else with him."

"No." The disembodied voice spoke like an echo off his ear. The same one from Spirea.

"What do you mean?" Sanje followed up.

"It's here."

"What is?"

"You don't need an extuiter. I think you need a priest. It's on me."

"There's nothing on you," Sanje enforced gently.

"It wants Skenkin."

"Look, I don't know what you're talking about. I can tell you that you did nearly put Skenkin inside a wall."

"What?"

"We don't have time for that now. She's all right. A man was seen putting something in the Constance water reserves. A man with long hair in a long coat. Is that who you saw on Spirea?"

"Yes."

"Can you tell me anything that can be helpful?"

"I don't know where to start."

"What made you lose your marbles, Varin?" Sanje aimed at the substance of what happened.

"I was fine, and then the voice got angry. It turned it a—" Varin was trying to figure out what was really most important. "My lip. He scratched me. He cut me open."

"Yes. You had a wound on your mouth."

"He dragged his fingers in a chemistry dish, and then he hurt me, and he said, 'Now you're really sick.'" Varin tried to remember. "Did he give me something?"

Sanje thought for a moment.

"We've got to find out," Sanje said as he stood and walked to the door, giving it three quick pounds. The door opened, and a medical technician stood before Sanje.

"We have to run more blood tests. I want samples drawn from both of us."

This was how they found the virus, comparing samples to identify the same viral signature in both Sanje and Varin. It had taken them weeks to find a sedative cocktail that could control Varin's powers. Though it was not permanent, it worked long enough for the breakthrough.

Varin learned that the city had been infected with the virus. Suicides and murders were up in huge numbers. People were confessing to activities going on in their work, business, and school environments, involving groups of people banding together to single out and torment individuals. Some of the murderers were people pushed over the edge who just cracked. They said they were driven by passions they couldn't understand to go on multi-person killing sprees.

Varin and other officials were administered samples of a cure, but making mass quantities was proving impossible. Varin closely monitored the medical staff who studied the isolated virus to learn its effect on biological systems. He thought maybe if Haytoo could make the infection real, perhaps he could reverse its effects somehow.

Finally, after several trials, Varin lay his hands on an infected woman, and she was healed. The process was not immediate, buts the worst symptoms were eased with surprising positivity— enough to help victims be calmed and on their way to recovery. When he lay his hands on the woman, he could feel the vibration of the poltergeist inside him. It seemed to be making him more powerful. There was a warmth and light in his hands when he placed them on the sick.

"Bring her to me," the voice of the dead extuiter said in his mind. Varin began to see what Haytoo had been talking about. The spirit was working with him to achieve his goal, but the spirit wanted to see Skenkin in return.

After explaining this to Sanje as clearly as he could, Varin shut himself in the enormous weapons-testing room again. In the isolation of that room, he sat down and tried to reason with the spirit, looking like some madman debating with himself.

"I cannot let you kill her."

"Is it her?" the voice responded.

"I don't know what you mean."

"Bring her to me. I'll help you with the city," the spirit told him.

Varin was deeply conflicted; he had seen the spirit's power and believed it could do what it was promising, but he did not want Skenkin harmed, or the child inside of her. He wrote a note to Skenkin and had it sent to her in another part of the catacombs. When she opened the note, it read:"Ansen wants to talk to you. He may want to hurt you. But if you come and face him, he will help me heal the city."

No one had spoken that name for years. Skenkin had never told Varin of her first extuiter. Her senses were overwhelmed by grief, realizing her young husband knew what the Clarens had been doing. If he revealed what he knew of her, her life could be destroyed. She did love Varin, but thoughts of running away filled her head. She thought of claiming Varin had lost his mind. It was only a matter of time before she would have to start living her life without him anyway, and it seemed entirely reasonable that she run away to protect herself and her child. Somewhere deep inside, she still clung to the hope she could have all of the terrible truth out in the open and be free of it, so they could continue their life together.

Varin was sitting on the floor with his head in his hands when his wife stepped into the control room alone. His back was to her. She pushed the intercom button.

"I'm here."

Varin began gently shaking as though he had decompression sickness. It was a subtle deep wavering, like a man with a neurological disease. His breath went in and out in short bursts. The extuiter was doing his best to stay steady, but the condition remained. When the spirit began to speak through him, it was as if it went directly into Skenkin's mind. Varin was hardly moving his lips at all.

"He wants to know if you knew."

In her heart, she knew what it wanted to know. Had she known he would be murdered? Her stomach churned with fear. She felt frail, disgusting. She did not want to answer him, but she did not want to make whatever this presence was impatient.

"No," she braved and then: "Who are you?"

The thick window of the control room cracked in one corner like ice.

"You know who I am."

"I'm sorry," she answered with quick sincerity, swallowing hard. "I didn't know, Ansen. I wanted us to be happy."

"Then how could you go with another man?"

"I didn't. I swear I didn't."

"There was somebody." Varin's voice strained with pain.

"No. I was… I was stupid. I just didn't think of you that day. I was scared. Everything was falling apart, and when my brother called, I went to see him."

The glass was not cracked anymore. It had only been an illusion.

"I'm sorry. I didn't want to lose you. I don't have all the answers, and I don't know what you thought, but I wanted you alive. I will always love you. You will always be in my heart."

Varin's body was still, his fingers tugging through the hair around his temples, then he too seemed to be weeping. But it was silent.

"Won't you come to me? Come to me and hold me, my love." The voice from Varin seemed to be a mixture of two—his and Ansen's. It was tender. It seemed honest.

She watched them there on the floor. His back was still to her, and the silence in the air was deafening. She felt the pitch of fear all around her body, but with a deep breath, she stepped out of the control room. After a moment, the side door to the weapons-testing room opened with a clack and creak. It shut behind her. She walked to Varin and stood before him, then slowly got down on her knees. She reached for the ghost inside of her new husband, taking the haunted spirit and its host into her arms. Varin's hands, trembling, rose to feel her face.

At first, he did not move. Without looking, his hands were on her face, searching the contours of her features. When he raised his head, Varin's eyes were closed, as if he was seeing with other senses. He mingled his breath with he's, and Ansen's features emerged over the surface of his face. Then the dead extuiter kissed her with soft, longing lips, reliving the passion they had shared. Suddenly his voice was in her head.

"Put my spirit on the water," he said. Varin was stilling. The shaking desisted. She looked at him breathing out a meek breath, and he seemed to come back to himself.

"Come with me!" she said firmly as if to strengthen him. "Now!" She reached for him fast.

Then they were standing before the Constance water reserve. Varin's eyes were open, but he was clearly in a trance.

"Put your hands on the water," she said to him. He knelt and did as she directed.

"Goodbye, extuiter," spoke the spirit in his head. The water began to glow with an amethyst light. First beneath his palms and then spreading farther and farther over the surface. When the glow faded, all the city, the stones, the starslides, the moon, and the stars came back to him with clarity. Varin watched Skenkin's features for a moment.

"It's done," he told her.

In the days that followed, inoculations were administered, and Varin continued to place his hands on those affected the worst. In some ways, his power had improved permanently, despite the departure of the dead extuiter's soul.

It wasn't long before the city's state of well-being returned. Haytoo was nowhere to be found, and even further expeditions to the surface of Spirea proved unsuccessful. His image was plastered all over the media on every planet.

Then one day, walking to his workspace at Liberty Square, someone bumped into Varin with the intent to give him a good stir, and while recovering, he heard Haytoo.

"What a show you gave," Haytoo's voice bombarded him.

Looking for a sign of the rogue extuiter, he picked up a signature of dark energy on a nearby thrine in the crowd. Varin pulled back the fabric of space and spotted Haytoo weaving through the people unaware of his presence. Varin was close in the chase.

"There's a temple on Spirea."

"I don't care at all about temples!"

"We are the shone men," he said, slipping onto a scotschoot, but Varin did not lose him. They were still unseen by those around them.

"You are a plague on men!" Varin tackled Haytoo, but as the contours of space are varied in the hidden side of reality, he did not realize he had sacked him right off the speeding scotschoot, which had no cover that day due to good weather. They were free-falling.

Varin waved his hand, opening a path to the world of physical matter. They were falling fast to a stone embankment in a Constance canal. Haytoo twisted Varin in the air to cushion his fall and made a soft patch of ground appear beneath them. They struck it with intensity, rolling off to one side of the waterway.

Haytoo slipped from Varin's hands, and before Varin could recover, Haytoo was running across the water of the sizable canal, making stepping stones appear and disappear rapidly beneath his footfall until he was on the other side. Varin clenched a wounded arm, looking up to find Haytoo standing on the other, side talking to him above the sound of the coursing water, and a fast-approaching shipping vessel coming between them.

But as Haytoo began speaking there was a disturbing sight. On a rocky crag, somewhat crouching behind Haytoo, there was a creature watching the egotistical megalomaniac. It was human-oid, its skin a fleshy white. Its head was oversized and bulbous, and its mouth a mess of fangy teeth. The thing crouched there, watching Haytoo, and as he began to speak, it used its clammy hands, heavy with long black claws, to tear open a slit in reality. It slid inside the black gaping hole, then the tear sealed up.

"There was a temple here! In Constance! They built their businesses on top of it downtown! I'll see you there!"

The shipping vessel passed between them. Varin began to run up over the ship, making steps appear and disappear beneath his feet, and high in the air, when he was sure he would reach Haytoo, some jagged part of the ship swiped past, causing him to fall. Tumbling downward he smashed against the ship rails until his body splashed into the water. He had to fight not to be sucked into the ship's engines. He survived, but Haytoo was gone, and again Varin had failed.

*

"Tell me that he gets this guy!" Evah exclaimed.

"No. He doesn't. Something worse happened."

"What could be worse?"

The bell rang in the distance.

"I'll tell you tomorrow."

"What about Galneea?"

"He got away with it. They limited his kepplequer properties in small ways, but the rights and ownerships were his, and nothing could be done to supplant his overall control. I'll tell you the rest tomorrow."

Chapter 14
The Maelstrom

The ceaseless revolutions of the planets could not turn fast enough to keep me from the most obscure patches I sought to explore. Over waters and into the nightclubs of this queer world I seeped: Seeped into its entities, seeped into locked rooms, over Liberty Square, and by some way of machinery discovered the presence of my desires. An anthroscope dream relator in the Constance Thwargg ward that relayed information back and forth between observation bay 17 and a sleeping chamber on Scabeeze. That is where I found Galneea.

The room was quiet and not too large considering it belonged to one of the wealthiest Scabeeze masters in the system. But this was common, for it was a place made for one specific cause: Thwargg psycho analytics. Included in this process were dream collection, reconciliation, and interjected manipulations to focus the waking conscious life experience. But all of this was a sham. The Scabeeze had no care to sleep in there and rarely did. These dream chambers and their machinery were formalities for the wealthy that the gullible Constance leadership believed were a part of a devout ritual practiced for the betterment of the Constellation of Spirea. Wealthy citizens like Galneea paid handsomely to have the Thwargg run simulated feeds instead of genuine content, so no one could ever bother with the contents of his head. On this night, what drew me through the workings of the Thwargg anthroscope was a rare communication.

Galneea lay his gangly body down beneath the anthroscope. A place that was too small and clearly never meant for someone like him with his big belly and long spindly extremities. He looked like an odd spider on a tiny tanning bed. A spider with stupid face tattoos to match his black eyes. He closed his eyes and an automation arm lowered, the sound of its motors humming. The mechanism injected him with something, and then the machinery came to life with pulsing lights that traced back and forth around the large screen hovering above his face. Sire Claren's face appeared on the grainy screen. Galneea kept his eye on him as he drifted into unconsciousness.

Then he was sitting in a white room on an overstuffed chair with a drink of some mysterious liquor on a table beside him. Sire Claren was sitting in front of him. They met in this dream state as they most often did, out of body where no prying eyes could discover them, in Galneea's subconscious mind.

"This extuiter has been found?" said the prominent business owner.

"She has."

"And what can she do?"

"We don't know the extent of her abilities. We have yet to question her."

"Then why are you taking my time?"

"An ambassador who has questioned her guardian reports she has made others see things. A new report suggests she has hurt another girl with extuited hornets."

"Well, that's something."

"If it's so, she's the most capable extuiter ever at her age."

"And at her age? What will she do for me?"

"I have a way to control her. It should be simple really. If we have an agreement, I will move forward with arrangements."

"You want to be Minister of Health Affairs?"

"You as Prime Minister and I as Minister of Health Affairs will reshape the Constellation of Spirea. The citizens who drag down this society will finally be useful. No more handouts destroying surplus. There will be an order where everyone will be put to purpose as it should be and not according to some foolish ordinances claiming to be compassionate. Give me Minister of Health Affairs, and we will go from there."

"The last time we played with extuiters, we had to destroy them. They are tempestuous."

"But right now, this extuiter is a child. Children cannot be held accountable by the law. I can make her do whatever we please, and there will be no repercussions, provided we keep it looking like she is only acting out emotionally here and there, if she is caught at all, and we will have years to complete our work. Children are an easy commodity to work with. I, personally, have been using children to do things for decades. They are useful in more ways than most imagine."

"Very well. But you better keep control of this one."

"Using the love between parents and children has nearly limitless potential. It is a skill I am extremely well practiced at."

"All right. If there's nothing else, I want to get my body off that damned anthroscope sleeping table. I think you should think bigger than side jobs for your tiny system. Let's do this right if we're going to do it at all. Create a package deal. I want a big package deal that moves the people."

Claren nodded. "Let me see what we're working with. I do have an idea. Before Haytoo lost his... potential, he showed some conceptual possibilities I had never considered."

"Well, get back to me. This society needs a hero."

Claren could not help but be perplexed by the idea of making a little girl a hero.

"Me." Galneea lifted the glass from the table and, taking a drink, he began to wake, then he was back in his chamber and white noise filled the anthroscope screen.

Chapter 15
Rituals

On the fifteenth day, Evah brought a book with her. It was a book about temples on our worlds and in alien civilizations like Earth. She had searched for what Haytoo called the "shone men" but found nothing. No religions that worshiped such a being. Seeing she was interested in these ideas, I picked up my story at the discovery of Haytoo's excavation.

*

On the evening of Haytoo's appearance in Liberty Square, Varin was troubled with many thoughts. That day he did not tell Sanje or any of the Constance officials that he had seen the extuiter. He wondered what temple Haytoo was talking about. There were no historical sites downtown. Before going home, he decided to take a walk where the nightclubs and cafes were, but there was no temple to be found. Expanding his search, he found himself in the older region of town maybe two or three blocks away. There was a fire burning down one of the alleys. He decided to take a closer look. Approaching, he could see homeless people standing over the fire for warmth. They didn't say much. From a corner came the voice of a wiry older man with grey hair.

"Hey, come on, man. What you got to eat? I know you got something." He was sitting on the ground against a grimy wall, alongside another man who kept smiling at his friend's behavior. Varin opened his satchel and pulled out some johacam fries. He handed the man the bag, who opened it to share with his friend.

"Hey! These are good. But they can only be eaten upside down. You see." He took one in his hand. "You have to turn it this way, and then turn it over and flick it two times. Not hard though. Gentle. To clean it fast." He flicked his finger two times over the fry. "Then it goes in like this." He turned the fry like a craft of some kind maneuvering in water, then opened his mouth wide, stuck out his tongue, put the fry on its white spongey surface, and slurped it in fast, chewing with delight. With his mouth still full, he continued his lecture, "Yeah! That's how you get the betters out of it. It's different with the green ones. Only the red ones work that way."

Beside him, his smiling friend casually tossed a couple in his mouth and shrugged at Varin, munching away.

"He doesn't know," said the wiry man. "He doesn't know. That's why he dies."

And again his friend threw a handful into his mouth. "Maybe," the friend said.

Varin started walking further down the alley. Past the fire, he saw a pile of rubble, and not too far away, a lit open door blocked by a wire fence. Peeling back a loose segment, the wiry man spoke up again with an excited whisper.

"Hey, man! Don't go in there, man! That's where the god Kushka lives! There ain't enough ventilation. My friend ain't come out since he went in there."

*

"I thought that everyone had a place in Constance. Why are there homeless people?" Evah asked.

"We don't know. For some reason, no matter what we do, there are always people who don't fit. They try even, but then they can't keep from going back on the streets. Many in authority say that they're sick in their minds, but I've met some good smart people who live there. I don't know. But the wealthy are often disgusted by them, and the working class thinks they just don't want to work, so they don't like them. Different people think different things. Once a great man said, 'Blessed are the poor in spirit.'"

"I don't see anything about a Kushka in here either," she said, flipping through the index of her book.

"No. That man had his own ideas about things. I guess every-body does, but a lot of people agree on a few things."

*

Varin pulled back the fence and peeked in at the door. Inside, he saw that the first floor was ripped apart, everything stripped to the foundation and bare bricks of the walls. On the far side of the room, there was a gaping hole in the floor. Light from the hole danced with shadows. Above it hung a pulley system and a rope. After a few moments, the rope began to sway and jerk, and Haytoo's head peaked out of the depths. With his back to Varin, he missed seeing the extuiter slip out of sight in the doorway.

Varin's turmoil was great, and he didn't know what to do. He wanted to see what this temple was and what it said about people like him, for he had had some strange dreams about his people and their temples, but knowing Haytoo, it would bring nothing but trouble and sickness. He didn't want to jeopardize his life for a murderer's fetishes.

In a few short minutes, he was standing down the alley talking into his kalodia to Sanje. Soon, a military team was setting up a barricade outside the building. The homeless were cleared out, and the perimeter secured, then the team captain called for Haytoo to come out. For some time, there was no response, so they sent in a fully armed team with orders to kill if necessary. Some were equipped with sedatives, the same one used to sedate Varin when he had lost control of his mind. They spearheaded the invasion with two concussion grenades. Eight men filed in, weapons ready, while Varin and Sanje watched from outside. Plasma shots were heard, and suddenly men were crying out in distress.

"Man down! Man down!"

It was as Varin had feared on Spirea. He knew the men were shooting each other, and he was filled with regret that he had let them go in. Then the shooting fell silent. There was nothing from the building for what seemed an eternity, then one of the detachment finally appeared in the door. His gun was dangling at his side like a useless toy. He was in a state of confusion. Varin was relieved to see someone was alive.

"He wants the extuiter! He has Rykes. I think everybody else is dead."

Medics scrambled to help the man.

"Does he want this extuiter dead?" the captain asked Sanje.

"No," Varin interrupted, "I don't think so. He thinks he's found something in there and he wants me to be some part of it. If I get close enough, maybe I can sedate him."

"I want my man alive."

When Varin entered the building, he found six bodies. Two were dead with disturbing gashes from plasma rifles; another two were still alive but barely breathing, having been victims of their own sedation darts; and a fifth was dead, his skin a sickening blue color. He approached the sixth man, who was frozen in mid-attack, encased in some kind of clear resin block that disintegrated to nothing when Varin touched its surface. The man's body collapsed dead to the ground, he too a gruesome blue.

Varin noticed there were other smaller holes dug into the foundation that had been abandoned and refilled. At the far side of the room was the opening that led to where Haytoo was holding Rykes. A scream came from the hole, and a bright light appeared, as if a fire had been started. Smoke escaped in a plume. Haytoo was burning Rykes alive.

Varin ran to the hole and peered inside. Rykes was at the far end of the chamber, tucked into a cove of some kind. Flames were on him, but he was not entirely ablaze yet. Haytoo traced a pattern in the air with a flaming bundle of some dried weed. His movements were meditative, as if they were a practice to focus energy.

Varin tugged at the thrines in the space before him, ripping open a path to the burning team member. He was on him fast, despite the dangerous drop to the chamber floor, pulling the man free from the cove and putting out the flames. Haytoo subsided his movements but made no advance on Varin.

"Let Rykes go, and I'll stay."

"I'm sorry. We're going to need him."

For the time being the man was tucked aside, still bound and gagged. He was bruised and bleeding from his head. Other than some burns on his arms, he would be all right. Varin tried to keep calm and find a way out of the situation or a way to bring it to a definitive end.

"It's a little hot in here. Do you think we can talk up top?" he asked calmly.

"No."

"What is it that you want?"

As he talked, Varin studied the rectangular chamber. It was about ten feet wide and twenty-five feet deep. The walls were long, smooth segments of stone with markings along their surface. It was fairly well lit by a couple of squatty floodlights stationed on the floor. At the end of the chamber, near the carved-out cove, lay Rykes' plasma rifle. Haytoo's burning thatch was now smoldering in the cove where Rykes had been bound. It looked like a sealed doorway. Haytoo grabbed a torch jammed into the wall and gestured for Varin to come closer.

"Come on. Look."

He held the torch to the wall, and Varin approached, his hand close to his hip where the sedation darts were packed. He looked to where Haytoo was shining his fire, illuminating some hieroglyphs on the wall. The image was of exceedingly thin men and a door. The men appeared supernatural and made of white light.

They trailed towards a being with many arms, and under the being's foot lay a slain, misshapen humanoid. A strange species. Haytoo pointed at the men of light.

"Here. The shone men. They come in from both directions and become this one. The god Urga. They are Urga's combined power."

He whipped the torch around to hold it beneath the archway into the ritual burning area. "Here! *Aiek Tham Kut.*" He pointed. "That Art Thou. And look!" He brought the torch back to the first wall to a line of glyphs right above the first. It showed a doorway above Urga, and the letters scrolled over the door "That Art Thou." He then turned the flames to a space between that segment of glyphs to reveal another patch of symbols. It depicted what looked like a burning sacrifice of white-hot fire. A man on fire. "A sacrifice to the god of death. To enter the door. To become one with the god."

"I don't know what you think you've found, but it doesn't seem right to me. You think we were made for death? Why not life? What language is this?" Varin spoke as truthfully as he could.

"Naaheen."

"Then what does this say?" Varin pointed to a patch above the other glyphs Haytoo had shown him—a patch above the shone men and Urga.

"*Seet Lhat Afhanda.* Being Consciousness Bliss. It's to do with the god of death. Don't you understand? Only in joining with God are we truly in bliss. We are only a part of God. One part. One aspect. But by joining him, we are all."

Varin could now see clearly that in the carved gate, or door, there were charred remains of at least one other body.

"You've done this to others?" Varin tried not to reveal his shock.

"I haven't got it right yet."

"Maybe you aren't sacrificing the right person. Maybe you have to sacrifice yourself."

"But there's clearly a priest present."

"But you said yourself, only the shone men can go in."

"I'm a little afraid to do that." He thought for a minute and then, as if connecting some logical threads, he said, "What if it only takes one. Ansen said you would go to Earth. I don't want to be here anymore. It makes sense that Earth would be the path. Have you seen visions of these things?"

"No. But it seems familiar. Like a dream. Like I've dreamed of this place. You said that Ansen traveled to Earth. He had to give up his body."

Haytoo was seriously considering the idea.

"I can't use you to practice on. Ansen didn't say I would go. But he never saw this—or did he? He said you could go. And of course, if he knew of this door, he would think I'd sacrifice you." Haytoo stepped towards the door, staring inside. He reached his hand in to touch the back wall.

"I don't know, Haytoo. Why don't we just walk away from this? Why do we want to be with a god of death?"

With his feet in the ashes of the dead, Haytoo ran his hand down the wall where it was scarred with burns. He felt a groove and began to dig at it. It gave way to the impression of a lever. Varin's heart was starting to pump fast. His instincts were telling him this may be very real: Something was going to happen, and it wasn't good.

Haytoo worked his fingers in over the top of the lever. It began to break free from the wall.

"Don't do it. Haytoo! Don't do it." Varin begged and commanded at once. Then he was grabbing a dart from his pack at the same time Haytoo pulled the lever out of the wall. Varin lunged at Haytoo to stop him, burying the dart deep in his neck, and they began to struggle.

Haytoo yanked the dart free. He had never fought in such a human way. Varin slammed him against the side wall of the door, but as he tried to wrestle the torch from Haytoo's hand, the door of the chamber faded to black. It was a passage to an empty black void. In the near distance was the freakish white creature

Varin had seen around Haytoo at the canal near Liberty Square. It waited, like a host ready for its guest, with its fangy mouth and bulbous head quivering.

Haytoo fell on top of Varin, their feet still close to the void. The extuiter freed the torch from Haytoo's hand, but with one last extuition, Haytoo encased Varin's head in a clear resin block, solid against the ground. He could not breathe. He could not move his head.

He took the torch and jammed it straight into Haytoo's chest, lighting him on fire and burning him severely. Haytoo recoiled with a shriek as his long dark coat lit up like tinder. The agony dispelled his final extuition, and Varin was freed from his suffocating fetter.

The cruel extuiter staggered deeper into the doorway, the flames abounding, and fell into the open space where the creature was waiting. Varin tried to grab him and free him from whatever fate this was, but the door filled with a burst of fire. Varin fell back and tried to cover Rykes.

The fire raged, spitting a torrent of flames through the length of the chamber. It was hot. Then the door yanked back its heat and light, fast and greedy, and the door reappeared in its former place. Haytoo was gone.

*

The bell rang. Felin looked to Evah. She was dismayed.

"What was it?"

"I don't know. But it wasn't good. It certainly wasn't bliss."

"Did he go to the god?"

"Haytoo wanted to be powerful, Evah. He saw what he wanted to see because he was vain. And I don't know where he went, but it wasn't to God."

"I have to go." Evah was confused and shaken.

"Evah? There's nothing to worry over about Haytoo. My story frightened you. I'm sorry."

Then Evah stopped cold, her presence rooted and stable as I had never seen it before. She looked at me, and for the first time, I could see her mother in her. Her eyes lit up like the solar storms on Deiphera. But they were not orange like her mother's; they were steel blue storms like her grandfather's.

And from her lips, like cold sables to the flesh, words slipped. "What do you know of these things, rat?"

"Evah?"

That spirit subsided. Then, like someone dialing back the intensity of a light, she was tender again.

"I don't… I'm not afraid. I have to go, Felin," she said, and she ran off, leaving her book behind on the ground. I scurried over to it with concern filling my guts.

"Evah!" I called to catch her, but she was gone.

The book was much too large for me to do anything with. I sat there a moment straining to see the open page, but it was lost to me. All I could see was some indecipherable mass. I ran back to my place up high, hoping she would return and unsure what to think of what I had seen in her behavior. All that I could see for sure, through the muddle of my dark sight, was that she was overwhelmed and deeply troubled by something.

*

The little rat could not see what was on the page, but I could. For I was there. I was finally feeling at home in Evah, and when I was not at my work, we were together as two parts of the same person, so I saw in the book what the blind rat could not. It was an image of a supernatural creature with many arms, and beneath it was an inscription that read: "Urga the Goddess of Death: Destroyer of Ignorance and Greed." But what scared Evah was what she felt she knew the least about: Herself. That's what shook her to the bone. You see, it wasn't a male god at all. It was a female, and she wondered exactly how dark the essence of her being might be. There was such a war raging in her head.

Could it be possible that she might become such a thing as what was on that page? She wondered if that was to be her fate. Could her true will be so sinister and her being so unimaginable that she became a goddess of death?

Chapter 16
Delta Waves

At 4:51 in the afternoon, the kalodia chimed with an incoming call. I was weary with anticipation since hearing that the Thwargg ward had news of Evah's whereabouts. I answered hoping it was Magistere Sanje with information, and by some grace, a plan for her to be reunited with me. But it was not Sanje. It was a sales call. A pleasant-sounding male voice, full of blithe.

"Are you ready for your perfect home among the stars? Imagine your family snug and warm from the coldest weather. Now, you only need to say yes to our limited-time offer. Feel like you're inside the comfy pocket of a cozy sweater right now. This insulation offer is ready to make your dreams as perfect as you deserve. So go ahead: Reach inside, and know that it's possible with financing arrangements that are right for everybody, then get ready to attain your perfect home by selecting five now to speak with one of our reliable representatives." Then without even a moment to make a numeric selection, the kalodia chirped off an awkward tone and disconnected the call.

Without thinking twice, I ran to my night chamber and tossed through the clothing on the foot of the bed to find my sweater. The same sweater I wore when Blouty Duthane visited me. I jammed my hand into the right pocket. Nothing. To see it through I plunged into the left pocket and there at the bottom was a small piece of paper. I pulled it out, and, unfolding it, a kalodia number was revealed. At first, I thought I recognized it as Sanje's number. Then I realized it was not. It was one digit off, to be precise.

When one finds such coincidences in matters that are usually otherwise unrelated, one feels obliged to follow through on the evident plan some coincidences suggest. Perhaps it brings on a state of shock to discover such activities, and like a reflex one follows through on their direction. Perhaps it makes one feel important to receive such special treatment, or very smart to put such things together. Perhaps it feels good to know something few others do, or perhaps it is all of these things that made me go to the kalodia and make the call. I was desperate to have my child back. Whatever reason, I did choose to call. And then after inputting the number, I felt terrible. It felt wrong. But I continued anyway.

The kalodia rang too many times for comfort, but just as I thought I might give up, the connection was made. There was a tiny sound of static feedback.

"Nine," said a woman with a firm and formal voice. It somehow reminded me of my mother. Then the connection went dead.

Then, feeling all the worse for having betrayed Sanje, I called his number to cover up my indiscretion. Yes, I would talk to him. Ask him about Evah. And then any record of my dialing the mysterious number could be excused as an accidental input error. I hated this activity. It was the same way I knew the game plan when helping to direct Varin and Ansen. I noticed I was trembling to be in the midst of the activity.

The kalodia kept chiming, and a part of me hoped Sanje would answer so that I could tell him. I had no power, and as it always was, this was the power I had. To do these things.

The kalodia chimed and chimed and chimed, but Sanje did not answer. This communication was complete. I ended the call.

It was at times such as these that the world seemed to be under some supernatural control. Yes. There was a sensation in the body that felt as though everything was out of my control. Yet at the same time, it was me initiating what was happening.

At that moment, a draft rushed over my fingers and stole the scrap of paper into the air and onto the control center in front of me, dragging it towards a crevice between the equipment and the observation window. Amazed, I staggered forward with the thought to catch it before it disappeared. And though my thought was to capture it, I was slow. Somewhat mesmerized and someway wanting it to disappear where it could never be found. Then it was gone, and I do not know for sure if I let it slip away or if I had made the choice to push it over the edge of the panel. Well, it was, at least, out of sight and out of mind.

At nine that night, I went to the dream chamber, lay on the table, and activated the anthroscope. The automated arm swung towards me with cold precision, aiming its needle into my arm. Staring up into the monitor, I drifted off towards the perfect frequency of delta and theta brainwaves, somewhere between sleep and unconsciousness far, far from my troubles.

I was sitting in the little white room, in my favorite comfortable chair, with a sentimental drink on the table beside me, and before me, my father emerged from a grainy ghost into something that appeared solid.

"Skenkin." He fixed his eyes on me.

Something was different: This was not the trouble-free space it had once been. I did not like to "feel" anything here, in any way, for it made me realize all my conflicts were not dispelled in the presence of my father as they once had been. I tried to let go of my warring thoughts and find some sense of what was changing here, but what had changed was me.

"Father."

"Why have you done this, Skee? What good could possibly arise from turning your back on your family?"

I was silent, wanting to know all the comfortable platitudes he could deliver. I wanted to see if I could withstand them. I wondered what fabrications of morality he sincerely believed were true and what liberating insight of my own could free me from his rhetorical captivity.

"There is life for you still, Skee. There is an attainable future. We know where Evah is."

"She could have been found before. I can't allow her to be used. I cannot allow myself to contribute to any plans you have that do not serve her well-being."

"What well-being? Being lost? Having no connections? Having no mother? Has anyone else come to give you promises?"

"It is for the works we've done that I've lost her. It is because you see only plots to use the extuiters that she cannot be given to me. What philosophy is valid that condemns a child to unwanted service? Any life for that matter?" My words surprised me. They commanded a position I had not expected, but it felt right. I felt strong.

"You may yearn to disengage and relieve yourself of responsibility for the decisions that have been followed through on, but that is not considerate of your child and will not help to realize her greatest potential. What life is hiding alone? How much despair you must have known. I did not include you in the specifics of how your people would be utilized because they were complex. And frankly, you did not seem to want to know. You seemed to understand my intentions have always been to serve the best interests of social order and my family."

"An interest that will cause someone such as Ansen to give up on life may not be an interest well suited to enhance the best in society or your family."

"We all mourned Ansen. His gifts were a great loss. He just did not have the understanding to see there was a need for his skills, and some may be better suited to decide how those skills should be used. Perhaps I back channeled. But his gifts would have been used by those in power anyway. They would have been used by authorities that were really out of touch with the people of the Constellation—an authority that could not solve the simple problem of loss of life potential. These are authorities that survive and build their activities on impractical ideas. Impractical ideas do not assure everyone what is best. They do not reconcile the lost satisfaction. They do not amend the loss of satisfactory opportunity. Like Ansen, they do not understand the suffering they inflict on themselves to be without use. And, to the society, they should be able to serve in some way."

"But that is not the election of free will. It is not for you to make those decisions. You were not chosen to make those decisions."

"Did you love Ansen?"

"Yes. Maybe no. I learned to love him."

"Did you love Varin?"

"Yes."

"Oh, Skee. How many times did we sit around saying this or that could be different about the system we live in? About the choices that were being made? And it was as plain as that—we thought how wonderful it would be if you could marry someone who could make a difference. If I gave you the impression you were ever forced to do anything you did not want to do, I cannot remember you saying it was so. So a father says, 'Marry a certain kind of man,' and his daughter does. Is that an abuse of power? Infringing on free will?"

"I was too young to know what free will was. My free will, now, would not condemn someone to death because they are disillusioned."

"What a terrible way to think of things. You condemned no one. If you have regrets about something you did, you should stop hurting yourself for it. We are blameless. Ansen died the moment he gave up. And, what's more, through his continued resolve to make himself useless out of spite. He was a boy. And these worries are the thoughts of children who only want to elucidate their desire to feel good while giving up their responsibility to make good choices."

My father's voice released a burst of disappointment. Looking into his eyes, I could already feel a surge of remorse for disappointing the man behind them. I always did sympathize with his ideas. Maybe I did know about Ansen. Like I knew the piece of paper would fall into the crevice if I let it.

"All of this can be erased," he continued. "The man who has put you here will have no grounds for acting against you or me if you come back. You have a home of your own. Surely you are still collecting Varin's death benefits. If that's running out, we can come to some agreement. Come back to your life, Skee. I sent Blouty to you so that you could see there is a life out there for you. I know he has silly ideas about scooping you up, but that's no one's decision but yours. I will get your child back for you, and you needn't worry about any of these things. I assure you this: Your child will be sequestered for the Constellation system. And if you want to have anything to do with what happens with her, you must listen to me."

"No. No, I don't have to listen to you."

"Clearly they had not told you your daughter was found. Why is that? Who will have control of her? It will not be Sanje alone. It will be the body of the state, and it will be the greatest power of the state. If you think what has been done before is wrong, then come and have a say. We can do something more positive together. Don't… don't leave yourself out in the cold. With the history of the extuiters as it is, you'll be lucky if your daughter is not simply institutionalized in some manner, and left to do nothing. Or made incapable of doing anything, in order to secure the safety of the people."

I could see my daughter as he spoke, incapacitated on some drugs and alone, and now I really was afraid. Afraid my father could not lose.

"Fine." I gave my resolution for the time being. "I'll meet with you in a couple of days, and we'll talk then." And I despised myself for not being smarter.

"I warn you. You must be careful what you say to Sanje if you think you are going to go poking around for your options. There is an inevitable procedure in motion now, and the longer you wait, the less chance you have to help in deciding your daughter's fate."

I had no answer. It felt as though he was right.

"We can do something better. I guarantee that, Skee. There can be a bright future. Two days. I will see you back here. Four o'clock."

"Two days. Four." I lifted the sweet drink to take a sip—that projected prop of my favorite special treat when I was a little girl. Being trapped in my mind with him made me want to be sick. Being stuck with my own failure to make life right again made me sick of myself.

Before I slipped to the salvation of my solitude, my father leaned in. "The only way to make this work is to say yes."

I awoke. The word "no" wearily halted at my unyielding lips. I did not know what family even really meant anymore. I rolled off the table, heavier from the drugs than ever before. It had been some time since my last infusion.

I walked into the lounge, shoving my arms inside my sweater and wrapping it around me. The waves outside were crashing hard on the promontory. The solar winds glowed in the sky. I listened to hear the voice of conscience inside me. I had allowed my father to be the voice that guided me for so long I did not know how to hear my own reasoning. I guess I was searching for wisdom. Something that could give me direction—some communication from myself that would tell me what really should be done. But there was only silence. Silence and the crashing waves.

Then my finger was on the kalodia.

"Connect to Sanje," I heard myself say.

I would tell him everything. I sorted through my thoughts to orchestrate what I might say—something that could make a difference. The kalodia chimed on and on. I could at least leave a message to inform him of the activity, collect my thoughts, and find some way of going through this in a way that could still give me a chance at some future.

The kalodia finally connected.

"Four," the formal woman's voice said at the other end of the signal, then broke off with that stifled chirp.

"Connect me to Sanje!" I threw my command into the kalodia, forcing back my concern.

The kalodia began to chime but cut off fast.

"Four," the voice, though it had not changed, with its formality sounded cold and insistent as an unbudging menace—a stalking counter-presence to my free will. The kalodia screen went white.

I had done this myself. I had likely entered in some hack. Somehow. Somehow the kalodia was no longer under my control, and I could not reach Sanje. I prayed that it would only be this way for a short time. Maybe they thought I would get upset and do something impulsive. Something hasty. Maybe they would release the kalodia the next day so that I could call whoever I wished again when my thoughts were clear. Maybe later that night. Or maybe, there would be no way for me to call Sanje ever again. Maybe he would try to call me, and on his end, it would only chime and chime and not be able to reach me. And to what end?

Two days. Two days. Two days and maybe the next Spirean man to deliver my rations would not have a kind story to tell me about Constance. Perhaps I would slip off the edge of the South Rock Promontory before then. That smiling Spirean. Or some other delivery men may take me away, or throw me in the shipping starslide and turn off the polar thrums. Perhaps that nice Spirean will deliver me some poison. Something in my food. Something on the sweetened brumble berries I love to eat in the morning and I will have a seizure, and there will be no evidence.

So my mind went on that way all night. And when I called Sanje's number again, that wicked woman assured me with her "four!" I may as well have ended my life as I had ended my chances at liberty. Now I had selected my fate. The same fate I always did. And I continued to torture myself into the rising of the Zaizon moon. Into the dawn with its grey smash of cloudy melancholy.

Two days, I thought. And my mouth was dry, my eyes like swollen radishes.

The waves kept crashing, and sleep would not release me from the torment of my thoughts.

Chapter 17
Aggregation

People don't really know what they want, I find. Evah thinks she wants her mom and dad, but I want to rearrange them. And as we shall be as one, somebody has got to figure out who's right. She may never really know and accept I am here. And as that is so, and she is far more sympathetic, I suppose some may think I am a malignant will. "Perhaps." That's what Mommy says. "Perhaps" I am this or "perhaps" I am that. There is something admirable about being a person who accepts who they are. Take Blouty Duthane, for instance. Now there's someone I can really respect. There's someone who really likes being important. And he will do anything necessary to achieve that end. There's no moral ambiguity about that. You know where he stands from the beginning to the end.

Like most humanoids, he spent a long time telling himself the morally shady motivations that drove him were not really in his control. People get overlooked, they get overstepped, and they get stepped on. They have to know there's an order to things. You get in line, then stab others in the back when it's safe. Be pure and valiant in appearance but able to forget those scruples when necessary. For a long time, he was ambiguous to himself, but not anymore. Now he knows he must put a boot to the head of his competitors to get where he wants to go. If he wants to be "somebody," he knows that there are going to have to be a whole lot of nobodies, and they must be treated as such. After all, you're either with them or against them. He's a loyal opportunist willing to do anything to make himself the top of the heap. He spent more than enough time getting shoveled around this way and that by authorities, who apparently knew what was best for him and his "kind." Now it was time for him to make a few calls of his own.

So, while Evah was watching the squirmy Scabeeze Galneea declare his run for Prime Minister on the Holy Heart TV, I traveled to visit Blouty Duthane. Soon Evah and I would become one, and the greater part of my liberty could be limited. I saw Evah's mother make her fantastic insulation connection. I even crept inside her little white room. I dared not give myself away, for that grandpa creature is one I wanted to better understand. These workings were, as far as I could see, not legal—to meet some poor creature in their mind and pinch them into doing your will. But that wasn't all those busybody Thwargg were up to.

Blouty Duthane was in the Laboratory of Regularity Algorithm Applications, assessing the combined ratios of Constellation inhabitants self-fulfillment through social behaviors. What made Blouty Duthane such a good employee was not only that he graphed his statistics with precision, but that he could also accomplish ulterior functions for the elite managerial interest. You see, on the other side of statistics for satisfying society-centered activity was an excess of private information about the masses that was funneled directly into Blouty's department. What people favored on average. Everything from the drinks they chose to get them through a busy workday, to the most popular trends in product colors they purchased for themselves and their loved ones.

Now, beginner statisticians thought much of the information was garbage because that's what they were told to think, but other more experienced workers understood it was prime knowledge that could be sold. It had applications in advertising, sales, and, at the current time, politics. Appealing to the wants, pleasure, and unquenched desires of the people could make a spider look like an illuminated, heroic, and relatable political frontrunner.

Well, on this evening, it was so that Blouty was kept on late to record and direct this personal information of the citizens to the office of Eine Claren's office. This is what he was told to do, and this is what he did, despite the illegal nature of such information farming. After all, this is what it meant to not be the shoveled but to be one of the shovelers. The exact kind of assertive actions an influential, self-possessed person committed themselves to do. *Smart, smart, smart*, thought Blouty Duthane despite his lack of legal impunity. It made him feel dominant. And that was important to Blouty Duthane.

There was one scarcely weighable perception that set Duthane's aggregation precepts apart from his predecessors. One he felt was going to make an exalted difference in the use of said information. His predecessors sought all private data. That included small, varying obscure choices. The former Thwargg in Blouty's position thought they were smart to include only a record of decision-making that people were not proud of—the fleeting decisions that revealed things about them they would never share with friends, family, or the public. The will and proclivities they were ashamed of. But what this character information did not account for was the choices people made that showed how they wanted to be better.

The old Thwargg guard thought to only use the information to appeal to the darkest aspect of the people; their deepest, darkest instincts. But this was cynical. Too cynical for Blouty's taste. Because at some level people believed they could be better. That they can change. So Blouty set his aggregation standards to data representing the world people might aspire to. He felt, in this way, political candidates' public personas should be created to represent what people wished they could be. He thought that was more efficient. Still, it was a manipulation of people's information and desires.

Most of the Thwargg elite, the ones practicing such abuses, saw little validity in Blouty's point. They believed people were as clean as their dirtiest choices. But this was the philosophy of authorities who created facades of character, so they could win the people, then go on doing what they really wanted: Benefit from the advantage. Provided that goal was achieved, they'd try anything Blouty threw down the pipe—for the time being anyway. It was a small difference, but Blouty was betting there was something to it. Enough to make him big in the wards.

Then, at 9:03 p.m., I gave Blouty Duthane a side game. He liked to bet with people's lives and fates, thinking they were only as valuable as ones and zeros on the dollar. Who knew how many faces Blouty could put on. I wasn't about to put a limit on it, especially when the side game fixer was me. So, on an input observation monitor, I sparked a connection to Eine Claren's little white room.

Blouty was surprised to see such a taboo act happening right before his very eyes. He, after all, had heard that such things went on, but it was believed impossible. It was something he, frankly, was a little afraid of. What if people were meeting him in his dreams and he did not remember? It was exciting to think of some other unsuspecting person being manipulated in such a way though. That was something he might enjoy doing for fun, and here it was.

Before him on the screen was the girl he wanted and the boss he wanted to be. He did not know why this was appearing in front of him. He did two things. He immediately ran a signal search to find out what bay console the interaction was being initiated at, and then he pushed record on the monitor drives.

He did as I thought he would. Blouty Duthane wanted leverage that could help him get the girl he wanted and maybe even the job he envied. There was a part of him too that thought, for some more sick-minded reason, that Claren wanted him to see this power over his daughter. He liked to feel such power. He felt loved—ingratiated and permitted to know the secrets of the woman he wanted.

One thing was certain. This was a pleasure he could never speak of. It would be something meant only for him. Moreover, something meant only for him and Claren. Such power.

He watched as she lost her fight—as she gave up all that she had to give up. It was through this subtle yet enormous pleasure he felt as he watched that he thought he finally understood the real satisfaction of the secret work he did for Claren, and the other Thwargg, who knew what power was. He was so thankful for this opportunity. This would give him special pleasure every time he saw Sire Claren. A pleasure that they had this secret— this unspeakable secret. And he would have a little insurance for when he was ready to make a vertical move in the ranks, or for whatever.

He made a personal copy of the white-room incident onto his kalodia and initiated a scan to record any such future activity. He then diligently finished his work and completed aggregating the final stores of information from the inhabited worlds into Claren's private hub.

What a night, he thought. And it was, indeed, a night that would change Blouty Duthane's life forever.

Chapter 18
The Harvest

Evah arrived on our sixteenth day together with the news that Galneea was running for Prime Minister. I was surprised Sanje hadn't told me. She was back to her old self—no sign of blue storms in her eyes. I continued as though nothing had happened, but I knew something was being decided inside her. The mysterious male voice wasn't nearly as active as it had been, and I felt sure my presence had something to do with the relief. No mention of trouble with menacing sights either.

I had one more story to tell, but I knew the more she learned, the more inner turmoil it could cause. She was making immeasurable decisions about how her gifts should be used. I only hoped I could help her see the most positive use for them. There were terrible things I had to share. And, though it was a tale of modest heroics, the real substance of it was likely to be disturbing. These were issues that made my heart heavy to speak of, and I could only imagine what she might be thinking. She hadn't asked if Varin was her father, and I hadn't told her. But I would have to answer that question soon enough and dispel the mystery of how I knew all these things.

My instincts told me the time we had left was short, and though I regretted it, I allowed the urgency to make me seem indifferent to her emotional struggle. I needed to press forward.

She needed to be prepared for the extraordinary fate she was about to meet.

"My dear Evah. You know I care so much for you. I feel my life was made for you."

"What do you mean?"

"Well, perhaps I will find some way to explain with my story. The things I'm about to tell you may be difficult to hear, but I can't see any other way to go on than to share them with you. It just seems best."

"All right. It will be all right."

I wished I felt as positive as her, but I did not know if everything would be all right.

*

It was six years ago, and Galneea was running for his planet's open magisteria seat. During his campaign, he notified the Constellation intelligence officials that he had received a visual message from an eco-terrorist group. Sanje and other representatives, including the Constellation defenses, met on Galneea's swamp planet to plan how the threat would be dealt with. They gathered at his industry headquarters to view the message. In it, a Hypathian man made a statement.

"We, the members of the Hypath Resource Egalitarians, refuse to be silent any longer. For decades, the Magisteria of Constance has enabled the Scabeeze to monopolize kepplequer resources system-wide. The Scabeeze masters mine and control the vast majority of resources, building their industry to make wealth for themselves, give kickbacks to government officials, and siphon off resources to power the planets of Scabeeze and Constance while leaving other worlds underserved and largely underdeveloped. On behalf of the people of the Constellation of Spirea that go on underrepresented in these matters, in protest against giving yet another greedy Scabeeze master with large kepplequer holdings an opportunity to run for government office, we will blow up all Scabeeze holdings on Deiphera. You have three days to establish a referendum diverting equal resources to all six worlds. If our demands are not met, all Scabeeze resources on Deiphera will be destroyed. To show our resolve in this matter, today at three, the first of these resources will be eliminated. On behalf of the Hypath Resource Egalitarians, we implore you to meet our demands."

His demands were impossible to meet. It would have taken months of planning to even prepare such a motion for voting. Several Scabeeze masters like Galneea would have had to cut through trade bureaucracy to coordinate an effort. As was threatened, at three o'clock, one of Galneea's barb-fish farms and harvest centers was destroyed on Deiphera. Hundreds of barb fish were killed, along with their babies. An entire protected habitat was decimated with explosives and ultraviolet light bombs that rendered the kepplequer useless upon exposure.

A defense team was organized to halt any further attacks, but their leads were few. The eco-terrorist group had no history to investigate and the suspect pool was overwhelmingly broad—it could contain anyone from Hypathia or Sabia. Even some Scabeeze could have been involved. Anyone connected with the industry was under suspicion. It could also have been someone with a personal vendetta against Galneea, since it was one of his properties that were destroyed.

The magisteria called on the Constance Thwargg ward to run a facial recognition search on the man in the visual message, but they found nothing that could positively identify a suspect. The investigation started a terrible seizure of thousands of Hypath homes and kalodia properties on the search for any viable leads. The message was played on news outlets in every world. No one wished to be a Hypathian in those days as there was no Hypath that wasn't under suspicion. The paranoia was thick. The threat had shown people how fragile life in the Constellation could be, and threats to kepplequer resources were an immeasurable blow to the confidence of the people and their economy.

Sanje received a message from Varin. The extuiter had urgent news that he could only share with him. They met back on Constance in Sanje's office.

"We need to bring up a stream of the visual message."

"All right." Sanje did so. A projection of the visual message lit up on the wall.

"Skip to the end," Varin urged. Sanje did, and Varin stepped in close to use his control pad. "There are digital hiccups in the rendering all the way through. But here at the end, when the man is exiting the frame, you can see the streaming shorts are more profound." Varin passed through the message frame by frame. The terrorist's image appeared to morph slightly. There were flashes, and when they cleared, a badly burned man in black was revealed.

"Who is it? What is it?" Sanje asked, amazed.

"I think it's Haytoo. The hiccups were extuition signatures. They were strange, but that's what it was."

Sanje threw himself back in his chair, feeling the doom of the frightening extuiter's presence.

"From the looks of him, he's been in the water. Or he's going in the water," Sanje observed.

"Oh, I don't know. Why do you say that?"

"That is a military-grade diving skin."

It was decided Varin would be sent to the seas of Deiphera for a clandestine search of the facilities. His experience with Haytoo had proven to be dangerous before, so he went to see Skenkin and his child with a grave concern he would not return. He wanted to be with them. He didn't want to leave.

*

I looked to Evah to see if this was difficult for her to hear. She looked at me but said nothing. Her eyes told me she knew who he was.

*

"I wish you didn't have to do this," Skenkin said, her eyes like storms of fire. She smiled with love and kissed him. "But I know you do." She ran her hand over the tight curls of his hair as they embraced. Varin played with his child and held her.

"Maybe you shouldn't go," Skenkin said. "I don't want you to go."

"Don't go, Daddy," his little one said. She always said that.

He wanted to reassure her. He wanted to reassure them both. He wished he didn't have to go, but he knew he was the most qualified agent to meet with Haytoo. For the sake of saving lives and resources, Spirea could not do without him going. So he was, despite the inner sense of doom he couldn't shake.

"Don't worry. It's only some work Daddy has to do. I'll bring you something back from the ocean in the sky."

He kissed them both, and with that, he departed.

Varin was taken to the defense catacombs outside the capital. It was a secret facility dedicated to the most radical tech of the modern age. When he was possessed with Ansen's spirit, that was where they had taken him. A doctor brought him into the submersion laboratories. Inside were submersible submarines, diving gear, skins, and computing technologies made for use in the water at extreme depths. She had him take off his shirt and sit down near an enormous tank filled with thousands of gallons of seawater. Inside were strange forms of sea life, including small multi-tailed creatures that lit up like light bulbs as they carved in and out of shadows.

"When's the last time you used your amphibian respiratory organs?"

"A long time. I was a kid." He remembered diving into the sea on Hypathia. Laughing.

"We're going to wake them up." She stepped up to Varin with an inoculation gun and shot an injection into his thigh. "This stimulant will help."

After a moment, four delicate creases on his left and right ribcage blew open. They spasmed until it was clear Varin had control over them. He flexed them in and out. Two gills rippled open on both sides of his neck.

"Nice and pink," the doctor said, examining them with a penlight. "They're in good condition. Use the stimulant to get 'em going every time you submerge."

Then he was diving into the immense aquarium, wearing a diving mask with a grated mechanism over his mouth.

"All right," the doctor said into a microphone. "Are you able to get air over your vocal cords? I need a vocal reading."

"Ye—" He breathed. "Yes. Wow."

"That's good. You'll want to keep your mask on at all times in the water. You were born for it, but we need to filter microbes and any other sea life forms. Your stomach, blood, and respiratory systems will be vulnerable. It's been too long for a natural immunity. If you feel comfortable, we'll send you down without tanks."

"Yeah! This feels great." Varin's slim body and long legs streamed easily through the water. There was something of the little boy he used to be in his voice.

Outside the tank, she gave him the rest of his diving skin.

"Take the mask with you to tech. They'll install more comms. Listen. Keep the stimulant gun holstered when it isn't being used. You'll have plenty to wake up those pretty gills. You need the stimulant. It's going to be the safest way to get them breathing. Guard it with your life. Only having this, the light tech, and small weapon, you're going to have a lot of physical liberty down there. That's going to be your best advantage. Stay alert and move fast."

In the tech lab, a militant gear head prepared to show Varin equipment that would help him move quickly through the barb habitats and mining facilities.

"You can't be serious. This guy's soft," the muscular gear head said.

"This guy's here," said Sanje.

"Stow that opinion and get to your job, soldier," commanded a steely military leader whose every motion seemed to cut like a knife. It was the major who had led the base command crew when Varin was on Spirea.

"I just don't see why you don't send in a cold fire team," the gear head replied.

"Because the last military team that went near the threat involved here all wound up dead. This man did not," the major explained.

"Well, do you work out?"

"Yes."

"Good and hard? 'Cause what you're about to do is gonna take some stomach. I mean, every time you use this gear, it's gonna feel like when you hit the wall in a heavy aerobic workout that isn't going to end for another forty-five minutes. You get me? You're going to have to come through the other side of this gate and be able to keep pushin' forward, man. It's going to make you feel like you been stretched on a rack!"

Varin stood his ground. "Just tell me what I have to do."

"All right. That's what I wanna hear. Come on."

The gear head led him to a clearing and knelt beside a small black digital box attached to a strap. It was portable. There were two screens on the device. Under each screen was a metal dial, and between them a numeric pad. He programmed the unit. There was a fast ticking sound as the dials wound, and a gate swirled open before them with bands of lightning flashing around the circumference. At the end of the twenty-foot range, another gate appeared, swirling in mid-air.

"This is a planck thurometer triangulator," the gear head said. "A special one, which is why it's gonna take a little more out of you than a regular PTT. This has a highly advanced strain filter on it so it can be used to make gates in the water. The filter keeps your matter from being joined with other organics that may flow in."

"What am I supposed to do?" Varin asked.

"You step inside, man! Geez, aren't you listenin'?" the gear head squawked. "Listen, man—"

Varin stepped into the gate, shutting the gear head up. There was a vacuum sound—*ffffoooom pluumb*—and Varin appeared at the gate across the expanse.

"How was that, sweetie?" the gear head said with a laugh. Varin was nauseous but held himself together.

He gave the gear head a stone-cold look. "Show me how to use this thing so we can get on with this."

"All right." The gear head showed his approval with a big toothy grin.

Soon, Varin was inputting codes on the PTT and adjusting the dials.

"Those codes will tell the PTT what kind of travel you'll be doing. Conventional short-range, underwater ranges, far distances of over a mile and then there's a space-travel setting for interplansetary movement. We want you to keep it as simple as possible. This has a filter like I said, but don't let any other large organic life travel through with you. I mean anything larger than your fist, man."

He started to lead Varin to his lab table on the other side of the room. "We're going to equip your dive skin with three monitor mikes in case anything happens to one. You'll have a backup, but believe me, these things are solid."

As he arrived at the lab table, a Planck gate appeared, and Varin popped into sight, startling the gear head. "Nice, man. Look. Save the showboating for when you need it. The reason you'll be miked with a connection to me is so that you get the right coordinates. I'll have maps and schematics of every inch of where you're going, so do everyone a favor and only use the PTT when we give you coordinates, and you have a confirmed 'Go.' Do you understand?"

"Yeah."

"It's important. I want my equipment back. You read? You don't want to create a door for yourself into a mud pile, man. 'Cause it doesn't matter how much you been working out, you will not be able to come back from that."

Varin felt the gear head's seriousness and nodded in compliance.

"My name is Dee. That's what you're gonna call me when you're down there."

As the extuiter departed for his duty, the major shot him a stirring look.

"However special you think you are, don't go foolin' around with the resources."

Varin nodded with puzzled caution, and soon, he was pulling away from the laboratories on a catacomb zip track. Varin looked on to the seemingly endless claustrophobic tunnel. The moody blue lights whipping past made him introspective. He'd never felt so abandoned by the still quiet voice within him. It was as if he was doing something all wrong, but he didn't know what.

After ascending countless levels, the car raced into the hangar bay. A military-grade Prowler 237 was firing up its engines, its stubby wings cranking up and down like a bird stretching for flight. Through the hangar door, he could see the surface of Constance. Starslides dangled from space, and the ocean world of Deiphera loomed in its stellar position. The sky was a vast expanse of periwinkle in the wake of the golden setting sun.

Varin felt uncertain of everything, even insignificant and small, in the presence of this galactic scene. He boarded the prowler, and it lifted off towards a starslide to the watery world.

Cracking into sight over South Rock Promontory, the engines made their cat-like wail. Gliding over the observatory, they came to a hover above the surface of the waters and began their descent into the Deipheran depths.

Varin watched the water overtaking the cockpit window and felt his gills twitch. His black diving skin covered him from head to toe, and he had holsters strapped onto each hip with snug crisscrossing belts. One held the stimulant gun, the other a high-powered plasma pistol that could blow a hole through a steel wall. The PTT unit was slung over his shoulder and locked into position on the belt behind his stimulant gun. He touched his finger to his temple.

"This is interceptor. Checking comms," the extuiter said.

"We read you, interceptor," returned the major from the catacombs.

"Copy that," returned the extuiter.

As the prowler carved through the tides towards the sea floor, a door slid open behind Varin. The team coordinator entered and moved in close.

"Our point of entry is the South Rock Promontory, ground zero of the initial attack. We have forty-three vessels scanning the ocean floor for abnormal heat signatures. Our theory is that getting the bombs and ultraviolet equipment very far from the shipping starslides is unlikely. So, our search began at the major port entries. There have been unusual readings in the field nearest the ground-zero perimeter. That's where we're going to send you in. You're equipped with two cameras, correct? One on your belt, the other at the left side of your skins face grate?"

"Yes. That's right. And lights," Varin confirmed.

"You find something and confirm the area's clear of threat, and we can send a team. But if you're going to take care of the defusing, we need you to keep those cameras on the device. Are you confident about the tools in your kit?"

"Yeah." Varin spoke with impressive confidence though he did not feel that way at all.

"Then they can walk you through any procedures from camp. Now, because of safety protocols initiated due to the apparent threat—and I don't know what that is, but it must be good—we have to stay at least fifty meters clear of the sites. So the camp will have no visual on you other than what you show 'em through the cams and the global positioning in the PTT unit. We're almost in range of deployment, so we need you in the submersion chamber right now."

In no time at all, he was in the chamber. Beneath him was an automated expulsion hatch.

"We are a go for submersion," came the voice of the coordinator through his monitor.

"Well, if there were a day made for doin' something, today's that day."

Water began to fill the tank. All Varin's senses were in a state of hyper-awareness, and a wash of memories filled his mind. He saw the stars around Skenkin's black hair and the animals of his child's mobile swaying to music. He remembered the rat that drank the water of his imagined shooting star. The metal in the tank was cold, and the colors stark. Every edge seemed jagged in the shadowy light. He felt a presence with him unlike ever before, and he thought it was God. It felt protective but angry, and he prayed the presence would be merciful. He remembered the tortured poltergeist from Spirea, and countless images of his child raided his mind.

He remembered standing with Skenkin at the Constance water reserves, exhausted from the fight with Ansen's spirit. He couldn't look into her eyes.

"I don't want to believe any of it. But it happened."

She'd taken his face into her hands. "What? What?" she said, but she knew he was aware of everything she and her father had been doing. She held her ground. She could not lose.

"Tell me you will never betray me, and I'll believe you."

"No. Of course not," she said.

The water was flooding up fast over his thighs in the chamber.

Like a shock to his brain came the sight of he and Claren sitting in the white room. Claren leaned his head forward, those blue storms in his eyes breaking deep into the hidden parts of him.

"The war is on Deiphera."

Then water was filling the little white room in his mind, rising and sloshing left and right, splashing off the vivid white walls. Varin rubbed at his eyes. He was sitting there staring at the old Thwargg as the water reached into his mouth. He spat out the imaginary water that seemed so real and it brought him back to the present moment in the submerging tank. He drew a big breath and sank beneath the rising water, yanking the stimulant gun from its holster. He pressed it to his thigh and released a dose. After a few moments, the air escaped his mouth with a burst of bubbles. Every muscle in his body contracted, unsure his gills would work, but they soon blew open. He thought of being a smiling child in the waters of Hypathia; of playing, and the mysterious comforting presence was all around him.

His body was flush with heat. This was not a summer swim. It was the cold of the deep; a swim in the farthest icy depths. He realized his suit was starting to work. Not only did it insulate, but it warmed him. He felt the salty saline of the sea pressing on him and thought this was what it must have been like to be in his mother's womb. Soaked in a realm of dreamy life. He tried to keep his focus on the task at hand, but he could not.

"Opening the expulsion hatch," said a voice on the comms. The words floated in his auditory cortex like a phantom memory.

Drifting off in a trance, he thought, *I must stay conscious now*, for something was pulling on him to sleep. That presence he felt wanted to take him away from this unstoppable process. All was still and silent.

The hatch opened, and his body shot out with force, ejecting him with prejudice, downward through the currents without resistance. It was like falling. The air in his lungs did not store in a fashion to repel the depths but to join them. In the moments that followed, he may have been unconscious.

He saw himself sitting at his desk, writing a report. On the screen, the words "illegal Thwargg activity." And: "I regret to inform you that my wife is involved."

He clicked a button, and the display read "upload." He had written a report and was sending it to Sanje, but something happened. There was a technical error, and the screen went white. That was only days ago, and he had not brought it up with Sanje. Part of him could not understand why he kept forgetting to share the information further. He feared the truth—that they were programming his mind.

He was conflicted, and part of him wanted to say nothing, but this was different. It was as if someone had rubbed out the impulse to talk to Sanje.

In the memory of the little white room, Claren extended his index finger and put it to his temple.

He opened his eyes, and the deep of the sea was a blue sooty void. He could not tell how far he had descended. The PTT unit beeped on his hip.

"Interceptor, you are entering the field," said the voice from far away, mingling with the sound of his heartbeat. For a moment, he could swear he heard two pumping hearts, but though he had gills, it was an absolute fact he only had one heart.

"We advise you to turn on your lights. Native entities are big, but they do not see well."

The sensory deprivation had dazed the extuiter. He strained to focus on the moment at hand. The currents shifted violently, and his body was whipped topsy-turvy into the depths by something. He couldn't tell what was up and what was down.

He tried to right himself as he pressed the button on the light attached to his shoulder. As the beam shone, he saw the tremendous shape of a second barb fish approaching through the darkness. It was a creature with giant eyes situated nearly outside of its body. It was long and flat, and behind it were multiple long tails. Along each tail were what looked like hooks. It had to be twenty feet long, its entire body luminescent with a brilliant blueish-white light.

As it pumped through the water, it shimmered with iridescent flashes, and strobing pulses of red energy moved from its skull to the end of its tentacle-like tails. Indeed, this was like a dream.

Varin's light redirected it from colliding with him. Veering up and to the left of the extuiter, it created a riptide that tossed Varin head over heels again. He tucked in his body and gave in to the tumble, moving in harmony with the forces of the sea. Then he was steady.

"Roger that. Lights on," he responded to his team.

Beneath him was the hatching field. Thousands of barb-fish babies danced in schools like flocks of incandescent bulbs, and lower down he could see a hot-pink luminescent bed of eggs, the oozing afterbirth mixed in with the black of the milling floor. This was where the resources were separated from unneeded junk. He could see barb fish breaking free of their eggs. Their obstinate drive to get out and swim with the other barbs made him think of his little girl, her sweet little smile, her hair all wild. He grinned with amazement.

What was it? he thought. *What was it that made me write that report?*

He could see his child's body stretched out on the dream table. She was connected to the anthroscope, and her mother was standing over her. He was looking for Skenkin and opened the door to the dream chamber. She was sliding the child from the table. The child was groggy.

"What are you doing?" he asked abruptly. Skenkin was caught and couldn't lie properly to make sense of it.

"Nothing." She smiled. "We were just playing, weren't we, sweetie?"

She poked the child in the tummy to make her laugh. Use of the machine was forbidden. There was no telling what it could do to a child's conscious identity to be connected to the dream technology. He didn't know what to do.

"Okay," he said to her. And that was it.

"There's a hatch twenty meters in front of you," a voice said over the comms. "That will take you to the first source."

"Copy that. Searching." The barb fish babe he had been watching broke free of its gelatinous egg, darting off fast. "Won't my light hurt the resource, command?" he asked.

"No. Don't worry about that," replied the major.

He imagined the automated anthroscope arm injecting his child with its sedative.

The mill floor was a blaze of glowing material confusing to his eyes. Another hatchling was beating its head wildly against the inside of its glowing gooey egg. Others slipped around him like a swarm of rapid fire.

"I see it."

"It's a sliding lever." He unlocked the hatch and pulled himself under the grate, still submerged in water, then closed it behind him. The first device was already visible.

"You're on top of the reading, interceptor."

Varin examined it. It wasn't elegant; it was big and clumsy-looking.

"What is it?" he asked.

"Give us an image."

"What?"

"Back up, man! Back up!" squawked Dee. Varin did. "Thank you!" Dee commended. The comm was silent a moment. "Hm, my God, that's an improvised flash bomb, Mr. Muscles. We're turning on your head camera."

"There's a timer."

"All right," Dee continued. "The bomb specialist is coming online."

A steady, focused voice cut into the line. "Interceptor. There is a break box under the timer pad?"

"Copy that. I see it." It was a yellow-colored metal enclosure. The muck of the sea was all over it. "Why does this bomb look so old?" Varin asked.

"It's environmental build-up. We need to identify all ingoing wires. From where we are, we only see two. We need you to check it."

Varin did as directed. "No, that's all."

"Let's open her up," directed the specialist.

Varin pulled a wedge from his tool kit.

"We need you to close your eyes in case there's an unidentified trigger."

He slid the wedge up into the groove and closed his eyes as he jimmied it open. There was a snapping sound.

"Here we go. The box is opening."

When the box broke open, there was a discharge of internal units unpacking. He could hear a breaking sound, then digital blipping.

"That's good. Keep your eyes closed. We'll walk you through this."

Varin heard a hiss like a match being extinguished and an accelerated beeping.

"Keep your head up. We need to see the display on the timer."

He opened his eyes to see if he was pointing the cam in the right direction, then closed them tight again in case the unit blew. The beeping accelerated to a single tone and then, as his heart began to race, the unit shorted out. There was silence. He backed up as far as he could to avoid any discharge, but nothing came.

"What's going on, command?"

The comms were silent and then finally the bomb specialist broke in.

"Interceptor, this diffusion is complete. Either this one was a dud, or your work just got a whole lot easier."

"That's it?" He opened his eyes. Looking up through the milling floor, past the flash bomb, he could see that barb fish hatchling piercing up out of its jellied bubble and slithering free into the open sea.

"Good work, interceptor."

"All right. I'm going to give you coordinates for each one of the readings so we can get you through this site and onto any other discovery reports." It was Dee's voice. Varin felt a huge relief to be moving on.

Dee read coordinates; Varin put in the travel identifier code and turned the dials. The PTT gate opened. It was unnerving and painful going through, but after the first leap, he felt confident. The terrorists were smart enough to put together something dangerous, but the three following flash bombs flooded without a hitch. Then he came to the first firebomb. Varin was told it was a particle splitter design, but the break box had flooded on this too and everyone was confident the mission was going to be a success.

One after the other, Varin shot through the PTT gates with building ease, but he began to notice his eyes were blurring and his heart rate was accelerated. His chest was starting to burn when he breathed.

"Tell me I'm getting out of the water soon. I'm having some physical abnormalities."

"The doctor thinks it's the high level of oxygen in the water. It's pure. And there's a lot of pressure down there. The last unit is in the firing chamber for the kepplequer lines that operate the mining facility's power cells. Let's get you in there, and you can take a break."

He set a gate to the firing chamber where it was dry, then took off his mask to have a much-needed rest. Taking a deep breath in through his mouth, he steadied himself and waited a moment for his vision to clear. But there was little time to spare, so he put the mask back on and was back to work fast on another particle-splitter bomb. It was attached to a wall lined with kepplequer cells in the hot claustrophobic firing chamber of the generators. This was where the mine burned its main source of energy, and he didn't want to stay there any longer than necessary.

"I'm ready. Let's do this," he said to get their attention.

"Let's open the break box."

Varin moved closer to the device and began to wedge it open. He noticed another stream of fibrous wires attached to it, unlike any of the other devices. The fibers started to pulse with light as he was cracking open the box.

"We have a problem—this one is different. We have activity." The particle splitter lit up.

"Yes, we see."

Looking to the timer pad, Varin could see it short in and out and then begin a ten-second countdown."

"Clip the wire from the break box to the accelerator."

Varin did, but the particle splitter started to show a spinning light inside the clear housing case.

"All right," Dee said. "Put in the code two-two on the PTT pad. That will give you a reverse path on the current coordinates."

"I didn't notice them. I'm sorry."

"Never mind that, man. Push the go command on the PTT. You've got to get out of there!"

The light in the particle splitter casing raced and grew brighter. Varin pressed go on the PTT. As the gate opened, the bomb combusted in a hot yellow blast. The pressure from the explosion started to lift him off his feet as he stepped back through the gate, and he ended up under the water in his previous location, slammed up against the mill wall. Some large, heavy shrapnel blasted through the gate, jamming into the wall and pinning him down, and he let out a howl. It was the last of his breath. He couldn't pull the stimulant gun free, and he was on the verge of drowning.

Writhing in pain under the pressure of the shrapnel, he was using all his might to keep from taking in water. Then his gills blew open, and he received a rush of oxygen, but his eyes whited out with tracers. The rush of oxygen had overstimulated his retinas.

He jerked the shrapnel free, releasing himself, and was relieved to discover the shrapnel had not pierced him or his suit, though it had hit him hard. He was sure he had a cracked rib. He was going to be all right, but his eyes were still blurry. He had sustained a head injury too, and his oxygen sickness was none the better for it.

"Dee, get me somewhere dry."

Dee gave him coordinates, and in a minute, he was in a hall on the upper level of the operations department. He peeled off his mask.

"I barely did anything to that unit. I swear."

Around him, the mining facility was rumbling from the explosion. The walls shook and a few feet away a lighting fixture blew, sending sparks shooting into the air. Outside, the sound of churning steel could be heard then finally everything settled.

A screen at the far side of the operations room powered on. The eco-terrorist was on the screen.

"Are you seeing this?"

"Yes. It's on all the media outlets."

The terrorist spoke. "Our agent has alerted us to your activity. That was a warning. Now we are going to bring the war to you. If you infiltrate further facilities, the losses will be unimaginable." The screen shorted to black.

"It looks like we have a mole," said the major.

"Are there miners in the facility?" Varin asked.

"No. Everyone's been evacuated."

"What's the damage, command?"

"The resources are safe. We have no loss of life. And it looks like the event was localized so we should be able to contain it."

"Well, that's good."

"What's your condition, interceptor?"

"Everything's fine."

"Are you sure we shouldn't bring you up?"

"No. I'm ready to roll."

"Copy that, interceptor. We're going to give you coordinates to the next facility at West Rock. Has there been any sign of the threat we were to be concerned with?"

"I think that was him in the visual message."

"Switch up the PTT for distance travel."

As he did, he thought of the message—*We are going to bring the war to you*—and considered his new memory of Claren in the white room. *The war is on Deiphera.*

He wondered why he was having this memory. Was it real? Were the memories he thought he had in the weapons facility real? The ones in that same white room so long ago with all that backward talking. It couldn't be real. He hoped to God they weren't.

It was the only denial of memory experience he had dedicated himself to, and it was that denial that gave him faith that any of his life was real. That it wasn't put on. Was he lying to himself to hold on to his life with Skenkin? He wanted his child to be happy too. It was the same with the knowledge that Skenkin was messing with his kid's mind, using the anthroscope. He let it continue, not wanting to believe it. Wanting to hold on to some optimistic idea of what love should be. If God had anything to do with children, surely he couldn't allow a mother to risk destroying a child's mind? Haytoo had said she was a monster, and the tortured poltergeist thought the Thwargg and Skenkin had betrayed him. He was afraid. He was in denial. Things were more complicated than he wanted to admit.

He put in the coordinates for West Rock and stepped through the gate, but before he could do anything else, base camp shot the command, "Hold your position, interceptor."

He was in the underside of the milling fields at West Rock watching the little babies slam their heads silly to be free of their birthing eggs. One seemed to have been stuck halfway to liberty for some time and was giving up, so Varin reached up through the milling grate to help it, grabbing hold of the broken part of the egg. It was two times the size of his head. He worked at tearing it open, and the barb kid bopped to life, rattling in the crevice.

Varin couldn't tell if the barb had accidentally dug into his hand with the sharp bits on its tails or if there was some chemical reaction from the egg, but something was starting to burn his hand. He could see a gaseous fume spitting off his glove like he'd put his hand in acid. Recoiling from the egg, he banged his hand on the metal grating then ripped the glove off. Finally, the harsh reaction rescinded, and the glove had kept his hand safe.

The tiny barb shot free, its bunched tails pumped with their little blades to join the others. He squeezed his hand back into the glove. That was the last time he would put his hand next to a barb fish, even if it were to help.

His eyes were filling with blinding rings of light, but it only lasted a few seconds before clearing again.

"What's going on, command?" They had been silent too long.

Varin began to feel that odd presence again. With it came a sense of doom. Something was wrong. His instincts were telling him that if something was going to happen, it was now. He felt laden in danger.

"Command? I'm having a really bad feeling." Images of his kid flashed through his mind. She was saying, "Don't go, Daddy." Then the presence he was sensing made him feel like it was going to keep him safe, whatever happened.

"We have a report of a device found in the Constance reserves. Interceptor, we're going to need you to abandon the current facility and get to Constance."

"No, I have to do this," slipped from Varin's lips as if he was talking to his child. In his mind, he was picking her up to hold her in a bear hug and kiss her on the head.

There was feedback on the line. He let out a yell.

"Time's up," crackled through the comms but it wasn't command. It was Haytoo. Nothing else was said. The line was silent.

He saw Claren pushing his finger up to his temple. He didn't understand these memories, and he was struck with fear because, at the same time, the presence was alerting him there was trouble at hand. Then he heard activity from the nearby device.

"Command! We have an urgent situation!" He started swimming towards the device. "Command! I'm in front of the device here at West Rock. It's live!"

The flash bomb had come to life, and the digital reading was counting down from three minutes.

"We have an active device, command." He jammed his wedge into the break box and tore it open. It flooded, and the digital readout died.

"It's flooded, command. The flash bomb is out of commission. Give me the next coordinates, Dee!"

"I can't do that, man; we gotta get you out of there."

"If they're all set to three minutes I can do this! Give me the coordinates!"

"Hold on." After a moment Dee spoke fast and serious. "All right. But you gotta be ready to take the exit coordinates when we send them. You understand? We don't want to lose you, and we need to get you to Constance"

"I copy. I copy. Let's go."

He was off to the next device. When he got there, it was as he had thought. The other bombs were counting down from the same time. He disarmed as many as he could then he finally reached one that only had twenty seconds left. Varin jammed his wedge in, but he couldn't bust the box open. The timer jumped to ten seconds, shorting in and out. He wouldn't let it go. He felt so close.

"It's time to go, interceptor! Put in the exit coordinates now!"

Varin let up on the box and started to dial in the exit numbers, but it was too late. The timer reached zero with a piercing beep that could be heard even under the weight of all the water. He didn't know what explosion would accompany the flash and kicked off the grated wall, turning to shield himself.

The facility was destroyed. It wasn't a flash bomb. It was worse than anything they expected. The milling floor blew out with a terrible force, setting of a chain reaction that blew a countless number of flash bombs and other far more savage devices. The giant barb fish and their schools of babes were overtaken by the explosions and metal debris, the mining walls collapsed, and there were no survivors.

PASSAGES

Chapter 1
Contingency Among the Barbs

The farm, the mining facility, and reserve tanks were obliterated, but it was not the facility at West Rock. It was on Constance.

Varin realized the bomb he was defusing wasn't going to explode. He waited for the other devices to go off in the West Rock facility, but none of them did. There were no explosions from the particle bombs. There were no great flashes of light as bright as the sun.

"Interceptor?"

"It's nothing. Nothing's going off here. I need some air. Give me the position for the particle bomb."

"30.258 to 47.28345." The voice from command did not sound happy.

Varin stepped through the gate to the particle bomb and took off his mask. He was shaken with fear. He looked at the particle bomb. The display read 00.00, and it was beeping wretchedly, then the display fizzled to a blank screen. Command was silent.

"They're all decoys. These things aren't real, command," Varin said with dismay.

The line was silent. Then, finally: "We lost the only farm on Constance and more than half of our reserves."

Varin was horrified. The image of Claren filled his mind.

The war is on Deiphera.

Then he knew the war the old Thwargg meant. The war in him. The war that kept him on Deiphera. Surely, there was nothing he could have done in such a short time on the capital world. If he had made a gate to Constance, the best he could have done was minimize the damage. What was this presence he felt? The one that told him it was going to keep him safe. The presence that seemed to fill his mind with thoughts of his child telling him not to go. Maybe it did keep him safe as it had seemed to say it would, but it was at the cost of significant loss. Perhaps there was nothing he could have done on Constance but die. What was becoming clear to him was that these bombs in Galneea's farms and mines were likely all decoys. The bombs were old-looking. Covered in the muck of the sea. They may have been put there to cause destruction but not by terrorists only days before. Maybe for some insurance scam or something else. Everything on Deiphera might have only been a ruse.

The confusion of thoughts was starting to rip him apart—the fear that Claren may have planted suggestions in his head to keep him on Deiphera. But for what? He even questioned what this angelic sensation was. It seemed to want him away from Constance too. After what he'd seen in Haytoo's temple, maybe this presence he felt wasn't an angel at all.

*

"You think the presence was a demon?" Evah interrupted. Her tone was deep. Her eyes were glowing with faint blue storms again.

"It's hard to tell, Evah. Such things are scientifically unsubstantiated."

Evah was still. She put her head down and stared at the ground.

"But Varin thought it was something from God," Felin said, trying to allay her concerns that Varin, or anyone, should have to contend with such things as demons.

*

"Were there any miner casualties?" Varin asked command.

"Everybody is dead. Everything is dead." reported the major with simmering emotion.

Then Varin heard other voices. And, though everyone was supposed to have been evacuated, someone was there. Many *someones*.

He followed the sound down a hall, where he found a hatch. He cranked it open gently, and on the other side, he could see a large archway that led to a pavilion. The smell was awful. The smell of cigars. The smell of rats. The smell of Scabeeze miners. He pulled at the thrines of space and enclosed himself in secrecy. Some were playing poker around a large table, while others lounged about on chairs and sofas looking at their kalodias and watching a projection screen in the air. On the floor, their pet rats were running around free. Big fat black ones. He had heard these were favorite pets for the miners.

On the other side of the pavilion was a hallway with offices.

One Scabeeze lounging in a chair input something in his kalodia then raised his head.

"Hey, hey, hey, hey, the show's on." He was a little urgent. Nobody seemed to care.

"I bet the weirdo new boss won't last long," said one of the Scabeeze gamblers and threw a chip on the hearty pile in the center of the table.

"I'll see your bet. I think we should start a pool. Never seen a boss so hands-on in the mill floor," said another.

"I don't even think he really works here. Galneea has something goin' on on the side," said another.

"Yeah. Let's start a pool," said a fourth.

"Yeah. I can think of something I'd like to start a pool about," said the first and started to laugh. The others joined him. "No, no, really, that guy's stupid. That's my pool," he sniggered.

Behind Varin, the hatch he had entered through creaked back open. It shot chills up his spine because he felt like it was that presence again telling him to go back. He doubled back a little way from the pavilion door.

"Command, I am putting in a code for interplanetary travel. I want coordinates for the remaining Constance reserves."

"That's not something we advise," said the major. Then Dee got on the line.

"Look, man, it's really dangerous. I know you want to go and try to save the day over there, but the interplanetary functions have a lot of problems. There are starslides. All kinds. Shipping and commuter."

"Listen to me, Dee. Please. If I had been there, I might have been able to minimize the damage. You know that. I'm willing to take the risk. If I had held my position at the last facility, it would have been something to consider. All these damn bombs were decoys. If I hadn't seen the first start its timer, I wouldn't have wasted our time on any of them."

"I have to see what I can do. Let me see if there's a viable path."

"All right. I'm going to check something out here. Somehow, some crew was left behind. They're carrying on like it's their day off. Get me those coordinates."

"I'll get back to you." And the line fell silent.

Varin put in the interplanetary code then attached the PTT to his belt, and he was on his way into the pavilion. All his senses were on fire. He felt as though he was literally vibrating with adrenaline. He felt larger than himself too. It was a feeling he'd had when Ansen's poltergeist was inside him.

As he moved through the pavilion, he thought he might nearly levitate, his feet touched the ground so lightly. He shrugged it off as something to do with the absence of the water pressure.

Crossing to the hall, he began to check the offices one by one, staying out of sight. One had nothing going on in it. The next had no one in it, but there was a holograph display running some content. He nearly moved on to the next office, but he realized he was in the holograph content. It was running in a short loop. He moved to investigate the projection. It was him, typing a message into his console at home, but the point of view was that of the console screen. There must have been a camera inside it.

He knew immediately what this was. It was a recording of him preparing his report on illegal Thwargg activity. Then the moment of him trying to send the report. Now he knew there had been no technical error as he had thought. Someone had control of his console.

The image cut to a close shot of his child lying on the dream table. She was sleeping. The camera perspective was from the anthroscope. Her eyes were moving rapidly behind their lids. A wave of sorrow washed over the extuiter. *It was true*, he thought.

"Are you guys seeing this, command?" he spoke into the comms, but there was no reply. "Command one? Are you reading this? Can you see this?" But there was no response.

The recording feed cut to an image of him sitting in a small room and before him was the eco-terrorist leader. It was a small room, like the white room but different. It was the same office from the terrorist's visual messages.

"All you need to do is follow up on Deiphera," said the terrorist.

"All right." he heard himself say in the recording.

"Whatever happens, stay on Deiphera. Do you understand?"

"Yes," he said.

Varin could not believe his eyes.

"What are you showing us, interceptor?" Now, the comms were back, and he knew they were seeing this visual message.

"I ca— This isn't right."

"What isn't right?" asked the major.

"None of this is right," he followed up. It was then he realized he had to be more careful with his words. Anything he said now could incriminate him. For all they knew, he was mouthing sympathetic eco-terrorist statements. The line broke into static and shorted out—the same feedback he'd heard when Haytoo's voice crackled in with, "Time's up." The comms went silent again. He did not even want to ask if they were there. The only thing he figured they'd seen was him meeting with the eco-terrorist.

The recording cut to his goodbye with his family.

"Don't go, Daddy," said his child. At that moment, he realized if they had a recording of that, they could have been broadcasting it on the comms earlier. But he didn't think it was that simple or benign. He was having trouble distinguishing what was real and what was the workings of his mind. He did not want to believe it.

He continued watching. Skenkin ran her finger inside a little box as if to grab at something small. Then she was embracing him, and he could see her plunging her fingers into his hair; putting something in his hair. He reached up and dug around a little. There was a tiny piece of metal. A chip that seemed stuck to his head, almost like a tiny knot in his locks. It was too small to be a listening device. But a tracker—it could have been a tracker.

"I know you have to go," she said. And now he knew she had helped him to be used. Maybe by her father. It must have been. But was she really saying he had to die?

The war is on Deiphera. He thought of the stoic Thwargg, giving him an unconscious suggestion in that little white room.

He thought of pulling out his plasma pistol and blowing his head off onto the wall. He never had thoughts like that. He was trembling. They could have sent him to his death on Constance, but they were doing something far worse. They were going to make him a patsy for their scheme, destroying his faith in everything he held dear.

Despite the overwhelming feeling of betrayal, he was not going to kill himself, but he had to get off the West Rock facility. Fast. The way things were going, he wondered if Claren had planted an urge to kill himself. He had to remain calm and logical. He didn't know if he could trust his own instincts in any way. Maybe they were trying to provoke him into doing something completely out of character; something stupid that would make him look rash and guilty.

He knew he had to expose all of this—if anyone would believe him after the show with the eco-terrorist he just sent to command. There was no telling what the fallout would be post-truth. The Scabeeze were carrying on like someone had won a big bet. The comms were dead, and he didn't know how he was going to get a transport out of there. He had to find a shipping bay. There was nothing else in the office with any information. Not even a recording source to take for evidence.

He stepped back into the hall. At some point, he had opened up the space that was hiding him, and he could be seen. Still, no one seemed to notice him from the pavilion. Looking down to the other end of the hall, he could see there was one office left, and then beyond that corridors. He folded the space around him again and began to walk to the other end of the hall, hoping to find a way out, but deep down he knew he was probably never going to leave this facility. Not alive anyway.

Varin continued along the hall, and when he came to the final office, he gave little more than a glance inside. All he could think of was getting off that facility.

"Come, brother. You know as well as I that to another like you, you can be seen even hiding in the air," the eco-terrorist said from behind a desk in the office.

Varin unwrapped himself from the space in which he hid.

"And what are you hiding?" Varin said.

"Nothing. You know who I am. You're right on time," Haytoo said, still appearing as the terrorist. He stood up from behind the desk, putting his hands up as if to say he would be peaceful.

"In time for what?" Varin asked.

A visual powered up on the wall to the left of Varin and they both approached to observe. A news feed was rolling, showing an aerial view of the water above the second Constance kepplequer reserves. Great flashes of light and huge plumes of water burst into the air. A reporter could be heard.

"Oh my God. Oh no. We're looking at what appears to be the destruction of the second kepplequer reserve here on Constance. That is the last of the reserves here. My God. We can't even begin to imagine what this will mean for Constance. If you're just joining us, we have lost the last of the power source that keeps the capital going." The camera continued to pan around the installation.

"Why do you dedicate yourself to such things?"

The image on the screen changed to a news affiliate.

"This is a tragedy. We have not only lost the resources here on Constance, but as you know, if you've been watching, thousands of barb fish have been killed in the only kepplequer farm we have here. There are reports that the Extuiter of Constance was likely a conspirator working with the Hypath terrorists. We cannot confirm yet, but some reports have been received suggesting there is another extuiter plotter. We understand that the magisteria will be making an announcement soon."

"Looks like tough times for Constance. But don't worry, that planet of locusts will get their precious power. They may have as much as three days before things start going dry and the starslides start shutting down and the lights and so on. If they play it right, the most essential parts of the social continuum will survive a week, maybe two. After that, there's going to be a new man of the people who will save the social order, gain their love and trust, and be on his way to being Prime Minister after he is elected to the magisteria."

"Galneea," Varin said. "Why do you care if the Scabeeze master rises to power?"

Haytoo expelled a disappointed sigh.

"It doesn't matter who's in power. The will of the people will be heard and treated as it usually is." He looked Varin over. "You're an agent of a system, and your perspective is emasculated. We are so much more. You saw that temple."

"I saw you go to hell."

"No."

"How did you come back?"

"I returned through another door on our home planet. On Hypathia."

"And did you find your bliss?"

"There is no bliss. There is only the presence of our own power. What we generate. What we create."

"Tell me." On the screen, a clip of Varin could be seen. The one he'd already seen: The clip of him sitting in the small room with the eco-terrorist.

"To answer your question, working with Galneea allows me to do what I want to do, for now. Your system is a mess. It's a mess of lies."

"No. No, I mean, what did you see? Where you went." Varin steadied Haytoo.

"There was nothing. Nothing for a long time. It was the black you saw. The blackness seemed outside of time. It went on—I don't know how long. Longer than the time that passed here. I did nothing but wait at first. I could see my burned body in a doorway. It lay there inviting me to go back to the world. And then I walked. I walked away from the door, but it followed me. It was always there behind me. Then, from the blackness, I discerned a throne. And it was my throne—my throne in the mystery. In the black. Then there was food, and then victims for my hate, and they died horribly, sweetly, and there were women. And I thought I might make a race of Hypaths in my kingdom, in the black. But it was not my kingdom. Though I could have stayed there beyond ages, it was not my kingdom. My kingdom was here, and it had to be found. So I entered back into my mortal body, and I returned."

"There was only black or was there only what was in your head?"

The screen cut to a clip of them standing in the office, watching the destruction of the Constance reserve.

"I want to show you something," Varin said. "Take off this extuition."

The image on the wall cut back to a loop of the explosion, but the sound was no longer playing. Haytoo's extuition faded, and he stood there before Varin with all his scars. His face was destroyed, one ear burned off.

"Be still," Varin said and raised his hands to Haytoo's face. First, he removed one hand, and Haytoo's ear was there where it had been missing. "Do you see?" he asked the mutilated man, and Haytoo put his hand to his ear with some amazement. Varin placed both hands on his face. Haytoo winced, his jaw dropping in an expression of pain. Varin took his hands away, and Haytoo's face was healed, the scar tissue chaffing off like dead skin. "Now, why haven't you done that for yourself?"

"How long will this last?" Haytoo interjected, brushing away the damaged skin.

"It depends on whether you can accept it. This is what I have learned to do since you made your virus that needed to be healed." And, indeed, this new strength in his powers was some imprint left upon Varin by Ansen's poltergeist. "This is what I do most of the time in my work now. I've studied the body. The bodies of all races. I've learned what goes wrong and what must be reversed. And there is more. There is something I have found in the faith of others. What have you done with your time? Created pain? Sickness? Created an empty kingdom in the blackness outside of the living? I have found people have their own gifts deep inside them. What cannot be scientifically reversed. Some were able to work with my power to materialize healing, from images inside their mind, and it becomes real to them. They continue to be well. Then there are others. They always go back to their illnesses, their deformities, the moment they leave my lab. What I have been able to figure out is that some people... some people can only see themselves as sick. They can only know sick thoughts. They cannot see anything *beyond* sick."

"Oh." Haytoo thought deeply for a moment, then began to laugh. "You are going to be my biggest regret."

He continued to laugh, then took a deep breath to clear his mind.

From down the hall, the crowd of Scabeeze miners could be heard stalking towards them, their feet falling cloddishly over the cold steel floor.

"Who won the pool?" asked Haytoo.

"I did," said a smiling gruff-voiced Scabeeze with brown scaly skin, all lanky in body. He was clearly ready to play rough. The others crowded close behind where he stood in the door.

"I came in second!" said a shorter Scabeeze who seemed pleased with his performance. That one had a stun stick in his hand. Down on the cold floor, one of their fat black rats scampered in. Sniffing around, he crossed the floor into the office.

Varin knew the time for talk was at an end. He did not know how he was going to take all these opponents at once, but he knew Haytoo was the most dangerous. As experienced and potent as his powers were, he rarely trained to use them in defense or offense. It was the essential mote of ideology that set him apart from Haytoo, and in such a circumstance, it would be his undoing.

Without a thought, he twisted his body fast and hard, sending an elbow straight up into Haytoo's chin and nearly knocking him out cold as his body slammed onto the desk behind him. He continued his turn, grabbing the lanky Scabeeze in the doorway by the shoulder and sent a right knee, like a battering ram, up into his guts.

The short Scabeeze behind him drew back his stun stick to give Varin a fierce shock, but Varin swung the lanky Scabeeze sharply into the door frame, nearly breaking the short Scabeeze's arm. Before the stun stick had hit the ground, Varin extuited the wall closed where the entry was. The substitute wall slid down like a guillotine lopping off the short Scabeeze's mangled arm. As the appendage bled out and twitched on the cold metal floor, Varin ripped the gravitation pack off the winded lanky one and, with all his force, shoved him upward into the ceiling. Being light then, without his pack, the gruff Scabeeze nearly broke his neck as he was slammed hard into the steel framework above.

Varin kept moving as fluidly as he could to grab the gun from his holster and send a blast in Haytoo's direction. It missed, tearing a huge twisted hole in the steel floor, which revealed some sort of maintenance shaft. A flood of water started in the shallow service area. Haytoo lunged towards Varin, ramming him up against the wall.

Varin was tripping over the bloody Scabeeze arm beneath his feet, his boots making a sickening screeching noise in the fresh blood. He extuited a tight eyeless mask over Haytoo's head to blind him. But it was too late. Suddenly, Varin was howling in nightmarish wails. Looking down, he could see Haytoo had some sort of long, sharp object in his hand. It was stuck all the way through Varin and into the wall behind him.

Haytoo fell into him with the thrust and was frisking around Varin's wound to discover what his lunge had yielded, still unable to see. His hand slipped around Varin's back, groping over the dangerous metal instrument of torture he had made and his fingers got caught up between the PTT unit and the wall. Varin was screaming savagely, and with a force that nearly made him black out, he drove his head into Haytoo's face, right between his eyes. Haytoo reeled back, and as he did his hand whipped across the PTT dials, setting them to some unfathomable destination, but Varin could scarcely hear the zipping sound of the rapidly clicking dials through his pain.

The plasma pistol flew across the floor into the maintenance shaft, where water continued to flood, so with two hands, Varin reached for the spear that ran through his kidney and into the wall. He pulled it out with the last of the force he had within him, then fell to the floor, hitting his head again on the metal with a cold, abusive bang. His sight was turning to black. Shades of shadow. He did not know if blood was in his eyes or if the oxygen sickness was finally tearing his retinas apart, and his sight wavered in and out of a glazed light. He grasped for something to defend himself with—even something to steady himself. Though he could not keep his eyes open, he fought to keep death off of him, but he was losing that battle too.

Haytoo tore the mask away from his face and kicked the extuiter so hard in the side with the gaping wound that the dying man recoiled in a shock of pain, flipping onto his back. There was a beep from the PTT unit. Varin was dangling precariously, in a sickening knot over the large hole in the floor.

Looking up, he saw Haytoo for the last time. His deformity had returned, and he stared at Varin with hate, lifted his foot, and stomped on the extuiter, who fell nearly completely into the service shaft, barely keeping a grip on the twisted grating of the floor. His hand reached down to try to stabilize himself, and suddenly, the plasma pistol was in his hand. He raised it and shot off a blast.

This time he did not miss. Haytoo's shredded arm was barely hanging by the flesh of his shoulder, and on the right side of his chest was a gnarled gash.

Varin squeezed the trigger again. With a slick flash, the roofing beams slammed down onto Haytoo. Behind Varin, the ground opened up into a planck gate, and he reached his hands out to each side of the maintenance shaft to keep his weakening body from falling through the gate, not knowing where it could lead. Looking up for something to grab, he saw the black rat toiling on the edge of the hole. Varin could not escape. He was watching the rat lose its footing into a squirming dangle as he lost his grasp and the extuiter disappeared through the gate.

Light flashed all around him as he plummeted through the mysterious space. This was unlike the other gate jumps. It was a racing tunnel of light. Maybe stars. Maybe pure light like something pulled into a black hole, but he did not disintegrate.

Suddenly, the tunnel branched off into a somewhat bigger one. He thought it was possible he crashed through a starslide, but the tunnel was so long. Then all around him, he saw white faces. They were like slivers of light. He thought of Haytoo's obsessions in the temple. Those shone men. The white creatures watched him as he sped fast through the seemingly endless vacuum. They were traveling along with him when he blacked out.

When he came to, he was in a strange place. He recognized nothing. In his weakness, he fought to heal his eyes so that he could see better. His own vision was like a planck gate—electric bands swimming around in circles; in the center a blaze of light.

He could not heal himself; he did not have the strength, so he stared at the alien world around him. He was on an island. He could see a body of water and in the distance a brilliant city. Its towers were like gleaming light. In some ways, it reminded him of Spirea—the abandoned metropolis between the guardian mesas.

Looking up, he saw a woman. A great towering woman. She wore a crown, and in her hand was a torch. He thought of his daughter. In his dreamy haze, he wished he had traveled through time. He imagined the woman was his daughter. Something triumphant. But no, it was a towering carved statue.

By the look of it, he realized he was on Earth, but it appeared far more advanced than drawings or images he had seen depicting it. This was a sophisticated world. The city was like nothing he had seen in all his experiences.

Some people were drawing near. They were so clean, so human, and yet they walked past him as if he might be invisible. Indeed, he was there and too weak to hide himself, but they scuttled past him like some unnerving vagrant, passed out on the tidy green lawn that surrounded the perimeter of the island.

The woman who was leading the group raised her voice enough to draw any witnesses back to her lecture on the grounds of the prominent statue. A couple of kids stared a few moments, but they looked away too. No one so much as pointed to him. He was bleeding out. This was like a slow death in the beautiful sun of a dreamy world that looked so brave; a world of immense possibility. Then he fell into a deep sleep.

He woke to sparks. His body was being shocked by some small flying droid.

"Please move on!" the warm, human-sounding voice of the droid said. "This is a no-loitering zone. The Liberty Security

Force has been alerted to your presence. Please move on. You must move on. You will be detained if you do not adhere to this warning."

The droid knew somehow that he was awake but didn't seem to know he was dying.

"If you have been injured, medical attention will be administered upon dispatch report."

Varin looked down, and to his surprise, he saw the big black rat sitting on his chest.

"You fell in," Varin whispered to the rat that did not seem to mind the droid or any of the business around him but looked up into Varin's face when he spoke.

*

"You see Evah, I lied to you before. That wasn't me on Constance when your father met your mother, and I didn't go to Spirea with your father. But I had fallen into the planck gate with him. I wanted to go home, and so did your father. But something happened that no one expected: I could see his memories, and I clung to him as I clung to myself. To my life. It's not every day that a rat does such things. Or knows such things. I think never before.

"He tried to get up, but he could not at first. He saw the PTT unit beside him—it had broken free from his belt. He pulled it in close and pressed go. The gate opened on the same coordinate path back to Deiphera, and the droid backed off into the air as he pulled himself to his knees. He tried to come back to you, Evah. He made his way back to his feet, but he could barely move. I remember he was holding me in his hands, looking at me. And then I was back in the tunnel of streaming lights, and he was gone. I was returned back to the facility on Deiphera, and conscious in a way I had never known. It was as if I were him. But I am not your father. I don't know what happened to him.

"I eventually found a way to Constance, and though it took an indescribable amount of effort, I was able to talk. I went to the only person I knew that could help me. I went to Sanje. And then you were brought here. Your mother didn't know where you were taken because we did not know if she would ever be able to be free of her father's hold. Then I was brought here. And this is why I say... my life was made for you, Evah. Because I have no past or future but to know you. But ssto be here for you. I was born into consciousness with one idea: To find you and to help you. And I don't know why but somehow, I think, the presence of your father brought you to me, and though it is strange, it seems it could not have been any other way.

"There was one other sign of my connection to your father. I was losing my sight when I arrived back, and like a light, it has gone out waiting for you. I think somehow your father is seeing through my eyes. Or I through his. I sometimes wish so badly that I could see you. But it... it just isn't possible. I have often thought if I could see, perhaps I could extuit, but I have been able to do no such thing. I do not have your father's gifts to save you. To help you or protect you. I wish I did."

Evah was quiet, still, and her eyes were storms again. If there were two persons within her before today, I think they were starting to become one.

"I don't feel well, Felin," she said, sitting on the end of the wooden bench. "My head hurts. I need to go to the med lab."

"Don't be afraid, Evah. I know that this is many things to hear, but you aren't alone." I tried to say it with good intent.

"I will see. I will see what there is to do." This voice had the texture of deep, unwanted wisdom. And I wished that I were dead. That I had not come back like this. I thought I was her secret guardian, but now I feared I was her sickness. I think sometimes we believe we're doing something for all the right reasons and it turns out it's not that way at all. I hoped this wasn't one of those times.

"I'm so sorry, Evah. I wanted to help. I didn't know what the right way was. All I knew was that this is why I was here, and things being so out of the ordinary—out of the ordinary like you are—I couldn't give up."

The bell rang, but she didn't move. Not for a long time, but I stayed with her.

"What happened to Constance? After the kepplequer was destroyed?"

"The city nearly came to a halt. Much was as Haytoo said. First, they started shutting down certain starslides and lowering power availability to public transports. They shut down certain sectors of Constance that made less contribution to state funds. And that spread far outside the capital. But then Galneea came forward and made a statement. He offered free kepplequer and prepared kepplequer cells to share. He brought Constance back from a disaster, and the people loved him. He became one of the most powerful men on three worlds, with interests that extended to the others as well. He was elected to the magisteria, and he had many loyalists from every race. Both rich and poor. It could not be proved he was behind the destruction of the Constance resources.

"Not only did he get himself elected into power, but he cut special deals with the government and transport companies to get big rebates, discounts, and credits in exchange for his free kepplequer. The deals he made for his help will make him and many others in his business circles immense amounts of wealth for many years to come."

"I have to go. They'll wonder where I am. I'm going to go lie down for a while," she said.

I walked to her and put my paws on her legs to be close to her and show her I cared.

"I will be right here for you, Evah. With all my life, I will try to be where you need me."

"I want you safe."

"Go rest, Evah. Maybe tomorrow we will both have answers. Has Father Segura told you what time the Thwargg ambassador will see you tomorrow?"

"It's in the morning; I'll tell you what happened at lunch."

Then she took me up in her hands and held me close to her. I could hear her heart beating, and it was like a haunted memory for some reason I could not place. I crawled up onto her shoulder and, holding on to her hair, I put my nose to her cheek, sniffing for tears, and nuzzled my face to her ear.

"There is nothing you need to show them of your gifts. You decide what is best for you," I said, but deep inside, I wished she would conceal every sign of her powers. But I also feared I could not give her all the help she needed. "You must always remember who you are, Evah. You are a kind-hearted Hypathian girl. You have a mother and father who loved you in the best ways they could. You are not alone, and you have a choice. You always have a choice. Always come back to remembering the people who have given you their best and me. Things may get confusing but remember: You are Evah. Not what anyone else thinks you are or what they think you should be."

"Thank you, my friend," she said, placing me gently on the ground with a pet of affection. Then something dawned on her. "What about the toy animals and the voice?"

"I wasn't sure at first. I thought it could be Haytoo. But now I think the voice is your father's. The toys, the man with the leaf. I think they're just memories. Or extuitions you're making without knowing you're doing it. Putting things together somehow and trying to rationalize. I had thought that since I was seeing like your father might see, that maybe I was making it happen. But I'm useless when it comes to extuitions, so it couldn't be me. I think your father is trying to reach you somehow. It is possible."

"Where do you think he is, Felin?"

I tried to think of something to tell her but could only give her the truth.

"I just don't know, Evah."

168

Chapter 2
Refined Reachable States

N ow, Evah was searching to reclaim the whole of her past experiences and find truths that had been lost. She searched her mind for memories of her father. She searched for memories of her mother. But it was as if someone had built a fortress in her head, excluding her from the past she longed to reconnect to. She wondered if being placed on the anthroscope so young was the cause of her corrupted memories.

Although I did not think it was the reason, I wondered if that was how I was created; like some dissociated sliver of her person. No, it could not be, for I am bigger than some fractured piece of a whole. There must be another reason. If anything, she was a fractured part of my being. She could seek to remember and comprehend only the finite nature of experiences: A face watching over her; a leaf with its sense of color—its reference of detachment, the qualities of decay, and the passion of natural processes. But I could do so much more.

She was only beginning the search I had embarked upon long ago. Her time was centered in a comparative study between the knowledge she could connect to and the stories she was an audience to, but her mind could never reach as far as my presence in her aware state, with its formalities and captive condition of moral responsibility. And now, the farther she explored with her imagination, somehow, the more finite my potential became. We were in this way becoming one consciousness. But I was connected to the spirit of our loved ones—not only the physical—to something vaster; something cosmic. It was a wrestling match, as of late, to keep command of all my reachable states, as her definition of what a reachable state was became more limited.

So, through the small gaps of her imagination and pondering, I continued to escape, for the time being. I had emptied Felin's mind and connected through his experience to the shared beings of our past, and all the places those beings connected to, I could reach as well. My spirit was informed by our father. I had not understood how much. And still, I was of the eternal. I could not move through all of space and time, but I could reach the places my spirit had been carried to. I was aware and could make all these connections a passage for my knowledge, but I did not know why. The potential of my consciousness was more than most living things could imagine. Was this—my world, and all encompassed states known to me—here for my dominion? How could it have been any other way? For what good is it to have the knowledge of so many things, if it is not to exercise some command over them?

Haytoo believed something. He thought the system of the Constellation of Spirea was not made to command such beings as we. If anything, they should serve us. We should not be made subservient and used by lesser beings. Our father believed in service, and that is what destroyed him. And who was right?

When I awoke years ago, I was not alone. I was with my father in consciousness. I did not want to be alone now, but I could not find him. I could sit on the corner of a desk in the Constance Thwargg ward. I could stream through the currents of waters on Deiphera, on Constance and even Hypathia, or perch in the dead world of Spirea upon a mesa overlooking the old metropolis. I could mingle with the air around the starslides between worlds, wander in the sleep chamber of that filthy Scabeeze, be a spying fume in the hideaway where my mother cried for fear of her own web of lies, or hunker amidst the glowing eggs of a thousand luminescent fish. I could even find my way inside Sire Claren's little white room. I could do all these things and more—even sniff the scent of Blouty Duthane—but I could not find my father, nor conjure him with all my abilities.

I traveled back through a whipping hole in space to Earth; I seeped into the fertile soil of that cold planet, the soil where the traces of my father's blood had fed its worms. I played with the salty blue waves between Liberty Island and that future city. I even raced up to the crown of that chiseled lady with her torch to find some sign of him. There was no temple door to blackness or to hell. There was only the unyielding search.

But the nightly gaps wherein my tiny child body slept were coming to an end before meeting our new fate. Even I was becoming a passenger of time now, my choices narrowed towards exercising power in the constraints of time. I stole her life energy away now and then, leaving her detached and vacant; like the vacancy of grief. I was always awake. I was always watching.

Chapter 3
Subject Protocol

A s rays of the golden Eagle sun warmed the dewy morning cool on Constance, Cordia Stangsdon, Thwargg First Class, stroked her hand along the crease of her woolen first-class suit's left lapel. She walked through the deep bays of Constance Ward, where third-class Thwargg, in monochromatic jumpsuits, adjusted their anthroscope interjection apertures for final beta insertions into citizen batches under their time-zone assignments. As they input psycho architecture, designed by second-class sadjudicators and diagnosticians, Cordia Stangsdon, completed the necessary abnormality reports for her shift. Her stations were on daily interjection targets.

Today was a special day. She had been bestowed an exceptionally high honor. She was going to interview the first female extuiter candidate in ward history. It had likely been over two hundred years, if not longer, since the last known female extuiter had existed. The ward system was only 175 years old. According to Cordia's research, the oldest known extuiters were women, though no one seemed to care to talk about that. It was the Thwargg way not to be moved by such odd facts. "Logic above all else," was the Thwargg motto.

Cordia made her way to her office. She needed to check for any unexpected final shift orders. The file container on her door was empty so she took a moment to have a look at herself in the mirror before going to make history. She was impressive, or rather, satisfactorily impressed with herself. Her suit was clean and sharp; the dancing orange flames in her eyes were bright. She did not think of it too much, but she was attractive, with fair blue skin, dark hair, and a lovely shape for any Thwargg girl. She had heard the extuiter was half Thwargg, and she supposed she should make a positive impression as a successful, upstanding, polite girl who knows how to follow directions.

It was then, as she admired her hair in the sunlight that shone through her office window, that she noticed a note on her desk. Opening it, she discovered it was from upper management. There had been a change of plans. That day she would not go to Holy Heart School to conduct an interview. That day she was going to acquire the female subject, overriding all mandated protocols. That day, Evah Ahtochi was to be moved to Constance Ward indefinitely.

Chapter 4
Incendiary Forms

I jammed my head into the hole of the east church wall that led down to the playground. Maddy Poole was due to begin her late morning rehearsal at any moment. Though I suppose she was gifted with her instrument, the honking revelations of sound she pressed into my skull with her pointy fingers were unbearable. I had given up on extuitions and taken to tucking my head in the wall for comfort. It was either that or abandon the church altogether. Now I meditated on mountains of cheese or a creamy sandwich. That was a pleasant way to sublimate my discontent into a world of dreams. I placed my head comfortably into my dingy escape hatch and was beginning to drift off to some tantalizing fantasy when the church door was flung open wildly.

"They've come for me, Felin. They're taking me away." Evah ran inside. The door clapped shut behind her.

I was thinking lovely thoughts of a glazed lemon torte.

"That's nice… What!" Now I was on alert. I banged my head on the top of my hole in bewilderment.

"They came. They're here. A woman Thwargg. She's as nice as cardboard. And she says she's taking me to a 'wonderful place' called 'the ward!'" Evah was talking like a criminal on the run, and it was exactly the right tone as far as I was concerned.

"This isn't the way it's supposed to be at all! Not at all!" I said with amazement. "I'm going to have to talk with Sanje as soon as possible." I started towards the planck gate. "You have to wait here—"

The door opened, and I wished it were Maddy Poole, the organ player, but I knew it wasn't. I turned back to find Evah, but my eyes failed me. I could see the glaring light flood the doorway around a wisp of a shadow, then the door whined as it squeaked closed slowly behind the strange woman. Immediately, the air was filled with a musky perfume.

"Oh my God!" the woman gasped as if restraining a scream.

There was a shuffling and some clumsy thuds from the far side of the church where I usually met with Evah. I tried to find her, but my eyes fooled me due to the glaring light. All I could see was a mass of shadows.

"Well. You are something," the Thwargg woman forced out with a titillated tone. "Can you show me the little girl, please."

There were continued odd thuds from where Evah stood. *Show her the little girl?* What did that mean?

Then, Evah was standing there in the light of our blue-sky window.

"I'm not going to hurt you, Evah. Do you understand?"

"Yes. I was just praying."

"You were? Do you always look like that when you pray?"

"I don't know what you're talking about," Evah said as if the Thwargg would sound crazy reporting whatever she'd just witnessed.

"All right. Do I have to call Father Segura, or can we be friends and get along?"

"I guess." There was a silence. "I guess we can be friends."

"Have you ever left the school, Evah?"

"Yes. We went on a field trip to the Natural History Museum once."

"Well, that's what this is going to be like. You may even get to meet some very important people because I can see you're a very special girl."

It was a Thwargg woman. Her eyes glowed like Skenkin's.

"You promise you'll bring me back?"

"I can't promise you anything. But I can promise I won't lie to you, Evah. I have to follow orders. This morning I thought I was going to visit with you here for a while and that would be all. Then someone said that I should bring you back with me. Important people. You know, it's possible you may not want to come back."

"No, I'll want to come back. I don't want to go with you. I want Father Segura."

"Evah, Father Segura has orders to follow too. And he will say the same thing. Let's be friends. Please. I would like to get to know you."

"Are you going to take me to see my grandfather?"

"Your grandfather? Who's your grandfather?"

"Sire Eine Claren."

"Sire Eine Claren?" To this woman, the name was like that of a god. "Well, if that's your grandfather, then why are you here?"

"Because he's a liar and he probably killed my dad."

"Well, I'm sure that's not true. Who put these ideas in your head?"

"My angel."

"Your angel? Do you… talk to angels? Do you talk to a lot of angels? Or is there only one?"

"I'm not crazy," she said deftly.

The Thwargg woman let out a frustrated sigh. "Ohhh. Look, little girl, do want to go with me and have a nice day or do you want to be stubborn and have someone who isn't nice come and get you? Because they will."

"I'd like to see 'em try."

This was not going well at all. I wanted Evah to hide her gifts, and here she was on the verge of threatening these people who did not have to be nice. I couldn't believe they'd only sent one person to get her in the first place. I was poised to witness something terrible, and all I wanted was for Evah to go peacefully. There was a long silence.

"Fine. I'll go. I know my angel will be watching over me, so you better be good."

"Okay. I like to think I am good. I'm going to open the door and wait for you to walk out. Then we're going to take a scot-schoot ride." She opened the door and stepped out, leaving it ajar.

Evah started to move towards her waiting escort.

"I will be watching, Evah. You're going to be all right. Remember: Be kind. Don't try to hurt anyone," I said, and she heard me. I was sure of it. But when she reached the door, her shape changed again—a great big flopping shadow. Finally, it occurred to me to get my special goggles so that I could see her better. I raced to the wall and pulled my goggles free from my stash of odds and ends, put them on, and searched to find her, but all I could see was the door bouncing to a close.

I had to know what she was becoming. Without another thought, I darted for the hole in the wall. Losing my balance, in my haste, I banged stupidly down the cascade of lumber inside the wall like a rubber ball. It's times like this my big round body does help me. Flopping to a halt on the ground, I was off in a dash. Luckily the door had not clicked to a lock or I would never have been able to dash out onto the playground as I did. Indeed, that was not something I ever did, especially in these weighty goggles. It was dazzling in the light of the sun, and I had to stop a moment to focus my eyes and make sense of all the remarkable information that was jamming into my visual cortex.

"Oh, wow!" I said, adjusting the goggles, my mouth agape. "Say, that's pretty neat!"

I looked around for Evah and the Thwargg woman, but I couldn't find them. Everything was like mad rushing streams of sunlight in endless shades. It was beautiful, all the particles on fire.

I couldn't find them, but I knew where the scotschoots picked up and I was off again with ferocity. My tail was banging every which way, my feet smacking along. My fat body bounced about and cried out for me to slow my chase, but I could not. My eyes wide with rushing yellow fire, I huffed ahead at top speed, and barely noticed as I passed two children.

"Eww! A rat!" a shocked little girl popped off.

How rude, I thought as I continued my sprint out of the playground and onto the concrete walkway. I slipped fast as I hit the new turf, nearly losing control and sliding into the street. The neural patterning helmet was still a little awkward for me, making my coordination all willy-nilly. Some woman's snarlfoppit nearly took a bite out of me as I regained my pace. It jerked after me in a craze of barks but met with a hard stop at the end of its chain, letting out a yelp.

There they were. I saw the form of a little person pass in front of that undeniable Thwargg shape, but my eyes went haywire with the glare of the sun and some strange flashes of fiery particle streams shot out around their indiscernible forms. I could smell the wonderful food of a street vendor and thought that would be a good place for dinner sometime, but my drive was not averted. Though I did squeeze in a mental snapshot to remember the spot.

I heard a public scotschoot hovering into the sidewalk bay up ahead and to the left. If nothing else, maybe Evah would see me. Then she would know how much I cared.

I came to a stop and looked on twelve or so feet ahead of me, to try to at least catch a peek of Evah. It dawned on me that if she were some strange shape, others would surely be reacting. I saw the Thwargg woman stepping up onto the open-air scotschoot, and as she moved aside, there was my Evah. In the sun, I could see the shape of her face. She was beautiful and sweet and wise-looking—a being of golden fire, but that was just my goggles, of course. And then I saw it—something else. All around her like a specter, like some giant hydra. It was a twelve-armed creature standing at least ten feet tall. It seemed to not only be behind her but growing out of her, and not a single person reacted in amazement or fear.

I thought perhaps it was a feature of my goggles to see energy forms that were not physical. Or it was an extuition only for me. Her great arms swayed above and around her, and there was another face. One that was not kind. One that commanded with dread.

Evah stared at me, unmoving, but her other self, arms all fluid in movement, was a nightmarish vision. An atrocity of being ready for havoc. In one hand, there was a plasma rifle. In another, a metal rod.

I couldn't take my eyes off it. My rear hit the ground like an anchor as I gawked in wonder. It was a living image of Haytoo's "god of death." In shock, I could not move, and the scotschoot pulled away like a chariot of gold upon the air.

Chapter 5
Locus of Control

In the hours before reaching Constance Ward, Cordia and Evah were witnesses to mysteries of disintegrating social order on three worlds. Cordia escorted Evah through the Constance water district. Along a river bed that was out of the way, whole families were living homeless. Their camps seemed to be unregulated. Stopping to talk with some of them, Evah was amazed to discover that due to the kepplequer tragedy five years before, many displaced workers had ended up as beggars. Having to choose between paying their debts or feeding their families, they lost their homes. Many stayed near the water district because the climate was more suitable for outdoor living, and it was close enough to wealthy homeowners and business centers that begging was more sustainable.

Besides these and others who were out of work, there were disabled people that could not keep up with the demands of competitive work environments. Businesses could not create viable employment for people like them that effectively served their bottom line of turning a profit, so they were left to the elements and, often having no family to help them, became mentally ill after falling into despair. Indeed, many of the various homeless groups suffered this fate.

They continued through the outer region of the entertainment district, and then to further outlying areas. Along the way, they talked with other groups of the poor. Some were migrants from different worlds who faced language barriers as well as bigotry from citizens who did not want them on Constance. Many had come from other worlds in search of a better life, often from underdeveloped planets far behind technological and educational curves, and Cordia explained that many had had to do terrible things to survive. She used the word "exploited" to describe that work. These people, too, seemed weird or strange. It was becoming clear to Evah that being broken-spirited and living in such desperation, they might all be considered, by some, unfit mentally. Or unfit for society in general, and because of this, they were ignored or passed over all the more.

The Thwargg escort seemed to be following special instructions that she kept tucked inside her crisp blue and grey suit. Every time she read the page, she would reset their course on some new scotschoot line. She was constantly checking her kalodia as if she had a schedule to keep.

On the scotschoots in the outlying area, many people seemed dirtier. They talked to themselves and struck up odd conversations, stranger to stranger. Being so new to the world outside Holy Heart, Evah had never seen such behavior.

There was one disabled boy in a wheelchair that rattled off wails and strange honking noises. She had been looking at the old buildings, wondering if somewhere before her could be the alley that led to Haytoo's temple. Could these be the streets where her father had talked to the beggars and saved one man out of a battalion?

Evah tried hard to focus on those issues, but she was distracted by the wailing boy and could barely think at all. She realized he had no control over his condition, and she felt sorry for him but wished he'd disappear, so she didn't have to feel so uncomfortable—so disgusted and sad at the same time. Then she was regretting the notion of being disgusted, recognizing the powerlessness of the boy and all the suffering people. Not only the disabled and the ones that mumbled to themselves, but the elderly as well. The ones who could barely mount the scotschoots in their antigravity chairs, and those dragging their bodies behind wheeled metal frames.

Then, in the near distance, there was a rumbling boom. Coming to a stop where the buildings were old and dilapidated, Cordia put her hand on Evah's shoulder, letting her know it was time to exit the scotschoot. They walked up the block a little way to a clearing. It was an old park that had dried up and withered. Not far from them, on the other side of the park, were old buildings surrounded by fences.

"Stay close and look over there," Cordia said, pointing to the fenced buildings.

There was a screeching alarm, and then another boom and some of the buildings in the distance began collapsing in on themselves. An entire block was demolished. Evah was amazed at how clean the destruction was. It seemed so effortless. Another alarm screeched, and another building fell, this time closer to them.

"There's going to be a new experiment," Cordia said and started moving on to the next block. Evah was dazed by the goings-on but tried her best to keep up. They passed an alley that reminded Evah of Felin's story, but before any further exploration, Cordia mounted another scotschoot and they were off.

A lean man who looked like he was made of leather from being exposed to the sun so long mounted the scotschoot. He smelled of urine and something Cordia referred to as booze. The leathery man struck up some of that strange talk with another rider. The other man did not know him but, rather, seemed to know the world like he did. Their clamor made Evah's heart feel like an open gash. The leather man was loud, as if all the world was his audience. He seemed angry. There was a tone of outrage, perhaps, at his own hopelessness. It began to reach deep inside the young girl.

"Oh, she let him die," said the leathery man.

"Yeah," said another.

"All the things she coulda done." The leather man put his chin up in the air, proud. "A little pile of whimpers. I'm in my little diapers, Daddy. What could I do?" The other man nodded in agreement. "You know what I'm talkin' about?"

"Yep."

The leather man looked right at Evah, and at that moment I came forward, to protect her. To poise her in the storm. Here she was, open with compassion, and the dark spirits mocked her from the other side. She was dumbfounded by the relevance of his words. I extuited a fly landing on his forehead, and he smacked himself on the face. This didn't shut him up either.

"I wonder if she's ever gonna wake up?" the second one said to the leather man.

"Yeah, that's exactly what I'm talkin' about. Here it is right in front of her and she ain't gonna say nothing! You watch."

The scotschoot came to a stop. The leather man stood up sharply and walked off the scotschoot, disappearing into the Constance outer edges, still swatting at the aggravating fly. It was his good fortune to have left. I was prepared to do something far worse.

Something unexpected started to well up in Evah—she felt ashamed for the first time. She thought about the leather man's words and wondered if she could have saved her dad somehow. She wondered if it was her fault—if he was murdered so that she could be taken by the Claren family.

Another man hopped on, followed by a girl, and his words flew up in the air. "Yeah, it's where you're goin'!"

Evah felt overloaded with information. She thought of how horrible things seemed at school sometimes. The times when she was bullied and ignored because she was different. She knew she had not done anything to deserve so much meanness. And now, with all the stimulus of the world around her, she felt like something was pouring through the seams of reality to assault her with cruelty and blame. She couldn't escape the thought that she didn't fit in and that in too many ways, she was the same as all these people. Outcasts. Outsiders. None of them, including herself, fit into the simple world. Not the world she had been taught to know.

She wondered if it made her "mentally ill" like the others she had seen earlier. Felin had said something about "sickness" and what did he mean? Was she recognizing her sickness? Was this chatter coming through to her the workings of her imagination or was something talking to her through the people?

She considered how she never seemed to have control over her relations at school. She wondered if it was like that for all these people? Did they not have control over their suffering—over the brazen shades of humanity that seemed to slip around from person to person? If not, who had control? She often thought how stupid she must be that she could not make her life at school better. Perhaps all these people felt that way too. Did they know how to make things better? Would it make a difference? Was this just the cruelty of life, making distressed creatures of people and echoing through them like some super presence? It could not be the God she had been taught about. Did all the suffering they shared make them understand things she did not know? Some people seemed not to "work" like her, not to fit, and this otherworldly coarseness was blowing through them in an unbridled force. Is that what shone through her? Like when she'd tortured poor Pearly with the hornets.

Then she had a thought that scared her more than anything else. She thought of the Haytoo virus. That these things she was experiencing could easily seem like symptoms. But maybe Haytoo had these experiences. That psychopath. Could it be that his creation of the virus had been informed by similar experiences he'd had? It was something more than some Sharvannan moment of clarity. Maybe she was like Haytoo.

I wanted to reach her and tell her there was something from the other side that caused suffering and used those who suffered like toys in a cruel game. There, in that time and space, she felt the "sickness" of degraded life reflecting back on her, and her young Hypathian mind could only hold on to one aspect of sanity.

Could I heal them? she wondered. *Like my father? Could I make things better? And not be like Haytoo?*

Instinctively now, Evah knew there was a source to the misery of the world. She feared she was a component of that source and did not want to be. She did not want to be a demon that had driven her father to his death; a goddess of the dead. She was sensing our shared being, sensing that before she walked and talked, she had traveled with me as a part of her father in the field of interconnected consciousness.

Yes, I said to her. And she heard me like a whisper. Like the voice she'd heard at school. The one that was like her father calling her name.

I could only get so much as one word through to her. I wanted her to know she was an entity of unfathomable experiences. But this only made her self-searching more confused. She thought my *yes* meant she was a goddess of death, for that is what she was thinking at the moment my word bubbled up to her aware state. I might have said *no, not that* to her, for I did not think of myself as a goddess of death, though I am flexible on the subject of punishing the living. I might have said *no,* but I did not. For I understood something no one else did—not even Evah. Deep down inside, she wanted to be such a powerful being. For with such a presence, she could command others with dread. And that was all right by me, for in such a form we could commence with activities I knew we had to do.

"This is our stop." Cordia broke into the swirl of Evah's contemplations and they exited the scotschoot.

Her mind was eased by the interaction with Cordia, and she was thankful for it. She savored the mortal indulgence of eating lunch. A mundane thing to do for a goddess of death. But still, her mind worked. She ordered all her favorite foods. There was so much of it she couldn't help but think it was enough to feed her and two other kids from the water district.

Then she got to ride her first starslide. She thought this was something great and was starting to feel somewhat herself again.

They walked onto platform U5 to Hypathia. The line moved quickly. There was a family ahead of them in line; a father, a mother, and a child. Up ahead at the point of departure, an array of wild lightning flashes streamed in varied directions. She looked to Cordia with her glowing eyes and for a moment imagined she was with her mother.

There was a man with a long coat amongst the shuffle of people. In her mind's eye, it became the man from her vision with the leaf. He was looking at her, but amidst the passing of other travelers, he was lost again. But for a brief moment, he appeared. Perhaps he was a flitting thought in her mind, but it was as if it were real. I realized this may have been what I was searching for: A communication from our father.

When Evah reached the starslide, she was guided by the hands of the slide attendant to stand on a round tile in the platform floor that read, "Place feet here."

"It's perfectly safe," said Cordia. Then she and the attendant stepped away.

"Clear for transport," the attendant said in a matter-of-fact tone and pressed a button on his command console.

Some words from the scotschoot rattled back to the forefront of Evah's thoughts: *It's where you're goin'!* Then with a strange vibratory shock, Evah felt her chest spring forward, and in the blink of an eye, she was snatched away. There was a great white light and streams of what looked like white circular solar flares streaming together, two by two, becoming one, then she was standing on another platform. Another attendant shuffled her to a nearby place where she watched Cordia snap into sight behind her.

Hypathia was a tropic planet. The air was heavier. Warm. Wet.

Evah felt something rippling on her neck. She thought of her father's gills and felt to see if she had some too, but there was nothing there. Beyond a grove of trees, she could see a large structure made of stones and an observatory dome. This was a different kind of destination than the others they had visited.

"This is what we call underdeveloped," Cordia said.

There were no elegant historic cobblestone streets, or paved roads, no food vendors at all, and the starslides looked few and far between. The dirt roads and rough, broken-looking homes were cramped together in clusters.

Walking towards the stone structure, they saw flocks of children—children that looked like Evah, but with easily visible gills on their necks. These children wore shoes that did not fit them, if they wore them at all. They begged Cordia for money, and she refused them with ease. Although she did give some candy to one, who turned and shared it with his friends. They seemed so happy. They were laughing.

Then they reached a great courtyard of grass and towering stone slabs half buried in the ground. It was an ancient foundation, laid by some lost civilization, that appeared to be roughly pyramid-shaped. Their destination was at the top—an observatory that had clearly been built much more recently.

"What is this?" asked Evah.

"It's an old city built by one of the first known civilizations in the planetary system. This was once a pyramid used in religious ceremonies. A temple," Cordia said as they walked upward along the layered rows of ancient stone and grass. Evah's body tingled. She was at once in awe of the planet and terrified by the coincidence of being in such a place, remembering Haytoo's obsessions. She felt deeply connected to the planet as if she, too, had an ancient past now.

"Why have you brought me here, Cordia?"

"Because I was told to. We're going to look at something through the telescope. The ancient Hypathians used to observe the stars here. The structure is built in such a way that the sun rises over the top of the pyramid in a special place on the first day of summer, and the observatory was built in honor of the ceremonies they had on such days. Apparently, there are some views of the nearby nebula that can only be seen from here. They used to think stars were born there, like babies. They called it the Pillars of Creation."

From the top of the pyramid plateau, Evah could see more construction fences and sizeable heavy equipment that was making a level foundation—a large cleared area like the demolition site on Constance. She was overwhelmed by the view. On the surface of Hypathia was an ancient forest, and a distant landscape of countless ancient stones. In the sky above were the brightly colored Pillars of Creation, a half-moon, the Eagle sun, the planet of Constance and the red planet Spirea.

Standing there, taking in the extraordinary sky, something happened. As her eyes moved across the horizon, Evah was momentarily blinded by a flash of light. It appeared to be something like a solar flare pulsing from the Eagle sun. For a moment, everything was bright, and then she felt something enter her body. The flash of light slipped inside of her. It went into that vacant part of her chest that felt like the emptiness of a demolished space. She did not know its exact origin, but she knew it entered into her. Vibrations stirred through her body. She looked to Cordia, who was unmoved and did not see the entity mingle with her. There was the sound of whispers then she was still again before the theater of the sky and the humid planet. She knew what had entered her was a powerful thing that she dared not speak of. Now we were three.

They went inside the observatory to peer at the surface of the dead world Spirea. Looking through the massive telescope, Evah was able to see the haunted realm of buildings once clearly magnificent but now an endless cemetery of waste. She considered the awe her father must have felt on that zip track amidst the suffocation of decay and poisoned air and searched the surface for screaming beasts. She observed the shipping starslides that led to vast moving fields of junk and mechanical sorting conveyor belts, charting strange courses through the expanse of the decomposing graveyard.

"The first center of the Constellation government," Cordia said. "The first Great Experiment. The world became overpopulated in many places, and the planet began to change. It became poisonous. They used forms of power that turned ruinous, and there were so many people concentrated there that society could not be sustained by natural resources. It was due to this that they migrated back to some of the original worlds and then finally the new capital was established on Constance. What saved the Constellation was the development of starslides and the discovery of kepplequer. With the starslides, people could spread out across the system more easily, leading to less concentrated areas and a safer use of resources. Spirea is still studied to this day. Some precautions could have been taken so that the resources were not overused, causing the deadly changes in the planet's surface and atmosphere. Of course, some changes were to be expected as a natural order of development, and it's hard to say if any one mis-judgment was the deciding factor. That's what we learn anyway."

Evah listened to Cordia and with so much to see, so much to experience, she did not think too many times of striking fear in Cordia's heart with some frightening extuition. There was already enough in reality to cause fear. And the fear she had known for so long at school, and in her life, somehow did not seem so terrible anymore. Then Evah asked a question I did not expect.

"How do you watch people's dreams?"

"It's customary that in every home there is a place where they can be watched. It's complicated. We use technology."

"But what about the people who have no homes. Or even the people here on Hypathia? They don't look like they have any technology."

"That's a good question. They are further disconnected from society in that way because for most of them, there is no way to receive essential treatments to help them maintain a social equilibrium."

"Equilibrium?"

"They can't find a way to belong. They are left with too many problems to be productive; to belong. They have too many troubles or old ways of thinking that make it impossible. I'm sorry. I'm trying to make it easy to understand. A long time ago, people felt bad, or their brains didn't work right, they didn't like the world they lived in, or they had uneducated ideas about things. For a long time, it was all about the Great Experiment that brought different alien races together, but that was focused in one place. The center of the system. The capital. First Spirea, and then Constance. Efforts to reach out to all the planets and incorporate them into the same social order… well, it was an afterthought.

"But some couldn't give themselves over to the common social practices that defined the Great Experiment. They used to give them medication to overcome issues they could not deal with pragmatically, or sometimes little medical procedures on the brain. Then we developed technology that allowed us to help people by directly connecting to their brains for a kind of programming rather than taking out resistant brain segments. It helps to unify people. Now, the homeless have little anthroscope resources to help them. Connecting to an anthroscope is a civic duty, but if they can't because they don't have a place to go, then they are out of sync with the rest of the Constellation. Some can still get medication, but these people need help. Together with the magisteria, we have been able to build public-use dream facilities, but most of them have limited capabilities. And to this day, those limitations are a big problem."

"But I thought people didn't have to be on the… anthroscope if they didn't want to."

"That's correct. But the poor and the citizens on other worlds tied to their old way, more than anybody, needs anthroscopic aid. And really, the youth do too."

"Can't that hurt children?"

"Oh, that's nonsense made up by liberal groups trying to make a buck with scams and emotional rhetoric."

"What's rhetoric?"

"Ideas used to convince people of things. I personally think that all children should be on the scope as soon as they've developed motor skills. Think of these poor aimless children we saw today—running wild with no shoes on, begging for money, for food, or candy, and running to their old broken-down homes. If they were in line with the anthroscope project, their parents would be productive, and the kids would be too. They'd probably have higher kepplequer rights. Everything would be different beyond belief. People want kepplequer, technology, modernity—they want society, and then they're useless to it. It's a waste of resources."

"But why are there people like that on Constance? Don't they want to be useful?"

"They just can't get it together, kid."

Evah wondered if it was really the people who failed society or if society was failing people. She thought about things going to waste because society didn't need them anymore. Creations that were made to be used, sometimes only once, and then thrown away or abandoned. She thought it seemed the same for so many of the citizens she had seen that day. Just other things to be sent to the graves of waste and fire on Spirea. *The Great Experiment?* she contemplated. She wondered where she and Cordia really stood in the progression of time. When would they be considered a waste of resources—obsolete? She wondered what would happen to them. But she asked no more questions. It was time to return to Constance Ward.

Chapter 6
Closed Circuits

I couldn't sleep all night. By some mercy, I finally dozed off, and when I woke, it was already mid-morning. My head was heavy. I felt like some numb, scarcely real presence floating on the surface of life. I barely had time to get dressed, brush my hair, and wash my face before there was a bang at the bay doors where provisions were packed in. I checked the monitor to see who had come. It was the Spirean man. His D-39 shipping vessel was crammed onto the rock at the mouth of the starslide. I observed his looks and watched his smile for telltale signs of a murderer. I considered hiding and pretending to be gone.

"Ms. Claren! It's awfully cold out here! Are you there. It's Bakia! I have your supplies!" His voice clamored through the speaker system. "I don't think it would be a good idea to leave these things outside with the conditions the way they are!"

The conditions? What conditions did he mean? My mind was swirling around the meaning of every word he spoke, searching for threats.

"I wouldn't want them to get washed away," he said with a kind tone.

I was so tired. Physically, yes, but more than that, tired of being controlled with callous logic. Trapped by the apathy I lived with, which allowed such manipulative logic to claim its possession of me and everything in my world. I had been so desperately trying to hear my own voice. My own authority. But what I was realizing now was that voice could only be found in action. Or in response to action. But what tore me apart was not knowing what action to commit to in the first place. I was frozen. Doing what I was told and living within the parameters of what knowledgable persons established was always the easiest way to live. I'd thought I would rebel a thousand times, but it did not work out, for circumstances were only created for me to be successful if I supported the arrangements set for me. And in other ways, I did not want to rebel because I did not want to risk betraying something right and valid only to lose everything.

"Well, I guess I could just come back another time! I'm sorry I—" Bakia took his finger off the intercom button and, giving a final look to the camera, retreated back to his D-39.

Now that was the truth. He would only come back. *Someone* would come back. Maybe Bakia was all right, and next time somebody who wasn't would return. Maybe my chances were better now. Besides, I still hadn't betrayed my father entirely. We did still have the meeting this afternoon.

Like a mechanical arm losing control of itself, my hand shot out, and the bay doors sprang open.

"Ms. Claren!" Bakia smiled. Then, seeing me in only a thin dress, he said: "Oh, you're gonna freeze in this temperature! You go inside, and I'll bring these supplies in!"

The icy wind pressed around my body, and I was soaked by a rush of rain. I stared for a moment through the chill then silently turned and went back inside.

After a while, all of the shipment was brought in. Then, from the kitchen, Bakia called, "That's everything, Ms. Claren."

"Please come in here, Bakia!"

When he entered the lounge, he found me in my heavy coat, warm cap, and boots.

"Everything's all finished, ma'am." He walked in, looked around a little, and said, "Oh, it certainly is nicer in here."

"I must go to Constance, Bakia. You must take me to Constance," I said firmly with dry reason.

"Well, that isn't allowed," he said in his carefree way.

"What do you mean it isn't allowed? Why isn't it allowed?"

"Well, it's against the rules to bring people on shipping vessels. If you got hurt, I could lose my job. It's a liability issue, you see?"

"Oh, Bakia. What if I told you I'm in danger here?"

"Well, there's nothing to be afraid of here. I mean, other than getting wet I think the only way you could get hurt here is gettin' blown off the outlook." I watched his face. "That's why you're supposed to stay inside. I mean, no one else is coming through that starslide. It's out of commission. It's not supposed to be used by anybody."

"Are you threatening me?"

"No. Of course not! What could make you say such a thing? Look, I don't have anything against you. I shouldn't have even come in here. I'm sorry, lady, there's nothing wrong. I'm on my way."

"What if I told you somebody else has already been here?"

"Well, that isn't possible. This is a special route. Nobody knows about it. You understand? This is my route. Oh, you're gonna get me in trouble for nothing. I didn't do nothing to you."

"Why didn't you come last week?"

"I was told you didn't need the usual shipment. I don't know—I figured you weren't here or something."

"Well, someone made a delivery."

"Well, that's impossible. No one's supposed to know you're here."

"Somebody knows."

Then there was a long silence. Bakia believed me, but he did not know what it meant.

"Did they threaten you?"

"Bakia, these people don't make threats. It would give their plans away. Do you understand what I'm saying?"

"Okay." He clearly wasn't sure what to think. "God, I'm gonna have to make a report about this."

"Who are you going to make a report to? The same person who told you I didn't need a shipment last week?"

"Huh. What are you saying? That's— You sound— That's silly!" He watched me for a moment, and I did not move. "Oh, man, I don't wanna have anything to do with this." He started walking to the exit.

"Bakia, I need your help."

He stopped and thought, looking down at the floor.

"Oh, brother," he expelled. "Man, I have another shipment to deliver." He thought a moment. "I'll help you. Come on."

With great relief, we were off. Though I truly did not know where I should go. Sanje didn't want to tell me anything, and though I did not want to believe it, I was scared he was involved. It could have been that listening in on my meeting with Blouty was really only meant to set me more at ease, thereby allowing my father and his connections to have their way with me. Why did he keep me in the dark about everything?

I helped Bakia with his final shipment, then he smuggled me out of the Constance hangar. I told him that for his and my protection, he couldn't make a report about anything I had informed him of. I told him to keep making the shipments as if I had never left.

I hopped on a scotschoot to Liberty Square and paid with money Bakia gave me, keeping my head down and avoiding interaction with anyone unless absolutely necessary. I had decided Sanje was the lesser of two evils. I wanted nothing to do with my father. I even feared that the sedation needle on the anthroscope could be dosed with a deadly level of medication. My time and my options were limited, but now I was on a path of my choosing. Though, in truth, I knew I may be leading myself to death or prison.

It had been some time since I'd been with people. Anyone could have recognized me, being related to Constance Ward and their dogged master. I felt ashamed, and I could not pretend. I felt completely out of control. It was as if any person talking to me might know I was a traitor. To my father, to my husband, and to my child. There was no way of knowing how much was known of my recent activity. Or in what circles the rumors may have been moving. My only security was the knowledge that no story of the Thwargg abuse of rights had broken. It was possible my father and his conspirators were keeping everything silent.

I walked across the wide stone foundation of Liberty Square. When I saw a Thwargg woman, I covered my head to remain anonymous. She wore a first-class suit, her eyes blue like my father's. Her hair was black. In my heart, I wished I was her. If only I could be a hard-working Thwargg woman going home from my shift to my family. Going home to my little girl and husband.

By some grace, I made it to the doors of the Office of Magisteria and slid inside. Further luck was granted to me when I approached the desk of Sanje's assistant.

"Why are you here?" he said and quickly stood from his chair. "Come with me."

He led me to the Magisteria Hall.

"Magistere Sanje is not here. He's on important business, and I don't know when he will return." He walked with me a short way towards Sanje's office. "I will contact the magistere and have him return as soon as possible. His door is unlocked. Please go inside and shut the door behind you. I hate to do this, but it's best you don't turn the lights on. We don't want anyone seeing you through the glass door. Go ahead." He pointed for me to continue to the office and returned to his post.

I tried my best to be invisible. Some other magisteria were rounding the corner only a few feet ahead. I quietly opened the door, slipped inside, and tucked myself away beside the door as the officials passed. It was dark inside. Looking near the desk, I could see a peculiar swirl of electricity floating above the far end of Sanje's desk. I had never noticed it before. It was odd that Sanje would have some entertaining light. I made my way to a chair where I thought I might not be seen, then from the shadows came a voice.

"Ms. Claren?" said the mysterious presence.

I did not respond. *My God*, I thought, *they're all in on it. This could be someone here to kill me.*

"Please don't hurt me."

"Stay right where you are. Pull your cap down over your eyes. Believe me, you don't want to see me."

I did as the voice commanded. "There. It's done. I swear, I can't see you."

"Good," came the voice again. It was peevish, and weird, and that terrified me the most. It was a voice I had never heard, but it came from someone who seemed to know me.

"What do you want? Are you here to kill me?"

"Maybe."

"I knew you were watching," I said, starting to tremble.

"Keep your voice down, Ms. Claren." The room was silent for a while. "What do you know about Evah going to Constance Ward?"

"Nothing. I-I don't know anything. Is she there now?"

"Yes, Ms. Claren. Now I suggest you keep your mouth full of lies for somebody else. We know you're a liar. And we know all of the things you've done. If you want to stay safe, you'll tell me everything. If it sounds right, maybe we'll keep you alive."

"What do you want to know?"

"You think your father is a murderer?"

"No. No. Of course not." It was my father's people. I knew it.

"Oh, yes he is. That's the last lie you'll tell me."

"I don't know who you are. I'm trying to stay alive. I want to see my child again."

"Staying alive and seeing your child are two different things."

I could not respond to that. What the voice was really suggesting was that I was going to live but not see Evah. *Prison maybe,* I thought. And I was faced again with the reality that all I could do was hope for my child's freedom from my father's plans. And I knew to talk now could send me away forever, but it could free her too.

"Go on. What do you want to know?" I said.

"Tell me about the little white room. The one you get in through the anthroscope."

"My father designed it. But he isn't the only one who uses it." I sighed because it was a heavy burden to have known of this for so long. "Many people have visited the white room. Most have no idea that they have."

"Did Varin visit the white room? And Ansen?"

"Yes."

"Why?"

"People who go there that don't know are given commands to follow. Others have their minds fixed, so they forget information. Things they know that could hurt the people my father works with. They are subliminal suggestions they will never remember."

"And what if they do remember?" the voice interjected fast.

"Then my father wants them to remember."

"Why?"

"It's his way to bring them into the group. But some reject it. And if they want to tell, they can't. Because they've been given a suggestion not to. It hurts the minds of some people. They are terrified, I guess, to know what's being done to them and others, and yet they can't remember when they want to. When they want to talk about it."

"Is that what happened to Ansen?"

"Yes." My breathing was shallow now and I was filling with remorse. It was one thing to be a silent participant but another to speak of it. I could not bear the truth.

"And Varin?"

"He gave Varin many suggestions." I couldn't help but weep. Because of who I was. Because I felt how hollow all my life had been.

"When he was murdered?"

"Is he dead?"

"Ms. Claren."

"I don't know. His body was never found. I hoped he wasn't. I'm sorry—I really didn't know."

"Stop crying, Ms. Claren. You don't deserve to cry."

But I couldn't stop. I tried to weep more gently.

"Is that why you put your child on the table, Ms. Claren? So your father could tell her things?"

"I only put her on a couple times. I'm so sorry that I did. I didn't want to give her to him."

"But you did, didn't you?"

"Yes. It was always the plan. And he shouldn't be allowed to talk to Evah. It could be dangerous."

"Well, it's too late for that now, isn't it?"

"I don't know. My father wanted to talk to me today at four. That must be why."

"Why?"

"He wants me to help 'handle' her. He's told me if I don't she could end up on medication. They could do something to her brain—something that can't be undone. Permanent. The Constellation system is afraid of extuiters now. He says they will want to control her. My God, it's already almost too late—it's already two thirty." I stood up in shock.

"Wait! Sit down, Ms. Claren!"

"What will they do if you walk in there? Think."

"They'll stop me."

"We need Sanje. And he needs cause. He has no official reason to stop the proceedings. He needs proof. And you are going to be proof, to begin with. We cannot risk you being detained by the Thwargg. You know too much. I know he's killed before and I know he's used you. In a cruel way, I guess. I think there may be nothing he wouldn't do. There's certainly no reason he'd stop talking to her because you show up there. We're going to have to hope we can get past this. Let's finish this up."

"What is this?"

"This is your confession. Now tell me about Galneea."

"Yes. He's the one." I didn't even want to say his name. He cleaned up people who talked about him. He cleaned them up *permanently*.

"He's the one? What does that mean?"

"He's the one who wants to rule the Constellation of Spirea. And my father helps him. Few people have been able to make the capital expansion work in all of the inhabited worlds. He does it with wealth—with plans that hurt people who get in the way. My father respects his power and initiative."

"What has your father helped him do?"

"Many things. I think Galneea was responsible for Ansen's death. That's what really brought them together. And some extuiter that worked for my father. You want evidence. There is one connection my father had to Galneea. He made a large investment in something Galneea was working on. It was a large sum of money that he never got any return on, or rights. It was payment to kill Ansen. I only put it together afterward. I don't think I could really believe it at the time. But since then my father has used Thwargg technology to help Galneea win his magisteria seat, and he's going to do the same to help him get elected Prime Minister. I know that, but I don't know how you'd ever prove it. If some consideration could be given to me, I might suggest someone who could know something."

"Who? Blouty Duthane?"

"Yes."

"Tell me of Sire Claren's connection to Varin Ahtochi's death."

"Varin tried to expose him. To Sanje. That's why I came to Sanje in the first place. Varin trusted him.

"I'm glad you trust him. You can tell him about the tracker you placed on Varin before he went to his death.

"I know you don't understand, but my father is a powerful man. He helped me... You don't say no to my father if you want to keep the life you have."

"No, Ms. Claren, you don't say no to your father when you want to keep the life he's made for you. You don't say no because that would be breaking a contract of conspiracy."

"I know that I love Evah."

"I wonder. Love doesn't make assets of children." Now the voice seemed to change—I began to hear Varin's voice softly doubling over the peevish tones of my unseen interrogator. It shook me, but not understanding the mystery I said nothing.

"If I tell Sanje everything, will it be clear I do not want that for her? If I do that, will it be clear that her well-being means more to me? That her life means more to me?"

The interrogator made no sound.

"I only hoped we could have a new life together, but it's become clear to me that I may never be free. I only hope someone will take some pity on me."

"You're going to tell Sanje everything you've told me with as much detail as possible. That would be the first really good thing you could do."

"Can't I make some sort of deal?"

"If it were my decision, they'd drown you at the bottom of the Deiphera sea. Lucky for you, that will be up to Sanje. Now get comfortable and be quiet. Wait. Tell me this. How did you contact your father when you were on Deiphera? Everything you did was being watched."

"Blouty Duthane left a note. On it was a number. I called the number and it told me a time. Then I met him, the same way Galneea meets him: through the anthroscope, in the little white room.

"There's something you haven't asked me. Something that you should know."

"What is that, Ms. Claren?"

"What it was that made me risk being exposed by coming here. If I wanted to confess, I could have talked with Sanje over the kalodia. When I called that number, something happened. It somehow gave them control over the kalodia on Deiphera—in the station. I could no longer control who I could call. Do you understand? It isn't only Galneea involved—there is someone else. Someone who can control communications. Maybe military. Maybe intelligence agencies. I was afraid for my life when I couldn't contact Sanje. If precautions aren't taken, I *could* end up in the Deiphera sea. And no one will know the difference until it's too late."

"I assure you, Ms. Claren, we will look into that. If you will be true to an agreement with Sanje, I will make sure he sends someone to watch over you. Will that give you peace?"

"Yes. Please."

"All right."

Silence fell on the room, and we waited. I was glad. I was glad to finally be able to tell Sanje everything, but I feared for my daughter. I feared what that man, my father, could be doing to her mind, and I hated myself for being the creature I was. Privileged. Privileged to think it was my right to do these things to people all my life.

We waited. And waited. But Sanje did not come for a long time. I must have dozed off because suddenly the door was opening and the lights going on. I looked at the clock on the wall—it was three thirty.

"Ms. Claren, what are you doing here?" he said, walking to his desk and setting down a stack of papers. He seemed to be distracted by something on the floor.

"I have to tell you everything. My father must be stopped. There are many details, but I am supposed to meet with him on Deiphera at four."

I told him all that I could in the few minutes I had, and he recorded my confession in a visual message. I told him about the murders of Ansen and Varin. About Galneea and the elections. And I made it clear I was telling him because I thought my life and the life of my child were at risk.

Whoever had questioned me was gone.

"Perhaps it was one of my investigation team," he said. "If there was someone here, I'm sure they will return."

We agreed we would meet again for more details. I told him everything that needed to be known if I should disappear. I made sure he knew I felt at risk, and that my communications were being controlled. He encouraged me to return to Deiphera to meet with my father. A transport was called, and within fifteen minutes I was back through the Deiphera starslide. But I was late. I was late! And I did not know if he would be there to meet me, if he would know I had been on Constance. If he would know I had betrayed him. I couldn't bear to be alone. I couldn't bear to be myself.

I was only five minutes behind. I rushed to the dream chamber and started the anthroscope, and the arm swung in with its dosage. The dosage I thought could kill me.

Chapter 7
Right Angles

Constance Ward was constructed to impress any viewing audience with a sense that it was established in a classical era, at the time when the first seeds of society's ideas were sprouted. In fact, it looked older than other buildings around it at Liberty Square. Though all the buildings there were constructed to demand respect, Constance Ward was special. It stood seventy feet high with enormous columns that reached from the foundation to the ceiling overhang. Looking at it, one would wonder what technology could have been used to erect such a monumental sight. It aimed to steal away with the astonishment some ancient master civilization might command, assuming the dignity of a structure that continued to stand for thousands of years. But rather than quarried and carved stone, it was the work of masons managing impressive molds. It was a fake. It was the sort of indulgences new generations of society often built to demand respect and provoke reverent thoughts like, *As it was in the beginning, so it is now. Please place respect here.*

When Evah entered the ward, she wondered if it was as old as the pyramid on Hypathia, but what she found inside was not ancient stones but an institutional lack of imagination more dedicated to cost efficiency. The interior was as romantic as a health clinic. Cheap thin tile, white paint, and halls of inexpensive white lighting. Cordia took her up the elevator from one floor to another that looked so much the same Evah thought she could get lost in the endless divergences of similitude. No one walked the halls on the floor of the building they arrived at. It seemed whoever worked there was more than happy to stay at their desks and never be seen. Either that or the building had been evacuated, for it lacked any warmth of living beings or any energy of working presences.

They rounded a final corner to find a striking older Thwargg man standing with two persons in lab coats twenty-five feet away or so near an open door. Evah felt a rush of blood insider her chest. There was a pounding in it she wished she could switch off that rose in intensity the closer they moved to the waiting figures. Another older Thwargg man stepped into the hall and began to walk towards Cordia and Evah.

"You've done a good job, Cordia. The interview will be handled by someone else." He stopped them a few feet from the waiting men.

"You should know she was exhibiting some physical manifestations."

"Yes, all right," he said dismissively as if her presence had little value to anyone.

"It may be prudent to have me involved. Since I've established a—"

"No. I'm sure that management can handle the situation." The Thwargg turned his smiling face to Evah. "All right. Come along, little girl."

Evah followed the man, and Cordia stayed behind. One of the men in lab coats drew a syringe from his pocket and prepared the shot to be administered as Evah watched. She was brought to him in preparation for his business, but the old Thwargg with tempests of blue light dancing in his eyes held up a hand.

"No. That won't be necessary. Will it, little girl?"

Evah was unsure of anything, but with a distracted shake of her head, she assured the old Thwargg she would be good.

"All right. Let's step in here." He gestured for Evah to proceed through the open door. On the other side was a small white room with a table and two chairs on opposing sides. "Have a seat," said the Thwargg, and she did. Beside one chair was a bag that looked heavy and full. She chose the other chair that faced the door. The Thwargg sat down and placed the syringe on the table, then pulled a clipboard from the bag and set it in front of him with a pen.

"Are you hungry?" the Thwargg asked.

"No."

"Good. You went to Hypathia today?"

"Yes."

"Good. And you traveled around Constance?"

"Yes."

"All right. Good. Did you get along all right with Cordia?"

"Yeah."

"Well, I'm glad to hear that." He circled something on the page in front of him and made a notation.

Evah began to search the old Thwargg's face, wondering if he was her grandfather. "Who are you?"

"My name is Eine Claren." His words were clear and straightforward. Even cold and clinical. She wondered if he cared at all that she was his granddaughter. She could not hide that she knew who he was.

"Do you know who I am?" he asked with no pretense.

"Yes."

"Hmm." He was silent for a moment. "And who am I?"

"You're my grandfather."

"Who told you that?"

"A friend." Evah knew that she could not reveal Felin. She pointed to her head and tapped it two times.

"Really? Well, that would be something new. You don't really have any friends, do you?" He stared at her for some response. "You have some talents that the other children do not. Is that right?"

She nodded. "Yes."

"I understand you like to be mean to children with your gifts. Is that right?"

"No."

"But you did hurt a little girl, didn't you?"

"I didn't mean to."

"Well, we shall see. You understand I know everything about you. You have a history, and that is here. Whatever you think you know, or whatever you think this is, we are here for one purpose."

"What's that?"

"We are here to see if you have any talent that the state should be concerned with. I don't really think you have any talent. Do you?"

Evah wanted to hide her talent so she could leave and not be troubled by this man, but it was impossible. In that instant, without so much as a millisecond of contemplation, she had changed something. She hoped it would go unnoticed. She wanted to change it back, but she couldn't seem to do that. At the same time, she wondered if she had done it at all, it had happened so fast.

I was happy to be getting on with it.

Claren's head nodded gently, down and up. His face was no longer that delicate blue. Now it was an ashen gray like dead flesh, his refined eyes changed to huge bloodshot things, his jowls big and bulky. On his face was a sickening carved smile, his teeth big, his contorted face the shape of some demon. In its stillness, it was the unshakable twisted countenance of something evil, with deep, wet depositories of saliva in its grin. He looked at her squarely.

"What do you see, little girl?"

I moved to the front of her mind to confront him, the light of our own Thwargg eyes stirring in our glare. Our voice was rich with the resonance of multiple inhabitants. "I see the truth, old man."

There were three solid pounds on the door. Claren slid his chair back and stood up, then walked to the door and opened it.

Another Thwargg man stood in the doorway. His face, too, was instantly transformed to the likeness of a grinning demon. He was visually overwhelmed for a moment, by the hideous face on Claren's person. Claren simply looked at him and shook his head a little, then peered hard over his shoulder at Evah. He took a clipboard from the other man and signed a document, then gave it back. He then turned, reentered the room, and sat back down.

"Shall we continue?" he asked as if preparing himself for something. "Do you realize that what you put into the world is a reflection of what is inside you?" He looked her over for some response. "Is this what you have inside you? Are you filled with devils?"

Evah said nothing.

"I have things to share with you, but not while you are playing games with me. I have ideas I want to talk to you about, but not while you are doing this." He waited again for some response. Then, going to scribble another note, the pen fell onto the table. His hand was a shriveled, muddled mess of broken bones.

"There are 206 bones in most bodies in the Constellation of Spirea," we said to him. His face refused to give up the grimace of pain he was clearly stuffing back.

"I can't help you get back to your mother like this. Wouldn't you like to be with your mommy, Evah?" And suddenly she felt she was staring at herself. The deep, dark hidden part of herself that she feared—socially crippled and a horror to people. Before we could allow her remorse to weaken her resolve, we stirred her rage, and he saw the perilous depths of our abilities. The goddess of death was before him—tall as the ceiling in his heartless hive, like some stone monster come to life, eyes bleeding the fire of damnation. We reached out and grabbed him with two of our twelve arms, lifting him high in the air above his seat.

"You used our mother to kill our father," we said like a spat of boiling water. With our horrid glare reaching inside him, I pressed the muzzle of a plasma rifle into his temple. Just like the one I'd emptied from Felin's mind. "Do you feel like having your brains blown against the wall?"

Evah was a glorious, frightening vision. With one finger, I pressed the charging button on the rifle and it made its whine, but she would not pull the trigger. My rage pulsed through her commanding grasp, but she absorbed it back inside. Back into her guts. She withheld, against my satisfaction.

"No, Evah," the old Thwargg said. "It's not true. You must put me down. If they come in here, everything will be lost. They will destroy you. We have a chance at a new beginning. Everyone."

Suddenly, Claren was back in his seat with his face and hand restored. He looked to the corner of the room, where there was a camera, and put up his restored hand, to tell whoever was watching not to trouble them.

"You have a chance to do something wonderful. Would you like to do something wonderful? Then you can be with your mom, and you can help make the world a better place. Wouldn't you like to do something good for the world? For all the Constellation of Spirea"

Now Evah was weak with self-hate and confusion. It would have hurt her to continue in that way. She was ashamed and afraid of her power. No matter what was going on in her head, she knew she could not take on the entire world. She didn't want to. I could sense her thoughts. *I'm just a kid. Where am I gonna go? What am I going to do?* They were pleading with us. I only wanted to scare the old Thwargg. We let her have her peace. After all, I still wanted to see what plots this phony had in mind and where it would take us.

"Evah, don't you want to do something good and see your mom again?" he dared to ask a second time. And in the silence, Evah was cracking with self-defeat.

"I do."

"Good." He waited for a moment then reached into his bag and pulled out a long piece of metal. It looked like a rust-covered iron rod. He set it on the table. "Do you know what this is?"

"No," we said, but Evah was nearly mumbling into the table.

"This was made by an extuiter. Do you see it?"

"Yes," we answered.

"Its elemental compounds are unrecognizable."

Evah ran her finger along the heavy, slender metal piece. "Did my father make it?"

"Yes. Yes, your father made it. Before he disappeared." But Claren was lying. What was lying in front of Evah was the metal weapon Haytoo had used to cause our father's fatal wound, but she didn't want to know that.

"My father isn't dead?"

"Well, there's no evidence of that. He had many things going on, your father, and then he disappeared. He may return. Or we may find him."

"Can you help me find my father?"

"I think, together, there is little we could not do." The room was silent. "Do you know how old I am?"

"Why?"

"I am nearly 150 years old. Do you know how many extuiters I've helped?"

"Three."

"No. Good guess though. I have helped four." But again, he was lying. Unless he was including us.

"All the extuiters have been different. They have all had talents that changed into specialties of a certain kind. I personally believe that much of that was happenstance. They became obsessed with one experience or another, and that became what they wanted to do."

"My father helped people."

"Well, they all helped people in one way or another. But do you know what they all had in common?"

"What?"

"Before they were trained, their minds played tricks on them. They thought they saw things. They thought they heard things. Really, it was a painful torment. They needed to be helped so that they could focus. The extuiter has an extraordinary mind, but until they know the power of that mind, they are preyed upon most wretchedly by what they don't understand

are deceits of their own imagination. Illusions. Powerful fantasies usually generated to make up for the pain they feel in their
loneliness."

And this is what happens when you pepper your lies with
truth: The innocent are misled.

"One extuiter I helped thought they had friends in their head.
I say that, Evah, because I see you are suffering from that. I'm
sorry. Being away from your family, feeling alone, and being an
outcast at school must have hurt. Did it?"

Evah did not want to agree with him, nor did she want to lie,
and so she was silent. She had known tremendous pressures and
wanted to understand how to be what she thought of as "normal."
She wanted to know how it felt to be like other kids. She wanted to
know what it felt like, even a little, to be like Pearly Shyen.

"You are not alone."

Claren reached into his bag and pulled out a hefty book of
pictures. He opened the pages to images of Hypathians. They
were in their forest habitat. The colors were so vibrant—the trees
and soil and sky. There were smiling children. There were strong,
experienced mothers. There were beloved fathers, standing with
silent wisdom. Then he showed her pictures of pyramids and
temples, then images of stone carvings that depicted humanoid
bodies merged with the appearances of animals. Hypathians
with headdresses and masks both terrifying and wonderful.

"Do you see all these people? You are not alone. We all have
tribes. That gets lost in our new society, where so many ways of
living come together. But you have a place in the Constellation
system too. It is an honored place that you can be proud of. Now,
we think you're ready to begin your training. Being so young, I
believe you may be the most powerful extuiter in centuries. Do
you believe me when I tell you I think you're special?"

Though it took some thought, she finally said, "Yeah. Yes, I do."

Something was happening to Evah now. It was not that she
did not want to know the truth anymore, but that she wanted to
belong more.

"Would you like to continue? Can I show you something else?" She nodded. "Yes."

"I think you can do this, Evah. I think you can make something that can remain." Claren took another book from his bag, placed it on the table, and slid it towards her.

Evah sat up and looked at the cover. "Architecture?" She opened the book to look through the first pages.

"That's right. We want to do something for the people, Evah. We want to help those who cannot help themselves. The poor. All those people you saw today. They need someplace to live. If you can do this, there is no limit to the ways we can help them."

"It's something so big. You think I can do that?"

"The most powerful extuiters were not alone. They had other spirits that joined with them to help them accomplish their work. I think you already have spirits with you. You are powerful. There is a reason power is given to those who would otherwise seem meek. I believe if we start small and focus on what we want to create, before long, you will be making wonderful things. But you have to be able to control your gifts. You have to be in control of the forces that join with you. Can you do that?"

Evah shrugged with uncertainty.

"Evah, do you want to be in control?"

Again, Evah gave an unsure shrug because she just did not know if she was in control.

"We'll start small. Extuit a model for me. If you can at least give me a structure then perhaps we can work together from there. This will be an endeavor for a new era in the Constellation of Spirea. Are you ready to try?"

"Yes."

"Good. You're going to see your mom very soon."

Claren picked up the syringe and prepared the shot.

"What is that?"

"It will help you sleep. I need to get you under my eye. Give you a checkup. Everything will be fine. Do you want to do these things?"

"Yes."

Claren took her arm in his hands and administered the shot. In moments, her eyes were blurring. The door opened, and several Thwargg filed in as we slipped into blackness.

Chapter 8
Kingdom of the Naheen Mothers

Before the beast was put down in his pit, before the age of the Christ, even at the beginning of the age of Spirea, there was the Kingdom of the Naaheen Mothers. When the sons of Thwargg had come to Sharvanna and them, collectively, to Spirea, having already met the children of Sabia, the Pillars of Creation still shown its lights on Naaheen. In the thick forest, under the turning of the stars, the spirits of eternity came down upon Naaheen in their season, and from its heavenly brothers and sisters, the nearby planets, the water of life could be seen flowing into the hidden mysteries of Naaheen.

An expedition from the four tribes pierced the cloudy skies into the realm of the timeless Mother. Near the seat of her rule, in the Forest of Eshlam, the ancient travelers set down, and Thydon and Ezkaysha set forth to secret themselves into the city. The towering arbor gates were lush and sultry with unfathomable peace. A female child ran across the road into the thicket, drawing their attention to a fulcrum in the wall. In it, there was a lever. Ezkaysha, pulling at the lever, observed their first miraculous sight.

Upon its loosening, the giant gates evaporated like mist, and in sleepy repose, the breath of Elohayyam swayed the giant trees of Naaheen beneath the coming night. They happened upon the people, the Children of the Water, who demanded no secrets at all to enter. They worked and praised in bliss. Objects appeared and disappeared for the calling of their use, as it was common to the Children of the Water, but to the travelers, this was the second miracle they'd beheld. On the faces of the people, spirits were painted here and there, like animals, disarming to the mind; fanged and bull and goat. But though this was the land of soil, tree, and stone, their fashion and technology seemed contemporary to the coming aliens. Many wore bright garments, yet some were nearly naked. They stood by, watching the children of the stars, who were relieved by their welcome.

In the twilight, the city rose before them like an endless wonder. The third miracle. Along the ground, great stones were fashioned as promenades, and in and out of the water went the Mother's children. Three pyramids of stones towered into the horizon. Above the foundation of carved stone and soil, the brilliant city was strewn, a layer upon the old history. Brilliant lights of some mysterious source glittered around the modern out springs—structures more exotic and modern than their own, they found. Vessels floated upon the air, over the waters and the promenades, and buildings that looked like precious metals curved and arched, more refined than any art in all the known worlds, their grand windows made of something like the purest transparent gems—emerald and sapphire; even something stained with beautiful markings like translucent jasper.

The chatter of the language was like the musical singing of birds. All around, the Children of the Water could be seen in their pavilions and homes, buildings of sweeping sculpture like that in a dream. In the light of the city, and the light of the heavens, the buildings reflected a luminescence like a brilliant powdery moon. Orbs of light dangled in the air above parks like amethyst stars, and in their light, the stone pathways showed the glow of gold. The travelers witnessed all this and knew there was some magic at its source, like a heavenly spirit.

At the center of the city lay a stone temple, and from its heart came the dancing light of a fire. It was as if the travelers were expected, as if they knew where to go, and where they were meant to be. They had known hard lives; toiled, conquered, and bled to shape the solar system to their aspirations.

But as they walked the peaceful way up to the temple entrance, they were suspicious. "Surely, it could not be, but we belong here."

A woman was sweeping the steps as they ascended, and a caravan of men stood staring up into the light that came from within the temple. When the travelers were close, without so much as a worried or contentious glance, the onlookers parted. It felt like there was a divine wind, against which no obstinacy could arise. Thydon and Ezkaysha stood at the threshold of the temple. They beheld each other. The woman behind them swept. The men adorned their eyes with the holy vision.

"Perhaps they are reading the light of the flames," said the Sharvannan Ezkaysha.

Everything in Naaheen had a place, and every place had a function. The seven men in robes standing on the steps were the Witnesses. They were the first in the Circle of Creation. It was their place to witness the Chamber of Creation, where the living were brought forth and suffering was known.

Lifting their eyes to the Pillars of Creation, Thydon saw first the lights of the Waters of Heaven—white drops of light dispersing from the Pillars of Creation among the stars, and flowing into the temple top. As they had seen from their homeworlds. One would come, and then the heavens were still for a time, then another came. Some strode rapidly, yet some seemed to swing into the temple repository.

Thydon and Ezkaysha, seeing the temple inhabitants had no binding on their feet, worked up their courage and took off their boots to walk on the holy ground. Here they beheld the Mystery.

As they came into the Chamber of Creation, before them in a quarter circle were three women, and two men, kneeling in five of eight marked places. One woman moved over a space and gestured with her hand for the two visitors to sit in the opened areas, and they took their places in the Seats of the Heavenly Bodies.

To the right of the woman who gestured to them was an eighth open seat. The Chamber was circular, and around its perimeter were the Guardian Spirits. These were devotees in masks of every animal, and in their hands were metallic staffs. At the tops of the staffs were long spearheads as sharp as razors and pointed as the teeth of magmakytes. They were not young men and women but old. It was their allotment before creation to bear the passing of the tides of time, and defend the Mother from it, as it was the night before the day of the summer solstice, and the Harvest of the Souls.

Before the quarter circle of the Heavenly Bodies were two mothers sitting, one to the left and one to the right of the Disk of Gardens, which was seven feet in diameter and rested in the floor of the Chamber of Creation. It was the duty of the two mothers to turn the Disk, and present before the Timeless Mother of Naaheen the appropriate garden for each appropriate soul she sent forth. There were seven gardens around the edge of the Disk and another in the center.

The Timeless Mother of Naaheen was all aglow. She sat at the top of the Disk of Gardens and was the fire of life whose light filled the Chamber. The witnesses watched from their place on the steps, beneath the striding of the souls that came from above. The fire within the Mother and about her was the life of the Waters of Heaven that had rested in her for one year. Her head was thrown back in a holy trance, her eyes amazed. They appeared like the clearest sapphires and like flowing jasper from her head. From her body bands of light swayed and undulated in the rhythm of Elohayyam's breath upon the leaves in the Forest of Eshlam. At the seat of her heart emerged each individual soul, and each individual soul gave forth itself into each individual garden on the Disk as presented by the mothers. Her hands were open with love, and the souls came forth in her state of trance.

To the left of the giving of the souls, sat Sorrow and Sin in constant babble to one another. What their sex was could not be detected. One brutalized the other in a stream of cruelty with words; the other wept and blathered in streams of victimization, and their enchanted cacophony of woe and harm traded back and forth between them. Now one Sorrow, now one Sin, interchanging to and fro without end.

On the right of the giving of the souls were the Three Martyrs. They seemed stretched out in suffering, bearing the burden of all causes. Their robes were fair, but their bodies tortured and withered, and they seemed to float on the air, staring upward to the heavens. They were men and women, and their suffering satisfied the horrors of the beings of flesh and the torment of the demons. Together with Sorrow and Sin, the quarter circle of the Heavenly Bodies, and the Three Martyrs, this made up a half circle around the Mothers of Naaheen.

Behind the Timeless Mother was the Crystal. This was a man floating in the air beneath the opening at the center of the temple where the Waters of Heaven drew in. The drops of light entered into him, and he became brighter with each one; an amethyst color like the mysterious stars that floated above the parks in the outer city. They were the unborn souls of the coming year, and he was the receptacle. On the day of the Harvest of the Souls, he would give them up to the Mother of Naaheen, the Mother of the Unborn, and a new year would begin.

This ceremony of the Evocation to the Gardens went on for hours. Thydon and Ezkaysha observed, and Ezkaysha prayed along with the first five Heavenly Bodies. Thydon would not submit in such a way because, though he thought the Mystery compelling, he would not commit his prayer to such a practice. In truth, he prayed for little reason at any time. He was a tenacious being who devoted himself to the logic of sciences, and to him, there was no mystery to causality. Nor did he want the burden of any mystery added to it.

The ceremony continued through the night to moments before dawn. As always, Sin and Sorrow punished each other, the Martyrs suffered, and for this night, the Guardian Spirits stood and would not give up their post.

Then the moment arrived when the Timeless Mother was all but empty, save the blessed souls that would be given unto the Heavenly Bodies so that their interconnectedness with the Eternal Presence could be renewed. The undulating bands of exquisite light were resolved, and the fire that consumed her was all let out. Now her whole person appeared like flowing clear jasper.

The Mother stood to give up the blessed souls, and the Chamber of Creation was filled with the amethyst light of the Crystal. Indeed, the magnificence of the brilliant purple light was a glory to behold. It seemed to fill the space like water.

The Mother of Naaheen, the Timeless Mother, wore garments and wrappings around her head that could be seen now. They colors were cool to the eye, but the headdress was also threaded with colors bright and shimmering. First, she came to the empty seat in the quarter circle. Her open hands and her heart charged with the heavenly fire, and into the empty seat, she administered the light of the soul. It danced upon the air above the open seat then extinguished itself as it was delivered to the mysterious eighth heavenly body, and so the giving commenced to the first man representing the seventh heavenly body. Her hand and heart flared, and the soul was placed into the man. He trembled and shook in ecstasy then collapsed in a sleeping trance.

The Timeless Mother continued to all the Heavenly Bodies. Men and women alike were rapt with ecstasy and put into a trance. Finally, she approached the first of the two travelers. Looking to each other, both were fearful, but Thydon wanted nothing to do with it.

She came to Ezkaysha, and though he was afraid, he allowed the Mother to give him the gift. He too shook, and to Thydon the rapture seemed a violating seizure. A possession if nothing else, if he believed in such occurrences.

When the Mother stepped to Thydon for his time, he drew his gun and shot her, but his defiance was not complete. He took up the spear of the Horse Spirit and, with astonishing and blasphemous crassness, struck the head of the spear on the stone to frighten the Mother, who stood with her wound flowing thick, her body at its weakest, having given all those souls to their Gardens. Sparks flashed up into the air from metal on the spear, and then Thydon swung it hard, lopping off the Timeless Mother's head.

The Guardian Spirits and the two mothers fell upon the body of the Timeless Mother, crying out in their language as they held her head and lifeless body. The repetition of the Mother's name fell out, one cry on top of another.

"Urga! Urga! Urga!" This was the way of the death of Urga, Mother of the Unborn.

Thydon swept up his companion Ezkaysha, who was still in his trance, and carried the man out of the temple over his shoulder. As he did, the magnificent city perished, for it was by the Mother's power and will that many things existed. Like fuses, all the buildings began to smolder out of sight. Vessels that flew above the waters and over the promenades crashed and disintegrated. Yet some things remained, though they would be stolen away and lost to eternity. In confusion that day, the Children of the Water let out cries of horror and woe.

Thydon dragged the barely conscious Ezkaysha through the empty archways of the dissolving gates. They were not ravaged by the Children of the Water or troubled in any way, for their mourning was so great, and it was not in their nature to harm the living. Thydon found even their craft untouched, and they ascended into the sky and returned to their home Spirea, where Ezkaysha's blessing would be delivered to his people, the Sharvannans.

This was the divine dream imparted to the sleeping Child of the Water and child of the sons of Thwargg, Evah. It was the history of the end of her father's people, before their subjugation, and henceforth the being of the known universes was interminably scourged with burning and profound complexity, as could not be comprehended by the mortal mind.

Eine Claren had seen snatches of such dreams of the lost world of Naaheen, but never so much as this. He witnessed them in the dreams of other Hypathians and extuiters once known as the Children of the Water and the people of Naaheen.

The child lay on the Thwargg dream table connected to the anthroscope. Claren's eye appeared giant in the magnifying glass attached to the brain-activity scanner. This is what it meant to be under his eye. The activity pleased him, as did the dream.

"Hmmm," he murmured as he drew back to watch the girl on the table.

He pulled out a twist of cherum from its pack, rolled it up like a tiny scroll, and tucked it in his mouth to chew. It tasted as sweet as honey in his mouth.

Chapter 9
No Quarter

The raucous crowd pressed in on Evah as she and her supporters made their way to the Hall of Magisteria for examination in the extuiter selection hearings. Safety guidelines for the hearings had been dashed into chaos due to press leaks from the various camps of Prime Minister candidates. Concerned citizens from every planet had flocked to the proceedings to demonstrate on behalf of impassioned causes, and the media had been whipping up social angst for two days with rumors that the first extuiter had been identified since the Constance kepplequer reserves tragedy. An extuiter plot was still widely believed to have been the cause of the trouble all those years ago, and now the public was baring their teeth on the matter.

Concern was heightened when Evah's name started to drift around the news platforms. She was, after all, the daughter of the prior extuiter, who was generally accepted to have worked in collusion with the eco-terrorists that had caused the Constance disaster.

"Evah, did your father conspire with eco-terrorists? Do you have an opinion about kepplequer resources?" shouted one reporter, striding in to get her clip for the evening report.

"She's a little girl!" cut in her mother, who was already well ensconced in the procedures. Father Segura stepped in and pushed the microphone away from Evah's face. The girl was in a state of awe, not having realized how many people had deeply passionate ideas about the extuiter program. The swarm of the crowd was stifling; she could barely breathe.

"I don't know. I don't know," shot from Evah's mouth in awe.

"YOUR FATHER HEALED ME! I BELIEVE IN YOU, EVAH!" cried one woman with the zeal of an exalting fan.

"The reports are true. This extuiter is part Thwargg!" one reporter spoke into a camera. "Get a shot of her eyes! Get a shot of her eyes!" he demanded. Evah looked into the camera pensively, and indeed her eyes were filled with icy storms.

As the guards pushed their way forward, Evah observed the different groups. Some flew signs. "Extuiters are the Evil" plastered the crowd in many places. A group of Hypathians stood amidst the rumbling crowd. Many of them just wanted to see the new extuiter, but some of them too held signs that read "More Power for Hypaths." Another group held signs that read "Sabia the Forgotten World." Seeing them all in their panic, rage, and joy, Evah could not imagine what she could possibly do to live up to the expectations they all expressed so passionately.

The doors of the hall slid open with a jolt, and Evah was relieved when they kept the crowd from crossing the threshold. Skenkin held her hand tightly. They made their way across the shiny marble floor and Evah realized this was the temple of Constance. Everything was polished and sanctified with a love for order. The columns rose way up to the carved ceiling and its painted frescos.

They strode through the grand doors at the end of the first great hall. Before Evah was the ornate magisteria bench, a grand structure where each of the sixteen magisteria of the eight planets had a seat. In front of the overbearing bench of the magisteria was a table where she and the others were to be questioned. She was to be seated before the bench, divided from the clamoring audience. The crowd around her chattered with unnerving energy. It was decided that by selection of lottery, some reporters and crowd members would be permitted to witness the proceedings. There were other officials, too, with their assistants, including two Prime Minister candidates.

A robed man entered from the magisteria chambers and came to stand before the impressive bench. "Oyez, oyez! The Great Hall of the Magisteria of this fine planetary system will be called to order!" shouted the man with blustering force, and everyone rose to their feet. Fifteen magisteria entered and took their seats. It was the first time Evah had seen any of them, including Galneea. She stared with mixed emotions and overwhelmed humility. *My father did this*, she thought. *He stood before the people in this way.*

The magisteria were seated, and the blustering man in robes shouted again. "This committee for the selection of extuiter is now in session!"

Everyone sat in synchronicity that seemed imbued with a kind of worshipfulness, Evah thought.

"The committee will come to order," said Galneea and smacked his gavel down with commanding pitch. "We are here to determine the readiness of the candidate for extuiter and to discover the appropriate action moving forward, should the candidate be found acceptable. We will begin by interviewing the Thwargg responsible for the first assessment of the candidate and then move on to a discussion of peripheral concerns and talk with the candidate herself. Let's begin by bringing forward Sire Eine Claren of Constance Ward."

Claren approached the examination table, sat down, and organized some documents he had brought with him.

"Sire Claren, you have prior experience with the selection and training of extuiters, is that correct?" Galneea continued.

"Yes. That's correct."

"And you have interviewed and examined the well-being of the candidate to be considered here today? Evah Ahtochi?"

"Yes. I have examined her."

"Is this girl a viable candidate for the extuiter program."

"Yes. I believe she is."

"And do you have any concerns we should be advised to consider in this procedure?"

The Thwargg thought for a moment, and then he put forth, "Yes, well, she's having some identity issues."

"Are these common issues?"

"Yes, I think so. We have never had an extuiter so young, or one that is female. There is a considerable amount of data we don't have to weigh against her."

"Let's get directly to the point. Is she a danger to society?"

Evah felt self-conscious. She realized everything that would be said about her here would end up all over the inhabited six worlds. She felt a little embarrassed for everything she had come to think on her own, right or wrong.

"No," Claren said, "but she must have close, experienced observation and guidance."

"Why? What is the nature of her identity issues?"

Now Evah would finally be the freak everyone at school thought she was. *Everyone will laugh at me. Especially if they hear I think I'm some twelve-armed goddess of death.* She wanted to disappear.

"Well, that is a private matter for her teachers and mother to know as we work with her. I can assure you these are no more unusual than the issues I have experienced before," Claren said with confident authority, and for all she had heard of the man and all she thought, she longed for experienced confidential guidance like his.

"I'm sorry, Sire Claren, but you do understand you're going to have to be more direct with us in these matters."

"No. No, I don't. This committee has overstepped its authority by inviting press and private citizens into these proceedings, and that is not an acceptable forum for such questions to be answered. I can assure you that all my experience with the extuiter program—and that is vast—gives me a comprehensive understanding that this girl is like any other candidate and does not pose any more risk than any candidate before her. You will have to take that as important wisdom for your consideration. This girl has gifts, and learning to understand and direct her gifts is no easy task. She deserves our confidence. It is paramount at this time in her training." Claren was as stubborn as an old horse on the matter.

Another of the magisteria leaned into Galneea. They conferred quietly for a moment as Galneea covered his microphone. There was some polite nodding, and then the chair of the proceedings spoke again. "That's acceptable for now, Sire Claren. But you will be acquiescent in submitting proper answers to any questions we may bring before you in private. Is that understood?"

"I understand. I will be as honest as I can, of course, with all matters relevant to these proceedings."

"Fine. Let's continue. I'm going to open the floor to the other magisteria, who will have five minutes to question you."

"Thank you, Magistere Galneea," said the Thwargg.

The proceedings continued in much the same manner from one magistere's questions to the next. Some inquired whether the program should continue at all, as the last two fully trained extuiters had failed to continue being productive government constituents. They attacked Claren as having suspect influence over the former extuiters, and one even demanded he remove himself from the training process because he was the young candidate's grandfather.

Finally it was agreed that if she were to be formally brought into protective custody and trained, then Sire Claren would only act in a supervising position, to which Claren agreed. But, because his presence had been instrumental in the development of the program, his guidance would still be in demand should they proceed.

Evah thought maybe they would assign Cordia to her schooling, but they did not. What she did not understand was that Cordia's presence had simply been a tool used to evoke her desire for her mother and a willingness to cooperate with her when they were finally reunited.

All was going as planned. Public opinion, and the social pressure to fit in, even in her newfound occupational circle, was too threatening for her to allow grudges against the people who could protect her. Even those who had killed her father, and though her conflict continued to give her pain beneath the surface, there was a part of her that did not want to hold on to animosity. Claren and Galneea were counting on her desire to be happy, and accepted, to make her give up her doubts.

Inside, Evah's allegiance was being ripped in two directions. On the one hand, there were the stories that Felin had shared with her, which she believed, and on the other hand, her mother and grandfather kept seeming to show they had her best interests in mind. The truth was that, deep down, she was angry at her father for leaving for Deiphera so many years ago.

Her inner turmoil was hurting her so badly she felt sick to her stomach, and she needed to keep herself busy with other things just to be able to keep moving ahead with her life. Inside, Evah felt like she had to make a choice about where her loyalties should lie. But, unable to really deal with that, she started leaning in assertively to the challenge of extuiting detailed architectural models. The more successful her extuitions, the more distance she felt from conflict, and being able to reach goals was sometimes the only thing that kept her afloat amidst her inner turmoil. She sought any source of relief from thoughts of the past that had not yet been resolved.

The magisteria moved on to "peripheral matters." First, they called Father Segura to testify about her scholastic aptitude, her general learning potential, her social interaction, her home life, and behavior in the home environment. He told them he thought it was right to put Evah in the program, that she was a gentle girl, and where she belonged was with her mother. It was during Segura's examination that questions revealed it was Magistere Sanje who brought Evah to Holy Heart Orphanage and School. The judges had opened an investigation into Sanje's activity, which is why the magistere was not present.

To further examine whether it was right for Evah to be accepted to the program, they called her mother to the examination floor.

"Ms. Claren, you are the mother of Evah Ahtochi?" opened Galneea.

"Yes. Though my name is legally Ahtochi too. That was the name of her father and my husband. I stopped using the name due to threats after my husband's disappearance six years ago."

Evah watched how steady her mother was under so much strain. She was calm and graceful, and she hoped she would be so well collected if she had to speak. For the first time, she was considering that her mother, too, lived with dangers.

"Pardon me. Ms. Ahtochi, are you aware of the demands that will be made on your daughter should she become an extuiter for the Constellation of Spirea?"

"I am. It can be a demanding education, and it is a commitment that she will be called to honor for many years, if not all her life."

"Do you now or have you ever had any connection to eco-terrorist groups, Ms. Ahtochi?"

"No, sir. Not that I'm aware of."

"But maybe you have?"

"No."

"Have you any knowledge that your husband, Varin Ahtochi, was involved in any way with such groups, or did he ever express to you his concern over matters such as the worlds Hypathia or Sabia being cheated of resources?"

"Sir, I did not have any such knowledge, nor did my husband ever express such concerns or beliefs. It should be noted for the record I have been examined extensively on such matters at former proceedings and have been exonerated of any involvement. I stated then, and I state now, my husband had a kind and brave heart and served the Constellation of Spirea with unceasing dedication. That is the man I—"

"That will be enough, Ms. Ahtochi. I have limited time for my questions and understand you will be forthright with any questions I ask. They are in the best interest of the Constellation. I have two questions that must be answered. The first is: Do you want your child to be submitted to the extuiter program?"

"I do not mean to skirt your question, but that is really a question that must be answered by Evah. I do know that in all the eight worlds there is no one known to be like her. I fear for my child's safety should she become an agent of the state. I have already lost one family member in service, and I do not want to lose another. I also have concerns that if she does not have proper guidance, she may be in great personal danger, both emotionally and mentally. And I hope should she not be accepted or if she chooses not to enter the program that her gifts will not be neglected, but that she will receive auxiliary help in some way for her well-being."

"That's a big responsibility to place on a child—asking them to make a decision that will affect the rest of their life. Don't you think she needs to be guided?" Galneea pursued.

"I can only help her to search her heart and mind to find what feels right for her. What kind of person or parent would I be if I forced her into a life of—"

"All right, all right, Ms. Ahtochi!" said Galneea and smacked his gavel down. "Have you discussed this with her?"

"Yes."

"And? What does she have to say, Ms. Ahtochi? What answer have you helped her find in her heart?"

"She would like to be involved."

"I have one other point to address, Ms. Ahtochi. It is my understanding that six years ago, shortly after your husband's death, your child was taken from you. My understanding is that she was really abducted and that the man responsible was Magistere Sanje. A probe will be questioning him shortly, and that is the reason for his absence here today. He has been forced to abstain from the proceedings and is under threat of imprisonment should you testify against him. It *is* your position that Sanje is responsible for your child going missing, correct?"

Skenkin seemed lost in thought. She stared, thinking deeply.

"Ms. Ahtochi? Please answer the question?" Galneea leaned forward, as did several of the other magisteria.

"I'm sorry, sir. This is an emotional subject; it's difficult for me to talk about it. I haven't even had a proper chance to talk with my daughter about it."

"Please answer the question, Ms. Ahtochi."

"Several years ago, I lost my husband. I was overwhelmed with grief and I trusted Sanje. He was a friend to us. I entrusted our child to Magistere Sanje, and my sorrow was made all the deeper when, at that time... I lost everything. I was not well, and in my grief, I could not reach my child. I could not see through my pain to be the mother Evah needed. I feared for our lives, and I couldn't take care of her. I wanted her to be somewhere people wouldn't suspect who she was. And so because of these concerns, I asked Magistere Sanje to take my child and place her somewhere safe, with the hope that one day I would have the strength to reunite with her. It is the most difficult decision I have ever had to make. I told no one the truth, not even my family. I can't believe how strong Magistere Sanje has been to keep this to himself all these years."

"Ms. Ahtochi, I have notations here that you have suggested a predator took your child. Are you disagreeing now with your own statements?"

"As I said, sir, it was a dangerous time, and it demanded secretive and unorthodox methods. I apologize to the magisteria and the people for any confusion. I believe she has been well cared for. There will be no complications due to this unfounded dispute. Magistere Sanje should be released from custody immediately."

"Are you sure, Ms. Claren—Ms. Ahtochi? You aren't going to change your mind tomorrow?"

"No."

"Ms. Ahtochi, if you are under threat or duress that is causing you to make such a statement, I can assure you the perpetrator will be met with deft reproach. You will be safe, I assure you. All you have to do is tell us that Magistere Sanje is responsible for putting you and your child in danger."

The air was thick with tension. "No. That would be wrong. That's incorrect. Magistere Sanje acted on my wishes; he was helping my family."

"Okay, let's move on. I'll open the floor up to my fellow magisteria." And Galneea did, despite his evident discontent.

Whatever had happened in that exchange, Evah could see it was not what the magistere had been expecting, but this was precisely what Claren wanted Evah to see. Though there may have been some truth in it, they knew that every play they made had to improve their chances of Evah's reconciliation with Skenkin; they wanted to strengthen Evah's resolve to be a willing participant moving forward with their plans.

The committee continued, asking Skenkin if she thought she was fit to mother now. Then they asked if she wanted to be with her daughter in whatever environment they chose to keep the young extuiter.

"I want to be there for Evah if there is a place for me and she wants me there."

The proceeding went on for over two hours, and then it was decided the young candidate would be invited to the floor for statements and answering questions. Evah was nervous but applied all her focus towards staying at ease the best she could. She was concerned she may extuit something inadvertently in her nervousness. The new spirit within her and I were still present inside her, and she was beginning to understand that we could surprise her with acts of our own will.

"Please state your name for the record, young lady."

"Evah Ahtochi."

"Ms. Ahtochi, do you understand why you are here today?"

"Yes, sir."

"And why is that?"

"You want to know if I should get into the extuiter program."

"Would you like to do that?"

"Yes."

"Why?"

"It just seems like that's what I'm supposed to do. What else am I gonna do? I've got these things that I can do, and I want them to be used right. I wanna do something good. I don't know. I want to be somewhere I'm supposed to be. It looks like this is it."

"Do you realize this will be the beginning of something you will likely be doing long after you grow up? That it's a choice you will have to live with the rest of your life—and not one to be made lightly?"

"I understand."

"You say that you want to do something good. What is that?"

"I've been told I shouldn't talk about the things we plan to do. I don't want to disappoint people."

"Can you give us some idea?"

"I want to make things for people. People who need it. I want to help people."

"That's a big ambition for such a little girl."

Evah shrugged, unsure what to say.

"Would you like to show us something today?"

"Well, this is a lot of people." Evah thought for a moment and then she looked to her mother, as if to ask if it was okay. Skenkin nodded.

"Now, you're going to be nice, right?" said Galneea.

Evah nodded. "Yeah. All right, everybody, close your eyes." She gave them a moment to do so. Evah closed her own eyes for a moment, and the third spirit within her shot into the air. "Okay. You can open them now.

When the crowded opened their eyes, they found a giant star, ten feet in the air above the floor, between the bench of the magisteria and the examination table. The crowd was amazed. Photographers tried to catch the star in an image, and the people talked to one another.

The star seemed to oscillate with the rhythm of a beating heart, its radiance hypnotic, but it quickly collapsed, became white-hot and exploded into hundreds of smaller stars that blanketed much of the hall. At the center appeared a sun, and the crowd let out a stir of shock, clearly afraid something could go wrong. The blanket of stars in the air above the hall began to circle around its source and then, swimming through space, became a fantastic spiral galaxy, spinning on its access with long stretching arms in a methodic fluidity.

"Make a wish," Evah said, and one of the stars shot from the spinning galaxy towards her mother, exploding into a flash in her hair, where it became a tapestry of tiny stars all about her long black locks.

The galaxy continued to swirl in the air as Skenkin stood to make sure everyone could see the stars in her hair. Her orange eyes danced, and the stars amidst her hair made her appear like some deity of the heavens. It was just like that night with Varin so long ago. All the crowd was amazed.

"Let me see," Evah said, thinking a little. Then the hall lights seemed to dim. The turning galaxy and the stars in her mother's hair were bright in the air, and Skenkin lifted a thick lock of hair to observe the stars clinging around it. She looked at Evah, wondering how much her child knew of the past or if this was only coincidence. Then suddenly the stars all collapsed back together again, and after hanging in the air a moment longer, the amethyst spirit sprang back inside the little girl, and the lights returned to normal.

Some of the crowd laughed with amusement; some sat a little terrified. Some even clapped. Galneea's gavel struck hard.

"That'll be enough! I don't know what to say. Thank you, I guess."

Evah thought he was disappointed. "I mean, I want to do better things."

"No, that was quite impressive, little girl. I'm going to have to move on here and open the floor to the other magisteria."

It was decided after a short private conference that Evah would indeed be accepted into the extuiter program as the first female extuiter in its history. The news was already out across the inhabited planets by the time the hearing was over.

They made their way back through the exterior hall and onto the steps of the revered building where a crowd of reporters waited to see Evah. Flashes filled the air as she walked towards them, her mother holding her hand tight. Then Skenkin let go to allow her to say something to them if she wanted to. A hail of questions filled the air. One reporter upfront put his microphone to her mouth.

"Evah, how did everything go today?" he asked.

"Well, they were all pretty nice to me. I think I'm going to be the next extuiter."

"Are you excited?"

"Well, yeah. It's good. I think it will be good. But I don't think it's going to be easy. I guess we'll have to see what happens."

Evah was starting to feel confident, but her time in the public eye would not last long. In the air, the flashes cracked brighter than her dreamy amethyst star. Then Evah was on the ground, and the people nearby rushed in to be near her collapsed body.

Skenkin rolled the child into her lap and could see that the young girl had been shot. Though it was not some terrible weapon that might have disintegrated her fragile body, it was bad enough to be fatal.

The crowd pressed in as order turned to havoc. This was the last photo op that would ever take place for the young extuiter.

As medics lifted her body from the ground, a red garnet stone slipped from her hand to be trampled and lost.

Chapter 10
The Pale Realm

T he veil of darkness obscuring Evah's sight dissolved to reveal
the beckoning sky, and her body rose fast up into the air.
From the heights of the sky, a female angel descended to
meet her. She was softly clothed in garments that appeared scant
and transparent, and her body was light, her hair long. She was
natural, and her skin was pale, her long dark locks heavy and
lovely in the air. Together, she and Evah began to race towards
the clouds. The fast wind snapped and whipped around them,
and the cloudy sky of Constance became a clear and far-reaching
blue that soon dissolved into the colors of space as they lifted
higher and higher.

Looking into the heavens before her were the final layers of
some far-off clouds, and beyond them, though in the dark of
space, golden bands of light raced and bent around a male figure
who seemed to be made of a vibrant radioactive dust—a vivid
dusty pink, scarcely holding its shape in the blast of bending rays
that surrounded him. One might imagine he was under currents
of water. His white hair was like bands of lightning that seemed
to float around his head in the depth of some mysterious waves,
like a shroud of multiple dimensions. His chest was bare, and the
clouds appeared like clothes, while his eyes were bright exotic
suns. As Evah rose, his hand gestured for her to approach. Her

sight grew dim, and then she was on his shoulder, and the folds of his hair were like soft locks waving around her.

They seemed to be soaring through the sky, the sight of him still somehow blurred and obscured, as if extraordinary collisions of time, light, and space were converging to reveal his visage to her mortal senses. She was near the sight of his face, near his cheek, and as he raised his head like something radiant in the grace of the world that bears the immeasurable weight of unlimited adoration, there was an inexplicable depth to his being that seemed heavy in its indefinable vision and experience. Then Evah could see that he was weeping. Witnessing his sorrow, she looked to the sky ahead and could see a masterwork of fantastic clouds floating in the deep expanse of the blue sky. Her sight dimmed again, and he was gone.

Drawing open the shade of her awareness, this time, she could see a secret lagoon in the dark of night. She stepped towards the water's edge. The light of a moon was on the water and its reflection in its fullest state. Around the lagoon were lush green trees and tall plants. Their presence was only visible by the illumination of the moon. At the far end of the lagoon was a gentle waterfall over a short slope of rocks that flowed into a shallow body of water. From beyond the gentle fall came a white light from some mysterious world. She thought that beyond the rocks was heaven; she could sense that the soft glow of light was the radiant emanation of the last kingdom.

She was moving over the water towards the far curving bank lined in green plants. She must have been floating because she made no splash and did not disturb the water. When she reached the far bank, she could hear a rustling from the dark of the plants and trees nearby. A man was running to the water's edge. His hair was long and knotted, his face bearded and his body clad in a long, dirty white garment. She could see he was in a panic—that terror was upon him. Blood was all about his body, in his hair, and covering his arms and hands. He fell to his knees at the water's edge and did not acknowledge her through his suffering but stayed collapsed on all fours. She could see that on his head was a crown of thorns, and in his derision, she knew who he was and why God wept. His was the suffering of all mankind. His was the humiliating suffering of God himself.

Evah began to move towards the small running waterfall at the end of the lagoon. She reached the rocks and began to climb, but her endeavor to move up into the light was becoming mortal and labored. The stones were sharp and hard, but she did not feel them too much. She was rising up to the illumination of the mysterious pale realm, and as she reached up to the top stone, the light grew bright... and then it was no more, and her time before the realm of heaven was done.

Chapter 11
Apostasis

"Evah?" I waited for her to answer, but there was no response. "Evah," I said. As a rule, they don't let rats into military hospitals. Or any hospitals for that matter. I didn't know how much time I had. Sanje had brought me in for a visit, having stowed me away in his business satchel. We had been there for an hour, hoping Evah would return to consciousness.

"I'm sorry, my friend," said Sanje to comfort my disappointment. "She's lucky to be alive and really what she needs now is rest." It had been two days since Evah had been shot and nearly lost her life.

"If all of this was a publicity stunt for Galneea's Prime Minister run then we failed her, Sanje."

Since Evah's departure from Holy Heart, I had been in the dark about everything that was going on. I spent endless hours waiting in Sanje's office, and countless hours biding my time at the church. The authorities had released Sanje due to Skenkin's remarks both at the sequester committee and a separate probe into Sanje's involvement in Evah's move to Holy Heart. She had denied her father's and Galneea's requests to condemn him. As much as it was difficult for me to come to terms with, Skenkin and I were apparently, now, officially on the same side. I still didn't trust her, but she was going to be one of the most valuable witnesses against her father.

"All right. I guess we should go," I said and stepped towards the edge of the bed so Sanje could close me up in his satchel. Then Sanje gestured to Evah, whose eyes were starting to flutter a bit. I scuttled up beside her face, and as I had so wished when she awoke, I was there, sitting near her shoulder, my little hands upon her temple. I nuzzled my nose to hers, sniffing for good health.

"Evah?" Her eyes did not burn brightly.

"Hi," she said and swallowed hard.

"Get her some water, Sanje." The magistere did.

"Hello there, Evah. You're going to be all right. You're in the military hospital on Constance," the magistere told her. "You've been sleeping for—"

"Where's my mom?" Evah interrupted clearly in pain.

Sanje continued to reorient her to the world. "She's home now. When you were stabilized, she went home. She had been waiting here for the last two days. She needed to go home and get some rest and clean up, but she'll be back, I'm sure. Felin has missed you."

"I have. I'm so glad you're all right, Evah," I told her.

"We're going to keep you safe. No one else is going to harm you. I can assure you of that."

"You're Magistere Sanje," she said.

"That's right."

"Thank you for helping my family."

"You're welcome. I know things have been rough for you and I'm sorry. The government of Constance is going to keep you safe."

"They're going to put you and Skenkin in a protected house on Hypathia," I added.

"Really. Will it be nice?"

"You'll have everything you need there," Sanje told her.

"What about my training?"

"The Thwargg will visit you there. Not so much at first, while you heal, but soon every day."

"And if you want, Evah, you can take me with you," I told her.
She was silent; everyone was silent for a moment.

"It will be all right. I've had a complete check-up. Remember, I used to be a pet. And you don't have to worry about me talking in front of Skenkin. It will be our secret."

She was silent for what seemed like the longest moment ever.

"It's not that. It's not any of that," Evah finally said.

"Then… what is it, Evah?"

"I can't be two people at the same time, Felin. I can't be in one place and think different things," she said, trying to explain her feelings.

"What do you mean?" I encouraged.

"I know you have your ideas about my mom. I know you don't trust her. But I do. I need to trust her. I need to have a home, Felin. And if you're there, I'll hate it. I'll hate her."

"Huh." That was all I could get out in my astonishment.

"What am I supposed to do? How do we know what we're supposed to do, Felin, when all the choices are so difficult?"

"There has to be some wisdom that we trust. You have to search deep, deep inside yourself, Evah, to find the truth that's right for you. Everyone has their own truth. Sometimes we're on a ride that's not of our own making, and we must remember who we are until the end. It's going to be all right. Go and do the things you need to do, but remember you will always have a place in my heart."

Then I threw myself on my back with my hands behind my head. "Well, it's kind of a relief. I've been meaning to do some things around the church. And anyway, I found a way up onto the counter where Maddy Poole puts the donuts on Sunday morning."

"Um, and we will have the investigation to work on—" Sanje attempted to redirect my disappointment.

"Yeah, that too," I said nonchalantly, trying to take the strain off the situation.

"Your mom will be working with us." Sanje was attempting to prepare Evah for the future, should everything turn serious.

"And listen. What's most important is that you focus on the things you need to do. Your training is important, and as much as I wish I could be there to see—" Evah started to speak, but I asserted myself. "I understand."

My effort to be reassuring was a success. I believe she knew my foremost concern was the same as it had always been: That she be all right.

It was then that Skenkin returned. I did everything in my power to put aside my feelings of disdain for her that I knew did not truly belong to me by any natural means. In attempting to do so, I understood what Evah had meant when she said she couldn't be two people. I remained lying over Evah's arm and stayed quiet. She looked at me, and I nodded inconspicuously and sniffed the air like some average rat who could not understand anything that was going on.

Skenkin crossed around the bed, looking on. "You brought her a rat?"

"Well, the word was around Holy Heart there was a friendly rodent type that Evah had entertained herself with from time to time," Sanje explained, though I'm sure it wasn't true at all. "It turns out he's domesticated, but he must have run away at some time from whoever he belonged to."

"Oh, yeah. Do you want the rat, honey?"

Evah looked to her and, without speaking, shook her head with a put-on smile.

"Yes, no… I won't be leaving the rat. I guess I've grown fond of him, so I'm going to keep him. We were on our way out; I have to get him home." And with that, Sanje picked me up and slid me back into his satchel. "We'll be on our way and give you two some time together."

I felt Sanje rise, lifting me up in the air.

"I'm so glad to see you're awake. Does it hurt much?" Skenkin said as Sanje carried me away.

Chapter 12
Structure & Light

Though our disdain could not be vanquished, this was our most beautiful age yet. We dug our feet in the soil and ran beneath falling waters. Evah was wild and in love with the times, stirring up pleasures with the other children on the edge of the Eshlam Forest. In the near distance, the structures of her ancient mothers served as the horizon vista before the morning sun that shone up into the vault of the skies. At dawn and dusk, on the world of Hypathia, the lush green leaves of trees taller than could be imagined were the background for her days of joy. Now she was healing, and she was strong. In the morning, she played then returned to her mother's arms, and life, and all things, felt just right.

The Thwargg had sent two education ambassadors to begin their work with Evah. They met in the afternoon for two hours at a time. Then her mother taught her other subjects to keep her education current. One of those subjects was architecture. She learned about woods and metals and different kinds of glass—about design and foundational structure, how to apply mathematics to concepts of engineering, and how to use light effectively. Even her dreams were filled with the construction of homes and buildings.

She had been extuiting models for months. Each time they became more complete. They were even elegant. The more she exercised her ability, the more her skills improved. There was a point she'd believed she could never achieve what was being asked of her, even on a small scale, but as she learned to harness the energy of the harbored soul within her, her goal became more attainable.

On an afternoon in late winter, a season that was like any other on Hypathia—warm—she was playing beneath the Cyclone Orchids, and the song of Kofutu, a neighboring musician, was ringing in the air when she saw her father's spirit. He was far in the distance amidst the trees, where the magic light played between deep shade and golden radiance. His figure seemed like an illuminated being, and he looked so young and handsome. In her head came that voice from the year before. The one that had lingered in her mind sometimes in the field at Holy Heart.

"Little queen," he said, then, turning to walk away, he vanished into the thick of the forest, the deep of the shade. Evah was overwhelmed with emotion and, giving without thinking, pursued the spirit of her father, passing the grand tree that was always her marker to go no further.

On the other side, not too far ahead, was a path that had long been overgrown. It was familiar somehow. A man was walking on the path, his back to her, so he did not see her. His long dark hair ran over his shoulders and he wore what seemed like some native white garment. She did not follow close for fear of finding herself in trouble, but she did pursue like some little cat, wild in the way she was.

The path led between two giant stones, and on the stones was what seemed like ancient timber. She had seen this in her dreams.

The man turned towards her prowling place among the low plants. She ducked fast, so as not to be detected, but saw him plainly. It was the suffering man she had found before the Kingdom of Heaven when she'd drifted between life and death not long before.

Standing up from her hiding place to see him properly and be certain, she could not find him. He was gone. *Surely*, she thought, *this is some sign and I must be brave.* She walked on through the corroded gate, but still he was nowhere to be found.

A strong wind blew through the swaying trees that seemed to bow then stand and bow again in a hypnotic dance. Not too far inside the ancient premises, there were carved stone figures, a little way off the path. Evah approached them. One seemed to be a man floating in the air, and beneath him, sitting in what appeared to be some sort of prayer, a woman. She seemed soft and peaceful. The growth of the forest had overtaken the carvings. She pulled away some ivy to better see her discovery.

Then the familiar voice came again. "Evah," it whispered. And looking in the direction of the voice, she could see what appeared to be an old stone structure. This, too, was suffocated with overgrowth.

"This is not the cradle of death or stolen dreams," came the voice of a woman. Standing there, where she had not been before, only a moment ago, was the person who'd spoken. Her jaw was strong and square, her eyes penetrating, and her body thin, yet shaped with taut muscle and ligature that resembled the untamed roots and vines of the forest. She was in her fifties, Evah guessed, but as you know, when you are young, anyone older than twenty-five looks ancient.

Evah was petrified and did not move.

"You have seen, little mother. It has been wrecked by the ages. Clean away the destruction then you will receive, but you must tell no one."

Evah looked to the stone structure.

"There," the spirit woman said. Then, without a sound, she was gone.

After assessing the work that would have to be done to clean the stone structure up, Evah turned and headed for home.

That night, lying in bed before she slept, she had a psychic feeling. It was as if the woman was calling to her. She was consumed with the need to return to that place.

The next day, after her lessons, while Kofutu played his string instrument and the neighbor children made percussion instruments of all they could find, and danced, Evah slipped away to her hidden place and started cleaning the stone structure. She did this for many days during that winter. The work was not easy, and sometimes she was filled with fear thinking about what she might discover lurking inside, but she remained brave.

After twelve days, the space was cleared and even washed with supplies brought from home. She understood then that the structure was some sort of sanctuary. The construction was simple: There was a stone foundation and four carved pillars, with a carefully carved stone slab above for a ceiling. In the center of the ceiling was a circular opening, perhaps a foot and a half in diameter, and on the eastern side of the structure, there was a direct view of the largest pyramid, where the observatory could be seen. On the north side was a spring that pooled gently and streamed into the depths of the old city.

Connected to the hole at the center of the ceiling was a metal ring. It had once been supported by three chains, but only one was still attached. The other two dangled down freely.

Evah climbed up to the top of the sanctuary and made her way to the opening. There were two hooks in the stone where the two additional chains attached. She reached inside, drew up the ring, and readied the chains to be connected. There were grooves in the ring where something must have sat at one time, suspended from the ceiling.

She hooked one chain up with no problem, but the third was missing a link, so she pulled a tie from her hair for a makeshift connection. She even got the length right for the ring to sit level.

Just as she was about to drop the ring inside the opening, however, a loud buzzing dashed past her that she thought was a bug of unnatural size. She jerked back from the hole aghast, thinking for sure she was about to be a late lunch for some hungry damselfly, but looking up in the direction of the buzz, she saw it was a hummingbird. It zipped back and forth, its wings a blur. It was not afraid of her and flew in close several times. Intrigued, she stood to watch it, but when she was firmly on her feet, it zipped away towards the deepest region of the old city.

"Huh," she uttered.

In the distance, other ruins protruded from the fertile Hypathian soil, all covered in the knotted vines of the old forest. The bird disappeared so fast it seemed unreal. Then, as she stared in its direction, the harbored soul within her sprang forth, racing ahead like a loosed thack ball down over the side of the sanctuary structure. She ran after it, throwing herself down on the edge of the sanctuary roof to look below and see where the spirit had gone.

Peering over the edge, the light that came from within her was still as a stone, levitating in mid-air over the waters of the spring. Beneath it, she could see that small items along the ground were levitating as if it had some gravitational pull, including a leaf that looked like a scotschoot.

She made her way back to the tree she'd used to climb to the roof and made her way down. After her descent, she expelled a frustrated sigh. "Oh! The ring!" She had forgotten to lower the ring down and now she would have to climb back up again.

The light suddenly shot quickly to the right a short distance, and where it went, more objects in the water and soil popped up into the air. She went closer, and it moved away. This time gently, evenly, it floated back towards her and then away again, further downstream.

"I don't get it. You want me to follow you?"

The light whipped back towards her fast and bobbed up and down as if to say yes.

"Oh, brother. Okay. But it's getting late, and I have to go back home soon."

The light shot downstream again. With another sigh, she began her pursuit, and so it went, slowly moving on towards the heart of the old city, all the while lifting lightweight objects in the air as it traveled along.

Evah was beginning to feel a sense of familiarity with the environment. There was a sense of synchronicity, and in her head images of the sacred dream began to appear like flashing memories. The memory of the Mystery and the Mother of the Unborn returned to her—it was as if she was meant to be there.

Then it was as if she knew what she was going to see next as they turned through the twisting curves. She thought, *I'm going to see a lake*, and sure enough only fifty yards later, after climbing through a knot of plants, the view opened onto the place where the spring ran. It was a giant lake, and though the jungle was so untamed, now she could see long walkways of refined stone in the distance. From different regions of the lakeshore, three more white lights soared through the air to the first that had led her so far, and they all merged into one. Being a bigger orb then, it moved over the water, causing it to tremble and race upward like strange rain in a fast cycle. It burned three times brighter and drew slowly towards her.

Evah stumbled back a little, adrenaline pumping through her body. The light charged towards her as quickly as the hummingbird had. Unable to stop the collision, Evah tried to jump back, uncertain of what such a power would feel like inside her, but the only difference she felt was a humming vibration. Then she noticed that she was floating a little way off the ground as she gently moved backward in the direction she had leaped. She was levitating.

"No way!" she said. Her mind was more than a little blown. "Uh... you know I can't be doing this all the time." She bumped up against a tree gently, and her floating came to a stop. Her feet touched the ground, though just barely.

After a short while, Evah was mastering her newfound ability. She turned a flip in the air, and then found that she could float above the ground in whatever way she pushed herself. Before long, she was starting to enjoy her fun, floating on her back above the ground, when the light shot out of her body again, and in a snap, she hit the grassy dirt.

"Hey!" she yelled at the light, exasperated. "Don't do that again! Or you can find someone else to hang out with! Ouch."

She rubbed her shoulder and dusted herself off, then noticed the light was hovering over the water again, in the direction of some structure atop steps on the other side of the lake. It shot back and forth out to the depths and then back to her.

"Phhh! That's a big jump!" she said, then looked the lake over, thinking. "Hmm." The light shot back inside her, making her float again. "Well, if ever there was a day to do something, I guess today's that day."

Evah took off her shoes and, with a great stride, took a running leap into the air over the lake. It was as if she had wings on her feet. She strode long and fast over the shimmering surface, but she could not sustain the lift, yet when it seemed sure she would be taking a most unwanted bath, Evah bounced back off the water with a splash. She did this again and again with an irrepressible jubilance.

"I am walking on WATER!" she cried.

As she soared above the water, the hummingbird zipped past her head again, flying fast into the scene ahead.

Easing down on the other side of the lake, she applied all her focus to her footfall, allowing herself a way to walk on the ground again with some confidence. She approached the small building at the top of the steps, but the entrance was covered with fallen rocks and other debris from the crumbling structure above.

Looking through an opening to the interior, she spotted something that looked like a giant gemstone. She had heard that people had looted the ancient sites for antiquities to sell and thought how strange it was that no one had stolen this treasure. It was carved into angles, a clear pinkish stone, but she didn't think diamonds got that big. Then she noticed there was a metal ring near the stone with a chain attached. That's when it dawned on her that the ring at the sanctuary with its grooves was a stone setting perfect for such a gem.

From above the structure came the grimacing snarl of some wild cat. A cold shock shot through Evah's core and every hair on her body seemed to stand up straight in a report of fear. It was a zaggar. They called them the child stealers; they were a predator with no match.

Evah felt her innards turning to mush and she felt as if she were going to ooze right into the gaps between the stones. She wished she could.

The giant beast leaped down onto the landing of the steps, boxing Evah in at the collapsed entrance. The zaggar's paws were the size of Evah's head, and through its bristly sanguine coat, its muscles flexed like machine works of heavy fluid steel. It presented its glistening jaw slung low, as if encouraging her to struggle.

"Please don't eat me."

The zaggar licked its chops, its claws seeming to peel forward, ready for business. It stepped in close to taste the air around Evah, and the child could count the whiskers around its nose, all splayed back in a growl that further revealed its weapons.

Evah was no longer thinking at all. She was quivering and the rush of blood to her head was making her see stars. She was barely present at all when the great light from within her came forward from her chest and the menacing cat stepped back, eyeing its new foe with uncertainty. Then the tempest of destruction faded from its eyes, and it became docile. After peering at the light for a moment, it stepped back and lay down before the amethyst star, it head lowering in submission.

"Oh, that's good. Good zaggar," Evah whispered. She watched it stand, turn around in the other direction and lie down again like some sort of guardian surveying the view from the top of the steps.

"Hmm. That's weeeird, but I like it."

Hesitantly, Evah turned back to the entrance and placed her hand on some of the debris to see if she could make it even budge, but it was useless. Then the light flew back inside her and the stone she was touching rose off the ground. She looked back to be sure the zaggar was still behaving. There the cat lay, surveying the clearing, and beneath Evah's hand, the immense stone maintained its levitation.

"Oh, man, this keeps getting better all the time," she said to herself and directed the stone to a clear distance before lowering it to the ground.

After moving several pieces of debris this way, she was able to reach inside. A giant snake slithered away from her, as if making way for her.

"Hello. That's big enough to eat me too." Evah was impressed with her welcome but thought it prudent not to stick around. She made her way inside the ruins just far enough to grab the stone. There was a giant disk on the ground with carvings on the surface, and on seeing it, more memories of her dream came back to her, but this was not the temple. This was only another sanctuary. She picked up what she thought at first was a gem, then realized it was some sort of quartz. The clearest quartz.

Evah turned and exited the sanctuary. The zaggar stood and, without looking in either direction or at Evah, began marching forward. Evah took up after the giant cat's lead, though she wasn't sure at all where her protector was going. They walked along a stone promenade and then onto a dirt path, when the cat stopped and stepped aside. Through the tangle of vines and plant life before her, Evah could see a path that led back to the sanctuary she'd first departed from.

"Okay. I guess I'm going to go now. Stay here—"

The beast gave out an unbridled roar that shook Evah's bones.

"Okay. It looks like there are some laws in motion here. I'll be going," tripped from her mouth a little fast and apologetically as she stepped through the tangle of plants and was on her way.

Returning, she entered her sanctuary, and with a gentle bounce, she was in the air beneath the opening. Working the ring down to the lengths of the chains, she placed the quartz rock securely within its setting. It sat there like an unlit lamp.

Touching down to the ground, she watched the crystal, expecting some new wonder to transpire, but nothing happened.

She scanned the view of the sanctuary for some sign and listened to the air for some sound or voice, but though it was peaceful, with the cool breeze and the shade of the coming night, nothing out of the ordinary happened. She looked up through the opening, but there was nothing but the sky.

"Well, after everything else, that's a little disappointing."

She listened and watched again for a while longer and wondered if maybe she hadn't done something the way it needed to be done. She remembered the story of Haytoo in his temple on Constance. He had done some weird ritual or something so maybe there was some ritual she should do.

She sat peacefully beneath the crystal like the carving of the woman. Still, nothing happened. Though the place was filled with serenity, and the vibration from the light inside her gently hummed, there was nothing too fantastic. She wondered why there was an opening above the crystal at all and thought maybe something had to come in through there.

In her mind flashed a memory from her dream: The illuminated man beneath the opening in the temple drawing lights into himself from the night sky. Her thoughts troubled her. For one, she did not like the idea of having to come here in the middle of the night. Although she did feel she would probably be protected, sneaking away from her mother for long periods in the evening would be tricky, to say the least. But what really concerned her was that the man in her dream seemed asleep, or something, and in the power of the lights. She was afraid of what all that power could do to her. Floating around in the air was fun, but what was happening to that guy in her dream was more than a little far out. To see it may be one thing, but to *be* it would be something else altogether. Would she be able to return to normal after something like that happening to her?

"Okay. Well, I'm gonna go then."

There was no response, supernatural or otherwise. Night was falling fast and she had to make her way home.

Chapter 13
The Perfunctory Eruption

"We know," Blouty Duthane heard from the other end of the kalodia. The call interrupted him in the last thirty minutes of his shift at the Laboratory of Regularity Algorithm Applications.

"Hello? Who is this?" His voice was filled with arrogance, masquerading under the guise of a good-natured fella. A recording of him played through the kalodia. "You've done the things you had to do, Skee. We all have things we have to do, and you did that."

"There will be a vehicle waiting for you in Liberty Square. This is a ride you do not want to refuse." He gave no reply, and the silence signified he was uncomfortable. The connection ended.

We had a transport waiting for him right outside Constance Ward. We weren't going to be subtle. At the least, Sanje and I wanted his bosses to be aware he was dealing with unknown entities. We were about to unsettle the power and practices of one of the oldest institutions in Spirea's history, one that had roots reaching much deeper than before it was identified as Thwargg Ward.

Within minutes, he shuffled through the back entrance of the Hall of Magisteria, plodding his way, under armed escort, to the office of Magistere Sanje. Upon entering, he found the magistere sitting at his desk.

The office was dimly lit, and there was no one else around. The marble floors and cold architecture in the hours after dark made it seem more like an ossuary than a building of public affairs, and walking into Sanje's office gave one the feeling of penetrating one's own tomb rather than being granted a prodigious privilege.

It was warm. Too warm for his Thwargg first-class coat. We anticipated he would stay buttoned up in every way and certainly not take his jacket off. We wanted him to sweat, and he obliged us with his self-inflicted discomfort. From where he stood in the doorway, he could see little more than the shaved head of a quiet man in robes, like some harbinger of death in the shadows. Then I—a fat black rat—stumbled through the pool of light that faintly illuminated the ominous man's desk, and silence pressed on the atmosphere with corrosive suspense. Sanje did not bother to look at him.

"Blouty Duthane. Former custodial manager of Psycho Architecture, Thwargg Ward, current supervisor of the Laboratory of Regularity Algorithm Applications, Constance Ward."

"Yes." Blouty stayed near the door, uncertain what to do.

"Sit," Sanje told him.

Sensing the man's dissatisfaction with the situation, Blouty did as he was told.

Sanje touched the control panel of his visual monitor. A projection played on the wall. It was a recording of Blouty Duthane sitting on the couch in the South Rock Station lounge. "Is this you?"

Blouty drew an audible breath through his nostrils.

"Yes, that's right!" Blouty said with inappropriate zeal and a smile. "Why?" His zeal continued with the aim of breaking the tension. "Is there some question I can answer for you regarding Ms. Ahtochi?"

"Yes. This office is excavating gargantusaurus bones."

Blouty was puzzled and disturbed by the phrase, not knowing what to make of it.

"Really?" Blouty chased after the logic of the mysterious words.

"Yes. One that we are currently dusting off was lodged in the not too distant past on Thwargg. It's a bone of undeniable mass. An investigation into a conspiracy between the Thwargg judicial system and the Thwargg Ward Psycho Architecture Department that manipulated the unconscious minds of first- and second-time offenders to get them doing final clench offenses and thereby getting themselves put away for long periods of time. Getting them to turn on each other in deals to lower crime rates. It seems like a good way to control crime and destroy organized networks, but it is a violation of due process. It's a violation of citizen rights that preys on exhausted, emotional minds of persons who have been taught to do little else than make ill-begotten decisions under pressure. The more vulnerable victims were the many children of those offenders. They were taken by social-service branches and used as pressure points to compact the psycho architecture input in their parents, causing rash behavior. They were used as hostages to bait and upset their offending parents. I understand an extended purpose for the unlawful activity was to diminish government spending on financial social aid. Anthroscope procedures and unconscious monitoring are mandatory for criminal offenders, is that right?"

"Yes, it is. But what you're suggesting is preposterous," Blouty said with an old-chum kind of smile.

"Crimes are always preposterous until people are in prison for committing them. Your department was Psycho Architecture at the Thwargg ward. Is that right?"

"Yes."

"And now you have a nice big raise and promotion. Is that right?"

"Yeah."

"It's not easy getting moved to Constance Ward. Any position there is a coveted one. Is that right?"

"It is."

"You seemed proud of your move to Constance Ward when discussing it with Ms. Ahtochi. Mr. Duthane, I must inform you that this meeting is being recorded for future lucidity in discussions between the Magisteria of Constance. Do you understand?"

"No, I don't like that at all."

"Why?"

"Well, uh, it could make me look guilty of some offense."

"We already know you're guilty. We are here to discuss something new. Make yourself useful, and we are prepared to exercise leniency."

Blouty stood and walked to the door. He looked out at the armed guards standing watch in the hall.

"You could walk out that door. But you will finally know what real due process is. You'll feel the full weight of this office in the prosecution of your offenses. This visual recording I have of your visit to Skenkin Ahtochi is enough proof alone to give you two years in prison."

"That's absurd! She is a childhood friend."

"No, Mr. Duthane, she is a witness protected by this office. Your presence there indicates a threat to that witness, and that is first-class tampering."

"What do you want?"

"Eine Claren."

"You're talking to the wrong person. You see, what I do know about your investigation into ward activity on Thwargg is that it cannot be pursued by Constance law. That's lower-court Thwargg activity. You have no authority over the way other planetary governments are run."

"There are strict Spirean laws regulating psycho architecture throughout the planetary system, but the easiest activity to prosecute is yours. Others will go free, but you won't. Your life will be over. Your position at Constance Ward will be gone, along with its perks, and by the end of it all, most likely your pretty house on Thwargg too. How ya gonna get the girls then?"

Blouty was silent and rolling his head around to release tension in his neck.

"The worst part of it will be that those you collaborated with won't trust you anymore. They won't know what you have given up about the processes, about the secrets. You tell me, are they dangerous people when concerned about their money and freedom? At the least, you will be cut off, and who knows, living such a desperate life, like your victims, you might find yourself in an endless cycle of going to prison and getting out, only to go back in. Who knows what that feels like, that desperation? It could make you do silly things, and one little suggestion on the dream table and who knows what you may find yourself doing."

"That's ridiculous! Those people were lowlifes and drug addicts who couldn't even take care of themselves, let alone their dirty little neglected children. They made no contribution to the world but being a nuisance in the street, fighting at bars, and falling down drunk in the road, and making more and more little people just like them. Those people are like animals. Witless things, with no self-control."

"Maybe I'm talking to the wrong person." Sanje pressed his control pad to stop the recording, stood up, and walked out the door. I fumbled into the light, watching him go.

Blouty was in his chair again, now radiating pompous disgust like some grisly immoral discharge. Then he looked at me and said, "You stink, little rat."

I sat up, my big belly extruding, and rubbed my head as I teetered on my duff.

"Go stick it up your starslide, buddy," I said squarely, and out into the cold halls of the magisteria building shot Blouty Duthane's cry of horror.

"AAAAAAHHHHH." It bellowed out of him like the pitched wail of an emoting tenor; a perfunctory eruption.

"I'm glad you feel that way. You think this is weird, you better get ready. 'Cause you can bet yer sweet little Thwargg suit your reality is about to melt before your eyes."

"What are you?"

"I'm the one that bites. You think your technology is good? You won't believe the things we have. Our bugs are everywhere. Don't you feel 'em?" And though I said this, it was as if something else was guiding my words.

Suddenly, Blouty Duthane was patting and frisking down his ears and his neck and looking at his hands wildly as if something were crawling all over him. "Ahhh. Ahhh. Ah. Stop it! Stop them."

"What is it? What? What I do?" I asked, quick and serious. I didn't know. Though I realized as the words shot out of me that I sounded wicked.

I stood on my hind feet and quickly rubbed my eyes, then my hands were waving in the air at him. "What! Did I do something? I think I did. I did it. I did it!"

I was so happy with myself! I think I made an extuition! Ants, maybe. Maybe it was ants. I don't know, but it was great, and then all of a sudden it was over.

"I'm tellin' you, buddy. I'll give you psycho architecture." I leaned in with a crazy stare to cement the act and snarled, dangling teeth in a grimacing menace.

Blouty Duthane was sitting terrified in his seat. I could smell his fear. I think I even smelled a little urine.

Wow. All I could think was, *Wow, I did it; it happened.*

I refocused myself as fast as possible. "This is your last chance. You're going to tell us everything you know about Eine Claren's activities. And any connection your office has with Galneea. I'm betting someone like you knows all about the little white room Claren takes people to when they're on the scope. Spill it."

Sanje opened the door and walked back to his desk. "My God. What's the matter with you?" he asked in a matter of fact tone. Blouty was hunched in his chair, staring at the floor.

Under the cover of shadows, I mouthed to the magistere, using my little hands emphatically to explain, *I made an extuition. And he lost his mind.* I was silent but could barely contain my joy. I don't think he could read rat lips. But it happened. I knew it, and I guess that was enough for me.

But Sanje got the sense that there had been a radical shift in Blouty's condition and prompted the recording to recommence.

"Is there something you want to say, Blouty?"

"The network is unending. I walk into a dining establishment, and they're there. I don't tell anyone where I'm going. They're at the nearby table. They don't talk to me directly, but they say what I need to do. Sometimes they leave clues on interactive sites on my computing console. Anyone who is on the dream table is vulnerable, myself included. They can change digital information then change it again, so no one ever knows information was disseminated or altered. I think there's organized crime involved. The social system and courts are doing what they need to get something out of it, but organized crime gets information and the manipulation of people to gain profit and security. My point here is that no one is safe. I am not safe. Nor Skenkin. You saw what happened to her little girl. The extuiter. There are few rules for these people. Rules are like playthings in their system of favors."

"Are you saying that the assassination of Evah Ahtochi was the work of these people?" Sanje asked.

"My point, I guess, is that getting people to do things like that is not too challenging for them. Right now, the focus is in largely on the Prime Minister election. I know that Galneea wants to set the stage for an extuiter program comeback under his rule. Let's just say, I know she isn't dead, the little girl. And that was the plan. To use her when she is instated for some sort of running platform. And more than that: They want to make the little girl feel that Galneea and his associate Eine Claren are her protectors. You see? She will fear being hurt again, and that's how they'll control her. And her mother."

"Did her mother know she was going to be shot?"

"I don't think so."

"What do you mean the focus is on the Prime Minister election?"

"Well, I know that much of the data I harvest from the masses is used to manipulate public opinion for the benefit of the candidate they want elected. I don't know why they don't simply program the people through psycho architecture—telling 'em who to vote for. They could. And maybe they have. I guess that people are still subject to traditional beliefs, and the influence of people around them, so directly telling people what to do with big social decisions is still subject to historical positions. Like Hypathia and Sabia demanding development and resources. I like to think what it means is that to do big things takes a lot of coordination, and they aren't powerful enough to corrupt everybody. It gives me some satisfaction knowing that everybody in the Thwargg establishment may not be dirty. Many of us genuinely think we're doing something good for society, when it comes right down to it."

"But this harvesting of information is being misused?"

"Yeah. They build public images according to the desires of the people. It's the same with the child being shot. There is a deep-seated fear of the extuiters, and to see her brought down a notch was cathartic for the people that they plan to capitalize on in a sweeping change of opinion so that they can get them behind some fantastic social platform."

"Do you have any proof of any of this?"

"Well, I know my specially harvested data goes to management—to Eine Claren. And it's not protocol. But what disturbs me most is what your little friend was talking about."

"I don't know what you're referring to."

"The little white room."

"Oh, yes."

"It's long been rumored among the upper classes of the Thwargg wards that such a place existed. If you can call it a place. It's a constructed virtual environment. A platform in the anthroscope program structure where unconscious minds could be met and treated or communicated with in a way that could never be witnessed in the real world."

"Yes. Tell me more about this white room."

"Well, I don't think it necessarily has to *be* a white room. I think it could be whatever they want to project into it. I don't know who built the internal environment or how many people use it, but I do know that Eine Claren uses it."

"How do you know this? Have you been there?"

"Well, that's what's so disturbing about it. I don't know if I've been there."

"Then how do you know it exists?"

"I have recordings of Eine Claren using it. I haven't been on the anthroscope since I saw it."

"Isn't it a requirement of employment in the wards to submit to weekly scopes to ensure better well-being?"

Blouty laughed a little. "You're kidding."

"About what?"

"I did what the rich do. I run loops. Surely you must have been offered such an option."

"No. I will confess I don't use the anthroscope anymore."

"You're fortunate to be in such a position. You know that they're rolling out implants for the common population on Thwargg in the not so distant future. Then there will be no need for anthroscopes or dream tables. It's the Thwargg ambition to make implants mandatory and then surveillance mandatory for everyone. But the technology hasn't been developed for every alien race in the system yet."

"I've heard such a rumor. Tell me about these recordings."

"They're all on here." Blouty pulled his kalodia from his pocket and placed it on the desk. "I have nine recordings. Three with Skenkin, five with Galneea, and one with Evah."

"The girl? It's illegal for children to be on the scope."

"It's from her discovery examination. More of a pep talk than anything else, telling her it was time to find her ancestors. He wants her powerful. But the Galneea meetings are what you want. They talk about something big happening to change the perception of the extuiter program and the need for "someone to do what has to be done." It's vague, but I think that's about the assassination attempt. The rest is about their plans for the ministry."

"The ministry."

"Galneea wants the Prime Minister office. For business. Money. Claren wants to be named Minister of Health."

"Thank you, Mr. Duthane."

"I guess I'm a witness under the protection of this office now."

"Do you want to be?"

"Just as long as you put me somewhere a little safer than South Rock Promontory."

Sanje picked up Blouty's kalodia from the desk and leaned back to observe the Thwargg. "Well, we shall have to see."

Chapter 14
The Incumbent

Morning is the cool of the day on Hypathia. In the air, through the open windows, one can hear the wild birds, and filthy bugs that possess the activities of the planet before the sultry fugue of its atmosphere overcomes our senses. I could be on South Rock Promontory, Deiphera, and have more pleasurable hours, or on a lost patch on Sabia, still obscured from the public eye with Evah. For reasons I am now learning, my father wanted us here. He wanted Evah in the cradle of her people's history and in their way of life. Neither of us speaks the language, and watching Evah play with the local children is like watching a bat try to mingle with ostrickses. But she is happier than I have ever seen her, sparse as my mothering memories are, though it was not our pleasure my father had in mind when he put us here.

There is some ancient spirit here. A voice of the haunting, lost ways of the ancient people. Though the books tell us it was a blood-loving religion of swarthy tribes, there is a heart here that is tender, and through the din of chaos and the undeniable struggle for domination and survival that is the wild milieu of animals and plants, there is an untapped, secret spirit of creation. That is the aim of our pursuit: For Evah to find it, become a part of it, and wake the creator within her.

This morning I heard my daughter's voice when she woke. She called out with the concern of an innocent child who had lost a tooth.

"Mommy? Mommy? Mommy?"

When I entered her sleeping chamber to determine what the matter was, I could not have been prepared for what I saw. Her window was open, she lay in her bed, and all around her were wild animals. On her pillow, a brightly colored, monstrously sized bird, flapping and stretching its wings, while furry, indigenous creatures nestled in close, and on the floor at the foot of her bed was an enormous black cat. The cat observed me for a moment, thumping its tail on the ground, and in my head, it sounded like the beating of some extraordinary drum. Its yellow eyes and tremendous head possessed an unnerving command. It considered my presence as if it wondered whether it should eat me. Licking its fangy chops, it stood like a guard before its queen and seemed to be telling me my place. Then, with sleepy laziness, it turned towards the window and pulled its powerful body out over the ledge.

"Okay. Come on," I said and put out my hand for Evah to leave the bed. When she did, her company rose and bustled, and as Evah and I exited the room, another of the creatures could be seen crawling out the window. I shut the door tight.

"Why did you open your window last night?"

"I don't remember," she told me.

I believed her because she seemed as confused by this strange event as I did.

I sighed and then I could hear something like bickering coming from outside. A man and a woman were frantic over something. I told Evah to stay put and went to the front door. There was a small crowd: A man, a woman, and maybe two or three children. I walked out to see what was going on, as it seemed there were no dangerous animals around.

When I rounded the corner of our house to where the people stood, the woman approached me, rambling in her native tongue. She wasn't mad, though I couldn't say what her state of mind was. There in the clearing, around the back of the house near Evah's window, I could see some sort of strange hut, unlike anything I had seen before. The surface was like some shimmering metal or like a pearl. It had a curved shape, and though it was no taller than the house, it was a spectacular alien peculiarity. One might consider it to have had four walls, if they could be called that, and there was a jeweled appearance to what were apparently windows. I was afraid to go near it. Being concerned some terrible animal was lurking in the nearby forest, I ran inside and shut the door.

Peeking into Evah's chamber, I found the animals were gone. Even the gigantic bird.

I shut the window. Standing there, I could see the remarkable pearl structure. It was amazing, but deep inside, I was afraid because this was something I did not understand or know if I wanted to understand. This was something way beyond my powers as a mother, as a Thwargg—maybe as a mortal. This is what my father wanted. And though the power growing in Evah may have been greater than anything in the eight worlds, I did not know how to control it. Feeling lost, I connected a call to my father.

"It's happened," I told him. "She's made something in the middle of the night and I don't think she even knows how she did it."

"Oh, Skee. You sound hysterical," came his voice from the kalodia. "Is it solid?"

"I don't know," I told him.

"Well, go rap on it! Does it look like it's made out of something children play with?"

"No! No, not at all."

I walked outside and carefully looked to see what creatures could be lurking.

"Hold on a minute."

I walked up to the structure fast and, scared, reached out my hand and gave it a fast couple of bangs. Feeling my knuckles hurt a bit, I retreated as fast as I'd approached. "No, it's solid. Like weird solid. It looks like it's made out of pearl but it's as hard as rock."

"That's good. Is there a door?"

"I don't know. I don't exactly feel safe around it."

"For goodness' sake! Why not!"

"Because there was something else. There were animals."

"Animals?" As always, my father talked to me like I was ridiculous.

"One of them was enormous. It could have eaten me, it was so big."

"In the little building?"

"No. In her room with her when she woke up this morning. There were animals, and there was the building, if you could call it that, outside her window."

"I'm going to come and see you. Clean up the girl. There will be no lessons today."

I took Evah into the kitchen to make some food. I didn't know what to say to her, and she was silent. I prepared our dishes then, turning round to bring them to the table, I saw Evah as I had never seen her before. She was watching me, wondering what I was worried about, when I dropped the dishes in shock. Evah looked down at her feet. She was levitating six inches off the floor. She looked up at me like she had done something wrong.

"Oh," she said. "Oh, yeah. That's happening. I can still walk on the ground though, Mommy."

"Please do! I don't want to see you do that again. Especially when Grandpa's here."

Hours later, a private transport arrived. It was an official vehicle of the magisteria. I thought Sanje had come and was relieved to know my father was trying to work with him. Then the door opened, and Galneea stepped out.

Some of the neighboring children went in close to see the fancy vehicle and who was inside, but guards stepped out and immediately shewed them away. The daunting magistere wore dark robes—the color that represented his people's planet. His body was wiry, his belly big and his head a great bulbous brown fleshy wad. He wore his gravity modulator, and when he walked, he seemed to float in long strides like a king of the most offensive specters. And, of course, there was my father with him. Like a glorified household pet around his beloved master.

Galneea was already starting to glisten from the humidity. He patted the dewy sweat from his brow while trying to keep the appearance of respectability, but we all knew he was a dangerous, twisted creep, and I hated my father for bringing him to our home.

Within what felt like seconds, he came inside and roosted himself in my favorite chair. Evah sat on the couch, hugging the arm tightly to keep herself from rising into the air.

"Now, little girl, you're a talented little girl, aren't you?" said the contemptible Scabeeze in a manner that awkwardly masked his disdain for children. He pulled a box of candy from under his arm then rose, all cumbersome, to toss it on the table in front of Evah. "What's your favorite candy?"

"Jiggle bears."

"Hmm. Well. These are good too." He returned to his seat and twisted a dial on his chest to generate more gravity for his comfort. "Ahhh," he released with pleasure. "We're going to do big things, kid. We're going to work together. I will be Prime Minister, and you will be my extuiter. Now, how does that sound?"

"Well, if you win."

Galneea and my father looked at her, offended. Then Galneea laughed—a low growl that went on far too long.

"Yeah. When I win." The room was silent for a moment. "I hear you made something for us last night."

"Well, I didn't make it for—" Evah could feel the men staring at her; she was starting to get the idea that everything was supposed to be for them and they were always to be the winners. "Yeah."

"Good," Galneea said. "Well, we look forward to seeing it."

"Okay. Great." There was silence again, then Evah looked to me, and it was clear she didn't like what was happening. "Maybe you should show him, Mom."

I rose. "Yes, yes! Let's do that! Evah, you stay here."

I took the men outside. I thought for a moment that maybe one of those cats would be around and it would eat them so we could be done with this, but no.

After some examination of the building, it seemed clear there was no door, but when the men pressed in close to one of the less oblong walls, it evaporated, making an opening barely large enough for them to squeeze inside.

"That's clever, but it will never work. We can't have that going on. It would make the people nervous. They wouldn't trust it."

"Yes." My father nodded.

Galneea lifted a fist and banged on the ceiling three times. It seemed he was trying to break through it to the outside.

"Well, that's good."

"Mhhmm," my father agreed.

"The windows are a bit silly."

"I agree. There is a kind of tradition to that, I think. I'll talk to the girl. She's a child, you know?"

Galneea banged on one of the windows with his thick knuckles. "Shouldn't they open?"

"Hmm. Yes, of course," my father concurred.

"Are we going to have to lay a proper floor in every one? We need to keep the budget down."

"Hmm. Yes."

Then they were on their way to leave without saying a word. Or so I thought. My father walked Galneea to the transport, then returned to the house while his business partner waited in the cool of his vehicle and headed straight to Evah's room. She was standing, but on the ground, luckily. She moved to her vanity chair and sat. My father stood at the window, looking out onto the alien formation.

"You're going to have to apply yourself more diligently, Evah." He began his talk without looking at her. I watched him from the doorway; he looked like a shadow in the light. "This is lacking some essential things."

"Like what?"

"Like a door." He kept his back to her. "And a floor. And windows that open but keep out the elements. Plain windows will be fine."

"Okay."

"It must be bigger. Much bigger. We will clear some more trees. Next time bigger than the house. Do you understand?"

"Yeah," she said hesitantly.

"Well, then what's the problem?"

She shook her head a little. "I-I've never done these things before."

"Well, whatever you're doing, something is going right. You need to keep it up. Whatever it takes, you need to push through it."

"I'm just… I'm a little scared."

"Of what?"

"It's all new, and it's happening fast."

"Can you do better? Do we need to get you on the anthroscope?"

"I think I know what to do."

"Good." Then he turned to me. "You see that she keeps on doing what she's doing. That is what is most important." He turned back to Evah. "And I understand you had some friends in your bed with you?"

Evah didn't know how to react. She looked like she had eaten some of Galneea's twisted candy and had a sour stomach.

"No more of that. That isn't safe. You'll get your mother eaten. No more."

She said nothing.

"All right. Good. Carry on, you two."

He came near and nodded his approval to me, and then, with that, he made his way to the transport, waving and smiling as he climbed inside. Watching them go, I wondered how much of this pressure Evah could take. I wondered how much I could take. But it was as it always had been.

Chapter 15
Submission

In the ease of sleep, as the morning sun rose above the Hypathia trees, Evah was scarcely troubled by the argument her mother was having on the kalodia. Grandpa wanted her to take a transport he had sent. But she did not even wake when the door shut loudly. I had blocked her ears to ward off any disturbance, for our time was near, and though I did not like her grandfather, I planned to use his ploy for my ascension.

Evah woke to the sound of saws buzzing brutally upon the ancient trees outside her window and rose to spy a great tree crashing to the fertile ground. No friend of the wild could visit now as her window had been sealed shut permanently.

She noticed then the quiet that ruled the house. There were no sounds from the kitchen of water running, or pans banging, or dishes clanking. She did not hear the kalodia making sounds like some secret whispers from a far-off realm, as it often sounded when she first rose from sleep. The air was empty of music or the sound of something amusing being watched. It was late in the morning, and her mother had not woken her as she usually did.

"Mommy?" Evah said with what force she could muster in her sleepy spell.

There was no response; the word seemed cold and lost in the vacuum of silence. She noticed that, outside, her creation was still standing. Despite her efforts to "apply herself" as her grand-father had ordered, she was unable to revise the construction she had achieved the first time round. She felt like a failure, unable to control the ability she had received.

The day before she had taken a long walk and did what she could with the other children to distract herself from the little creation, hoping that if she did not focus on it, it might disap-pear, but it endured.

She noticed something different about her physiology then—the spirits within her were not making her float as they had the day before. Something was different. Her stomach was hurting, actually rather severely—hurt as it had never hurt before.

She walked to the vanity and observed herself in the mirror. She thought she looked older, taller maybe, but more than that she noticed a little glow of yellow behind the blue storms of her Thwargg eyes. Then she thought, ever so faintly, she could see a band of light that waved around her for a moment. It almost looked like a tail or something, then it was gone.

Something drew her mind to her brush. Perhaps it was only that she needed to do something with her hair, but then she started to meditate on the brush. It began to tremble, then rose up off the surface of the vanity. She reached out her hand and snatched it before it could sail any higher.

"Mommy, I don't feel well!" But there was no response.

She marched out to the living room to find her mom. "My stomach hurts," she said, expecting her mother to be there, but she was not. Now she was getting worried. Then she noticed the front door was open. She did not want to raise her voice, concerned that someone might be alerted to her vulnerable state. She looked out through all the windows but saw her mother nowhere.

It was then that Evah began to consider her grandfather's words. *You'll get your mother eaten*, he'd said. She considered the size of those cats that were drawn to her. They didn't want to harm her, but who knew what they would do to her mother?

She began to look for blood but found none. There was no sign of struggle, but the door was open. *Maybe Mommy tried to get something out of the house, and it took her.*

Unhappy thoughts began to spin circles in her mind. She could see her mother being attacked and dragged off by the huge cat that had been in her chamber the morning before. But she did not want to think of anything bad for fear she might make it come true—if it hadn't already. Surely her mom wouldn't leave her alone. Something must have happened to her, and it was her fault. Could it have been the neighbors; the upset woman outside the day before? She had done something in front of the children that drew too much attention. Not an extuition, but there was a bird that she'd wanted to see, and it had gone to her. The children had been amazed, and she'd liked the feeling of being special to them. Maybe they'd told their parents, and they had put it together that she was the Extuiter of Constance. Her stomach throbbed, and she was afraid for her mother.

Ever since her adventure to find the crystal in the ancient city, the sanctuary had been calling to her. That's when she'd really started to worry. What if the woman spirit of the sanctuary wanted her to return? Or the suffering man? Or the spirit of her father? Or the weeping God from her journey near death? She was afraid she had not done as she was meant to do. What if the power behind all these things—maybe the lights; those spirits—wanted her to return and they had taken her mother? These were mysteries she did not understand.

These gifts had been given to her, and it was a delight to do fun things with them, but what if there was a price? They had read the books written about her ancient culture and thought they were half-truths at best. Was it possible the stories of the Goddess of Death were fact, and her mother had been taken as a sacrifice? For even then in her confusion, the sanctuary was clear in her mind. The face of that woman was clear in her mind—the woman who appeared and disappeared so strangely.

Deep down inside, she knew she was supposed to return to the crystal and the sanctuary, but she was afraid. What she told her grandfather was true. *It was all happening so fast.* And tears began to fill her eyes, for there was a burden she did not want to accept, but she knew she must. It was the calling of her people. It was the calling of the extuiter, and no one else in all the worlds of Spirea could answer these mysteries. She wanted her father. She wanted him to hold her hand into the mystery. And she wept because life is scary.

For all the shapes of this world that make us unhappy, that shake us up, that give us hurt and grudges to hold on to, when we see past them, there is a destination we are heading towards, and we do not want to go alone. It is this way even for extuiters. Maybe especially for this extuiter. Though, I suppose it is this way for every mortal who is aware of a unique and unexpected calling that has only to do with them.

Evah washed her face and put on some clothes, then she started out for the sanctuary, leaving the empty house behind. By the time she was getting close, the sun was rising to its highest point in the sky. In the distance, she could see some activity of lights. The amethyst lights.

One popped over some of the tall plants as if to get a look at her. It traveled along with her a few steps then shot off in the direction of the sanctuary. She noticed the forest was quiet—no birds were singing; no bugs were buzzing or clicking. She could hear the sound of the spring running its cool water over the rocks and into the stream. She wondered if she might find her mother there, held hostage and possessed in some supernatural dismay, or worse, murdered there as some offering in a show of cruelties to the flesh that only the most wicked mortals make.

The thick of the forest broke open to the view of the sanctuary. Now, its four pillars and stone slabs of floor and ceiling were home to a show of extraordinary lights, and the crystal hanging in the center was full of amethyst stars. It shone brightly and pulsed, the sanctuary full of its presence, the light shimmering, and golden rays slipped all around.

Above the sanctuary, like eight or ten enormous fireflies, were more of the amethyst lights. They spun round like things caught in a cyclone, dipping in and out of the opening of the roof.

Evah stopped near the carved statues she had cared for and cleaned, and looked at the levitating man and the woman in the trance below him. She took a moment there before the sanctuary to remember what it was like to be a child. Her little body ached. She knew her skin and bones may be forever changed after she entered the sacred place, and she stopped to think of the moments she had known love as a child. There were thoughts of her father she did not think she could find. They were kind. And there were loving thoughts of her mother too. Then the sound of Kofutu's jangling string instrument played in her head, and she remembered what it felt like to dance with the other children in the afternoon shade, and how they all banged with unhindered passion on everything they could find to make their percussive bliss. And with this joy in her heart, she crossed the threshold into the sanctuary that brimmed with the bright energy of its numerous souls.

At first, she saw the light all around her. The crystal was somehow twisting back and forth. She could see the forest, but only for a few moments. The sun reached its highest place in the sky, and its light entered the sanctuary as a concentrated beam into the crystal, the amethyst glare and waves of gold saturating the space as everything outside disappeared into blackness, and day became night.

Evah sat beneath the crystal, hugging her knees, and put her head down. She noticed the dark was on the floor then, and the lights were slinking and sliding around. Suddenly standing before her was the woman who had given her the charge of clearing the sanctuary. In the air, there was so much silence it seemed they were in the vacuum of space, departed and adrift from Hypathia. Only a gentle *tink, tink, tink* of something bobbing against the crystal could be heard, and then that too was gone. The face of the woman of the sanctuary filled her mind.

"The spirit of the horse still betrays you. You will not find what you seek here. You are not the Mother of the Children of the Water. You are the Crystal, for you are the first to come. The functions of your people will take a hundred years to be rebuilt after being vanquished for so many centuries. The Children of the Water are scattered. Even now, there are others like you, but they do not live in lives where their gifts are novel playthings. They live hard lives, and to them, their gifts are like hearing or blinking—daily motions to survive. The judgment will be yours: Should they come home or will the worlds be swallowed up? Too long now have the doors of creation been closed, and in the passages, the spirits of the hungry run loose; the spirits who betray the creation. Now they are here."

Evah looked around and saw there were creatures like demons in the dark around the sanctuary. Time and darkness swept around them, and they appeared as something revealed in a storm of sand. Now a part visible and then another, but still it could be discerned they were a multitude.

"Now they try to reach their wickedness into this world through the living. The weak-minded and confused, the suffering and the abandoned, who would abandon themselves to be free of pain. The hungry rob through them to reach this world."

Then the spirit mother brought Evah's focus back to her, and she was relieved. "The Children of the Water can no longer walk the passages between the gardens. Even a thousand years ago, it was only for the new spirits on their journey to becoming. Now, those spirits have rested on the breast of the Kingdom of Naaheen too long and must be born or return home.

"You have seen the cities of the sons of Thwargg and the sons of Sharvanna. All the body of creation is dismembered, confused, and rambling in the quick of the shadow outside the spring of life. Outside the garden. The builders of this realm have sought to reconstruct mysteries of the everlasting in the working of their science and equations. Gods unto themselves. Should we continue past the end of worlds again? Now the time is coming. But ask: Ask that of what troubles you."

"Where is my father?"

"He is but a servant awaiting your call. When it is your time, you will know. For you have seen all these things. The water of life you will carry must go to the kingdom above the falls where you have not entered."

Then the ground was no longer beneath the weight of Evah's body and hundreds of spirits came into her—the longing of tens of thousands of years of experience all together. Then we went out through the vascular system of the cosmos, and as we were in relation to the realms of the known worlds, we were in relation to the farthest and most unconsidered regions of space. We visited the fountains where consciousness emerges, the unsuspected places of origins that gave up the benefit from conflict pressed out of other places and times in the multiverse.

Evah's body abounded to the ceiling and unwittingly tangled near the chains of the crystal. Then all that went down seemed to go up. Her person was ignited with the source of a million dreams lost in the Naaheen landscape for all those years since the murder of the Mother and the end of her people, and it shone out of her as the light of a star. The sanctuary was like a craft—a vestibule onto the chasms of eternity, to where the mortal is brought as a witness of the endless length and depth of existence's gauzy presence.

When the fulfillment of the long-awaited convergence into the Living Crystal was complete, the sanctuary returned to the Forest of Eshlam. Now the child levitated above the stone ground in a suspended trance. It was night, and though darkness was all around, Evah appeared like an illuminated being whose blood and tissue shone like the mantle of a lantern. The sounds of the forest had returned in a thriving, pulsing rhythm.

There was a disturbance through the tall plants, but whatever creature made noises stopped to watch for some time and made no movements. Then another person was in the sanctuary, unwrapping a long garment from around their body. It was Kofutu.

He wrapped the levitating child with his garment, untroubled by pain or shock. Nor was he seized by spirits or guardians of the forest. Evah was bleeding, though she had no wounds; the young girl had started her first menstrual cycle.

Kofutu closed her eyes, which had been sprung open in shock, and, holding her in his arms, he brushed his hand up under her chin and closed her mouth. She was weightless, and neither sank nor rose in his embrace. He brought us back to Evah's mother, who had been awaiting her return for hours. Skenkin had been afraid to raise too much attention in the populated region. She did not want the broader population of the people to know who Evah was, or what was going on. Nor did she want to draw the further attention of her father, so she spoke only to a select few. Kofutu, who was loved by the children, was the first she'd talked to of her daughter's disappearance.

Kofutu carried Evah to her room, but her state of weightlessness was unchanged. They placed her above her bed to catch her should she fall from her suspended state.

"She is not sick," Kofutu told the worried mother. "This is what the neighbor woman was yelling about the other day. It is like something from old stories of the people here."

"How long is this going to last? Do they know?"

"They know nothing. We know very little anymore," Kofutu said with the defeat of a lost culture. "But you must be careful who you tell. I don't know what could happen. This power must be treated with care. There are surely laws. Laws of the unknown. They must work their ways."

Skenkin could not leave this circumstance uncontained. She was concerned about Evah's health. She contacted Sanje, who arrived with a small medical team. There was another of the magisteria with him to witness what was happening to the extuiter. Sanje could no longer leave himself exposed to rumors and allegations that he was in some conspiracy to control her, so the female magistere watched on with the others as the medical team checked Evah's vitals and determined she was in good health. Afterwards, the magistere witness left, and Sanje remained with the medical team in case there was an emergency.

In the middle of the night, Sanje awoke to the sound of thuds. He jumped up, expecting to see someone trying to break in the front door, but there was no one there. Heavy rainfall had moved in from the direction of the sea, on the far side of the old ruins, and was tearing at the roof. Looking out the windows on to the front of the house, Sanje discovered a thick fog hanging in the air. Then a terrible bang shook the house further and there was a loud shattering of glass.

He met Skenkin in the hall near Evah's chamber. With a racing heart, he stepped forward to open the door, but there was no intruder. The bed beneath Evah was now hovering a foot off the floor, and to the right was the vanity table, its mirror jammed up hard into the ceiling. The gleaming shards of the shattered mirror dangled through the air like a frozen cascade of water.

In her shock, all Skenkin could think of was how dangerous the glass could be for her child. With shaking hands, she rushed in to clear it away, but as she plucked a jagged piece from the air, she turned to tell Sanje something, and four shards darted at her fast, lodging deep in her skin. She collapsed back towards the door in terror as the vanity slammed to the ground like it had been thrown by some raging giant. It nearly crushed the sometimes erring mother. Sanje brought her out to be treated by the medics, who had already awakened due to the ruckus. Her wounds were not serious; the shards had not struck any major veins or arteries.

"I don't think she meant to do it," the mother said as her wounds were being cleaned. She was trembling.

"Skenkin, I don't know if she's in control at all." Sanje tried to be steady, speaking with a mixture of sympathy and unmistakable concern.

Evah, in fact, was not in control. But I was there. Watching. This was the conflict she had wrestled with for so long, spilling out into the world. Deep inside, she wanted to show her mother how dissatisfied she was with her ambition and the betrayal of her father. The forces working upon Evah overwhelmed her senses, but I could see and did not try to stop her. This was a power no one could contend with, and soon, if she would give her will to me, it would be mine.

They did not enter the room again until morning. When they did, they found any further secrecy was going to be impossible. In the large clearing of land outside Evah's window was another extraordinary structure. This one towered over the house by a fully developed second level. It was made of the alien pearl substance, and the windows still had the appearance of jewels. This time, though, there was a transparent sliding door. When one waved their hand near the windows, they evaporated, but nothing other than air could enter or go out.

I wanted our grandpa to be pleased, for there was still, I hoped, another story to be told between us. Sanje was overwhelmed by the manifestation and wondered how long it would remain, if it was an extuition. He was uneasy exploring it, though he did with trepidation, for he understood, though he had not seen the dreams of the past as Claren had, that this was a power of indefinable seriousness. A power hitherto unknown by modern science and far beyond the bounds of the extuiters he had known.

Before long, there were crafts in the air above the new structure, and the Spirean news was flush with amazing stories to disperse among the people.

Evah had to be moved. A military convoy was brought in, but no one knew how to handle the young extuiter. They did not know what would happen to the vehicles or surrounding environment wherever she would travel.

After much debate, it was determined they would bring out a crate to contain her. It was made of heavy dark metals with only one door and a small barred opening for a window. It measured perhaps seven feet high and six feet wide in either direction. Skenkin's heart ached at the thought of such a contraption being used to contain her daughter but agreed for Evah's safety and the safety of others that it must be done. By placing the containment unit up to Evah's window, armored guards were able to move the girl, who was still light as a leaf on still water, inside.

Crowds and the press had gathered to see the source of the fantastic things going on, but no one made any official suggestion that what was being kept in the metal box was the extuiter. Guards were appointed to keep watch over the pearly miracle, and the convoy departed.

TERMINUS

Chapter 1
Asylum

The opulent blanket of silver clouds in the Constance sky sent light spring showers to the ground, pricking up the chalky tones of the old outer city. Dilapidated buildings stood like abandoned monoliths, formed by a people who no longer wanted them. In places like this, you could find the lower-income populations surging into the leftover ruins of the region, pleased as faux nouveau riche to finally be getting their still-standing, if not illustrious, piece of the pie. It took a brutish spirit to survive here, under the oppression of desperation. The most exemplary brand of faith was demanded to quell the pains of survival and the temptations of criminality that slinked in every shady corner, jeopardizing whole circles of families.

It had been two months since Evah's immersion into the deep mysteries of her people. Some elders on Hypathia still held on to fragments of their history. They said the light of the light rested in the heart of their ancestral people until they were delivered to their lives among the mortal gardens, but the ritual needed more than one person. They did not know what would happen if others were not found to share in Evah's burden.

Many officials of the Constellation government had no desire to see such a joining of mystic figures. Some wanted Evah destroyed, citing if such a way of life was dead, then for the sake of the living society, there should be no Hypathian rebirth. They had kept my daughter in the catacombs of a secret military facility deep beneath the ground near the capital. Now, we were being moved in a convoy to a Constance construction site meant to be one of the inception points for what the newly elected Prime Minister called the "Reconstruction Era." The new extuiter was to create free housing and medical facilities.

News had spread through the system of Evah's survival and the building she had created, but that was nothing in comparison to what was being asked of her now. Galneea was relying on the successful extuition of three enormous complexes as the foundation of his "reconstruction" plan because his platform for the Prime Minister race was to produce a foundation of support for the poor, then redistribute essential resources on previously underdeveloped worlds such as Sabia and Hypathia. Really, though, he was expanding the business interests of his longtime partners by giving them all secure holdings in the infrastructure of two new worlds: New cheap labor, new government kickbacks and war profiteering in the recurring skirmishes of quickly growing unstable regions plagued by political and tribal conflicts, not to mention the disparities over newly coveted natural resources. If he could make them money with planet development, he was sure to reap the benefits when he moved back into the private sector.

Evah's new gifts were now in demand, but what she had inside of her was a mystery to all of us. It felt like we were trying to put a rope around a twister; a wild thing that existed for its own purposes, sacred though they may be. These were not things I could guide my daughter through—I could barely communicate with her at all. A new presence had consumed her entirely; she was not the girl she was before.

Sanje and other magisteria initiated investigative probes to undo corrupt circuits of power in the Thwargg wards. The aim was to expose colluding individuals from organized crime and dirty businessmen from all worlds of the system, then charge corrupt politicians. But people of prestige, like Galneea and my father, rarely see the inside of a jail. There are laws that protect them and representatives that protect them even better.

When the probe concluded, thirteen mid-level Thwargg managers and three upper Thwargg managers were indicted; a couple of judges from Thwargg and Constance too. The entirety of the networks Sanje tried to hold accountable was too vast, and the investigations fell apart, having lost momentum. I think it was inevitable the investigations failed because even somewhat decent public officials will often protect the dirtiest of their fellows. Perhaps out of loyalty and reverence to the common risks they all take "for the good of the people," or out of fear they would be brought down too for some petty transgression they'd committed at one time or another. It takes a lot of courage to stand up and be heard when all your brothers and sisters might turn their backs on you and make your life hell. Luckily, Sanje was not murdered or jailed himself as some rebut for his courage, for he was our last honest friend in the government.

Blouty Duthane did not fare so well, losing everything he'd worked so many years to earn. He pulled through as a star witness but had to walk away from the wards forever, his property seized and sold off by the government. Everything was liquefied then the funds were secretly sent to him where he was living a new life on Sabia.

My father was exonerated of any corrupt connection to paid-off dream loops for the rich and powerful, and of any direct link to private information harvesting. Everything he did looked like clean bureaucratic processing, though he did have to pay a fine for using experimental Thwargg technology. "The white room incidences," as every press outlet had begun to call them, only boiled down to a few business meetings and familial interactions, according to evidence, and my father claimed he was experimenting with it as a new form of communication.

It could not be proven they were conspiring to stage an attempted assassination on Evah's life either. Even in the deep fractured places of their unconscious minds, they refrained from self-incriminating phraseology. Cleanliness is close to godliness, and they did love to think of themselves as gods. It is those with cunning tongues who can without fatigue tend to the assurance of their own worshipfulness all day and night.

The evidence Blouty offered was weak, and the assassin claimed the motivations were his own—that it was an act of revenge for the displacement of kepplequer workers after the Constance terrorist attacks. Even my own testimony made no severe damage to my father's reputation. Due to the dynamics of my relationships with my father and Evah, my statements were submitted without appearing in court. They were found uncorroborated, despite the white room evidence.

The investigation could not hamper Galneea's political drive either, and though some vowed they would reopen investigations once he was free from the laws protecting him from being indicted as a sitting Prime Minister, I do not think he will be burdened much further anyway.

And so it is now that Galneea and my father are Prime Minister and Minister of Health.

Since my father's release, having Evah moved to the development site was his first show of force with the full cooperation of the Prime Minister. He commanded his constituents in government as he had in the wards—a good show of might to let naysayers understand his ideas would be taken seriously. Together, the two of them kept the Constellation of Spirea enthralled with their antics, masters in a game of strategy.

The moment you'd think they agreed on some ill-reputed policy, opposing politicians would take a side against them and then the two would split. They'd stir up a circus with some name-calling rivalry and capture the support they had generated in opposition to their former positions, picking apart their naysayers with sly sideways tricks and dealing in rumors, the threat of bad decisions, turnarounds, and fear-mongering whenever they could. Then they'd grandstand in defense of popular issues, just enough to always stay on top in public opinion with the people.

Of course, to me, it all looked like the family politics I had grown up with. Being buttressed in such ways and forced in directions I despised were tactics I had known all my life. Now, here I was handling my daughter as my father had always wanted. I wondered how it was that people like my father always got the better part of their desires. With some people, nothing is withheld, and there is little that keeps them from taking.

Our convoy was nearing the development site on the side of town I rarely had a need to visit. It could have been some alien planet, it seemed so foreign. And though the convoy floated along with a confident sense of direction, I'd scarcely known where I was since we'd crossed the commons borderline. I only knew we were near our destination because a large portion of the city buildings had been demolished, leaving a gaping vacancy in the cityscape.

The top floor of an old hotel overlooking the demolition site had been prepared for Evah's arrival. The building had been cleared of unnecessary furniture, the walls stripped clean, and special lighting fixtures had even been installed. They lay in anchored furniture, in her suite, and the connected sleeping chambers. Everything was to be bolted down.

Turning onto the avenue leading to the hotel, I could see it was like a ghost town. The military cleared the surrounding blocks and we pulled up to the front entrance of our temporary abode. Somehow one man had found his way onto the walkway across from the hotel, but the armed guards swarmed on him to thwart any further assassination attempts.

He was lying on the ground, but he didn't stir when they approached, yelling commands. It turned out he was a sick, homeless man dying right there on the side of the road, and medics attended to him as Evah's heavy metal crate was unloaded from the transport. If she was near her little barred window at the time, she might have seen him as he was being treated and prepared for transport to a nearby hospital.

The crew moved the metal crate into the retrofitted entrance of the hotel. In the last month, Evah's appearance had changed. What had once been a silver light around her was changing every day to something more golden, and twisting bands of energy emanated from her body, undulating in the air. From the window in the crate, her light shone out like something from the sun.

The crate was elevated on graviton repulsors that helped it glide around with little exertion, and they took her up to her suite in a service elevator. Every entrance had to be retrofitted to allow for the crate's transfer.

They brought her into her suite, setting the crate down about fifteen feet from the glass doors of the balcony that overlooked the demolition site. Two guards remained, and everyone else was cleared from the room to allow Evah and I some time alone. I approached the door of her containment crate to speak with her.

"Evah?"

There was no response.

"Evah, you aren't a prisoner. This was the safest way to transport you, that's all. We didn't want you or anyone else getting hurt. I'm going to let you out now." And with that, I opened the door.

Though she did still levitate, she had now regained her ability to walk and, to make it easier, she was fitted with a gravity modulator similar to the type the Scabeeze used.

"Do you want some help?"

"No," she said, but she no longer spoke as other mortals did. One did not hear her with their ears. Now, her communications were heard in the mind. It was like the whispers of three hundred voices, both male and female, at once. I backed away to make room for her.

She walked out into her new environment. She was still only four foot three, but when she walked, it was the walk of a powerful woman. Her garment was long and loose, something like a nightgown hemmed at the knees. We kept her hair tied back for simplicity, if not to simply keep her from looking like some crazed thing.

The walls were dashed with a yellow glow, and all around the room were bending rays like sunlight shimmying through the refraction of water. She shone brightly, but it did not hurt to look at her.

The bands of energy wove around her in a slow hypnotic dance. She did not look at me, but I don't know that I wanted her to look at me, for the intent behind a glance from her might have dangerous repercussions. We did not know.

She moved sleepily towards the balcony and stopped within the archway to survey the empty landscape before her. The demolition site had been poured over with a foundation making it appear like a snowy plain that extended for two city blocks amid the evacuated containment area. It seemed like the sprawling, lifeless, hollow estate of some hermit king—though in this case, the vast empty estate of a newly fertile hermit queen.

"It would have been better at the temple," I heard her say in my head.

"What temple?"

"The traitor's temple. Haytoo's temple," the whispers chimed. The name sent shivers up my spine.

"Evah, how do you know that name? Is he one of the spirits inside you?"

"No. The spirits with me are pure."

"Oh... That's good," I mumbled under my breath.

"Grandfather's here."

There was a knock on the wall where the entrance had been knocked out and covered over with heavy drapes. The break in the silence startled me. I scurried to bid him come in. He had not seen Evah in maybe two weeks and when he did it was clear even he was overwhelmed with the sight of her.

"Oh my goodness," he said to himself.

"I think she can hear you," I warned him. "I think she can hear maybe... everything."

"Hmm." He looked at her with his personal brand of tenacity, as if he were summing her up. As if he could sum her up. Then he began to slowly walk towards her. "Evah? Can you hear my thoughts?"

"Why would I want to hear your thoughts?" the whispers rose—apparently in both of our heads.

"Well. That could be overwhelming. We have to be careful about that. Has she spoken anything with…" He gestured to his mouth as if he were pulling out words. "Evah, can you speak… uh… using your voice?"

But Evah gave no reply. She did not even turn away from the balcony to look at him.

"Well, we'll do it your way for now. Maybe that precious ability will return."

He walked towards her, and although it was an excess of ego that made him self-possessed, I was impressed. He stopped where it was convenient to whisper his will in her ear as they surveyed the view.

"This is all for you, Evah. Now is your time," he encouraged. "You will be pleased to know that your first structure still remains. You've done it, Evah. You have made something that will remain. We have moved our developers in, and they are at work now—"

"A home?" rang her whispers. "We've made a home for someone?"

My father was silent for a moment.

"Oh. Yes," he replied gingerly. "Of course. It will make a useful home for somebody." I knew he was lying. It was at this time I prayed to myself that she believed him and never found out the truth. My father was turning the creation into a public anthroscope facility.

"Thank you. Thank you, Grandfather."

"Now, we move on. Now you shine. Show the people of the Constellation of Spirea what is possible."

"I will," her whispers filled our minds.

"Do your best with it, and then we go back to Hypathia for the reconstruction inauguration. It will be a big celebration."

"Will it be on the first day of summer? That is when it must be."

"It could not be on that specific day. A couple of days after. There are some financial matters, backing, and some other matters that must be respected."

"The work would have been greater on the first day of summer."

"Well, let's see what we can do here. I want to show you something. This is something we must find a way to incorporate into the work."

He touched a button on his kalodia wrist band and a projection of the foundation-covered construction site sprang into the air. "There are four power access points here, as you can see, and six water inlets. If this is going to have more than one story, which I figure it will because I know you're an ambitious girl, the water must reach up to the top floors."

Then he touched the kalodia band again and a holographic projection of a building appeared over the site. Using his free hand, he gestured with commands to zoom in and out on regions of the site, then he turned the projections in different directions to make his points. "We have experts standing by who will be more than happy to consult with you about how these things will work best."

"Yes. If they will not be afraid."

"Well, they're going to have to have courage. This is far too important to leave things to chance."

"There are certain things I cannot change or achieve as you think they should be done. There is a natural process that may not heed blueprint demands. I will make a way for the water and some power use. These manifestations are not meant to be powered as you think."

"Then how are they to be powered?"

"By me, I think. And by the spirit master that has chosen me."

"Well, I can't say that I understand that, but you know what we need." Then he paused for a moment.

"What is it, Grandfather? Tell me what's on your mind."

"What if something should happen to you, Evah? I must insist you create the capability for power-source installations and lighting. It's too many demands to put on you. To sustain all these projects. And how long could you maintain them? If something happened to you, our legacy would be lost."

"Thank you. I understand."

"I want to give you something."

My father pulled a small box from his pocket and held it out for Evah to take.

"This is a kalodia band. Like the one here." He held up his wrist. "It has the specifications of the additional sites on Sabia and Hypathia, though the Hypathia site is a little bigger. You will see we have made the Sabia site identical in dimensions to this one, and the same in every way I discussed with you today. You can look at them whenever you like. What else can I do for you to help us get the things happening that we need?"

My father was feeling the strain of fulfilling the promises he had made. All the Constellation of Spirea was watching, and if this wasn't successful, he would go down as the greatest idiot in ministry history.

Evah turned and began returning to her crate, whispering in our minds as she went.

"You should have listened to me about the first day of summer. That is when the power will be the greatest. I know that site is more than twice as large as this. The waiting could damage me. And get me something soft to lie on. Right here. I must be close to the place of the beginning of things." She spoke her final words to him as she stepped back to her metal waiting room. "I will see your experts."

In the hours that followed, construction advisors took their turn having meetings with the shining extuiter, and though they had seen her little creation on Hypathia, they were hardly believers. But they were amazed when they saw her, for she was unlike anything they had ever come in contact with. These were the builders of cities, the builders of towers, and magnificent mortal achievement. What was speaking to them in their minds was a presence of unquestionable power, but still, they only saw a little girl who made things with pretty windows. All but one thought this entire idea a ridiculous impossibility. Only one. And it was not me, for I too thought this impossible, and despised my father even more than I already did, thinking of the demands he was making on Evah.

"Great Mother of the people," said one Hypathian man who had come to discuss, of all things, plumbing. Never before had I thought of the developments of sinks, toilets, and showers a holy subject, but this man seemed to. "It is my great honor to serve your needs."

"Welcome, my friend," she said. And when she spoke into his mind with these words, he got down on his knees. "I am not the Mother; I am the Crystal. I am only a servant too. Please help me. Show me how you would move the water through the palace from the heavens, and I will give you a blessing, if you will have it."

He brought out some diagrams, then samples of materials and finally explained dimensions that could help the creation be built upon and added to. Many of these things were not considered in the first creations on Hypathia because they were unplanned events. After his work was complete, he stayed a while longer.

"Though the blessing is already mine to serve you, tell me of what you spoke of earlier," he said with humility.

"Your wife is pregnant, is she not?"

"She is."

"Your child will be born a female. If you serve her needs, she will receive the spirit."

"I will."

"She too must decide it should be her destiny."

"I understand."

"You must name her Kahtura. She will be one of the three mothers should the time continue."

"I swear it will be done."

"You must go now, but be certain to bring your wife to the ceremonies on Hypathia. You need only be there to receive the blessing. Do not be troubled. They will not let you see me."

The man thanked her and left.

"It's almost time," she said to me. Night was falling. Through the balcony window, I could see that a vast system of clouds had formed, perhaps out over the nearby sea that led to the Constance canals. Evah lay her shining body down on the newly installed bed, and the lights were brought down low. Everyone was cleared from the room; the few that were permitted to see Evah.

"Goodnight, my love," I said and began to make my way to the chamber that was prepared for me.

"Mother. Mommy," she said. That was a word I had not heard in some time, and really, I'd expected never to hear it again.

"Yes." I returned to her. "What is it, Evah?"

"Will you stay with me?"

I turned to go and sit in a chair nearby. "Of course."

"Will you lie with me?"

I hesitated.

"I promise I won't hurt you."

"Oh, I know you don't want to hurt me—"

"It will be all right," she said in my head.

I approached her. I was afraid. There was so much we didn't know. Evah hadn't been touched, not even directly by a doctor, since her latest transformation.

I sat down on the bed. There was a warmth from her. I was lying in bands of energy that surrounded her body, but there was no discomfort. I hadn't expected her to need to be held. This tremendous power had consumed her, and I didn't know what she felt, if anything. She had become so shiftless on the surface. I saw no joy or tears; no childish antics. Only a stoicism of sublime power, but it was occurring to me per her request that the serene immovability upon her face was the expression of someone carrying an immense internal burden.

"What's the matter, Evah?"

"I don't know if I can do it, Mommy. I don't know what they will do to me if I'm useless to them and still look this way."

"You're beautiful to look at, Evah."

"But I know there are some who want to destroy me. I know they're overwhelmed. So am I. There's a force within me that wants to refuse their demands. I'm afraid, Mommy. Don't go away. Not for anything."

This time, beneath the more solid whisper of her words was another voice whispering, "Don't go away. She is with me." It was like an echo behind her words.

I looked out through the balcony window to see a white fog rolling in fast from the direction of the storm. Nothing was certain, even Evah in her power.

I closed my eyes and stretched out beside her, and my hand found its way to her arm. She was lying on her side facing the demolition site. I pulled a blanket up from the foot of the bed to put over me.

"Cover me."

I did, then I drew in close to her and held her. The light of her body was not bright. With my eyes closed, it was as if I were holding my child and not an ethereal goddess come to mortals. She was like any other child in my arms, though the bed was adorned in golden light and those bands of mysterious energy.

Then I was asleep. It was such a deep sleep. I dreamed; I dreamed that I was forgiven and that Varin had returned. He had only gone somewhere his skills had been made greater. And I told him I didn't want him to be an extuiter, and he and Evah were pleased. I could feel his breath on my ear when he kissed my cheek.

I closed my eyes to savor it, and when I did, there was another dream. My father was in prison, and no favor from the powerful or any manipulation could free him. They created a special prison for him and Galneea. In a dark place, he called out to me; he told me he was sorry for using me all my life—that there are better ways of love he had not considered. Better reasons to have people love you and need you; better reasons than to make yourself great power. The darkness all around us was unbearable. It was as if something was watching us—something that loved our pain and remorse.

"I do not know how long I will be gone, Skee. I may never be set free," my father said to me. There was a weakness in his voice. "But I am trying to find a way to be forgiven. There are ways of the world I did not know I should say no to, and I know it was that way for you because of me."

In the morning, before the sun was up, I awoke. The white fog was on the demolition site, and there was an electrical storm spatting and flashing inside. I thought, as I peered past Evah's body, that the miracle we needed was happening. I was so thankful. I lay my head back down and continued to hold Evah, then I fell asleep again.

When I awoke the second time, the sun was up. Evah stood before the balcony doors watching the site. I did not know what her creation looked like, nor could I see it from where I lay, but I knew something had happened the night before.

I stood up and walked to the window with anticipation. Evah took no notice of me. There was nothing there. Nothing. Nothing had changed.

I was terrified. My breath was shallow and fast, and I started to think of how I could steal Evah away from there; from all of them. She was still a light of power and mysterious extravagance, but there was nothing on the foundation of the demolition site.

There was a hard rap at the entrance. My father barged in without waiting for an answer to welcome him.

"What has happened?" He walked up to Evah. "This is very disappointing!"

Evah said nothing.

"What do you have to say, Evah?"

Then a swarm of birds filled the air high above the demolition site. There were thousands of them—starlings in a frightening swarm that twisted and contorted through the sky. There were so many it looked like darkness itself was raiding the day to steal away anything that lived.

"Are these your tricks, Evah? Is that your creation? Are you embarrassing me with a show of some stupid animals?"

The swarm shifted in an amorphous riot then swooped towards the hotel balcony. When it seemed sure they were going to crash into the building in a suicidal pact, they rose up like black rain in reverse, returning to the sky.

"I am inclined to leave you here in this empty city until you do what you are told. Is that what we should do?"

"Nothing more can be done here."

"Ever?" He looked at her with acidic spite. It was a look I had seen many times before—a hateful look like a weapon made to disintegrate all the aberrant atoms colluding to defy him.

"Do you know how much money it's going to cost to build these buildings now? No! We will wait. I am giving all that I can to make this world work for you. The worlds have no use for a strange queen who will not work for them. You are not a queen! You are like any other being of the six worlds, and you must give. You must give."

"There's nothing more she can do. She told you. Look at what you're expecting! You remorseless animal! Grazing on the ones who love you, the people who need you, to have your way with the world!"

"Oh," he sighed with contempt. "You think this makes you special, Skee? You think this entitles you to something special? To do nothing? You will work with her to GET SOMETHING HAPPENING. Now I have to go and face Galneea! I have to face the politicians with a thousand disgruntled plots!"

He recovered his composure the best he could. "Please, Evah. It's time. You must make this happen." He sighed again. "I put my faith in you. One thing I can assure you is I will not return here unless there is success."

My father left, and as he promised, he did not return. But he called. In my imagination at first. In truth, I am not a mother who finds that holding your child helps them produce anything of superior quality. That is not how Thwargg accomplish things. She wanted me to stay with her that first night, so I did. So in my mind, there were a thousand words with my father, and a hundred times he was right.

On the third day, my kalodia chimed.

"You know what has to be done. She will benefit nobody should this coddling continue. I know you understand me." Those were his words.

Evah needed more than a life in underground catacombs, and this was our chance to return to the world. She knew as well as I did that the world could be cruel. She had bled once already, and my remorse was making me soft. The burden was making me weak. A little disappearance act would be forgivable.

I was sure she knew—she said so little to me in the days after the first failure. Every morning I saw that damned white plow of virgin concrete. All I could see was white concrete, even past the light she shone. Past the miracle of her being she showed. All I could see was that gargantuan tablet with nothing on it, lying before our eyes day and night, the unwritten story of a miracle we so desperately needed.

I had imagined many times the most effective way to go. She would call *Mommy* to me, and I would be gone. Then her heart and mind would be charged again. With hate and sorrow, and fear, and she would be reborn after the darkness.

When I was ready to leave on the fourth day, she spoke to me.

"Being with you at night is the closest I can remember we have ever been," she said in my head.

She was right. I could say nothing; I had nothing to say.

"It's all right if you want to leave me."

My God she knew—I know she knew. And as I thought that, she went on.

"I know you're disappointed. We are here to do all you ever dreamed of. Why you wanted an extuiter for your... What? Why did you want an extuiter?" The whispers were quiet then. She wanted my answer—wanted to know what in me could control as my father controlled?

"For selfish reasons, Evah. It's easy to loathe my father, but I am not so different. How could I be? But choices have been made."

"And you are disappointed with the results. On Hypathia I thought the cats tore you apart in Eshlam Forest. If you went now, should I think Grandfather has murdered you—that the strong men in the passage outside have broken your body and your will?"

"I'll tell you something, Evah. It's not much of a delusion to think of such things happening. When I ran to Deiphera, I was haunted by how it felt to miss you. To have lost you."

"Really? Is that what haunted you?"

"No. I was haunted by the idea that I could have betrayed you. I was haunted by the knowledge that I could be harmed for disobeying some people who have too much power for their own good. I knew no other way to have you but to go back to your grandfather. To do so was to… it meant I must control you. But those… There are some who could hurt me. They could hurt you. And if I could make an extuited life, in my dream, you would not have such powers to make them want to use you. In my dream, we would not need them, and they would have no care to trouble us."

"This can change. How I am now, but it will not be the end."

I thought of being thrown off the promontory at South Rock again, though I realized that I used the fear as my excuse to do what I thought could get my way. It was the turmoil of a serial coward. Like a hypochondriac using illness to hide from themselves and the world and getting paid to do it. Paid sympathy. I used the conflict with my father to enable my own games, and here we were, and it wasn't a good way that we were in. Because it was born from manipulation before Evah was even created.

My impulse was to use more games to get farther away from the failure of my prior ones. One offense to cover up another. But they were all my choices.

"I won't leave. I'm here. And if it means nothing can be done that is being asked of you, then we will deal with it together. There is so much… power on you. A power that is coming *through* you. I barely know what to think of you. How to understand you. Search your heart, Evah, and tell me, what can be done with me here that you could do better without me? If there is something you could do if I ran away, something you could do if I were taken? Search yourself to find how you can do it with me here. Without games. Because I'm here. I'm not going anywhere. Do you understand? You don't need to be terrorized, and I won't be responsible for doing it."

"I've already done what I can do here."

"All right. Then we'll wait until they give up and call us back. I will wait with you. I will do everything I can to protect you: I will appeal to Sanje and the magisteria; I will fight my father until either there is no more fight in him or whatever end. If you say you have done all that you can, then so be it. I will be with you to face whatever we have to face."

"I'm sorry that it couldn't be different."

"I know."

They waited a whole week more. No one was permitted to visit, and I did not leave. Every morning everybody was filled with the same disappointment. The guards grinned at us, knowing our failure. I did my best to assure Evah that she shouldn't blame herself. Her appearance did not change back to what it was before her pyrotechnic appearance. Instead, the bands of energy around her became more apparent, and her color turned an orangey-yellow. She was more like a burning fire than something bright and airy.

For whatever reason, she studied the off-world demolition sites prepared for her as if she still had a hope of fulfilling my father and Galneea's demands. Then, as unexpectedly as the swarm of starlings in the sky that day my father left, the convoy came back to take Evah away. Everything was packed up, and she was carted out in her metal crate. No one would even talk to me about where we were going, though I overheard some men talking about returning to the catacombs.

Our convoy departed, and the empty hollow of the city area was unchanged, except that now it was a cause for doom—Evah's doom to isolation, perhaps, until she died. If she even could die. But perhaps it really was my own isolation that concerned me the most. In truth, neither of our sufferings would be so finite. We were Thwargg. We could both still live for 185 years.

Chapter 2
The Innocent

When I was a little girl, I imagined many things that made my days wonderful. I was a highly respected Thwargg. I was a beautiful heiress who everyone adored. Sometimes I ruled the world, and sometimes I fought great wars. I was a Sabian nomad and a Hypathian princess of the sea. There was no pleasure embarrassing, no joy too small. I was the maker of things that must be had. I was even a doctor. I made my hair into funny shapes that made me smile all day, and when night came, I imagined my exciting life with the stars as my guiding lights. I was the discoverer of new worlds and the scientist who knew about the relationship between particles and their relationship to me.

When my daughter was five, we called her a wild thing. Her hair was so beautiful and out of control. There was no end to her energy, and she did not want to sleep. She wanted to see every mystery. She painted pictures, and she painted me. She painted me with more importance and character than I had any right to possess, and I loved her for it. And if she would not sleep, I was so happy that she might curl up with me. Her big brown eyes reminded me of all the world there was to see.

On the night after we departed from the hotel, they took down all the barriers and let the people in. It was late. It was dark. It was time for the people to make their way back to their lives; to go to sleep and get ready for school the next day, and for work.

There was a story that got around, about a little girl who did not want to sleep. Her father read her a story, and they played with toy animals, making funny voices together. He left the room and she called him back. He tickled her silly and told her he had to sleep. She called him back again, and he sat beside her bed and made up some other silly tale. He even sang some songs—songs about her being the light of the world to him. And off he went to bed again. But when it seemed he could drift off and get some real rest, his little girl was standing in the door again.

"I want to go there in the morning, Daddy."

"Okay, honey, I promise, but you have to go to sleep now, sweetie."

"Did you see it, Daddy?"

"What, honey? What do you want Daddy to see?"

"It's a castle, Daddy."

"Pfff. A castle! Oh, that's neat. You gotta go to bed, honey."

But the girl hedged around the bed, and then she was at the window.

"Look, Daddy. Look at it," she persisted, holding up the shade of the window. He had taken nearly all he could take, but looking up to tell her to go to bed, he saw it too. Something that had not been there only hours before.

He rose and pulled up the shade, and the child was right. In that vast expanse, where the construction workers had kept the whole neighborhood up late at night and early in the morning, there was a pavilion. A great big one, shimmering pearly white in the light of the moon and the city street lamps. He could not believe his eyes. It was beautiful, he said. There were long curved arches and fountains, though they had no water in them. There were strange but extraordinary lamps that glowed like amethyst stars and did not seem to touch the ground.

"Get dressed. Let's go look at the castle," he said and woke up Mom. They walked out on the street a few minutes later, and they weren't alone.

It is said that there is a scientific phenomenon in particle physics that some things exist, but they do not actually become present until they are observed, or what is observed is changed by the observation. They call it "observer effect." It is a strange mystery. That something can be there all the time, and you don't know unless you're looking right at it, or looking at it in the right way.

I thought back to the morning of Evah's first creation when I heard that story. Well, after all the worlds had heard the story. That morning on Hypathia we all saw her first creation, but not until someone else had seen it first. And the second time, when Sanje was there, I realized now that someone must have seen that one first too: Children playing in the morning. The little girl who first saw the Grand Pavilion on Constance, she was a Hypathian child.

When Evah heard about her, she told me, "She's the Witness. She must come to see me on Hypathia the day of the inauguration. There are others."

The girl was a child of four years, like Evah, when she was wild. I told Evah that little children don't usually show up places because they are told by some stranger. So, Evah wrote a letter. Two, in fact. One was to her parents, thanking them for believing in their daughter and for being such loving parents. Then she invited them formally. She was so gracious. Then she wrote to the girl.

It read:

To my little sister,

I'm so glad you found my palace of the heavens. I knew you would. You are blessed with a gift that is so important to all the worlds.

The Extuiter of Constance, the Crystal

Chapter 3
Mannin Starengon

Two weeks before the inauguration ceremony for the Reconstruction Era on Hypathia, while Evah slept, I finally found the last necessary component for my ascension. I entered into Evah's senses, and when she recognized the discovery I brought to her, she spoke with her mortal voice for the first time in months. The shock erupted like a cracking seizure from her brain with a scream. It woke her mother, who ran to her in fear, only to hear two words escape her mouth.

"Mannin Starengon," she said in a tone her mother had never heard before. But that was all that could come from her mouth. After some convincing words in that chorus of whispers she used to mingle with mortal minds, her mother contacted our grandpa.

"She says she's seen a new structure that must be built in honor of the new ministry. She says it will be your true mark on the history of Spirea. She must have a meeting with Galneea."

"He needn't be troubled," the old Thwargg said. "I can speak for him."

"She says it must be Galneea. It has something to do with a Mannin Starengon."

The old Thwargg fell silent at the sound of the name and ended the conversation.

Hours later, there was a call on the kalodia. Galneea was in the catacombs and was going to meet with the extuiter. The room was prepared, and the guards let the new Prime Minister into Evah's quarters. But when he entered, he was not alone; he had brought Claren with him.

After being seated before Evah like a dignitary visiting royalty, he probed her intentions.

"Hail, little queen," the Scabeeze said sarcastically. "Or should I say the Crystal?"

"Hail, Minister," her whispers filled his head.

"I don't like that, kid."

"There is no other way."

"That's not what I hear. You had a nasty dream, I hear. You used that little mouth of yours to say some dirty words." He waited to observe her response.

"Do you know him?"

"I've been briefed. The question is, do you know him?"

"He is needed."

Galneea laughed. "What do you want, little girl?"

"He will make my power more complete."

"No," Galneea said more to bait her than shut her down.

"I know he is a criminal."

"Tell me about this vision you have had. A new building, I hear."

"I cannot do it without him. It is a monument. It will be the biggest tower in Constance. It will be the new Tower of the Ministry, which will last until the end of ages."

"Well, you have my interest. Why do you want him?"

"I will tell you something you already know. Great things are built upon the suffering of others."

"And this suffering is to be Mannin Starengon's?"

"It is a holy gift to be a martyr. It will be his redemption to the new kingdom after this world if he will accept this burden for the wrong he has done."

"Wrong? Oh ho ho… *wrongs*, child. Many wrongs. Many."

"Where is this tower to be?" Claren asked.

"You must break ground in Liberty Square. Prepare for water and power."

"Oh. Why didn't I think of that? This Starengon is dangerous, child."

"I know what he is. Bring him before me, and he will never be a danger again."

"Do you know where he is?"

"Earth," Evah's whispers came again.

"I don't like you knowing all these things." Galneea sized up the little extuiter for a moment. "No sense in holding our cards too close to our chest anymore, I guess." Then he turned to Claren. "Let's finish this business. Bring Mannin Starengon to the little queen."

"I would be remiss not to inform you that would be a terrible idea, sir."

"Why?"

"I think it's overreaching in a direction we cannot fully understand."

"Oh, I'm pretty sure we can handle it. When will this monument be made?" he asked Evah.

"I should think on the day of the inauguration. If you grant me this, I will create all of the sites on the night before the inauguration."

"All of them?"

"Organize celebrations at all the sites if you wish. It will be done."

"Will he be attending the inauguration like your other invitees?"

Evah was silent a moment. "No. He is not like the others."

"Oh. You must prepare us a list of your special guests. I hear you have been writing lately." Then Galneea stood.

"Will you be changing the inauguration to Constance where the tower will be?" she asked him.

"No. We have some social fixations to attend to. Bring Starengon. There is something else I want to tell you. It's good we're talking. We have decided to change the Hypathia inauguration to the first day of summer as you have asked." He started to leave but turned back to make a point. "You had better not disappoint me. I'm not like Grandpa. You don't disappoint me. I will be the only 'witness' you need that night."

"It will be done."

The Scabeeze minister left. Claren lagged behind.

"Don't be foolish," Claren said to us and followed after Galneea.

Mannin Starengon was a criminal of the most detestable kind. One had to be detestable to be in the Travelers Project. That was what they called the secret work being done to finally create a stable bridge between Spirea and Earth. A secret facility had been established on the burning trash planet of the Constellation system where they sent test subjects through the most extensive network of interplanetary tunnels created, using a combination of several technologies, including an advanced plank gate model. Our people had sent Hypathians and Sharvannans through because they were the closest in appearance to humans.

They began with criminal test subjects because of an extraordinary fluctuation in the space-time continuum. Sometimes a subject would show up in 1939 only to discover some odd part of him or her had been sent to 2235. Sometimes the body would be delivered to one time, but their consciousness ended up in another one altogether. So they used expendable citizens.

When they had stabilized the technology, the subjects were too valuable to destroy, and some were allowed to stay. They were to explore the world and send back reports on all their findings. Mannin Starengon had been believed to have escaped and gone on to a new life on Earth. Someone knew where he was though—he had not been lost to all.

So it was that this attractive though brutish man was eating lunch one afternoon at a street restaurant near the Bab al-Futuh, in Cairo when he felt a sharp snap to the back of his neck and toppled face first into his spicy liver and sausage sandwich. A vehicle appeared out of nowhere and came to a startling halt beside him, shocking the nearby patrons. Those who emerged dragged him into the vehicle and departed; the patrons tried to forget what they had seen and carried on with their meals.

When they finally brought Starengon, it had been three days and ground had already been broken in Liberty Square. Two body-armored men brought the prisoner in and threw him on the ground a safe distance from us. He had a hood on his face and his hands were bound. He wore blue jeans and boots with a leather waistcoat and had been treated badly. Beaten. Maybe worse. His right hand looked strange.

"Get this man a chair," Evah told them. They did as she commanded.

He sat there unmoving.

"You brought the wrong man back for another one of your experiments," came his voice in a low growl.

"What makes you think we are going to experiment on you?" Evah asked in his mind.

"Well, whatever you are, you aren't whispering sweet nothings in my ear. So what are you, and why am I here?"

"Are you Mannin Starengon?"

"Yeah. Mannin Starengon. But I been called a lot of things," he said snidely.

"You've murdered men?"

"If I say yes, you gonna eat me?"

"No. You've murdered men?"

"I try to keep busy." This did not please us. Starengon's chair shot upward, pushing him five inches in the air, then slammed back down with a *WHACK!*

"AARGH!" ejected from his mouth as the wind was knocked out of him.

"Or are you a terrorist?" We would not let him have control of our emotions, and though he tried to hide it, we knew he was shaken.

"Oh, you're something special. I haven't heard the terrorist word in a while. Aren't your people finished with that business? I did what I had to do. We had an agreement."

"The way things are, you may never be done with that business."

The man sighed but said nothing.

"You're here to make a new agreement."

"Do you know what I can do to you?"

"Why don't you do it to me?"

"Evah," said Skenkin. "I don't like this at all."

We stared at her. And in her mind, we placed one profound "Shhh!" with three hundred whispers, while lifting Starengon and his chair from the ground. This time higher. He hung in space four feet above the floor. There he dangled, turning slowly in a circle. We had perfect control.

"Well?" we continued. He did nothing.

"Well, I think you know as well as I do that I've been drugged. But you better keep a careful eye on that."

"No. No, I didn't." And saying that, we drew him to us and swiped away the hood, then drove him back again up into the air. It was not the man I had seen at the table on Earth. There before us was the burned figure of Haytoo.

"It is as I thought. Do you see, Skenkin? But what have they done to you?" We turned his docile body in the air to see him better. His head had a large bandage taped over the right side of his skull. "Yes. They did it."

"What did they do?" Haytoo spoke, but he was clearly amazed by the sight before him. A girl, shining like a sun, with swaying bands of light around her.

"They fixed you. They made you like them."

Haytoo lifted his hands to his head, feeling a three- or four-inch divot in his skull where his brain had been altered. We rocked the chair back slightly to keep him from falling as he slumped, fondling his skull. He nearly slipped out of his chair, but we rocked him back again—this time sharp and hard. "That Thwargg son of a—"

"What Thwargg?"

"Where is that spineless pig Claren? Bring him to me, and I'll *make* him spineless!"

We jolted him sharply forward to a halt and silenced him with whispers only he could hear. "Be quiet! You're looking for a fight you can't finish!" We spun him slowly to see the guards watching from the door.

"Claren gave you Starengon's place in the Travelers Project?"

"Of course."

"And the real Mannin Starengon? Is he... murdered?"

"You said it, not me."

"Oh... No. Where some people are is one of the greatest of mysteries to me."

"Who are you?" he said, hunching forward with his forearms on his lap and running his left hand over his hairless scalp.

"I am the beginning and the passage to the end." Still, only he could hear my words. "I am the way you have been seeking for so long."

He lifted his head to look upon us.

"Urga?" he said as he turned in the air to face me.

We retorted publicly, "That's trash. A fake history made up by the people who conquered our ancient mothers. She's buried and dead. Just another murdered mortal! Isn't that how you see the world? Your history was murdered by hands just like yours. A mind just like yours. It is me you seek now. Your kingdom is not on Earth, and though I think you are better suited for a world of burning garbage, it is through me you will come to the kingdom you seek."

"You knew they would do this to me?"

"I needed to know, but that is not why I called you."

"And who are you?" he said, looking over Skenkin. "That monster of a wife. Wait a minute. Are you the child?"

"Tell me. Tell me, please. Do you know where my father is?"

"No. I thought... I thought I would see him on Earth. I don't know why. He wasn't there. But Earth is a big place. I figured someone like us could get a lot of attention on Earth, but there was no mention of someone with abilities. But you know they aren't much different than us."

"What do you mean?"

"They destroy what they can't control. Most places do. Things they don't understand. That's why I didn't let them know about my power."

"You didn't kill my father?"

"I don't know. He is… He is a man I can't forget."

We searched him for the truth, but in some creatures, you cannot tell the truth from lies, or discern a reason from emotions they hold on to after they have done terrible things.

"You must forget that, as I must forget, Haytoo Valaire."

"What could you possibly want from me other than my head?"

"I am trying very hard lately not to murder everybody too. You're no exception. But I need you. Do you want a place in the new kingdom on Hypathia?"

Haytoo and his chair began to slowly float back to the floor before us.

"I don't know; it's pretty hot there."

"You're going to have to get used to the heat."

"Yes. What do you want me to do?" In that moment, the longing Haytoo harbored for his history and home, the one that had charged his search and cruel actions, emerged gently upon his features. In that moment, we gazed upon some fragment of remorse in the monster. A feeling of unworthiness. Humility.

Then we spoke into his mind so only he could hear again. "I think I need you to save me. Do not speak. No one else can hear these words. Only you can know. There will be a celebration the first day of summer on Hypathia. I think you will need to free me. It must be before the end of the ceremonies. They do not want Naaheen to rise again. You will not be able to do this without suffering. When the time is right to come for me, you will be freed. By me, your power will be restored."

Haytoo raised his eyes to look at us.

"Will you make your vow to me?"

"I will," he said in his mind, and with that, we placed our right hand upon him.

"You must bear my anger and sorrow for a time," we said so that everyone could hear us again. Energy began to transfer between Haytoo and us, a bright golden light surging around his head. He was seized with some trouble and his body clenched. Then he began to tremble, and a sound of horror rose to escape his lips, but it was stifled as he was overwhelmed in a trance that seemed to slam into him. He took our conflict in his muscles and bones and mind. The light shining from his head surged through his entire body, and then he lifted off the ground, falling back into a stasis in the air, floating there as if lying face up. Nothing more could come from him in his suffering.

"Take him to a nearby chamber. He must be close."

The guards moved towards Haytoo but hesitated to touch him as he was still glowing.

"The light will not harm you, and he is unable to."

One of the guards put out his hand and touched Haytoo. Feeling no pain, he gently pushed Haytoo's body through the air.

"Be careful with him and do not let him be disturbed after you've taken him where he must go."

It is so that some people seek for years to be a part of something while others simply find themselves in the middle of it naturally. It was so for Haytoo and my father as it was for Haytoo and I. What one wants, another naturally has. And it makes one wonder whether one is more blessed than another. Special. Was it a blessing for Evah to have such a strange relationship to the universe, that she was this important a phenomenon? We knew Haytoo had felt robbed of being chosen, but now that he was, one must ask if it was really such a blessing to finally be recognized by the mysterious source he longed to find, only to serve in the way he was now. One might ask if it was a blessing to have me as a part of their personality, for what should something like myself be for? It could not be that I was conscious, there and then, at the same time with Evah, in the same body as Evah, the girl who was to become the renaissance of the Naaheen kingdom. Clearly, this was my role. To rule. Yet I sensed her dissent against my darkest will.

"I must be alone, Mother."

"Evah. You must listen to me. If you aren't careful, you will have no allies. And I'm not talking about me," Skenkin said with urgency.

"What do you mean?" our whispers responded.

"Bringing that man into your inner circle is a betrayal. It betrays everything that Sanje has fought for on your behalf."

"His vision is too small."

"His vision is of integration. A loyal vision that cares more for you than my father or Galneea; whatever you're promising them. Think of all the questions Haytoo could answer. Did you know Starengon was Haytoo?"

"Yes."

"Did you have to choose him?"

"No."

"Then why, Evah? Why?"

"Sanje doesn't have the power to do what should be done."

"Is this revenge? Is that what this is? Who am I talking to? It's as if there are two of you. One is my daughter and the other I don't know."

"I could not tell you what revenge looks like. There are hundreds of spirits inside me and more than one voice."

"I beg you to reconsider what you've done."

"I don't know that I can. There is so much that is uncertain now. There are dangers I cannot clearly foresee. Where, in all the system of Spirea, could this new kingdom fit? How?"

"I can't tell you that. I don't even know what this kingdom is. But choosing to mingle with such dark agents can only be the beginning of something more ill-fated. If you continue this, everyone may side against you. Then what chances will you have?"

"I must be alone. No one can be trusted. Every effort I make is seen here. I have no choice but to search this power within me for the answer. I don't know what else to do. I don't know what they will do to you, Mother, but for me, I can't see anything other than the inevitable end."

Skenkin was still as much the victim of her paradoxical limitations as she ever was—powerless and only waiting to be victimized again. Evah did not want to contribute to the dark outcome she foresaw of Skenkin's inevitable loss to the powers that controlled her. "You will lose."

"Lose what, Evah?" she said with the fierceness of someone who knew how vulnerable they were but could not bear to face it. It was the bitterness of a person who, despite what they may show on the surface, truly feels they could not but fail if brought to the test.

"Me. You'll lose me," we said to her.

Skenkin's eyes dropped to the floor. She was going to say something, but she stopped. Finally, she turned in concession and left the chamber with a solemn gait. Finally, Evah believed Skenkin wanted the best for her, and that she understood the price that would need to be paid. It would cost lives, but Skenkin had her limitations, and those limitations were more reliable than her will to be free. Galneea and Grandpa were playing a deadly game of cards, and we needed death in our hand. There was a danger. Not only for us, but the others that were being called, but I did not think it possible to secure safe passage for all of us through the deadly coming period.

Evah understood she needed the deepest part of her power. I was prominent in her mind, and I revealed myself to her in a form she could understand. I was standing before the possessor of our body as a shadow of herself on that cold concrete floor. I held a shape for her someway between the image of her child body and the churning darkness of the cosmic dust I was.

"The end of time is coming," I said, and peered into her eyes.

"No."

"You can't stop it."

"There's another way."

She was startled by something about me. Like she had seen a demon from the black passages of the spirits. She put her hand over her mouth in horror.

"I'm more to contend with than phantoms of the forbidden world."

Evah sat down, and I was beside her.

"They want the power for themselves. They have already begun the plan."

"The mother of the sanctuary said there was a choice."

"No." Again I was before her, looking down on her with her father's eyes.

"We must try to do something. Help me. I know there's something you want more than the end of time."

"What? Love?" I held up my hand and her little monkey from that mobile she thought fondly of was swinging in her face with its teasing "Eeh, eeh, eeh!"

She swallowed hard.

"You want more fun and games?"

"No," she said. Then she could see her little chigraff crawling out from behind me on the floor with its stupid bouncy walk. "Come on, rhino butt. Maybe you'd feel better about it if you were a twelve-armed goddess of death." Behind me, the twelve-armed goddess rose up and snatched up Haytoo's chair in her hulking hands of carved stone. Her eyes like raging fire, she smashed the chair on the ground.

"No."

Everything was gone. The animals. The raging goddess. Evah made them disappear.

"That's your problem. You don't have any fun."

"There's something you want more," she said.

"I'm waiting."

"You want the kingdom."

I was sitting beside her again.

"I can't be all these things we need to make the new kingdom," she continued. "And you need me."

"The kingdom is already mine. Everything you do will only help me to have more of what I need. We are already saved; we just made sure of that. Haytoo can't fail. The world will be erased.

First will come the water, then the new world. You're going to see it my way soon enough."

"There's something in the Tower of the Ministry."

"What?"

"I don't know. Something. The spirits. Don't you hear them?"

"Oh, there's so much noise. You have no idea all the work I'm doing while you're sleepwalking."

"I'm always so afraid," she said. "So afraid of monsters. I never realized the biggest monster could be inside of me."

"Nice."

"We have to stop anything they might do to the others. I'll do what I have to. Maybe it's time to let the monster out. But first the construction has to be done."

"Right," I said with pride. "I'm good with that." And we were one again.

The closer it came to our own destruction, the fewer doubts she would have. She still believed there were redeemable qualities in the rulers of this world.

Together, Evah and I summoned up a record of the things set in motion by our captors and sought a way to send that record of concern to the only people Evah trusted. Our mother was right: Sanje would be our only other hope before everyone finally felt our real displeasure. Sanje or Felin. No one could know we were contacting them—our every move was watched.

We lay our tiny body down and searched for a way to burst out of this physical prison. She joined with me, and we tried to stretch into the field of consciousness. We stretched out with our mind to find Felin, using all the strength we had inside us. We focused together with our eyes closed, and though the room seemed to shift, and even the physics of the material world seemed to bend and loosen their rules, our mind could not enter into Felin's. We tried to send the whispers we so easily placed in all the minds around us into the consciousness of the rat. We tried to will it in countless ways, but in the end, there was always something preventing it.

Evah had never sought through the field of consciousness with me to see the things I saw. In the dark of our mind, we could see Felin on Sanje's desk. He was sleeping, but we could not wake him. Then we tried to reach Sanje directly, but again, there was something in the way.

Going back to Felin, we tried to shift some chemical response in his brain. Then we called on him like some sacred willing priest, as a protecting spirit, but there was no branch of contemplation that would connect to him. Every time we pressed in with our will, something happened that had never happened to me before. A flame appeared, dancing and flickering, and kept us from our goal. It drew all around the far-off shadowy image of our old rat friend.

Finally, Evah fell asleep in her meditation, having lost hope. She even prayed to God as she drifted into slumber. Wondering if it was her presence that had foiled our effort, I made my own attempt, but even I alone could not reach him through the fire.

As I rested my spirit, I fantasized about snatching up that fire and burning down the world with it. Burning up the snare of those who kept us as an animal to do tricks. Though Evah would not concede it true, I knew she hated the world as much as I did, for we were but captives in it. Now, my will would be done. But it would have to wait until the new sun on the first day of summer, for that is when our power would be the greatest. The sites would have to be created, and they would be the beginning of our new kingdom.

Chapter 4
Schizogram

'm so old and stupidly fat. And I measure my days by how fast I can get from one nap to another. I'm the oldest rat I've ever known. I was already old when I met Varin, and since then it's been nearly nine years. What was there left for a fat old furry friend to do now? I'd devoted all these years to someone who was gone, and I didn't know if I would ever see her again. I did not know how long I had to live. The greatest part of my life had been devoted to Evah. All those years, I waited, and then our time together was so short—a ride that took too long to arrive and passed too fast when it did.

Though Sanje's investigation was successful in some ways, I felt we had failed. I could not eliminate the greatest threats to Evah's safety. Everything that had been done to keep her out of the hands of Galneea and Claren now seemed a silly waste of time. Even keeping her from her mother seemed a misstep. Some circumstances were inevitable, it seemed. There were needs she had that I'd never considered, though I knew that without the path of life she'd had, she may never have achieved the great heights she was now achieving. It is hard to comprehend the radical progressions that make up the overall event that is our life in relationship to matter, time, space, and the mysterious unknown. I had not seen her since her transformation into what everyone was now calling the Crystal. To find her purpose, she had to let me go.

When one misses a person, the imagination plays many tricks. The whole of life seems a bundle of interconnected nerves. For me, I imagined we were communicating still, somehow, maybe psychically, and that my purpose had not ended. I believed I could hear her across the strange void of existence, in weird ways. I might see something like her face in a dish of food and conclude she must be thinking of me. I might smell a glillin flower and translate it as some message. I might hear her even in the words that other people were speaking. Sometimes it would be the texture of her voice mixed with another's or the use of words that I recognized, and I'd wonder if she was trying to reach me through another person.

I must confess I was down. And once one has experienced the depths of grief, one teaches themselves to believe that a saving grace can come in immeasurable and impossible ways. One thinks of there being no limit to saving graces as there seems to be no limit to the resounding vicissitudes of sorrow. In continuing to live, one can be tricked desperately by phantoms of hope. So I fooled myself, I guess, to think all of these things meant she still needed me and that we were now in some cosmic conversation.

Finally, though, I'd come to the conclusion that all of these weird connections were really only my ego crying out to itself to be healed and resolved. To finish my depression. Still, though, my mind was rife with rambling self-accusations and fantasies of reconciliation both with myself and the girl I'd lost.

I was lounging on Sanje's desk one afternoon, slipping in and out of dreams, and at the beginning of one such dream, I found myself in a metal box. There were bars that covered a small window where low light filtered in, and I noticed a stream of ants running along the window's edge. Looking back and forth between myself and the ants, I saw that they were growing. They were nearly as big as me.

Suddenly I was a pregnant woman standing before a window that looked out onto a lush green forest. I felt fluids streaming in my belly and then the movement of a child in my womb. In my mind, came the words, "Soon, Kahtura." I was a Hypathian woman on my home planet. My eyes scanned the forest floor that seemed so far away—so far away one would think I was in a tall city building.

My spirit moved in upon the scene of a little girl of maybe four or five. She was playing in some gigantic, fancy dollhouse made of pearl and gems. Then I was sitting in a moving vehicle with the child. There were others there. We were floating along in something like a tiny parade, but outside the vehicle were empty streets. Then there were flames all around us in the vehicle, and we had stopped. The door flew open, but I could not see who was there.

Danger was all around us, and through the door was a vortex of black space. The fire was being drawn into its void, and a battering wind began to ravage the interior of the vehicle. The void was a relentless vacuum with a mouth of twisting flames, and I saw the little child leave her seat, to be sucked out through the door into the vacuum of blackness.

I caught her hand and held it tight, trying to keep her from being yanked out into the nightmarish hole in the world, but the pull was so great that I too began to leave my seat. I was clinging with white knuckles to a handle on the opposing door, but a man who was in the vehicle with us—I think he was my husband—flew into the vortex of oblivion. I could see his body growing smaller and smaller as he was drawn into the endless dark, and I was crying out in grief and terror. Our bodies stretched out in the air on the verge of being stolen away.

When I awoke, Sanje showed me a piece of paper filled with words. He told me that in my sleep, I had started speaking. He said it was as if I were in a trance.

"Write this down, Sanje," I said.

"All right," he responded, a little taken aback by my odd, hypnotized tone of voice.

"They are going to take the mother of the Mother and the little girl who is the Witness. They will tell them they are going to see the Crystal—the Extuiter of Constance—on the steps of the ancient pyramid. While they are in the city, their official motorcade will be attacked. They will take the mother of the Mother and the Witness, and they will destroy them. They must be saved. They have already tried to kill the baby." Then I fell back into a deep sleep only to awake an hour later, not remembering any of it.

Sanje checked the records of official vehicles reserved for such purposes and found that there was such an order made, by Galneea himself. The order directed that a family be picked up on Hypathia, then go out of the way to pick up a family on Constance, before returning to Hypathia for the inaugural ceremonies.

So it was that just when I thought this fat old rat no longer had a purpose, I delivered a message from a source I did not know or understand.

Chapter 5
The Remnant

The stars in the sky above Hypathia had a dreamy strobe and coloration on the eve of the summer solstice. The Pillars of Creation seemed so close that one could cast a stone into the blueish-green solar spray. The pyramid observatory had been changed into a stately location for dignitaries that would come from every part of the Constellation system, and when we arrived with our mother, Evah and I were relieved to see the preparations. It meant the event was going to take place on the first day of summer as we had requested. We didn't know when the desperate final maneuver to control us would take place—only that it would. For now, we were focused on the construction extuition. Whatever was to happen, Evah believed the buildings must be completed.

First, they brought us to the observatory where a room had been prepared for us to make our miracle happen, but Evah explained we had to be closer to the prepared site. Everyone was obliging, and the good spirit was not diminished. They moved us to a platform that had been prepared for the inaugural speeches, at the foot of the pyramid before the edge of the Eshlam Forest. The soldiers erected tents for us there, beneath the stars, in the warm Hypathian night. Standing at the platform's edge, Evah and I looked onto the place where a grove of trees had been cut down for the new pavilion. It was the same site we had seen construction crews working on the year before when we visited the planet for the first time with that Thwargg woman Cordia.

Word had gotten around that there was Hypathian unrest stirring despite the Constance government's attempt to bring an equality of resources to the planet's people. They wanted the resources, and that equality was long overdue, but some cultural purists were outraged that we, the Crystal, were being touted as the gem of the integrated planetary system. They were angry that their cultural history was being further gentrified—that something spiritual was being used to build sites for the glorification of the reigning society.

The security team had prepared an electric shield around the platform to defend all participants in the coming proceedings. It flashed in skittering cascades of light every time some unwitting bug smashed into it mid-flight. We could see the large shield generators around the perimeter.

Standing there before the clearings, we studied the holograms of the off-world sites. Hypathia's foundation area was by far the largest, but the other sites were clearly of exceptional size too. First, we turned the projection of the Sabia site in the air before us, then with a touch of the wrist band, the Liberty Square site appeared. That was where we would make our most impressive manifestation. Bigger than any of the others, it would not sprawl as the Hypathian site. The tower would be a vertical wonder of levels and architectural curves. All of the sites were so far apart, and so far away, but Evah was convinced it could be done.

As we scanned the image of the Constance site, we could see it was a live shot. Armed forces defended the barricaded streets. They had closed the surrounding areas of all of the off-world sites in this way. Now, it was only a matter of when the great feat would be performed.

The feeling upon our body when we set the creation in motion was like that of an illness. It started as a mild shakiness. This being such a demanding extuition, we could already feel it coming on like a fever. Soon we would be able to do nothing else but lie down and sleep. When we did, the power would be taken from us like the draining of a reservoir. We could not foresee how great the strain would be this time. Somehow, all our emotional pain was being stolen into Haytoo's body, in the catacombs, across the divide of space. It allowed us to be stronger.

Our rage was stolen into him too. To think, that person into whom our sorrow and anger pored had been the source of our torment for so many years, that he was now to be our savior, boggled the mind. But Evah could not think too much about this unnatural turn of events. It bewildered her to consider she had nothing good to place her faith in. She wondered what that said about her. About us. We failed to reach our friend the rat or anyone better. She knew we were at a tipping point of nature, and she wondered what would become of her.

In the distant black sky, from the direction of Constance, came a loud *crack*! as a space shuttle carrying Galneea and our grandfather slammed into being on this side of a shipping starslide. I could feel their dreadful presence from the platform as their ship floated to a landing pad at the top of the pyramid.

Then our mother's arms were around our little body, and Evah was glad she did not fear us.

"Are you worried?" she asked.

"No," went our whispers to her mind.

"Good," she said and released us.

"You don't need to stay with me tonight. It could be dangerous. Great power will go out of me. There will be things you will not understand."

"Do you need me to go back to the observatory? I'd rather not."

"No. But you must be prepared. When will Galneea and Grandfather come?"

"In the morning. They said they would stay away to let you do what you need to do. I think they want to see what happens when the structure is made."

"Good. The time is coming soon. I want to get this over with. Tomorrow the spirits could leave me. After the people have arrived," we told her.

"Why didn't you tell us?"

"There are things that can't be disturbed. To let them know, they would think they are losing what is most precious in me, but this cannot go on forever. The spirits aren't meant to be in a mortal body so long. Not this time. Their deliverance is long overdue. If it does not happen tomorrow, I don't know what will happen to me. I'm becoming sick with it, Mother."

"Do you want to lie down?"

"Yes," we whispered.

A billowing body of fog was already rolling in over the ancient ruins from the direction of the Hypathian sea. The mist reached so high it mingled with the clouds in the sky that had started to form. It was like a great white wave crashing into the lush landscape, surging head-on towards us in slow motion. Soon it would come into the prepared site with its flashing electric storm. The time was close.

It was possible this would be the last event of our power for the time being. It could be that as we slept and the creation was done, some force of the universe would complete its cycle and steal away the spirits we hosted. This is not what I sensed would happen, but it was possible. I wanted to hold on to them and never let them leave us. Without them, we would be vulnerable until the next cycle began.

Our body was becoming sick, but the most troubling sickness was in Evah's mind. Her identity was deteriorating. This would be the final struggle before she gave in to me. She needed to be liberated of the spirits, and her body preserved for my command. Then the cycle could begin again. The old ways required a ritual mother to absorb the spirits and let the energies flow into the gardens of life. For now, we served as Crystal and Mother, and that's how it would be for another fifteen years—maybe another generation. Though we had identified another female who would serve as Mother, she had not even been born yet, and thus we could not know if she was to be *the* Mother. The one like Urga. Haytoo would have to protect me as I continued to serve in all functions for the coming years.

The deep of night arrived and the pristine white foundation nestled in the Eshlam Forest was filled with dense fog and the creeping storm. Evah slept and yet I still had some awareness for a short time. Our body pulsed with jolts of energy. Her mother, who lay nearby, was not disturbed. As the process neared its end we blazed like a sun and then our light faded, and as the inner fire dimmed, so did my consciousness, and together we all slept as in some enchanted spell.

In the dark of our rest, we thought we heard our grandfather but drifted off again. When we finally awoke Skenkin was no longer beside us. The sun had not yet risen.

"Come and see, extuiter," came a voice. It was Galneea. He was peeking in through the entrance of the tent. "Come and see. Come on."

Evah rose from her bed, and I could sense she was worried. We could not feel our gifts, and it gave Evah cause for distress. All the suffering Haytoos in the world could not eliminate every thought process that weighed what was happening.

We walked outside to find Galneea sitting in a chair, watching the scene before him in the Eshlam Forest. It was like a confused dream. Everything was still and quiet, except for the hum and chatter of forest bugs, and we noticed the electric field that guarded the perimeter was not making its spitting noises. There were no odd cascading flashes. Beyond that were powerful spotlights twisting their long beams of light up into the sky, and as they moved from one direction to another, we caught our first glimpse of the new pavilion. It was immense. The walls and the roof were long and curved. It must have been at least five stories high, maybe more. The amethyst light shone from inside. The entirety of the foundation site was filled. Evah let out an amazed laugh—a happy laugh from her mouth.

"Yes," said Galneea, sharing in her amazement.

"What about the other sites?" she asked, though still in the whispers of the mind. She could laugh but still make no words.

"You did it. All of the sites. You made them all just as you said you would."

He drew out a hologram pad and pushed a button on the screen, and a hologram of the Sabian site appeared in the air, turning slowly.

"Do you see that? That's Sabia. It even seems to regulate atmospheric pressure."

The hologram showed another building. It was white, like the one before them in the forest, and smaller, but no less impressive a work of art. Around the outside of the Sabian pavilion were more amethyst lights floating in the air.

"But this, Evah, this is truly— Well, it makes one speechless."

He touched the screen again, and the tower at Liberty Square appeared. It was impossible to say how tall it was or how many stories it had because it was simply too large for the camera to capture all of it. It was an exquisite monument that swept upward in sharp curves from the ground.

"They say the top is lit with more of these strange lights. I don't know about the color, but I guess it would be silly to judge such a wonderful creation."

Evah looked at her hands to see if the lights on the creations had been taken from her. It was not the case; light was still all about us. Now, though, it was becoming a deep orange, and the bands that swayed around our person were becoming red. Evah felt warm like she had a fever. Then, the moment of joy faded fast with the realization that the exodus had to happen soon. But what was worse was that we could not extuit. Evah tried to manifest a ruby stone like the one Felin had given to her all that time ago, but nothing happened.

"You've done it," she said.

"Oh. What's on your mind? Something not so nice this time, I'll bet. It's only temporary. Not like what we did to your martyr."

"Are you going to kill the child and the baby? I need them."

"I'm afraid they won't be able to be here. But what happens to them is up to you."

"Well, I want them here."

"But they can't be here. You see, we don't know what's going to become of these gifts of yours. We see what you've done. You have told us these things would happen, and they did. You've also told us enough to know the power could end. Now you've been going on about being some Crystal. That, and these other people you have selected, could be something that is too much for us to handle unfortunately. Do you understand? For the sake of Spirea, we can't allow whatever it is you want to happen to occur. We don't understand it, and it could be incredibly dangerous, so you're going to have to work with us. We've been watching you—the way you go on when you're alone. It doesn't look safe. It's like you're talking to yourself without words and we can't be sure what's happening. Your grandfather thinks you're talking to one of the spirits inside of you, but we both agree it looks like something very serious. And some precautions are going to have to be made. But you should be pleased, Evah. Even without your gifts, the creations remain. We'll wait a couple days and see how things turn out."

"Why isn't my mother here?"

"She's with your grandfather. She's been emotional. I thought it was important for us to talk. I wanted you to know what's going to happen. And I wanted to tell you myself."

He gestured to the two guards that had been watching the platform. One of them set down his weapon then they both stepped forward. "You've done good work. And we need to keep that work the way it is. You can rest now. Rest your mind. Rest your gifts. We're going to help you rest. We need you to behave. If you do these things, your friends will be all right, so please don't fight. Let these men do what they need to do."

The unarmed soldier drew an inoculation gun from a pouch on his belt.

"This is going to be simple. You'll only feel a prick. Then, in a few days, maybe you won't have to worry about being different from other children ever again. I know you'd like that. Do you understand? We haven't decided yet for sure."

"The spirits can't stay."

"We may want you to do some more work for us. What do you say? Do you want to be normal? Or do you want to help us some more?"

Evah said nothing for a moment, only looked at him. Then she spoke into his mind with those three hundred whispers, "I will tell you the secret of your everlasting glory. Some people can only see the worst of what could happen. It's like a prison of their own making. If you search and are not afraid, as most would be, in the places that seem the darkest, you will find the revelation of your power there. It will be a greater revelation than you have ever known."

Galneea nodded to the soldier to tell him to commence with his duty, but as he turned towards the young woman on fire with light, he was suddenly soaring through the air in the clutches of an enormous black cat. He slammed to the ground beneath the massive animal, which mauled him with its vicious claws. Before anyone could think, its great fangy jaws were around the man's throat, clamping down without remorse. Blood sprayed from the dying man as he screamed in pain and quickly pooled beneath him—a warm burgundy ooze that spread quickly. The man tried to struggle, but his life was robbed from him in seconds. The inoculation gun slid along the surface of the platform. Galneea grabbed it up quickly as the other soldier blew off a couple of fast rounds from his plasma rifle. The cat rose up to capture his next prey, but the shots were too brutal, and before the cat could reach the other soldier, it fell with a thump onto the platform.

Then Evah could see me standing before her in my dusty fume. "What are we going to do now?"

I could barely finish my words. Galneea burst through the image of my being to grab Evah by the hair. He drew her in close and jammed the inoculation gun into her ribs, shooting his victimizing drug inside us. We began to slump in his arms and he let us slide lifelessly to the ground. Then we could see and feel nothing.

Chapter 6
The Age of Miracles

Morning came on Hypathia the day of the inauguration. They had waited three days to ensure there would be no change in Evah's condition. More than abolishing the resurgence of the Naaheen ways, Galneea and Claren wanted to keep the power like something in a bottle that they could decant whenever they wished, so they aimed to trap the souls within us. I was finally awake in Evah after days of sleep. We had missed the solstice. They had kept her heavily drugged since her last extuitions; she could not so much as move, and even now, she was unable to extuit. It turned out the observatory, being utilized to welcome dignitaries also served as a suitable prison. Evah was their little queen in their tower. As I was liberated at least to move about the dimension of consciousness, I will tell you what I could see.

Skenkin was as much a prisoner herself, and she stayed close at hand to tend to Evah's needs. On that day after Evah awoke, Skenkin dressed her in the clothing provided—a princess's gown if ever there was one; a petty and flamboyant fashion made with fragile textiles and airy tulle layers that blossomed out from the hips to the ground. This was how they wanted the new Extuiter of Constance to be seen; a princess doll adored. With the fire from within that appeared to burn hot orange and red now, she looked like a fuel-soaked torch.

Skenkin fed and prepared her deeply drugged child for her march to the platform, where she would be presented as a willing consort to the pillaging of her people's spiritual gifts. Skenkin's arms were dressed in purple bruises from her wrestling match with the soldiers days ago—the night Claren left his grand-daughter to the whims of his honored Prime Minister. So as Skenkin and Evah prepared for their dutiful ceremonious act, I reached out to find our new Naaheen tribe members, and observe the condition of our would-be savior: Haytoo, the sadist. The murders were to happen this day—this morning. The Child, the Mother, and the twisted Martyr already had their death warrants signed. Galneea planned to nip all the buds at once and keep Evah as his fettered ward.

*

Saydacone Wivven, the gentle Hypathian plumber and father of the coming Mother, wondered why the official motorcade was picking he and his pregnant wife up so late when the inaugural ceremonies were to have already begun. A line of three vehicles pulled up to their home and retracted their graviton repulsors, lowering to the ground for easy entrance. These were beautiful, official Constance vehicles, all sleek and black and polished enough to see one's reflection in. Taking his wife Binnenbar by the hand, he felt as though she were finally receiving the treat-ment she deserved. He was modest about the honorary consid-erations but felt blessed. In truth, it was a beautiful day. The sun was shining, but it was not too hot, and the wife he adored was perfect in all ways as far as he could see.

"I love you, Binny," he said, because this is how he wanted her to know love—a privilege with many graces for those who devote themselves to walking a straight line in faith and dignity. I could see her through his eyes: She was smiling with pride.

In no time at all, they were in their seats and ready to go. Theirs was the most luxurious of the vehicles. A man approached the door as the graviton repulsors kicked back on with a hum, and the vehicle lifted into the air. The man opened the door and looked up at them from his place on the ground with a smile. I knew him, but from where? He was the major that had helped our father prepared for deployment to Deiphera years ago.

"Welcome aboard," he said. "I'll be running the defense for the motorcade today. You sit back and enjoy yourselves. It won't be long before we're picking up the other passengers, and then we'll be on our way to the event."

He closed the door and made his way to one of the armored vehicles that surrounded the government transport, and they departed on their way to the nearby starslide.

*

The crowd outside the observatory had grown well beyond two thousand people. There was only room for so many between the forest's edge and the platform, but still, the number was significant enough to make a lot of noise. Others were permitted to be in various areas of the surrounding Eshlam grove, and still more were situated around the new pavilion, waiting to be the first to enter. Hologram projectors were positioned throughout the various areas so that Galneea was sure to have his face in every corner of the celebration. Propaganda clips of Galneea and Claren being interviewed about the now-famous slogan "The Reconstruction Era" were streaming everywhere. Galneea could be seen putting on his most astute reproduction of modesty to represent a robust, forward-thinking leader. In between clips of him espousing his grand ideas of energy access to the jilted worlds of Sabia and Hypathia were clips of Evah standing on the balcony of the old Constance Hotel, looking out over the pristine foundation site where her first creation had been made. Giant words rolled through the air that read, "The Reconstruction Era: A Hope for All Peoples."

The day was not without its spectacles. The first were the projections of the beautiful creations on all three worlds, including the extraordinary Tower of the Ministry. Then there were ear-drum-cracking flybys of various military fighter crafts. Considerable effort was applied to stoking anticipation to as near a frenzy as possible, before the people would be permitted to catch their first glimpse of the great "man of the people" himself, Galneea. The Scabeeze would never be thought of as filthy thugs again. But the day was not without its troubles. There was a surge of protestors that made their way into the foreground of the festivities near the platform. They soured the air with chants of distressing slogans, making the event unpleasant for the people who'd shown up just to have a good time and get some food.

The line of dignitaries, including Claren, Evah, and Galneea, began their procession to the ceremony as a Hypathian woman stepped onto the platform to sing the Hypathian anthem. All of the people, even the unrested protesters, fell silent as she began to sing a cappella. Her voice was clear and rich. It qua-vered gently and all the people remembered their solidarity. Her song was like the most beautiful of arias sung in their native tongue—a bittersweet rapture that hung in the air above all the goings-on.

Chapter 7
The Errant Scribe

Sanje had ordered a military Prowler to be armed and prepared for departure. After assigning a military detachment in the secret catacomb control room, he shoved me into his satchel and lifted the strap over his shoulder.

"Wait!" I said.

"What is it?" Sanje stopped as he was making his way to the door.

"My glasses."

Sanje looked back at the control panel.

"I don't wanna miss this."

"Yes. Well. Here you are. Please don't leave those lying around just anywhere." He handed them to me, and we were on our way.

Before long, we were on the zip track in the catacomb tunnels, and for the first time, I was making my own memories on my first honest-to-God adventure. I jostled my way out of the satchel enough to get a view of the long track that extended out before us. A thin line of lights streamed above the track in the tight, round tunnel that curved out of sight into the distance.

"You better hold on. This has a bit of a kick," Sanje warned as he cranked back a control lever.

"Really?" I said with a smile. I could not control being rapt with wonder. "All right. I can handle it." And with that we blasted off like a rocket at such a speed I could not help but fly backward with a thump into the satchel.

"HOO, HOO, YEAH! NOW THAT'S WHAT I'M TALKIN ABOUT!"

I quickly made my way back to my perch with my goggles on. I didn't want to miss a second of this. We were flying through the same tunnels that I'd seen in Varin's memories. Though it was in flaring shades of yellow, it was the same long track twisting into the distance. As I looked on, with an ample supply of joy, I could hear a voice in my head like a far-off sound. It was a woman singing some beautiful song I did not recognize.

Then we were in the hangar bay of the catacombs. There were three military prowlers near the giant bay doors that led outside. The most heavily armed ship fired up, and a pilot appeared on its loading ramp as the detachment of armed military men hustled their way up to the craft. Three of the cold fire team entered the prowler, and one waited at the ramp to meet Sanje as he boarded for take-off. The Constance sky never looked so big. I had never seen this view myself, but it was the same as in my memories. Deiphera could be seen hanging in the air like a decoration of the sky beyond the array of dangling starslides.

"Wow!" I said in a whisper.

Sanje looked down as he walked along and, putting his hand on the edge of the bag, he said, "You better stow yourself away in there for a minute."

"Welcome aboard, sir," said the cold fire team's captain.

"Do we have visual on the objective yet, Captain?" Sanje asked deftly.

"We have identified the motorcade and attempted to make contact, but they weren't exactly pleased to hear they were being shadowed. There's a major in the security detail who has ordered us to stand down, but I'm guessing we're still a go."

"That's right, Captain. We're going in. The intelligence is sound."

Within a minute, I could feel we had come to a stop. Sanje had sat down.

"All right, team, we're lifting off," came the pilot's voice. I made my way back up to get a view, trying to be discreet, but I was clearly in plain sight as the prowler lifted off. We were in the cockpit, and I had a front-row seat for the flight.

"Uh, sir," said the pilot, nodding towards the strange sight of a fat black rat nosing out of Sanje's bag. Sanje looked to me.

"Oh, that. Well… it's a comfort animal. Helps me think," he said dryly.

I looked up at the pilot with my mouth in a broad smile, my tongue dangling, and my little golden goggles gleaming in the sun, then back to the cockpit window as the pilot drew back on the thrusters. The prowler roared as we shot into the Constance sky.

Chapter 8
The Devil in the Details

For every moment of control forced on us by others, for every tear we wept in sorrow because others took away what we loved, and for all the self-torment that rattled in our mind telling us to consent willingly to such egregious acts, we released vengeance. To sate the yearning left within us after our innocence and free-minded youth was stolen from us, for the benefit of others' dominion, we allowed darkness to reign. This is what it was to make a choice that shook the lives of many others. Though sometimes we cannot feel, directly, the satisfaction of justice, it is satisfying to start it in action. So we set our hurt free, in such a way as we did, with Haytoo Valaire.

Haytoo lay, suspended in mid-air, deep in his trance state when his killer came for him. An unwitting lab tech, who had been seeking his own glory, consented to administer a dose of life-ending poison. The supervising doctor in the test labs presented the opportunity to him after receiving an order from a top-level military supervisor.

So this is what it was to do real work in his field, the tech thought as he approached chamber 434, Bio-Technology Division. The tech was a central part of the animal testing process so the leap to terminating a humanoid Bio-Tech subject should not have been too difficult. Some people develop an emotional immunity to the cruel treatment of life forms that cannot defend themselves, and that was precisely the case with this tech. He was completely ready to dabble in murder.

The two guards at the door fired up the weapons on their hips as the tech approached. They had never used them here, but they knew what it was to be killers too. They checked the tech's credentials for good measure, then one of the guards stepped to the eye-scanner console and opened his right eye wide for the contraption to unlock the door. A loud high beep sounded, and the power locks hummed to silence with a click. The tech could see Haytoo floating in his limbo state—one of the strange and unusual things in this world meant only for men like him to see. The door slid open.

One of the guards stepped inside first, and the tech approached Haytoo, not knowing what to expect. The other guard stayed behind, guarding the doorway.

Pulling up the sleeve of Haytoo's right arm, the tech discovered it was an automated appendage made to look as real as possible so he stepped around the sleeping extuiter. Aiming the syringe into the air, he squirted a little spritz in preparation then lowered the needle to its goal. Suddenly Haytoo's mechanical hand was gripping the tech's wrist and squeezing hard, crushing the bones.

"What's that? Is that the good stuff?" sprang from Haytoo's mouth. He was still suspended in the air. "Gimme that!"

The tech fell to his knees in pain as Haytoo stripped the needle from his anguished hand. The guard closest to Haytoo drew his weapon and trained it fast on the extuiter, but as his finger moved to squeeze a blast into the air, Haytoo dropped to the floor out of his stasis.

"That was close," Haytoo announced as he drew back his foot and smashed the guard's right knee so hard it nearly collapsed in the wrong direction. The injured man dropped like a sack of stones beside Haytoo, obscuring the aim of the other guard. The extuiter picked up the fallen man's gun and blew a hole in the second guard still in the doorway, then a pulse of golden light strobed through Haytoo's body. The fatally injured guard was dragging himself into the hall, and the other still lay on the floor, screaming, near Haytoo.

The extuiter scurried to his knees before the bewildered tech. "Tell me how good this is!" And he jammed the needle into the tech's thigh.

"No, no, no, no!" he begged, and then his begging became a gagging sound. He sprawled out with a thump, enthralled in a grand mal seizure. White vomit projected from his mouth, then he gasped, gyrating in violent spasms. In the blink of an eye, Haytoo extuited a spear of that mysterious metal and plunged it fast as lightning through the closest guard's upper right chest, sticking it deep in the ground with a spark.

"Oh, you're lucky. It's been a while," he said to the stuck guard, who was still alive but pinned to the floor. The dying man's mouth hung open, his face in a state of shock. Little gasps escaped his mouth like a fish on dry land.

"Yeah. I like it. I think I'll leave it like that. Don't die too soon." He wiped some of the tech's vomit from his leather jacket onto the guard and looked up to see the man in the hall holding his gushing wound as he reached towards the eye scanner to activate the door's locking mechanism. The guard was stretching up along the wall with his hands, trying to bring his face to the scanner. He opted to slap the machine, which only shut the door. Haytoo rose to his feet, and in an instant, he was standing at the little viewing window in the door, watching the guard peer into the scanner.

"Oh, is that what you're doing."

The door locked with a screeching electronic tone, and the guard fell to the floor, bleeding out.

Haytoo turned back to the man pinned to the floor with his cold metal weapon and, kneeling down next to him, said, "I'm going to need something you have."

Suddenly the guard was screaming again when he thought he could scream no more as Haytoo removed his eye with his finger. "Sorry. Believe it or not, I do know what suffering is, but I'm late for an important date." He held the eye up to the scanner, and the door opened again. "Wow, I'm hungry!"

By the time Haytoo had reached the hangar bay, he had murdered thirteen men. The bay doors were still open from a recent departure, and the extuiter spotted that one of the two prowlers in the dock was heavily armed.

"MMM. Yeah. Lasers. I wonder how those work?" said Haytoo, pursing his lips as he admired his new ride. In moments, the psychopath was in the cockpit, powering up the vessel and scanning through the list of active starslides to Hypathia. He activated the graviton repulsors, raising the ship in the air. The prowler let out a rev as he pushed forward on the thrusters.

"Starslide 9-8B. Where the hell is 9-8B?" He was studying the navigation screen as he eased the prowler into the Constance sky. In his distraction, the left wing banged into the frame of the bay doors.

"Oops."

*

It was at this time something I did not foresee happening took place at the Liberty Square location. From beneath the recently relaid stone surface, near the entrance of the Tower of the Ministry, a bomb exploded, deeply scarring the front of the building. Three people were severely injured. I could not be everywhere. I could not stop it from happening.

*

The four-year-old Hypathian girl Natu stood on the back seat of the floating state vehicle. Her black skin shimmered softly in the Constance sun as she peered through the rear window onto the city. She stood between her mother and father as their ride made its course to the starslide—or so they thought, for it was sure they would never make it to the inauguration.

A sleek armored craft pulled up beside the state vehicle, moving sharp and fast. Its side door slid open, and a man who appeared to be from the Constellation military force drew something metallic off his belt and threw it fast onto the state vehicle. The magnetic charge stuck hard near the graviton repulsors as the state transport took evasive action.

Floating up high into the air, it was suddenly thirty-five feet above the street, and all the occupants were pressed down in their seats from the inertia. With all his might, Saydacone Wivven pulled himself up to reach the divider between them and the driver. He smacked the release button, and it shot down. The front seats were empty; it was a fully automated vehicle.

Looking through the front window, Wivven could see the major's armored vehicle was nowhere to be found, then, behind him, there was a loud thwack on the door closest to where the foreign craft had been. The noise was so loud that Binny let out a startled yelp, and little Natu looked on to discover what was happening as Wivven tumbled to the floor. The door of the state vehicle was ripped clean off clean, and a rush of wind blasted into the opulent cab with the glaring light of the sun. The car jolted fiercely, and Wivven jerked towards the opening but caught himself on one of the empty seats.

The charge sealed near the graviton repulsors blew, damaging the system along the right side of the vehicle. As fast as the blast coated the exterior with flames and smoke, the car began leaning towards the side with the missing door. All that was keeping the vehicle from a sharp drop to a sideways position was some bit of the repulsor holding on at the right rear exterior.

As the vehicle tipped, everyone inside grasped for something to hold on to, but Natu tumbled down, smacking face first into what was left of the right interior structure. She looked up to her mom with a bleeding, broken nose, choking on the black smoke from the repulsor system, a hail of tears bursting from her twisted face.

Binny, still strapped into her seat, reached for the girl, drawing her up into her arms. She was sitting in the seat opposite the missing door and wincing under the strain of the seat belt on her pregnant belly. The pressure was becoming too intense. She squeezed tightly on the overhead handle to relieve the pain as the vehicle gave out the last of its right rear repulsor and dipped into a sideways hanging position. Beneath her was a straight drop of thirty-five feet to the ground.

Attempting to reach out and secure his pregnant wife, Wivven lost his grip and plunged through the opening of smoke and fire to the street below. The state vehicle started to spin slowly out of control.

*

On the platform back on Hypathia, though she could barely move a muscle, Evah began to weep. She was nearly in a state of paralysis from the drugs they had her on. Still, we felt the loss of another Hypathian father.

The news of the bombing traveled fast to the Hypathian platform via security links. They were stalling the proceedings. The hologram clips kept rolling, and the lull in the festivities did not abate the crowd's anticipation. Galneea wasn't budging about claiming his moment of glory. He approached a technician at the side of the platform and whispered in his ear, then the holograms switched to a live feed on the mangled front entrance of the Tower of the Ministry. Plumes of smoke reached up around a sizable blown-out hole in the old stones of Liberty Square, and there were deep black scars in the tower's pearly entrance.

Galneea stepped to the podium to address the crowd. "Terror. This is how the weak in faith muscle their way into our free worlds—with clumsy, ill-fated atrocities," he began.

In front of him, the protective energy shield spat and flashed with cascading light effects as those silly flying bugs smashed into it unwittingly.

"This is how these unscrupulous fearmongers will tell you and me what is right—what we can and cannot do—and with such acts tell you that you are not safe. What you are seeing, these images, they are real. This is what the weak-minded among us did only minutes ago. When they saw this, the Constellation military wanted to sweep me away to safety. They wanted me to abandon you. Since the restoration of the Constance reserves and the reestablishment of safety for the kepplequer industry, the people have called me a 'folk hero.' Maybe I am. Maybe. If it means to stay strong and protect my planetary system from terrorists and remain generous with the wealth I have to save our hobbled welfare then so be it. I will proudly accept the title. That is what I am here for—not to be concerned with my security before the security of my people. I will not abandon you. Dark forces—EVIL—takes any face convenient to achieve its purposes. Before it was the Hypathian eco-terrorists. Now it's disgruntled Constance actors. Probably the same ones responsible for the assassination attempt on the finest example of your people's expression in the Constellation system: The Extuiter of Constance. One of your own people."

Some of the audience began to boo and hiss. It was the Hypathians angered by the misuse of the extuiter's gifts.

Evah was beginning to catch on to the truth that I already understood: that Galneea was blowing up innocent people in the same way he had so many years ago, in order to play the hero and claim the support of the people. The pain of the lies and the sacrifices turned our stomach. Oh, our hate, our hate for this world was welling with unstoppable force. Our mind was soaked in grief for the world being lost to itself interminably at the hands of this twisted master.

"I tell you this, even those showing disapproval now: This is the age of miracles! An age of miracles brought to us in the form of a little girl. She has worked so tirelessly to create these unmatchable feats of wonder she can barely walk. Look at her. There is the one who has helped me bring in this new age for Hypathia. Anyone who wants to step on that out there better look out for me."

There was an unusually big flash on the energy shield. One of the protestors had thrown something.

"I will get you. Anyone who wants to harm her. And there will be a reckoning beyond your imagination. Anyone out there who knows how fragile people such as your extuiter are—they'll get you. You better get yourself in line, because this is the time for Hypathia to triumph."

A military prowler cracked into sight in the near distance with a screaming roar. It moved slowly along carrying beneath it, in a net, the largest barb fish that could be subdued—a beastly spectacle to match the beastly spectacle of Galneea's pride. Evah thought it might be our savior, but it was not.

Flying in low was Galneea's final spectacle. The fish was a translucent pasty white, its body long and squid-like. Behind its enormous body were its many barbed, tentacle-like tails. They had put it to sleep for transport to Hypathia, and although twitches erupted through its massive body, it was in a deep slumber.

"Look. This is the future of Hypathia. Power for the people. There were people who said I couldn't do it, but I believed, and now the power is yours."

How we wanted to destroy this master of finance. The master of the sea, master of the people, master of the meek and disenfranchised, the master of self-glorification. But all the energy of our mind could not be focused to do our will physically.

Evah tried to stand but looked more like a rag doll being tossed up and onto the ground before her seat. She was disgusted with the sensation that she was only an inefficient puppet.

We slowly pulled ourselves to our feet like a drunk, and from us went out such power as we had not felt before. It was immeasurable. Evah was finally giving all of herself to me, and as she did, the waters of three worlds began to swell at their coasts. Giant tidal waves began rising to the sky on the not-so-far-off sea of Hypathia, beyond the ruins, over the port of Constance like a horrific shadow, and far across the galaxy on the eastern coast of America, where our greatest grief had been spawned. We reached out to end this troubling world with all its perversions of loyalty and tricks and hate.

The fiery bands of red about our body twisted and slapped at the air and the ground, and our light burned hot. Evah's eyes closed as the military prowler that carried the barb fish hovered above the crowd near the platform.

There was another crack in the sky. Haytoo had arrived. He could see our rage swelling in the sea beyond the ruins.

"What is that?" he said, observing the rising wall of water. "Looks like I'm here just in time." He pulled back on the thrusters to move in fast, heading towards the air above the crowd.

"This is a new beginning," Galneea continued. "Don't let anyone steal that from you," he said proudly, distracted by his impressive scene.

The thirty-foot sleeping giant that lay limp and dangling in its net was far too large for the power of the military craft. There was a fizz of smoking chemical reaction around the it—its acidic fluids were burning away the net under its tremendous weight—and a repulsive odor of rotting fish filled the air. The hoisting craft jerked in a rattle above the crowd, then the towing gear itself made a terrible grinding noise. The hydraulic mechanism was breaking in some way. A loud vacuum noise began to sound—something was sucking in air at the bottom of the ship.

In the cockpit of his prowler, Haytoo was fiddling with the firing system. A high-pitched charging sound filled the air.

"How the hell do you make these work? Fire, for crying out loud!" He slammed his fist down on the panel and two blasts shot from the laser cannons. He was trying to blow out the electric shield generators around the platform, but the shots were deflected by a magnetic seal. They ricocheted, banking into the sleeping sea creature's body in the net, and the acid reaction accelerated. Parts of the net were popping open.

Haytoo sent off another pair of pulses that streaked red through the air, striking the ground. The crowd started to scramble. He was flying so fast he couldn't get in another shot as he swept over the stage in a half hazard fly-by. He clearly had no control over the ship.

"Damn it!" Haytoo cursed.

Then the net holding the great barb fish gave way, and it was waking up fast from the pain. The creature broke loose from its restraints and plummeted to the ground, and people were screaming and running wild as they tried to avoid being crushed by the falling sea beast.

When it struck the ground, everything beneath it was destroyed. One of the generators powering the protective shield was smashed, and in moments, the shield was completely off, and the barb fish was making a thundering, squealing noise that pierced the ears. Its sharply barbed tentacles began to move with restless energy.

As he began his return approach to the platform, Haytoo could see the shields that kept him from reaching his fiery little goddess had been shorted. "Well, that works for me," he said and set down the ship as close as he could get to the platform.

Our senses dug into the swelling of the waters. Skenkin reached out to grab us and received a painful burn, her hand red and welted. She backed up fast to avoid further contact with the fiery bands that snapped around us.

Haytoo ran down the loading ramp as the laser cannons let off five or six rapid shots that made him dance with his hands in the air. "Hey, hey, hey, hey, hey!" He looked back at the ship for a moment. "Nice!" Then another of those metal spears appeared in his hand, and he started his run for the platform.

The barbed, tentacled monster was fully awake now, letting out grimacing screams. A horrific relentless bleating. Its tentacles whipped as wildly as the fiery bands around our body, but Evah was lost to all that was going on, entranced in the zenith of her power.

This time without asking, the military security was shielding Galneea with their bodies as they rushed the Prime Minister off the stage. Havoc was everywhere. Claren and the other dignitaries were scrambling desperately for cover, though some followed Galneea and his guards back up the slopes of the pyramid to the observatory.

Haytoo leaped onto the platform and with a spin of his weapon struck a straggling guard in the head, then encased him in one of his favorite devices for killing—a transparent resin block. The poor helpless man suffocated in an inanimate state of suffering.

Our power drew upon the seas, and the moment of destruction was near. Claren was dumbfounded at the sight of the murderous Haytoo using the wicked gifts he thought he'd taken forever.

Seeing Claren, Haytoo could not resist having his satisfaction with the plotting sire. A dignitary brushed past the old Thwargg, breaking his stare, and Claren turned to run from his executioner, but Haytoo was on him fast. He pulled back his instrument of torment and swung it hard at the Thwargg's legs, bringing him down without pity. He wanted to savor Claren's pain and would not end it fast.

The psycho savior commenced with his beating, swinging his weapon high above his head and bringing it down in a ruthless attack. The old Thwargg was crying out, whimpering and groping the surface of the platform, but Haytoo brought his weapon down again like some senseless primate of the wild beating down a dangerous predator.

Three pulses of light shot from our tiny body—three souls to where I do not know. Haytoo saw the strange eruption of sparks and realized my state of trance was turning into one he may not be able to free me from. Claren's struggling fell still, and he was at his most vulnerable, but the metal spear vanished from Haytoo's hand as he grabbed the old Thwargg by the collar of his first-class suit.

"I'm taking you to go, little piggy." He touched Claren on the cheek with the index finger of his mechanical hand and a gag appeared in the old Thwargg's mouth, a rope tightening around his arms and squeezing them without mercy against his torso.

Haytoo began to drag his captive across the platform to stir his goddess from her spell, and as he stepped before us, our eyes sprang open. He was about to say something when, behind us, a door opened onto the black realm where only spirits were meant to travel. Standing in the doorway were two beings of pure light, like slivers of lightning, all silvery-white. Then Evah was gone, and everything ceased to move. I could do nothing; I couldn't go with her. I was trapped in waiting. Forbidden.

There wasn't so much as a flinch in the scene. All around me in the stillness was the terror on the faces of the people, the unbudging, tortured beast of the sea, and the scarred, unmoving figure of Haytoo.

Chapter 9
The Pale Realm

I could hear the sound of birdsong; whistling and gentle squawks in unmetered time. Before my eyes, it seemed there was a veil of light, the color of the palest silver. It was so perfectly cool and comfortable that one might forget they even had a physical vessel. I felt as though I were an idea within an idea. There was no struggle, no tension. I was a spirit, one with the cool. A world emerged before me, full of light but somehow obscuring what was not directly focused on. It was like seeing through a crystal.

I was wearing the little dress and sweater I had on that chilly day in Constance when I was shot. Beneath my feet was rich soil and around me green plants. I might have thought I was on Hypathia if I didn't know that I was in the unseen kingdom. As I walked, the blurry silver light revealed a carved stone foundation. I do not know how far it went on. I could not see. On the edge closest to me, there was a stone funerary bed like something one sets the bones of heroes on in a tomb. On the surface was a man wearing black.

Then I saw a presence of fire. It sprang through the air, soaring between two tall torches that extended out of the foundation. It was conscious. Behind the man in black, one of those slender beings of light passed to a place not far off to the left. It seemed to be conferring with two others of its kind. One of them was more like a man, though he still glowed with a silvery light. The glow obscured his identity. Though I could not feel myself moving, I was drifting towards the man in black as he slowly sat up. He then hunched over, looking to the foundation stone with his legs dangling before him, sitting on the precipice of his resting place. It seemed he had been sleeping for a very long time. His skin was black, and his hair was tight little curls like mine. Though he had not yet looked at me, I could see he was the man from the passing thoughts and visions I'd had.

Then I was standing beside him, and though I was close, everything seemed to be obscured with blurs of light, silver and yellow all at once. And though I knew who he was, I could not focus on him clearly.

"I've missed you," I told him.

"I've been waiting for you."

"Where?"

"Here." He smiled.

"I'm sorry I had to leave you. I should have stayed home. I thought some other things were important to do. I didn't know I could never return."

I felt his presence. He was the dust of my dust; we were two of the same star. I wanted to speak with him, but I drifted in and out of waves of light. I knew they were the distorted waves of sorrow and misunderstanding that I could not see through.

"I had good reason to do all that I did," he said, "but I left you alone, and I'm sorry. You have been in my mind like a dream all these years. I didn't want to leave." Blinding waves of light crashed between us then dissolved and I could see him again. "You can't do what you are about to do, Evah."

I noticed there were no other voices in my mind. I didn't hear the whispers of the souls I carried, the taunting of demons, or the proud voice that had guided me since leaving Felin. My mind seemed clear of all those things. I was only myself.

"I have as much power over the end of the world as I have had the power to find you," I said to him.

"Choice is the greatest power you have when it comes to the end of the world, Evah. You've always had a choice."

"But there are others? The one I always hear now. The one I can't escape."

"It's your voice, Evah. She is you. You've been overwhelmed with difficult choices, and though there are other spirits speaking in all of creation, the voice that matters most is your own. You must allow yourself to be reconciled with the loss you feel. It is your voice that has the final say in your actions, in your part in the world. I know you've felt hopeless, that you've worried about the dead, and that you've worried about bringing justice to a world so far out of your control."

"I don't know where to go or what to do," I confessed.

"You only need to be right where you are. You needn't bother yourself with either the dead or revenge, but have hope. It's hope that helps the world endure. All the love you share goes on, and with love, all the world endures. I know you've felt different, but it's your differences that make you just what the world needs wherever you are. We all must live on. With the parts of ourselves that make us special and the parts that make us just like anybody else. We must live on with the things that we do right and the things we do wrong."

He reached out to me, and we were transported. We were standing on the stone foundation. His hands were on my shoulders.

"Is this heaven?"

"No, Evah. Not quite. I couldn't let go. Now I'm needed somewhere else. We both have to let go of these troubles. We are both needed. But I will see you again. You're more than I could have ever imagined." He brushed the back of his fingers across my cheek and kissed my head.

"What about the others? The baby and the child?"

"There is always another way," my father said. "We must try and have faith that what must come to pass will find a way. We must be ready to help in whatever way we can. But let go of the speculation and the worry. Give the best of yourself, Evah, and follow your fairest intuition."

"You have carried something for me," said the man in silver light, who had drawn close to us. "I'm going to take this burden from you, but I will allow some things that you have made to remain." With that, he put the tips of his fingers to my head. Everything started glowing brightly.

My father spoke a final time, though all I could see was light. "With your faith, your mother can persevere. I love you, Evah."

Then I was standing back on the platform on Hypathia. Haytoo stood before me, frozen in a suspended moment of time.

The remaining shadow of my lost spirit was there.

"What happened?" she asked me. "I want to know. I couldn't go with you."

"You're not forgotten."

"Is he alive?"

"He's alive. In eternity."

"I failed. I couldn't save him."

"Some people are not for us to save."

"So much was lost."

"I know." I looked upon the shadow of myself, and·she was gentle, with tears in her eyes. "There are others who need us. The ones who are with us must return. And there are others who are living. We have to let go. We must forgive ourself. It's time to go. This power was not for us to keep. They need our help."

"All right." And with that, the dusty fume of my shadow dispelled itself, and we became one.

The souls that were within me streamed up into the sky. When it was done, the world began to move again.

Haytoo said to me, "Are you ready to make our paradise?"

I felt at once empty and whole, and the light that had been all around me was gone. "Paradise is not mine to give."

And with that Haytoo disappeared from my view—swiped away in the clutches of one of the great barb fish's tentacles. The sea creature whipped Haytoo about in the air. First far then near again, smacking him hard against the platform. He was motionless, then a final light burst from his body, ascending to the sky, and the beast shoved Haytoo into the hidden mouth at the center of its tentacles, eating him whole.

"I didn't know they did that," I said, and suddenly I was swept up into my mother's arms as she carried me to safety.

Chapter 10
The Silence

O ur prowler was approaching the motorcade fast. They had changed their course and gone dark so they could not be tracked. When we caught our first glimpse of the motorcade, I thought we were too late. The sleek state vehicle was high in the air, hanging sideways and turning into a spin as it descended to the street below. There was a body lying on the ground between the two security vehicles. The security had come to a standstill, one in front and one behind, the empty space where the fancy wreck had been before it left ground level. There was a small craft I had never seen before buzzing around the capsizing vehicle like a wasp. It was armored and looked military. Then the deadly craft darted to the street, ready to make another attack.

"Firing," our pilot said, and we swooped in on the predator craft at a hot speed. Two phaser shots let out from the cannons hitting their target. The vehicle was stunned to a slow crawl long enough for our pilot to shoot off something like a towing cable that sank firmly into the enemy craft's side. We powered off our thrusters, sliding into a sweeping left bank, and then the towing cable pulled tight on the waspish craft and brought us to a halt, using the enemy vehicle like an anchor.

The loading doors of the prowler slid open, and the cold fire team was on the ground in seconds. The motorcade's two security escorts had remained at ground level, it seemed, the whole time the official vehicle was in the air. They waited in their defensive formation for the hobbled vehicle to crash down between them.

It did not crash hard—something had been keeping the vehicle in the air that had made for a slower descent—but there was no movement from the passengers inside.

Military men were all over the place. Three from the predatory craft, four from the motorcade security—including one who looked like an official—and our cold fire team. Shots were being fired from all angles. The cold fire team was making quick work of the three attackers, but everyone seemed to be from the same military force. The Constellation military was at war with itself.

When the three attackers were down, our cold fire team rushed in to take cover behind the wasp-like vehicle. The security force was firing on them. Even the official had opened fire on our men. I thought about Varin's memories of such violent events, and nothing seemed so terrifying as this. It was then I realized Varin's point of view was naïve in some way. No. It was my point of view had been naïve.

"My God, what are they doing?" the pilot said, leaning in with astonishment to watch his fellow men firing on each other. "Sir, I'm going to have to fire on that security detail."

"Permission granted. Please do," Sanje said.

We shot off two more phaser pulses that ravaged the lead security vehicle with a ravaging jolt. The security official sank two hits in one of our men, then in response to our attack on his vehicle, he put his hands up, waving to our pilot to stand down. Our cold fire team was attempting to take cover. They were deep in the conflict and mired in confusion by the attack from their fellow soldiers.

"Cold fire, you have permission to engage any hostile combatant!" the pilot told them. I could feel how conflicted he was to give the command to fire on his own people.

After a moment of uncertainty, one of our men threw a charge in the air at the rear security forces. The scene was nightmarish. When the charge went off, one of the security men was torn to pieces by the blast, and even through my golden goggles, it was a horrific sight.

There was an explosion on our left wing. They, too, were throwing charges, and all hell had broken loose. Still, the major was trying to tell us to stand down. He would wave at us then turn and fire on our men. Another of the cold fire team fell to the ground. Only two remained.

One fired another shot to the remaining soldier in the rear security team, who fell silent, then our team turned all of their focus towards the official and his remaining guard.

"I can't fire on the major, sir; I can't do it. There must be some confusion."

"I don't think there's any confusion at all. I need that man alive, Captain," Sanje said with awe in his voice, but it was too late. In that instant, as the major turned and started towards our ship, there was a *crack* and his arms slouched to his side. His body drooped, suspended on bowing knees for a moment, then fell dead to the ground.

Our two remaining soldiers advanced on the last guard with a final charge bursting into flames behind them, and the final shots sounded as our prowler touched down to the ground. All our enemies were vanquished.

After a moment of silence, Sanje placed his satchel on the control panel and started to exit the prowler.

"We need a medic team dispatched immediately. There are at least six team members fatally injured," the pilot ordered through the comms.

"There's a pregnant woman in the state vehicle," Sanje said. Then he was outside, cautiously moving towards the major. I scurried onto the control panel for a clear view.

It was a terrible scene, and after so much horror, the scene seemed menacingly silent. The quiet was deafening. A little child slowly wandered out of the state vehicle onto the street. She seemed lost. She was in shock. She started to cry, and then a woman was picking her up and comforting her in her arms.

Sanje checked the major for vital signs, but he was dead. The magistere then approached the state vehicle as a man stepped out with urgency. He was saying something frantically to Sanje, though from where I was the silence still prevailed. Sanje placed his hand on the man to steady him, and they stepped into the vehicle. The little girl started to settle in her mother's arms.

It was then my eyes could no longer withstand the rush of golden fire through my goggles. I took them off, and when I did, I couldn't believe my eyes. I could see! And my spirit was my own.

Epilogue

My name is Evah. I'm fourteen years old, and I am the Extuiter of Constance. My mind is quieter now. After my meeting with my dad on Hypathia, I no longer had the power to make those buildings. In fact, for a time, I couldn't do anything with my abilities.

Galneea and my grandfather both survived that day. They were afraid that everyone would find out all the things they were up to, but the only evidence of their wrongdoing was dead—the men who tried to kill my friends in the streets of Constance and Haytoo. There was nosthing left of him. They blamed the strange appearance of the aggressive prowler that day on Hypathia on Constance terrorists. They couldn't blame me. They didn't want people to learn they'd kept Haytoo alive all those years and hidden from the authorities. My mom and I kept our mouths shut, and they agreed to let us go until we were ready to return. It was a tacit agreement. That means secret.

Although one of the fathers of my little tribe died, everyone else survived. Kahtura was born, and her mother was all right. Natu had a really lousy day but her nose healed, and she held on to the part of her that made her special. Her innocence, I guess. Our friend Sanje placed them in protective custody. I didn't think they would ever really be safe, but after a while, they were released back to their lives.

Something happened—something I had a feeling about but didn't understand at the time. All the pavilions and the building I created on Constance remained after I could no longer make any more; they remained, the way my grandfather wanted, and some good things came from it. The kindest part of their ambition survived.

Galneea fixed up his tower and life moved forward, but one day, they both just disappeared. Galneea and my grandfather were in their tower, and then they were gone. It was a mystery to everyone. No one else disappeared; everyone else was fine, and the authorities couldn't explain it. So much good was being done at the other sites, even in the Tower of the Ministry, that no one wanted to upset that by closing everything down. There were investigations, and they asked me questions. But what did I know? I'm just a kid.

After the disappearance, my mom told me about a dream she'd had the night I made the Constance pavilion. She said in her dream, Grandpa was trying to reach her from someplace dark. He said he was trying to get back to her. Trying to be forgiven.

She had more of these dreams after the disappearance. I don't know. For now, I'm just trying not to worry about it all. I do remember the last words I said to Galneea though, and I've wondered what happened in that building of his. I guess I imagine that one day a door opened to that black world. The one where dark spirits run wild. Maybe Galneea and my grandfather went in. Maybe they thought they saw their glory in there. I don't know. I guess sometimes I think that's probably where they are. Maybe, like Haytoo, they stepped in, but they didn't come back.

The tidal waves didn't destroy Hypathia or Constance. There was some flooding. It wasn't easy for some people, but no one got hurt or died. They just got really wet. I'm glad I stopped; that I didn't do that. I've never wanted to hurt anybody. Those were difficult times, but I think I'm getting over that now. And I haven't heard any troubling news about Earth, though we still don't hear much about Earth at all. I do wonder about that place.

I've learned something. There was a part of myself I locked away, but not anymore. I know now that I can visit other people. That I can see things. But I have no reason to use this gift yet. Maybe I don't want to. There's a part of me that can go out into the universe, and maybe one day I'll be able to understand that better. I don't know how far I can go before I can't come back. Or when it might not be me who comes back. And I'm happy right where I am.

Sometimes though, when I see my reflection, or I catch a glimpse of my shadow in the corner of my eye, I think I see that part of myself in her black fume waiting for me to return to her and give her my power. It may be that dark being is something that will always be with me, and that to use the full extent of my gifts, she must be allowed to be free. I guess we'll see. There's been no call to serve as the Crystal or any demand for my most mysterious skills.

For now, I'm just living my life with my mom on Hypathia. No one seems to realize who I am. Anyone who may know, they treat me nicely. but I do look pretty different. No weird lights. For now, anyway. I go to school and have friends, and my mom works at the nearby university. Even my old friend Felin lives with us now. He really is getting old, and I don't know how much longer he'll be with us, but for now, he's with me, and we all have someone to love us. And the truth is, I can't think of anything better than that. For now.

T hank you for reading *Evah & the Unscrupulous Thwargg*. It's readers like you that enhance the reading experience of new works and increase their visibility. If you have enjoyed Evah's story please rate the book on Amazon and in your Kindle store. Your review can help the novel reach a wider audience.

After a short period of exclusivity on Amazon the eBook will be released on other popular platforms. Visit longoriawolfe.com for information on other works and an immersive experience that is sure to evolve. Again, thank you for being a reader and don't forget to rate the book. Your support can make all the difference.

CPSIA information can be obtained
at www.ICGtesting.com
Printed in the USA
LVHW040319250320
651140LV00020B/2403